SHE'S A JOLLY GOOD FELLOW

Sajita Nair was born into an Air Force family and raised in different places across India. She was commissioned in the Indian army in 1994, making her a pioneer of sorts. After a challenging and successful tenure in the army, she had a short stint in the corporate world in HR, before she took up writing. Her short stories, articles and travelogues have been published in reputed print and online publications. She lives in Visakhapatnam with her naval officer husband and their two children. This is her first novel.

W0232893

SHE'S A JOLLY GOOD FELLOW

Sajita Nair

hachette
INDIA

First published in 2010 by Hachette India
An Hachette UK company

Copyright © Sajita Nair 2010

Sajita Nair asserts the moral right
to be identified as the author of this work.

SRD

ISBN 978-81-906173-8-3

Hachette India
612/614 (6th Floor), Time Tower,
MG Road, Sector 28, Gurgaon-122001, India

Typeset in Meridien 9.5/12.3 by
Mindways Design, New Delhi

Printed and bound in India by
Manipal Technologies Limited, Manipal

MIX
Paper from
responsible sources
FSC™ C104740

*To the selfless men and women in uniform,
who make a world of difference*

Prologue

1994

On a world stage, when Sushmita Sen and Aishwarya Rai won coveted beauty pageants and heralded the arrival of the new Indian woman, Anju and I were all set to make some conquests of our own: by storming the last male bastion, the Indian army.

At the Officer's Training Academy, our Directing Staff, the officer responsible for the course of lady cadets, sternly informed us in the huge ante-room, 'Each one of you must choose your buddy. Your buddy will be the person who will stick with you throughout your training, and most often, beyond.' Since this was just a day after we'd all met each other, the task of choosing a buddy was a gamble.

I looked on as pairs formed. The long-haired, bubbly lady cadet with whom I had a one-day pact, suddenly floated away and paired with a short-haired, tall one who exuded the confidence of a lioness. A smarter buddy was certainly a better idea.

Soon, there was no one left – except Anju and me. I had overheard the others talk about her: she smiles a lot, opens her trap unnecessarily, sways her hips too much when she walks, she reads mushy romance novels – in short, she was guilty of doing everything that can get you rolling for miles – front-rolling, that is – on the boot-hardened roads of the academy.

But I had no choice. So I stuck with her.

Or rather, we stuck together.

Somewhere, our buddy-hood transformed into friendship. Our bonding happened during some of the toughest times, like when we crawled together on sun-baked gravel over touch-me-nots, front-rolled endlessly like a pair of wheels, circled the drill square running with rifles held high above our heads, shared half a bucket of water for our bird baths at camps, bent down ties-in-the-mouth when caught napping at the movie fall-in, stared into the starry night sky lying on tar roads counting DLTGH, Days Left to Go Home...

At our Passing-out Parade, we slow-marched together to the tune of 'Auld Lang Syne', emotions surging, eyes blearing as we neared the mast. It was together that we felt the high of commissioning, the weight of the gold stars shining on our shoulders.

And best of all, we learnt that we had been transferred together. We jigged, we hugged and swore we'd arrive in our new unit with a bang!

On a breezy September morning, I arrived, rather quietly.

But Anju kept her word.

1

Jump Starts

BANG! BANG!

I had been absorbed in snipping an upturned lock of hair that was sticking out from under my beret like a warthog's horn, when the banging on the door startled me out of my skin. In a place as quiet as Bengdubi, especially at night, even a knock on the door sounds like a 155mm Howitzer gun going off. I flew across the room to attend to the emergency.

A sobbing, shaking mass in a frilly purple poncho collapsed into my arms when I opened the door.

Anju.

'Oh, Diiiiips! Thank *God* I found you!' cried Anju. She was all over me, hugging me, pinching me to perhaps check if I was really there, and even kissing me, before settling to sob on my left shoulder.

'You can't even *imagine* what all I have been through,' she croaked.

'But I thought you'd come tomorrow,' I said, trying to pat her hair down, since it looked like she had been electrocuted. 'Wasn't your train delayed?'

She didn't say anything. Only her head continued to bob on my shoulder. I could feel a concoction of her bodily fluids soak through my academy dressing gown into my skin.

'Ahem,' said a male voice, 'your friend has had a bad day.' I hadn't noticed the officer who had accompanied her. He was of medium height, with a light complexion and a nose that could put Pinocchio to shame. 'She'll be fine now,' he said, wringing his hands.

'Yes, sir,' I said and smiled, suddenly embarrassed at the two of us standing there embracing like reunited lovers. I slowly peeled Anju off myself. Mud stripes and make-up ran down her cheeks, streaking her face like a Red Indian's. With that and her poncho, all she needed was a feathered headdress to complete the look.

I kept a straight face and patted her some more. 'Don't worry, Anju. You'll be fine.' She sniffed and nodded.

'By the way, I am Lieutenant Sandeep Singh,' said the officer, extending his hairy hand. I shook it. 'Please make yourselves comfortable,' he said as he motioned to the orderly behind him – there were more witnesses to this? – to bring in Anju's bags. Soon there were five suitcases of varying colours and sizes arranged neatly along the living-room wall, by the cane sofa-set. Their job done, the orderly left and the officer disappeared into the neighbouring room.

After a few more soothing words, Anju was persuaded to make her way to the loo – where she nearly burst out crying again when she saw herself in the mirror. She emerged a good half hour later, looking more like herself and less like a tribal warrior. A few sips of water and a few bites of chicken biryani later (Long Nose Pinocchio was kind enough to send us some dinner), she looked like she was ready to recount her story.

'So, tell me...' I said, fetching my medicine box and sitting beside her on the bed.

Barely had I said that, than tears started to well again.

'Oh! C'mon, don't be a melodrama queen,' I said, finally losing my patience. 'Do you want to tell me now or... what, is it tomorrow already?' It was a quarter past eleven and my eyes were getting heavier by the minute.

She sniffed and threw me a hurt look, then dabbed at her eyes with some scented tissue, smoothed out her pink floral nightdress, and finally began: 'My train reached Calcutta late. At first I thought I would have to wait until evening, since I had missed my connecting train. But then Guwahati Express was leaving in the afternoon. So I hopped in.'

'When did you get hurt? Just tell me that.' I knelt before her and began to pat at the dried blotches of blood on her elbow and her knees with a cotton ball.

'I'll tell you everything,' she said. There usually was no point in hurrying her since she was fond of telling stories, with the tiniest details and that too in a perfect sequential order. That meant I had no choice but to listen to her past midnight.

She continued, 'The first-class compartment was surprisingly quiet. I was alone in my coupé and couldn't see anyone around. There were no usual noises, just the sound of the train. It was really scary. I prayed someone would come... and...' She began to shake. The tears that she had held back until this moment came coursing down her cheeks.

All this, even before I had applied the fiery Dettol.

'What...?' I tossed the cotton aside and held her. 'What happened?' Her head hung low and her body trembled. 'Did someone come?' I prodded.

'Yeah,' she said, looking sombrely into my eyes.
'Who?'

'A p-p-peanut-wala!'

'Agh!' I looked away, unable to hide my disappointment. 'Is that it? I thought it was some dacoit or ghost or something.'

'But, it was as scary. *Believe* me!' She was talking rapidly now. 'At first he insisted on selling his peanuts. I refused, but the chap just wouldn't go away. He kept buzzing about me like a housefly, irritating me. Then I bought some, thinking he would go. But he stayed on, insisting that I eat them. And then... and then... he *forced* himself on me. I gathered all my strength and pushed him away. Then I pulled out my fruit knife and swung it at his face and yelled, "Keep off! I am an army officer." He felt the blood on his forehead, stared at me and walked away, lugging his tokri of peanuts.'

I was stunned into silence.

'Anju, you actually did that?' I finally asked, picturing her in the position she described. She would have made a cute ad for the knife, leaping out of a hoarding, stopping passersby with her soft, round face. She had a face that looked like a permanent smile was pasted onto it. Even when she was angry, I mean extremely angry, it looked like she was feigning it – the reason why punishment-happy seniors in the academy always had a pretext to take us to task. Being her buddy in the academy most times I had to join her in 'cutting the smile', a ritual which involved running the index and middle fingers across the lips like a pair of scissors, throwing the offending smile down and crushing it for several minutes, like children jumping up and down in a puddle to splash water.

Her head thrown back, she searched my eyes for praise and said, 'Yeah, I drove that jerk away.'

'That's my brave buddy,' I said, thumping her back. 'I am proud of you. Really.' Although I had this strong feeling that the chap fled because of what she said, rather than the action bit, now was not the time to tell her.

By now she was fairly composed. I took a fresh ball of cotton and dabbed some Dettol again. 'Is that when you got hurt?' I asked, rubbing the antiseptic on her wounds. She twitched a little and carried on, 'No, no. That was when I jumped from the running train.'

'What? You jumped? Stupid! Why? Wasn't there a chain?'

'I thought the train was moving slowly, but when I jumped, I was thrown off. That's how I got hurt.'

'Hang on, why did you even jump in the first place?' I asked, then added immediately, 'You were reading one of your romances, right?'

I knew that she found these candy books as irresistible as monkeys found ripe yellow bananas. In the academy, she read them in torchlight after lights out; she then snoozed during the next day's classes. Once, in the Military Tactics class, she even fell asleep – literally – during a punishment standing session: one moment she was standing next to me erect as a pole and the very next she had gathered in a heap on the floor. 'Impressive tactics,' the instructor had said.

'No, no, it wasn't that,' she said to me now, 'I felt so drained after all that happened with the peanut-wala that I fell asleep. Luckily the train had just started to move when I saw New Jalpaiguri flickering before my eyes. I threw my suitcases out and jumped.'

Her story had banished my sleep. Having dressed all her grazes, I was now sitting on her bed. An imaginary line divided our bedroom into my side and hers. We had a bed, closet and bedside table each.

'Well, you've had a long day,' I said with a sigh taking her hand in mine.

'No, no, it's not over yet,' she said, pulling away. 'When I reached the Movement Control Office which is supposed to assist defence personnel, the chaps added to my troubles by refusing to believe that I was a lady officer. They said that lady officers didn't serve in the regular army, only in the medical cadre. Can you believe it?'

'I can,' I said. 'When I got here, they found it hard to believe me too. But how could they repeat... Oh, the duty personnel must've changed. But didn't you show them your I-card?'

'I did, but they complained that the mole on my right cheek was too light for an identification mark.'

'They were right,' I said, 'especially because of your facial overhaul after that fall.' I chuckled at the thought of how funny she had looked.

'Oh, shut up!' she said crossly. 'You find it all funny, na? You can't imagine the state I was in. You know, it took me a dozen phone calls and such a lot of laboured explanation to finally prove my identity. Everything was so horrible for me. I thought you would understand.'

'Alright, alright. I understand,' I said quickly, patting her shoulder before the waterworks started again. 'I think I know the rest. You kept waiting until a Shaktiman came and picked you up. It bumped and rattled down the potholed roads dropping a few nuts and bolts along the way. You clutched at the seat but even that wasn't fixed properly. So, together you came bumping all along the 25 kilometres here... right?'

Anju gave me a vacant look. 'Actually I came in a Maruti Gypsy.'

'Oh!' I gaped. While I came in a vehicle of the description I'd just given her, she had the pleasure of gliding over the potholed roads in a sleek SUV, like a senior officer. The fall certainly had had its benefits.

We sat in the quiet, now looking away from each other.

Finally, Anju broke the silence with a couple of sighs and said, 'What a sad place for a first posting.'

Although I didn't quite feel it, I tried to sound positive. 'Anju, maybe it's not so bad after all. We haven't even looked around.'

'Look around? For what? Buffaloes?' She fixed her eyes on me with a stare of disbelief, then got up to bring in her bags.

If nothing else, it was good to see her in her normal form. And with her around, I kind of felt stronger. After all, we were just about to enter unfamiliar and unexplored territory. D-day was just a night away.

'I hope everything goes fine,' I said, as I opened her closet to help her arrange some of her things. An enormous cockroach flew over my head like a plane heading for a crash. I ducked and squealed at the loathsome creature. Anju, unlike me, remained unruffled, even as the creature landed on her dress. With a sweep of her hand, she brushed it away.

I must admit this was one of Anju's strong points – cockroaches. Rather, animals in general. She was the kind who could surprise a stray dog by walking up to it and stroking its head. Even in the academy, there were times when I felt genuinely proud of being her buddy, for her rare roach kinship. It was she who cleared these ubiquitous creatures from the trunks of other lady cadets when they ran helter-skelter as though under sniper fire.

Anju stopped arranging her clothes and looked at me. 'That cute officer is just on the other side of the wall, so don't make these funny sounds.'

'Cute? Who? Long Nose? Have you fallen for his nose?' I said, as she turned back to her task. Anju was also the kind who had a crush on every gentleman cadet that marched in the grounds of the Officers' Training Academy. One had intelligent eyes, another muscular arms, yet another a face to die for and still another a deep sexy voice...

'Hope you're not carrying too many of your romance books,' I said.

'Cute here means just nice... gentlemanly, okay,' she said, climbing into her bed. 'Remember those words?' She thumped her pillow, getting ready to sleep. 'We need to prove our mettle.'

Anju was quoting General Vij, the Reviewing Officer at our Passing-out Parade, who had described us lady cadets as 'pioneers creating history'. 'To conquer this new domain, it is important that you set the right precedent,' he had said. Listening to him at the Parameshwaran drill square, amidst caparisoned horses, personnel in their ceremonial best, curious press reporters and a shamiana full of beaming parents, I remember having felt two feet taller.

'Good n...i...g...h...t,' Anju yawned loudly into my reverie. 'It's been a long and tiring day. I need to sleep.' She stretched herself out.

'Good night,' I mumbled back.

Cicadas sang a lullaby nearby. I wasn't sure if Anju meant what she had said, about 'proving our mettle', since the umpteen suitcases told a different story. I knew they contained enough inflammables to set the little township on fire: stilettos, floral skirts, figure-hugging dresses and make-up kits were probably not what General Vij had in mind when he had advised us to 'set the right precedent'.

2

Double Up

D-DAY, DAWN: MY ALARM CLOCK SHRIEKED. I SLAPPED it shut. Usually I wouldn't have been this quick in the morning, but a cobra can make you more alert than usual – even if it is in a dream. I had just dreamt that I had been bitten by a cobra and was reeling towards death. *Subah ka sapna...* God! May it never come true, I prayed.

Groggy and bleary-eyed, I stumbled to the bathroom and splashed cold water on my face. Blinking a few times, I peered into the luminous black eyes in the mirror.

Post training, my face had changed: my cheeks had flattened out and my complexion had taken on a dark honey tan. The shoulder-length hair was replaced by a scruffy 'boy cut'. It was the easiest to maintain under a beret – no wastage of time or effort. My light flyaway hair often invited punishments in the academy. To avoid being bullied, I had devised a simple plan: with the beret on, I snipped off whatever stuck out with a pair of scissors. It worked fine – no stray hair, no punishment. Without the beret though, my hair looked like dishevelled plumage. Anju, on the other hand, insisted that her tresses be touched only by a beautician, even if that meant missing the occasional siesta. Guess that paid off. Hers was a neat blunt cut, level with her ears.

Let sleeping dolls lie, I thought as I looked at her. Asleep, she made such a pretty picture. Despite the tough military training, she still looked fair, delicate and feminine, with all her curves at the right places, unlike me. My body was mostly made of straight lines, the curves having nearly vanished. So while she was nicknamed Zulu queen in the academy, I was the Gentleman Cadet, GC. I was what they called the OG (Olive Green) type, doing everything just the way it was supposed to be done. Even when it was the punishment front-rolling session, unlike Anju, I never discreetly filled in haunches to cover distance, for the fear that getting caught would mean plenty more. Anju usually never got caught and even if she did, she almost always managed to escape. I don't know what exactly she did. Perhaps it was her dimpled smile combined with a seductive sway of her body and a sweet utterance of 'Pleeeeezze, sirrr...' that melted the hearts of the ustads and sadistic seniors.

'PT time!' I said, shaking her awake at 5.15 a.m. Dressed in spotless whites, we then jogged to the physical training ground, about a kilometre from the officers' mess where we stayed. The lawn spread out like a green carpet in the midst of the mess garden and the manicured hedge along the compound made a complimenting border. But the road looked like it could do with some maintenance. It was uneven at most places and with the surface tar worn, black stones jutted out.

'Careful,' I said, as I stepped on one. 'A sprained ankle the very first day can label us weaklings.'

'Oooh,' cried Anju. 'My knees hurt. And my body is aching from yesterday's fall.'

'C'mon, it can't be that bad,' I said, playing it down. 'Remember, it's our first day.'

'Yeah,' she nodded. 'We have to make the right first impression... and we shall.'

The PT ground was the unit football ground. Midway between the goalposts stood a large column of men in white, looking like white chessmen on a chessboard, equidistant and with ramrod straight postures. As we approached the column, I had this queasy feeling, the kind one gets when there are far too many eyes latching onto different parts of the body. To add to this, someone was waving to us.

'Isn't it the same officer?' asked Anju.

'Yeah, Long Nose. But why's he waving?'

'Maybe he's saying hi?'

'Stupid, this is a parade fall-in, not a college campus,' I hissed.

She looked at me. 'So what do we do?'

Just then Long Nose sprinted over, saying, 'Go back, go back!' All three of us came to an abrupt stop at the same time.

Startled, we looked at each other and then I turned to him, 'Sir, isn't it the PT fall-in?'

'Just double up,' he said urgently. 'C'mon, quick. These are the adam officer's – I mean, administrative officer's – orders.'

By now all eyes were on us. The whole unit was watching the scene. It would look funny if we just turned around and ran.

'Sir, but why? I mean... there must be some reason,' I persisted.

'Too many questions, huh?' His eyes bore into mine. He didn't have the kind and confused look of yesterday. 'If you must know...' his tone was firm and clear '...you are not in the proper rig.'

We simultaneously looked at our PT rigs. Everything looked perfect – spotlessly white T-shirts, shorts, sneakers and socks.

'Sir, but this is what everyone is wearing. We wore the same rig in the academy too.'

'Look, Second Lieutenant Deepa Shekhar,' the lieutenant rapid-fired, 'I am passing on the adam officer's orders. Get it? He says your presence is making the troops restless.'

'Sir, could we have a word with the adam... I mean, administrative officer?' Anju butted in, trying to make a last attempt to stay on.

Just then the administrative officer walked up. He was a stocky man with short curly black hair. 'What is the problem?' he barked.

'Nothing, sir,' Long Nose said. 'I was telling them to go back.'

'But, sir...' Anju tried to say something. The administrative officer cut her short. 'Both of you meet me in my office. Now, about turn and double up.' Disgust written all over his face, he then turned and walked away.

We had no choice, so we turned around too and ran back.

I felt like an idiot. I felt humiliated, like I had been stripped off my PT rig before the whole unit. I didn't mind if a pterodactyl picked me up that very moment and took me off into the Jurassic age. Anything, just anything was better. Anju wasn't feeling good either. She didn't tell me as much, but I knew because she was running fast with long strides, as though she wanted to go and hide in the loo.

Back in our rooms, we plonked down into our cane chairs. After a few quiet moments, Anju spoke up. 'What a sad first impression!' Her arm dangled across the armrest. 'Shooed away like houseflies before a whole unit... imagine!'

I gave her a rueful stare, sunk in the housefly moment. Unlacing my sneakers, I chucked them into a corner. My socks followed suit. I put my feet up on the glass-topped cane table, stretched back and closed my eyes.

'I am sure it's the shorts,' Anju exclaimed, her eyes lighting up.

I sprang upright. 'But that's our uniform. That's what all officers wear.'

'Then...' she said, looking glumly into my eyes '...we should realize that we are *not* like all officers.'

The administrative officer minced no words when we met him later in his office.

'You can't expose like that. Were you doing a fucking fashion parade showing off your legs like that? All those men, don't you know that they come from villages where women wear purdahs? For them it was a cultural shock. Do you realize that?' He went on for what must have been about ten minutes. With his heavy Hindi accent, 'expose' became 'expoje', 'is' became 'ij', 'legs' became 'legj' and 'realize' was 'realije'.

Both of us stood at attention, looked at him and said together, 'Yes, sir.'

I wasn't sure if the troops got a cultural shock, but he was certainly reeling under its effect. Maybe he came from Purdahland. I lost him somewhere, when suddenly there was silence. He seemed to have posed a question and Anju was looking at me as if she expected me to answer. I gave her an A4-sized blank stare. She then braved his fuming face and offered politely, 'Sir, actually we thought, we could...'

'Stop thinking, Second Lieutenant Anjali Sharma,' he bellowed. 'You are in the army now. All you need to do is take orders from your seniors and execute them. Understand?'

'Yes, sir,' Anju said.

'Stop living in a La-La land!' He shot angry looks at both of us.

'Yes, sir,' we said, in unison.

'You can leave now. And remember to keep a notepad and pen whenever you go to any senior's office.'

'Right, sir.'

What about the PT rig? He hadn't told us anything about that. A quick glance at Anju and a moment of contemplation later, I spoke, 'About our PT rig, sir... we are still not sure...'

'I'll let you know about that.' He cut me short. His pockmarked face then disappeared into a blue file, as if to let us know that he didn't have the time nor the inclination to advise us on what new addition to make to our wardrobes.

'Good day, sir.' Both of us saluted smartly and left his office.

'What a chap!' Anju said once we were out of everyone's hearing range. 'This Lala from La-La land is sure to make our life hell.'

'Hmm... looks like he's from the ranks.'

The administrative officer with his archaic outlook would certainly not be a pleasant man to deal with. But he held an important appointment and interaction with him was inevitable. Before meeting him in his office, both of us had taken care to be impeccably attired. We didn't want to be ticked off again for the way we were turned out. Moreover, we were to formally meet the Commanding Officer, the Second-in-Command and other senior officers. We had ensured that our Olive Green uniform had ruler-straight creases, the stars on our shoulders shone a bright golden, the black leather belt with its broad silver buckle fitted snugly on our waists, and the toes of our black DMS boots sparkled enough to reflect the faces of anyone who looked at them.

Our first formal interview was with the Commanding Officer, the senior-most officer in the unit, the king. All we knew about him was that he was Sikh. As we walked into his office, I felt like we were entering a mini-fortress, decorated with painted ammunition shells, spears as tall as me, about five feet six, and large potted plants a few inches shorter, about as high as Anju. A red runner bordered by smaller potted fan palms ran out of his office. The air here was so thick with ceremony that even breathing felt cumbersome.

I adjusted my peak cap and pressed the puffed-up scarf down into my shirt. While other officers wore the more comfortable berets without the noosing scarf, we had to be attired more rigidly since it was our first day, the day of official meetings – the day of lasting impressions.

My heart fluttering, I stepped onto the red runner. Anju was ahead of me. Suddenly, as if struck by lightning, she stomped her feet and jerked her right hand into a salute. The next instant, I carried out my best demo-type salute, the kind that would make my drill ustad in the academy beam with pride.

Standing before us was a towering Sikh gentleman,

in the most impressive of uniforms. He was perfection personified. His boots twinkled as if they were studded with diamonds, his silver-encrusted black shoulder strap gave him a regal aura, his turban had an untouched-by-hands look and even his moustache made the perfect angles of a flattened W.

This tower of perfection suddenly swung his baton under his arm, stomped harder than either of us and said, 'Jai hind, sahab!'

It didn't take us more than a second to realize that this impressive person we gave our smashing salutes to, was, in fact, the Commanding Officer's sentry, someone way too junior to us in the hierarchal rank structure.

I looked around. Had anyone seen our howler? There were personnel around, but all of them seemed to walk about purposefully, flitting in and out of offices.

We walked ahead as if nothing had happened, trying to stay dignified. 'Look before you jerk like that again,' I hissed to Anju. 'We just made fools of ourselves. Thank God no one saw us.'

'Why the hell did you jerk?' Anju retorted. 'Did I ask you?' Although she pretended to be irritated, I couldn't miss the smile dancing on her lips. I looked away, suppressing the laughter bubbling inside. But before we could reach the heavily ornamented teak door, we had both burst into guffaws. Then we hurriedly muffled our laughter lest the king enquire after the new sounds in his fortress. We waited a few minutes for the ripples to die before entering the Lion's den.

Colonel Gurcharan Singh Shan was a polished Sikh gentleman with a stern air about him, who spoke crisply and wielded his baton effectively. To me, he looked like an older version of the sentry outside. I consoled myself that our confusion was more or less justified.

'So,' he raised a bushy eyebrow at me after the formal introduction. 'Why did you join the army?'

If ever I was certain about anything in the army, it was this question. Perhaps the males in the Olive Greens thought we were misfits here, like penguins in the Sahara.

'Sir, actually... army...' I said, trying not to sound like it was one of my most well-rehearsed answers. 'It's different...'

'It's different...?' he intervened before I could explain further, '...as in...' His eyes searched for something on the ornate ceiling fan. 'What was that ad?'

'Maggi tomato ketchup, sir.' Anju was at her impressive best.

His hypnotic eyes flew down to her. 'Hmm... and what about you?'

'Sir, there's something about the army...'

'That's different?'

'No. No, sir... What I mean is... there's something that cannot be compared with anything in the civilian world...'

'Like the canteen?'

'No, sir, like the... glamour of uniform, the respect...'

'Glamour?' He frowned. 'You see glamour here?' I had this unnerving feeling that his baton would fly the next moment into Anju's face.

'No, sir...' Anju battled on, '...actually what I meant w-a-s...'

'Okay, okay, I get it.' He waved an imposing hand at us. A tense silence followed. 'Now, let me tell you young officers,' he said, the inflection and authority in his voice reminding us that we were face to face with the Lion himself, an angry one at that. 'Whatever your reasons might be, here all I am interested is in what you can do.' He leant towards us, and we shifted uncomfortably in our chairs. His eyes bored into our faces as he said, 'I'll be monitoring your performance very closely.'

We gulped. My chair was beginning to feel like a seat of thorns. I couldn't wait to get out.

'Meet the 2i/c,' he said, dismissing us. 'He will brief you on some important points.'

'What a khadoos boss,' Anju whispered once we were outside his fortress. 'Not that I expected him to be a huggable teddy bear or something, but he's a little too much!' I thought it was too dangerous to reply since we were at the nerve centre of the unit.

Two offices away was the 2i/c's or the Second-in-Command's office, where we headed for our second formal interview.

The first thing I noticed about the Second-in-Command was a bald patch on his head that I thought shone as much, if not more, than the toe of my boot. After the scary Commanding Officer, he came across as very friendly. The customary introduction over, he said, looking my way, 'I heard you crash-landed.'

'Cra...sh...? Oh, not me, sir, it was her,' I looked at Anju. She nodded, a gleam of pride in her eyes. She then went on to describe the whole incident in even more words than she had done to me. Thankfully the black telephone on his glass table-top rang. The peanut vendor would have to wait.

I threw her a disgruntled look. All she needed was a smiling face and she would take off on a yapping spree. She gave me a brief, stubborn stare and then pretended to look around.

Like the Commanding Officer's office, the Second-in-Command's office too, had an air of military pomp, with shields, mementoes, swords and miniature models of weapons and tanks. But to me, it felt that he wasn't carrying the weight of being the Second-in-Command very well, or else he wouldn't let Anju go on. The telephone conversation over, he turned to us.

'So, where was I?'

I took over. 'Sir, the CO said you had to tell us something important.' Anju's not-so-friendly eyes narrowed at me.

'Oh, yes,' he said. Then suddenly his face transformed. He rolled his eyes and curled his lips, contorting his face in a way that storytellers do when building the suspense. I leant forward, all ears.

'You are the first lady officers to be posted in this unit,' he said sombrely.

'Yes, sir,' we said.

'You see,' he put aside a green pen that he was holding, 'you need to be careful about a lot of things. Here, you will be surrounded by men and remember that you are constantly being watched. You must understand that a woman always attracts attention, especially when there are so many males around. So you need to conduct yourself well.'

'Yes, sir,' I said.

'Yes, sir,' Anju said, after two seconds.

'To assist you, we have appointed a good sahayak, one with exemplary conduct, since we have no option to provide you with a lady orderly. You see, we don't want to get into trouble on any account.' He paused for a moment. 'Frankly, I don't understand why they had to enrol women in the army. It's a tough life not fit for the weaker sex... well, anyway,' – he cleared his throat and clasped his fingers together – 'those are policy matters we have little control over. On our part, we have done everything possible. We have fixed a security grill in your verandah. All doors, windows and their latches have been repaired. We have installed a neon lamp just outside your room.' His upturned palms stressed each point with a jerky downward motion. 'Now,' he said, sighing, 'it's up to you to ensure your security.' He paused for a moment. 'Are you with me?'

'Y-y-yes, sir,' Anju said as she quickly fixed the pen she had been fiddling with back onto her notepad. I threw her a dirty look. This was the Second-in-Command's office and he was telling us some important things. Why the hell wasn't she paying attention?

'On your part, ensure that you don't attract unnecessary attention,' he continued. He then hesitated for a moment and said, 'Keep your things out of view of all males. Do you get me?'

'No, sir,' Anju said, before I could figure out the kind of things he was referring to.

'Well,' he paused before continuing, his eyes darting downwards, 'what I mean is your garments, ahem... your special garments such as br...'

'Got it, sir!' I sprang up from my chair; then sank back.

A tense silence followed. For a few moments, the important thing hung heavily in the air between the Second-in-Command and the two of us, among the glittering swords and shields. My quick interruption had also succeeded in getting his eyes from the region below our chins back to our faces.

He mock-cleared his throat and continued, 'All members of the Army Wives Welfare Association, that is, AWWA, will be there to help you, in case you have any gender-specific needs. We live like a family here and we are all there for each other.'

'Sir,' we nodded.

'And yes, before I forget. Please get full-length trousers made for PT, just like your OG trousers, minus the loops. We have a good unit tailor.' He scratched his bald pate and continued, 'Also, meet Major Prashant Bhat today itself. He will discuss some important professional aspects with you.' He then leant forward so that his three-tiered set of service ribbons brushed the table. Both his hands rested on the glass sheet. 'Is there anything else you would like to know, or tell me?'

'Sir,' said Anju, 'we would like to know about our appointment.'

'Don't be in a hurry, Second Lieutenant Sharma,' he said. 'You both have just come. We need to train you before placing you anywhere. Does that answer your query?' As we nodded reluctantly, he stretched back in his chair. 'If there is anything at all, don't hesitate to approach me.' He smiled.

'That was so embarrassing,' I said as soon as we left his office. 'All the things he talked about.'

'You were overreacting. We are women after all, and so, different from the lot.'

'We are officers,' I said, irritated. 'They must treat us like any other officer. Do you think he would've instructed Long Nose on where to hang his underwear to dry?'

'Don't talk rubbish,' Anju said, frowning.

'Rubbish? It's not me, it's you who talks rubbish non-stop. The man you told the unabridged version of the Ramayana to was the 2i/c, the damn Second-in-Command of this whole unit... Can't you just talk to the point?'

'I just said what he wanted to know,' she said, and looked away. 'What's wrong with that?'

We walked silently along the L-shaped corridor to Major Prashant Bhat's office. Flowerpots on both sides, painted a jarring red, stung my eyes. Even the green of the slender palms and the intricate patterns on the crotons failed to soothe. We stopped short of his office. Then I did what we had done before meeting all other officers. I adjusted my cap and slightly aligned the insignia on my belt to the centre. In a swift movement, I rubbed the toes of my shoes against the calves of my trousers. Anju chose to skip these steps, and instead knocked on the door.

A baritone voice said, 'Come in.'

Anju entered first, saluting smartly.

'Smart salute,' said Major Bhat. He wasn't looking at me. So I assumed the compliment wasn't meant for me. Both of us looked at each other, confused.

'Squat,' he said, pointing to the chairs across his table. Major Bhat was in sharp contrast to the other major we'd met, the administrative officer. This officer was in fact what you would call handsome, with an oval face, deep-set eyes and an angular jaw. He was lightly tanned and had an Ivy League haircut, brushed to a side. The most noticeable thing about him however, was his confidence. Had he been a little younger, he could well have passed for an MTV VJ.

His office too, unlike the others, had minimal paraphernalia – a table, an olive green Godrej cupboard and three chairs, one on his side of the table and two on ours, all of which were now occupied. A window on our left overlooked a road where an occasional pedestrian or motorcyclist appeared in the frame. On the wall was a grimy square clock that was slightly tilted. Below it hung an Army Postal Corps calendar, fluttering under the fan.

'So, who's who?' A cigarette held between his index and middle fingers wagged from Anju to me and back. Then, as if drawn towards Anju, he looked at her, 'So, you are…?'

'Sir, I am Second Lieutenant Anjali Sharma,' said Anju, bending her torso forward. I suddenly realized that he was attracted to her. In fact, even a moron could tell that Major Bhat was smitten. Anju had this kind of effect on most people, but no one made it so obvious. I was sure Anju hadn't sensed anything. That was her.

As for me, I felt one with the wall behind.

'And you must be…' he peeled his eyes away from her face to look at me.

'Second Lieutenant Deepa Shekhar, sir,' I supplied, sensing he would hardly have cared if I had said 'Madhuri Dixit'.

'Okay, well, let me introduce myself,' he said, tapping the cigarette on a glass ashtray brimming with ash. 'I am Major Prashant Bhat. I am the one who'll help you learn about how things work here.' When he spoke, his Adam's apple bobbed up and down, I noticed. 'In fact, I had a long discussion with the CO about the way you can contribute to the unit.' He puffed in, blew out a thick cloud of smoke and continued, 'I suggested that you be trained before being appointed anywhere. The old man said it was a great idea. You see, the old man depends on me for most things. I am not blowing my own trumpet, but the thing is, there's no one else here who has the experience and knowledge I have.' His pearly whites gleamed. 'In fact, you could call me his blue-eyed boy or man Friday.'

'Yes, sir,' we said.

'Okay, before everything else, I want to know something.' His eyes flitted from one of us to the other. 'Tell me, do I look scary?'

'No, sir,' Anju said immediately, flashing a dimpled smile. I had half a mind to nod 'yes' to give his inflated ego an unexpected prick. There are times when you want to add something to your To-Do list even if you could never do it. This was one.

'So,' he continued, 'don't sit so stiffly, like you're watching a horror show. I want you guys to be a li'l relaxed, okay?' His cigarette then pointed to our heads. 'You can take those caps off. Don't worry, they won't get lost on my table.' He laughed throatily.

Files, loose papers, manuals, pen holders and other stationery jostled for space on his table, now joined by our peak caps. I ran a quick hand to settle my wanton hair, in a bid to evade comments from the rock star. Despite the hairpins placed strategically in my hair like warheads, some strands still managed to escape.

But he didn't seem to notice. 'Okay, now... would you like some tea or coffee?' He reached under his table for the bell. 'You will be spending a lot of time here. So make yourselves comfortable. Tea or coffee?'

'Tea,' I heard Anju say.

I opened my mouth to ask for a coffee but promptly closed it as he said, *'Teen chai,'* to the attendant in grey who came in. *'Juldee,'* he added, in a fake British accent, and took another puff. Then his eyes settled back on Anju.

'So, how's it been so far? Be honest.'

Anju looked at me.

'Why are you looking at her?' Major Bhat said. 'I

am asking you.'

'It's been alright, sir,' Anju said, contradicting my expectations.

'Well, as far as I know it hasn't been... and dontcha lie to me,' he said in a singsong way, shaking his head. I thought he looked like a child actor who was grossly overacting. Anju seemed amused though.

He went on, 'I know about the leap from the running train, the incident at the PT fall-in, the mix-up at the CO's office...' Anju and I cringed at the last one. Surely he didn't know about our saluting blunder?

Major Bhat paused to read our reaction. Then he took another puff and continued, 'Surprised, eh? I know about the smart salute you gave the sentry.' He blew out some smoke and smiled like a man who had just attained nirvana. Both of our heads hung low. It was one of those rare moments when I was caught halfway between laughing and crying.

'See, I get to know everything that happens here,' Major Bhat continued. 'The thing is, you are the first lady officers to be posted here. Remember, you are in the spotlight. Everyone knows what you are doing, but no one knows what to expect of you and how to behave with you. So, all I can say is, be alert. And also... don't take everything to heart.' He nodded, looking satisfied with the lecture he had just delivered.

'Come, have your tea,' he said, motioning to the steel tray the attendant had brought in.

We held our saucers cautiously, with tea brimming over from the cups. He swept aside a file and made place for his. We waited for him to take the first sip – it was always seniors first. He then alternated between talking on the phone and signing documents that had been brought to him. Between his phone conversations, he took quick sips of tea and long puffs of smoke. I wondered how the smoked tea tasted in his mouth. Meanwhile, he went about his business with an air of self-importance, intermittently taking on the role of an instructor.

'There's the executive wing and the administrative wing,' he said handing over a dark yellow file to a waiting havaldar. 'The executive wing is where the action happens... issues, receipts and everything concerning stores. The administrative wing ensures discipline and welfare of the personnel, the non-officer cadre... the JCOs and ORs – the Junior Commissioned Officers and Other Ranks. The administrative officer is responsible for their discipline and welfare. And in our case it's Major Uttam Singh.'

A pockmarked face suddenly appeared before my eyes. I prayed I didn't have to hold an appointment in the administrative wing, under the administrative officer's direct line of fire. The executive side looked no better with Major Bhat at its helm. Was there no other wing?

'Ideally we would want one of you to be on this side and one on the other.'

That answered everything. I stared down at my notepad. My future suddenly looked bleak: there was no escaping Lala.

Not that the present was any better. Pre-lunch, post and late into that evening, we sat glued to the same twine and steel chairs, in much the same way. I was getting used to the disarrayed, smoke-filled office, Major Bhat's rumbling voice and the irritating flutter of the calendar.

'So, see you guys in the evening,' he said, getting up past sunset and stuffing three portly files into his briefcase. He was tall, well over six feet.

'Sir, in the evening?' the words escaped me faster than I had intended. I smiled quickly to nullify the negative connotation of the question. 'I mean... sir, in the mess...?'

'Yeah,' he said, shifting all his weight on his hands to close the briefcase. 'I hope you guys know there's a party.'

'A party?' exclaimed Anju, her excitement leaping out of her eyes.

'Yeah,' he smiled. 'Enjoy, since today you guys have nothing much to do.' He walked out of the office. Both of us followed him like chicks following a mother hen.

The word 'party' had sent Anju into another world. I was sure this could be a cause of friction between us.

'Excuse me, sir. I have a doubt,' I said.

He turned around, 'Yeah, shoot.'

'Sir, about our dress... I mean, we don't want to be ticked off for not being in the proper rig.'

'Oh! It's open collar.' Looking at my lost face, he went on to explain further. 'It means shirt and trousers but no tie. You must have worn it in the academy.'

'Yes, sir,' I said.

'But with the tie. Muftis, sir,' Anju elaborated.

'Alright then, be there by 7.30. A lot of people are eager to meet you.' He then kicked his fluorescent-green Bajaj scooter a dozen times, tilting it at various angles, before it agreed to oblige him with a ride. They looked like bum chums; my guess was they had started their careers together.

We saluted him. 'Good day, sir.'

'Ciao,' he waved, snaking away, his eyes lingering on Anju a tad longer than necessary.

3

Cheers!

ANJU STOOD BEFORE THE MIRROR IN A PALE PURPLE shirt and black trousers. 'Isn't it kinda weird?' she asked, running her hand over her combed hair.

'What?' I hurriedly tucked my cream shirt into beige trousers and slipped my feet into my black brogues.

'That we are wearing pants for a party.' She turned to look at me. 'Imagine! Baggy pants!'

'Think of it as our uniform. Come on, let's go,' I said, walking out of the room. I didn't want to dwell too much on the topic.

We walked up the cobble-stoned path to the officers' mess. In the subdued and well placed lighting of the long corridor here, the leaves of the potted plants looked soft, as though awash in moonlight. Even the pots here retained their earthy brown colour, unlike the jarring red of the office complex. Tastefully placed artefacts lined the corridor and the off-white walls were hung with classy paintings. I was certain that there was some female involvement in the décor here. Perhaps it was the senior officers' wives who gave everything here a soft touch.

An unpleasant voice suddenly wafted towards us from the mess doors, 'Is this the bloody time to come?

Are you the fucking guests? You are the junior-most around and behave like generals!'

Lala! We rushed forward. Long Nose and another young officer were with him as well.

'Sir, this was the time given to us,' I said, trying to explain things.

'When I can be here by 7.15,' he barked, 'you bloody well be here before me.'

'Sir, actually Major Bhat had given us this time,' Anju said.

He paused for a moment. The mention of that name seemed to have some effect on him. But he quickly got back into form. 'The next time you do this, I tell you,' he said, wagging a finger at us, 'I will come down heavily on you.'

'Yes, sir.'

'Sandeep!' He turned to Long Nose as his hand slid down to his crotch for a scratch. 'If this is your state, what will you teach these lost juniors?' He scratched some more. 'I want the menu card ready in the next ten minutes. I don't care how you manage it!'

Long Nose excused himself and darted out of the mess.

Lala then turned to the other officer. 'And you, Vishal, do whatever, beg, borrow, steal – anything. I don't care. Get that damn Johnnie Walker Black Label.'

Vishal, the officer we hadn't met formally yet, also disappeared.

That left Anju and me face to face with Lala. We looked at him for orders.

'Why are you staring at my face?' he barked. 'Go check the ante room and check that everything is perfect in queens.'

We headed to the ante room.

'"Is-taring at my phace!"' Anju mimicked Lala as we entered the luxurious-looking ante room. 'Huh! As if his cratered face is even worth a glance.'

'Shhh!' I said. 'If he hears it, he might come down heavily on you.'

'Yuck! If he does, I'll kick him where he scratches the most.'

We laughed and sank into a blue sofa. Blue seemed to be the theme of this room: the curtains, upholstery and carpet were all the same shade of peacock blue. Gold-framed paintings adorned the walls – beautiful landscapes, battle scenes, uniformed army men of yore and a portrait of a Tibetan woman. On a deep mahogany cabriole-legged table near the entrance, a heavy, black leather-bound book sat commandingly. I walked up to it. 'Visitor's Book', it proclaimed in golden letters.

'This room looks fine,' Anju said, following close behind me. 'Let me check the queens.'

Anju left, while I browsed through the pages of the visitor's book, taking care not to change its position. Glowing comments from generals, brigadiers and colonels on the hospitality extended by the unit during their visits filled its pages.

'Have you ensured everything is fine in this room?' I froze at the voice from the back. It was Lala.

'Yes, sir.'

He pulled out the blue pen from the gold-trimmed set of pens beside the book, took out a paper from his pocket and scribbled something. Perhaps he planned to give me some written instructions.

Lala's eyes glowered. 'This doesn't write,' he announced, waving it at me like a sword. The red pen, despite my frenzied prayers, didn't either.

'I want refills in both of these,' he howled. 'Get it from wherever.'

'Yes, sir,' I said, and turned to leave when he threw another spear my way. 'Where is the flower vase? Where are the flowers?'

'Sir...' I looked around hoping a flower vase would emerge from somewhere. 'Sir...'

'C'mon, speak up. Have you swallowed your tongue?'

'No, sir,' I said, and immediately felt silly that I actually answered that question. 'Sir...' I mumbled, '...I never saw one here.'

'You haven't? Look here,' he walked to a small table next to the sofa. 'Look!' He lifted up the boat-shaped glass tray and thrust it towards my eyes. 'Now can you see?'

'Yes, sir,' I answered once again, foolishly. Lala obviously couldn't tell the difference between a flower vase and a flower tray. But this was no time to highlight such intricacies of interior decoration. He placed his 'vase' back with a heavy thud, walked across to another table and lifted the newspaper. 'Where is the Sunday magazine?'

'Sir, it must be right there,' I croaked.

'Come, show me.'

I walked up and pretended to search for it, as if I had just placed it back after reading it.

'Irresponsible!' he grumbled. 'Is this the way you function? And where's that friend of yours?'

'Sir, she's in the queens.'

'Ensure all the tasks I have given you are completed. I'll be right back.'

He walked purposefully towards the ladies washroom. I spied from behind as he entered it.

There were a few moments of silence before a burst of abuses. A blue packet came flying out of the door. I recognized it as a pack of sanitary napkins. Another one followed, an empty tissue packet. Lala emerged with Anju following.

'Sir, I don't know who to ask to replace this,' Anju said.

'I don't take negative answers. Go find out and get it done,' Lala said, although he was in no mood to let her go. 'Dust, dirt, stink… and you tell me everything is alright?'

I ducked behind the door, clueless as to where to get the refills, flowers and Sunday magazine.

'Do you have a good handwriting?' someone asked me from the back. I turned around, alarmed. Was this really the time to assess my handwriting?

'See, I just got the menu card,' Long Nose explained, seeing my puzzled look. 'And now since the draftsman is not available I'm looking for someone who can write neatly on this. And I'm sure you can do this.'

'Sir, but I need to get refills, flowers and the Sunday magazine.'

'Oh! That's easy. You do my task. I'll do yours,' he bartered. 'Here's the list. Please don't make any mistakes.'

Long Nose gave me a black, thick-nibbed pen and an old menu card for reference, and left the ante room.

'Almond Soup,' I began to write very carefully.

Outside I could hear the voices of Anju, Lala and a third person: Major Prashant Bhat.

'Uttam, relax,' Major Bhat was saying in his baritone. 'What do you expect this youngster to do? Give her some time to learn how things work here. And in any case, most of it is the mess havaldar's job.'

'Yes, sir,' I heard Lala say, his bark having reduced to a moan.

A quiet moment followed. I was sure Anju felt secure under the mother hen's wings. No one could harm her now.

'Gurung,' Major Bhat rumbled. 'Where were you all this while?'

'Sahab, I had gone to get things for the party.'

'At this time? Bloody bugger! Pull up your socks. Get moving now and get everything in order,' Major Bhat thundered.

Then everyone seemed to have dispersed as there were no more voices. A short man came into the ante room with flowers and stuck them hurriedly on the pin. 'Jai hind, sahab,' he wished me before changing the refills in both the pens.

'Jai hind,' I said. 'Please place the Sunday magazine also.'

'Sahab, Major Bhat had taken it to read yesterday. He hasn't returned it.'

'Okay,' I said, relieved that two of my tasks were done and for the third, I had an answer.

'Gurung!' Major Bhat's thunderous roar shook the small man, as he switched on the air conditioner. He sprinted across the corridor to the main entrance.

'Can't you see the dust accumulated on the shield? Look, I can sign on it,' I heard Major Bhat say. 'C'mon, get it polished. We don't want our guests to think ours is a dheela unit. It affects our CO sahab's reputation.' Some more orders followed. All I could hear the mess havaldar say was, 'Ji, sahab.'

I continued with the menu card. 'Baked Cauliflower'. As I wrote the last item on the menu, 'Date Pudding', I sighed, relieved at not having made any mistakes. Long

Nose was pleased when he saw the card. He thanked me and carried it away, holding it carefully, as if it were a rare and precious work of art.

Lala appeared eventually and nitpicked some more. I braved all his vitriolic outpourings. It had not hurt so much when Anju and I were together at the receiving end. Just as I was beginning to wonder where Anju was, she appeared close behind Major Bhat. I was relieved to see her – doubly so because their coming also meant Lala's exit.

Major Bhat took a drag of his cigarette and exhaled the smoke slowly, looking around the room as though inspecting everything. He stopped abruptly at the flowers.

Anju seemed to read his mind and said, 'There's no harmony. Some of the chrysanthemums should be shorter. I'll just get it ready.'

No harmony? What was she up to? Was she volunteering to be a flower girl? Even as I looked on, Anju went about snipping a few leaves here, a stem there and arranging them with the expertise of an Ikebana artist. With her handiwork, every flower in the bunch looked stunning.

Apparently Major Bhat seemed to think so too. 'That's a fab job,' he remarked. Anju beamed like a child.

The party soon began to gain momentum as officers began trickling in accompanied by their wives. At 7.50, when the Commanding Officer's black Ambassador entered the mess premises, the mess staff ran helter-skelter to be in their respective positions. Major Bhat stood up, stubbed his cigarette, fanned the smoke lingering near his mouth and rushed to the main entrance. Anju and I followed him.

This was the first time that I saw our Commanding Officer standing. He was really tall – even taller than his sentry – close to six feet three or four inches. His towering figure made most of the other officers look like pygmies. When he cast a glance at Anju and I, we froze. For those brief seconds, anyone could have mistaken us for clothed trees. But the king mostly ignored us and expressed his desire to see the clarity of the cable connection. As he walked to the TV room, the Second-in-Command, Major Bhat and Lala followed him. When the king pointed his finger anywhere, all eyes flew there; when he turned, they turned; and when he stopped, they stopped abruptly, almost tripping over. As the troop marched out of our hearing range, Anju whispered, 'Where's the first lady?'

'She probably melted just being around him,' I whispered back.

'No, but seriously...' Suddenly her face lit up. 'Hey, have you seen Lala's wife?'

'No,' I said, wondering where she had managed to acquire her general awareness so soon.

'Okay, now as we walk across the ante room door, look at the second lady from left in the cream and blue sari. That's Lali.'

'Lali? As in Lala-Lali?'

'No, stupid, her smudged lipstick is blood-red, lal, and an utter mismatch with her behenji personality. Okay, now follow me.'

I followed her, curious to see Lali. 'Major Bhat introduced you to her?'

'No, just showed me. Okay, *bayen dekh*,' Anju ordered parade-style as we walked. I just about managed to catch a glimpse of Lali. All I could see was a small middle-aged woman in a heavy zari sari.

'What about Major Bhat?' I said, as we walked back to our original positions. 'I mean his wife... have you met her?'

Anju didn't see this question coming, but she answered quickly nevertheless, 'No, I haven't, but I think she's not here, or he would have introduced me.'

We joined the officers as they stood at the entrance, waiting for the guests to arrive. One of the captains suggested that we join the ladies, who sat gossiping loudly in the ante room. We managed to convince him that we were standing at the right place. By eight o'clock, the Commanding Officer and his troupe joined the rest of us to receive the guests. Even in the party scenario, everything was as per military clockwork precision. The hosts arrived 15 to 30 minutes early based on the seniority. Then it was the Second-in-Command's turn and within precisely five minutes after that, the Commanding Officer arrived. Now that it was time, the guests began to pour in.

Commanding officers and seconds-in-command of various units walked in accompanied by their ladies in dazzling finery. While each guest officer shook hands with other officers, when Anju and I put our enthusiastic hands forward, most folded theirs in a polite namaste, as if to say, 'Sorry-ladies-we-can't-touch-you'. Some even went on to add 'ji' to the namaste, adding to my ire. The 'namasteji' made me feel like Pappu-ki-ma. Only a few shook our hands and I respected them just for breaking away from tradition – quite like us.

The ladies however had a more varied reaction on seeing us. One of them hugged us tightly, planting a glossy kiss on our cheeks. There was another who stuck both palms on her cheeks and squealed, as though she were seeing a rare species of ape. One placed her plump arms around our shoulders and said how proud she was of us. There was another one who pulled us by our waists, wishing all the while that she could be one of us, if only they enrolled women in the army back then. Some commented that we looked smart, while others thought it inappropriate that women should mimic men in their entirety: career, mannerisms, attire and all. A few walked by, pouting at us. Then there were those who merely smiled dutifully.

A wave of silence suddenly descended on the waiting group. 'The general's here,' someone whispered. A cavalcade of black Ambassador flag cars arrived with the honoured guests for the evening, a major general, a brigadier and a colonel, the area inspection team. The Lion leapt forward to welcome them. His erect torso however, acquired a tilt now as he hovered around them. In his tame and dethroned avatar, he now looked more like a circus lion.

'Sir, these are the two lady officers posted in my unit,' the Lion said, moving briskly towards us. He had only introduced the Second-in-Command to the general and skipped all the others.

Suddenly all eyes were on us. I felt like we were being X-rayed. I wasn't expecting this kind of importance. Nor was Anju, since she immediately came to attention and nearly jerked into a salute. I tugged at her hand just in time and saved us some embarrassment – we were not supposed to salute without head gear on, but Anju seemed to forget everything when nervous. She probably took the drill ustad's words too seriously when he had joked: 'In the army, when in doubt, salute.'

I stood transfixed to the spot, awestruck at being face to face with a general for the first time ever. I didn't even notice when he extended his hand. This time Anju pinched my arm.

'I hope you contribute well to the organization,' the general said as he shook hands with us. He then walked away led by the Commanding Officer.

During the course of the party, we found ourselves to be the centre of attraction. Either someone was looking our way or someone was talking about us or someone was striking up a conversation with us.

'So, your training was at the Indian Military Academy, Dehradun?' asked a lady in blue as she floated towards us.

'No, ma'am,' said Anju politely. 'We were trained at the Officers' Training Academy, Madras.'

'So you are here for a five-year tenure?'

'Yes, ma'am, Short Service Commission,' Anju said.

'Okay. And how was your training? I mean did you have to handle guns, do route marches and live in tents like the officers?'

'You mean *gentlemen* officers, ma'am?' I said, not as polite as Anju.

Anju took over. 'Yes, certainly, ma'am. We handled a range of weapons, lived in tents, did route marches, physical endurance tests, horse-riding, swimming...'

Before Anju could list the entire academy curriculum, the plump lady we had met earlier in the evening walked over and swung her arms around us. 'Aaaww! I am so proud of you both,' she said, squeezing our heads into her bosom, suffocating us. She then released us, took our rough hands into her manicured ones and said, 'You are the brave new generation of women in our country who have broken the shackles of tradition and dared to venture into untested new waters...'

Did she just make this up or was she regurgitating a prepared speech, I wondered. She went on. And on. In a matter of seconds, she had raised us to a pedestal so high it made me dizzy.

The lady's voice quivered with emotion in conclusion: '...prove yourselves, since you are the ones who represent all of us in a man's world.'

'Yes, ma'am,' we smiled courteously. Everyone was silent for a while, as though giving the lady some recovery time.

'So, how do you like the army?' asked another lady in a brick-red sari, who had accompanied the plump constrictor.

'It's a great place to be, ma'am. Lots of challenges, a life of adventure, new places, people, new experiences,' Anju said.

'Did your parents agree to this decision?'

Anju and I looked at each other. Both of our parents had their reservations. My parents wanted me to complete my post graduation in physics and become a lecturer – the ideal job for a woman in their view. In a Malayali family that valued the teaching profession and academic pursuits higher than anything else, convincing them of my career choice was tough, especially since I was their only child. Anju's parents in Delhi had a problem of another kind. Since she had a sister two years younger than her, they felt that her unusual career choice would create complications for both of them in the marriage market. They had been upset when her very fair skin tone had darkened about two shades due to the training. Anju's parents would have ideally liked her to continue with her job as assistant office manager at a five-star hotel in Delhi, which she had landed soon after graduating in English. Anju had surprised them when she told them that she wanted to do something more exciting than grinning at well-dressed strangers.

Ironically, that's precisely what she was doing now.

'Actually, ma'am, they didn't agree right away,' she smiled, 'but we convinced them.'

'I knew it,' the lady said, looking satisfied for having successfully cornered us. 'No sensible parents can agree to let their daughter join the army, at least not in India. Our culture is not such that we let our daughters roam anywhere in the country, live anywhere, amidst men of all types! It's the *ijjat* of a girl after all.'

'Times are changing and we must accept the new changes,' said our plump constrictor, coming to our rescue. 'Women are everywhere now, conquering new heights...'

'Okay, tell me, Mrs Bhalla...' the lady in the red sari interrupted, 'would you let your daughter join the army?'

'I don't have a daughter, Mrs Das. But if I had one I would find nothing wrong in sending her,' said the plump Mrs Bhalla.

They stuck to their views. We changed ours – facial expressions that is – as we turned from one lady to the other. 'Excuse me,' I suddenly raised both my hands, trying to take control of the situation. 'Ma'am, it is our career choice and we are happy.'

Both stopped abruptly and turned to me. I shrugged, unable to think of anything more to say.

Anju pitched in, 'Yes, ma'am, we are happy.'

'You are too young to know anything about the world.' Mrs Das seemed to be in no mood to stop. 'How old are you, tell me?'

'Twenty-three, ma'am.'

'See, that's what I said. You better be careful and don't trust everyone around,' she advised us in a matronly tone. 'You people, I don't understand...' she said, concern written all over her painted face, 'you could have chosen brilliant careers. Why did you join the army?'

'Oh my God!' Anju suddenly exclaimed as though she had spotted a UFO landing in the vicinity. I knew she was up to something. 'I didn't even notice,' she said, her eyes wide open, fixed on Mrs Das's brick-red sari. 'Ma'am, isn't this the Baluchari... with stories from the Ramayana and Mahabharata woven into it? It's so b-eau-ti-full'

The other ladies joined in to admire Mrs Das's sari and pulled up the pallu to examine it. Mrs Das looked pleased with all the attention coming her way and forgot all about giving us advice. The conversation drifted to Tangail, Kanthas, Tanjores and Murshidabad silks. Anju participated keenly, while I was quiet. The kind of knowledge Anju had about all these saris, I was certain that she had one of each kind in her suitcases.

Although we managed to flee from this group, there were many more waiting to bombard us with questions and advice. Even before we realized it, we were face to face with the general and his troupe.

We stood before them as if facing a firing squad.

'So, where have you appointed them?' the general asked our Commanding Officer, twirling his grey moustache.

'Sir, presently they are undergoing an orientation capsule for two months,' the Lion said. 'Then we plan to appoint them appropriately.'

'Very good,' said the general, and sipped his drink. 'Do you think you can do night duty,' he turned to me, 'that is, inspecting guard posts at night and staying in the duty officer's room?'

'Yes, sir,' I said in my most impressive form.

'I see,' he said, nodding longer than I thought was necessary. I almost felt certain that he didn't see.

'I have my doubts,' he continued after a pause. 'I am not saying it is not possible, but it certainly will be difficult. Am I not right?' He turned to Anju.

'NO, sir!' Anju said, startling the general.

The general smiled, flashing his golden dentures. For the first time, we saw our Commanding Officer smile and to me, the first time ever, he looked normal. Now, since the general smiled, everyone in the group quickly took off their grim masks and put on happy ones, revealing their teeth.

One of them, an officer with salt and pepper hair said, 'Sir, 20 years back we could not even have imagined that women could wear the same uniform and rub shoulders with us.'

'Even if they wear the same uniform,' another lanky one said, as he shifted his weight from one leg to the other, 'they can never rub shoulders with us. You see,' he smiled, 'they are too short for that.'

The group 'ho-ho-hoed' like a bunch of Santas, the taller ones laughing more merrily than the rest. I hated to see my Commanding Officer shake and enjoy the poor joke.

'Let's not underestimate their capabilities,' the general said, waving away their bonhomie. 'We must understand that they are among the best in the country, intellectually, academically and mentally... perhaps better than us. In fact, I had spoken in depth to two of them at Delhi and I learnt that it was a desire to do something out of the ordinary that got them here. Am

I not right?' He turned to look at both of us and we nodded vigorously. He then turned back to his audience. 'Gentlemen, I will not be surprised if in the next ten years, I see them leading infantry battalions.'

The group nodded in pseudo agreement and put their grim masks back on. It was now our turn to smile.

We drifted away from this group and for the first time during the course of the party, were by ourselves, with no one clambering all over us. Our novelty must have worn off. At a distance, ladies paraded out of the dining room, their plates loaded with goodies.

'It's not going to be easy,' I said. 'You saw our old man laughing? All of them are so biased.'

'Hmmm.' Anju took a sip of her almond soup. She liked her tea and soup piping hot. 'I had always thought the officers would be chivalrous to ladies,' she said, 'but they are so rude to us.'

'That's because we are not just ladies, we are officers,' I said. Anju wasn't looking at me, but I could tell she didn't agree. I continued, 'But it looks like they are not ready for us. What do you think must we do to be accepted? Become like one of them? Try to be gentlemen officers?'

'That we can't, for sure,' she said, rather abruptly.

I blew at the rim of my cup to cool the soup. 'In any case, if we have to prove ourselves, we'll have to work doubly hard.'

'Not hard,' she took another sip as I looked on. 'Smart.'

'Smart?' I repeated. 'Look, Anju, if by smart you mean taking Benefits of Doubt and...'

'Hey, Dips, why bother about it now. We'll do it when the time comes,' she said, shaking her cup and draining it in one last gulp. 'Have your soup. It's yummy.'

Long Nose joined us at dinner time and amidst loud conversations and the clattering of cutlery, asked us what we thought of the food.

'I am enquiring because I'm the food member and so finally it's my responsibility,' he explained, biting into a dinner roll. 'Now that you are here, one of you can take over this department.'

'Is it required, sir?' I said. 'I mean, you are doing such a good job.'

'See, since this is the ladies' department, I am sure you can do it better. You may be able to give tips to the cooks or bring changes in the menu or better still, introduce new items in the menu. Well, anyway, that's not up to me to decide. Major Uttam Singh, the mess secretary, will decide.'

'Oh, in that case,' Anju said, shaking her head, 'one of us will find ourselves standing next to the cook.'

Long Nose laughed thunderously, perhaps more from the effect of having downed a couple of drinks.

'And what other appointments can one hold in the officers' mess, sir?' I asked.

'Wine member, property member, garden member... but in your case wine is out since the mess sec won't be comfortable with ladies handling daru.'

We smiled and nodded. From Long Nose we learnt that the Commanding Officer's wife stayed in Delhi, for 'the education of their two children'; that the lady in the brick-red sari was the unit's first lady, the Second-in-Command's wife. We also came to know that Major Bhat was a bachelor. When Long Nose divulged this information, Anju's wide-eyed expression made me wonder if she had choked on a bone.

Long Nose also informed us – to our amazement – that elephants from the nearby forests paid occasional 'courtesy calls' to the unit; and that when they came, all hell broke loose. They guzzled all the stocked rum by holding the bottle in their trunks and smashing it open before emptying the contents into their mouths. After the 'jumbo party' they usually went back 'happy'. 'Happy' meant 'drunk', I learnt. It also had superlatives like 'very happy' and 'extremely happy'.

Being our subaltern, Long Nose also thought it necessary to advise us on other important aspects.

'All colonels and above have a lipstick marking on their collar. Red lipstick,' he said.

'Red lipstick!' Anju repeated, looking amused.

'You know the red tabs,' he clarified. 'We call it lipstick.'

'Oh, okay, sir,' I said.

He continued in the same tone, his mouth twitching just a little bit, 'And the sentry doesn't have it.'

'Oh God!' we both nearly yelled.

After this party, the word 'party' lost some of its appeal for Anju. We learnt that it was as official as the office, if not more. As for me, the party made me realize that we would have to fight not external enemies, but internal ones. Lala's interference also increased, since eventually I became the food member and Anju, the garden member.

Three weeks into the orientation course, I was beginning to feel like muck, stuck in Major Bhat's office. I was no expert at body language but by the way he went about things, I knew he didn't want to include me. I was always an afterthought, a trailer, a mere obligation. Anju never sensed that anything was wrong. Nor did I ever tell her how I felt. She learnt most things faster than me and although I passed with flying colours from the academy, in the unit it was she who was popular, whom everyone praised. I was mostly in the background.

Somewhere along the way, however, Anju seemed to have got a whiff of things being wrong. One evening, as we walked back after games, she said, 'I think Major Bhat is not being fair to you.'

'Why, he's being fair...' I looked over at her pretty face scrunched in concern. 'What makes you think otherwise?'

She shook her head, 'No... I must tell him about this. He's not being fair to you.'

'Don't tell him anything about me,' I said sternly.

We walked along the corridor leading to our room. 'Actually he's a very nice guy,' Anju said. 'An army officer in the true sense... so smart and so knowledgeable...'

I wasn't looking at her, but she continued with the same zest. 'You know, the CO depends on him for everything?' She paused for a moment. 'Maybe he doesn't realize it at all.'

'Look, Anju,' I said, unlocking our door and pushing it open with more force than was required, 'I don't need any favours, okay?'

'You don't seem to like him,' she said from behind me.

I sank on the cushion. 'Looks like *you* do.'

'Ow, shut up!' she said as she turned and walked to the other room, a hand on her hip. 'Oh, these trousers... I can barely stand... and to play volleyball in these... The damned unit tailor!' she said, all in one breath.

The white trousers stretched unflatteringly across her derriere and threatened to rip apart.

4

Learning to Bark

DESPITE THE ANNOYANCES, I WAS BEGINNING TO LIKE the place, nestled among the Darjeeling mountains and scenic valley of the river Teesta. Anju didn't find the charms of a small town filled with natural beauty too attractive. She liked everything in a refined, sophisticated form, even nature.

One evening when the rains and cool breeze whispered their invitation to party, I found it irresistible. I dragged Anju out.

'Someone will see us,' she squealed.

'It's dark. No one can see,' I said, thoroughly enjoying myself in the evening shower. We danced in the rain and splashed water at each other. My joy also stemmed from the knowledge that training under Major Bhat was now in its last phase. Soon, I would be away from his overbearing persona. During the training, Major Bhat gave us surprise tests from time to time. Our ingenious answers often had him in splits – perhaps the reason why he enjoyed administering them more often than we would have liked. For some reason, he never found Anju's howlers as funny, stupid or irrelevant as mine.

'So, it's time for independent appointments,' he said one morning, taking a cigarette out of a pack. 'I have given you a large picture of how things work...' He lit the cigarette between his lips and blissfully inhaled the smoke. 'Now how you perform is left to you.' He smiled, placed the lit end on the ashtray and leant forward. 'I don't want to keep you waiting. I can see that both of you want to get away from me as quickly as possible. Right?'

'No, sir,' Anju said.

'No, sir,' I said out of courtesy.

'Okay, now here's how it is,' Major Bhat announced. 'Anju, you'll be in the receipts and issues wing with me.'

'Yes, sir,' Anju said and exchanged a smile with him. Unlike the other officers, he called her Anju instead of Anjali. I thought Anjali or Second Lieutenant Sharma was more apt. But since she found nothing wrong, Major Bhat called her Anju everywhere, even in front of the Lion.

He then turned to me. 'And you will be the Quarter Master, under the administrative officer.'

This didn't shock me, since I had been mentally readying myself to work under Lala all along.

'And yes...' He looked from one of us to the other. 'There's also another thing I would like to tell you guys.' He paused for a while and leant forward towards us. 'Behave responsibly. I don't want you guys to jump and dance in the rain like school kids.'

Anju immediately gave me an I-told-you-so look. Was he God? How did he know everything we did? And why was he so critical? I felt more and more that there were pre-prepared moulds for us to fit into and any behaviour outside of those was not tolerated.

Soon, I had an office to call my own, where people walked up and complained of ill-fitting shoes, overused torches and quality of rations, among many other problems. Files that came to me followed a definite route upward to the Lion. Most files I put up to Lala however, came back promptly with a 'meet me' curtly written. 'Meet me' usually meant 'be my whipping boy'.

Most people came into my office with real problems, but there were also those who dawdled around and peeped in curiously through the windows, making me feel like a rare animal, a macaque or something, in a zoo. Many times I had to haul them up and ask them what they were looking at. This was not mere asking though. It was barking, a la Lala. I was slowly learning the power of expletives, since every officer seemed to be using them to his advantage.

Anju was still under the mother hen's wings. Officially, we hardly met but whenever I had work in the executive side, I usually met her, especially around lunchtime. She seemed to be doing a good job but I noticed that she often dropped names, mostly of the Lion and Major Bhat. On the phone, when she talked to Major Bhat, I could immediately tell, since her dimples deepened. On the other hand, when the Lion called up on some rare occasion, she stood up and bent her torso forward.

'Why do you stand up when the Lion calls?' I asked her once. 'It's so funny and moreover what impression will you make on your staff? They'll be laughing behind your back.'

She puckered her lips and narrowed her eyes. 'I know. I must get over this idiotic habit. Okay, the next time I do it, just pull the receiver from my hand.'

I laughed. She smiled back at me, then placed some files in the out-tray and capped her pen. 'Come, let's go for lunch. Let's ask Major Bhat for his scooter,' she said, lifting the receiver. 'Why walk it?'

Before I could voice my disagreement, she had spoken into the mouthpiece. 'He'll be sending it across,' she said with a smile.

We had not bought a scooter yet and often argued about which was better to start with, a scooter or a motorbike. It was my dream to own a bike and I often told Anju this. 'A lady officer zooming around on a bike. Wow! Cool, isn't it?' I said.

'Sure! But what will happen if we have an official function and have to wear a sari? Imagine!' she said, and laughed, imagining it herself.

With no vehicle of our own, we usually covered distances riding pillion with our subalterns, Long Nose and Lieutenant Vishal Gairola. We moved about in a gang of four on their bikes. I was usually with Lieutenant Gairola and Anju with Long Nose. Together we rode to nearby scenic spots along the Teesta. Sometimes we rode to town just to have a cone of ice-cream. When Anju and I walked around in town with helmets at our hips, most people looked at us a second time to make sure we were not boys.

Anju didn't seem to mind this arrangement, but I didn't like the interested looks on people's faces when we zoomed past, setting the hill roads on fire. People in this small town were quick to make assumptions and most had paired us up already.

On Major Bhat's scooter, we headed to the officers' mess. Although I found it a tad difficult to navigate on the decrepit road, by my own standards I was doing quite well. The only practice I had was on a friend's brother's scooter, which I rode away from the disapproving eyes of my mother, who had a checklist of sorts that qualified someone as a girl. Driving, especially riding a two-wheeler with gears, wasn't on that list. Nor were so many of the other things I loved to do, like playing basketball – with boys.

As I rode on confidently, a uniformed person on seeing us promptly saluted us. I straightened my back and said 'Jai Hind' as was the norm. Almost simultaneously, Anju shook vigorously from behind and I lost my balance. We dropped in a pothole that I had been carefully avoiding and Major Bhat's oversized helmet slid down from my head over my eyes. Blinded, I lost control but managed to stop the vehicle, groping for the brake first and then the ground beneath my feet.

'What exactly were you doing?' I said, fuming, lifting the helmet back up.

'I just returned the salute,' Anju said, getting off from the pillion seat.

'I think you even stamped,' I said angrily as I looked around. There were already a few eyes on us. 'Now everyone will talk about the fall of the lady officers.'

'But we didn't fall.'

'When the gossip does the rounds don't be surprised when someone asks you about your fracture.' I kicked the old contraption angrily. 'Whatever we do makes news. Don't we know it? And people add their own namak, masala, mirchi. You get it?'

The scooter refused to budge.

'Look, Dips, you can't blame me,' Anju said, helping me with the tilt job. 'It's you who's not too confident riding the scooter.'

I had to accept that. When people knew you well, they read you even when you put up your best show.

*

'That officer who we met at the canteen,' Anju said, between the clanking of cutlery at lunch, 'you remember?'

'That Artillery one?'

'Yeah,' Anju said, leaning a little closer. 'Major Bhat told me to keep away from him. It seems he chases anything in a skirt.'

I spooned the rice and quipped, 'Thank God we wear pants.'

'Whatever!' she said. 'But we must not interact with him.'

'I won't. Don't worry about me. But you take care.' I served myself some kofta and concentrated on eating. Then I said as an afterthought, 'I think Major Bhat treats you like a kid, telling you what to do and everything.'

She lifted her head from the plate to face me. 'He's caring... a nice man.' She smiled and her eyes went back to the plate. 'That reminds me... we need to pack lunch for him.'

'Why? Isn't he coming?'

'He's busy. So he requested me. Moreover, that was the pact in exchange for the scooter.'

'Anju, I think you must not do these bum jobs,' I said, as we closed our plates. 'And don't be too easy with taking favours. They are always returnable, sometimes with interest.'

Three months had gone by and we were now used to the ways of the unit.

'How's Lala treating you?' Anju asked one Sunday afternoon. She was sitting near the window, plucking her eyebrows. She smiled as she asked, 'Does he come down heavily too often?'

'Oh! Lala,' I sighed. 'He must have a PhD in nitpicking. Whatever I do, he always finds some fault or the other.'

'You know what?' She swivelled around her chair to face me. Her eyebrows were two perfect arches. I thought of mine, like two squashed hairy caterpillars. 'Why do you keep taking shit? The more you take, the more he'll pile on you. Look at me.' She shrugged. 'He doesn't treat me that way now.'

'That's because you have your god-damn-father Bhat,' I retorted.

'It's not just that, okay. It's my attitude.' She was quiet for a moment. 'Try to be assertive, at least sound like you are,' she said, turning back to her task. I nodded, got up and turned on the tape deck.

'And that foul-mouthed CCME, Captain Shinde?' Anju asked, peeking into the mirror. Captain Shinde was the Company Commander, usually addressed as CCME, Company Commander Military Establishment, the man responsible for the discipline and welfare of the troops. The first time that I saw his office complex, it was so abuzz with activity that for a microsecond I felt like I was back at the Academy. Men in uniform ran along the mud track with their haversacks. Others were bent down on the tar road under the scorching sun. At a distance a few of them cleaned the barrels of their rifles by running flannelettes through them. The CCME was a very busy man, I assumed, since a horde of uniformed personnel, stood waiting outside his entrance to meet him. When Anju and I appeared at the scene, a dozen pairs of eyes instantly turned towards us, as if an unspoken 'Lady Officers sighted' alert had gone around.

'So far so good,' I said, flipping through some cassettes, and finally playing Michael Learns to Rock.

'And in any case, being an effective CCME is no mean task. I have seen him at work.' Right from the beginning, if there was any appointment I badly wanted to hold, it was this. I knew that being a CCME was both prestigious as well as challenging.

'I don't like that chap,' Anju declared. 'He swears all the time. Does he foul-mouth you?'

'Not me. But I keep hearing it all so often – MC, BC and sometimes their English equivalents. If I happen to be around him, he tells me that it's the only language the troops understand, which is why it is more effective.'

'I don't think so,' Anju said, wiping her eyebrows with a towel. 'He's obviously exaggerating.'

'Maybe,' I said, 'but he certainly has a commanding presence. The way he gives orders, the way he deals with their problems, the way he walks, talks... it's all very powerful.' I was talking to her back. 'And you know what? I have also started swearing. I find it very effective.'

'Really? I don't think so,' she said, dabbing powder on her upper lip and getting the tweezers in place.

'It actually is,' I said, trying to convince her. 'But to use it, you must have your body language perfect. I have been observing them closely. When they give someone a dressing down, they usually have their chin up, one hand or both on the hips or pockets, erect posture...'

'Manly postures,' Anju said, looking minutely at her face in the mirror.

'These are powerful postures and it gets results,' I said. 'I even tried it in my office. There was this guard, a doubtful case who looked at me from top to bottom and in the end, grinned as a greeting. I barked at him, one hand in my pocket, "Can't you see these stars? Bloody chap, don't you show me your bloody teeth!"

And you won't believe it... he gave me such a kadak salute. You try it.' I looked around for objects against which to demonstrate my newfound power to use certain words. So I abused the clock and a book.

Anju looked unimpressed. I used the f-word on the chair, powder bottle and suitcase. I had never used it before, so it felt a little odd coming out of my mouth. All I had used so far was the comparatively harmless 'bloody' and that too just on two or three occasions. Before using the higher ranked ones, I wanted to gain some more confidence. I thought Anju was the best person to practise with.

'It feels so crude, like Lala,' Anju declared, getting up to put her paraphernalia back on the dressing table. The dressing table was mostly occupied by her cosmetics. Although she hardly got the opportunity to use them, they were all there – make-up kit, lipsticks, combs and clips, compact powders and more.

My demonstration was still on. 'Look, crude or not, it has a punch... it works! "Bloody chap, fuckin' Bhat..."'

'That's not funny, okay!'

'I never said it was.' I laughed, looking at her dazed face.

In the mess, both of us had declared ourselves 'Maukatarians', learning from Long Nose that it meant eating as per mauka, occasion. Other than each other, Long Nose was the best company we had there. It was becoming obvious to me that he was zeroing in on Anju. On our impromptu trips to town, unit picnics and raids for home-made food at senior officers' residences, he secretly stole glances at her. Again, Anju never sensed anything.

Unlike Long Nose, our other subaltern, Lieutenant Vishal Gairola, of late, never made pleasant company. He was too loud for comfort and the most dominating in our group. We realized that he had a large male ego and some of his ideas were stuck in the middle ages. His resentment with us was becoming quite apparent. More often than not, whenever we met in the mess, he had a nag ready for every meal.

'Soldiering is not a profession for women. With you people around, I don't feel I am in the army. You dilute the esprit de corps.'

'Why should you have different physical standards? We get the same everything. We wear the same uniform, why the discrimination?'

'We never had this type of training in the unit. We were appointed straightaway. Why this special treatment?'

'If we can do night duties, why can't you?'

Some of these were genuine complaints. Physical standards for women in any army had always been a controversial topic. I had learnt that all feelings of disgruntlement among the men stemmed from this basic aspect. Hence, Lieutenant Gairola's complaint came as no surprise.

Anju and I decided to do something about things that were in our control, like volunteering for night duty. But the Second-in-Command thought otherwise.

'We don't want problems on this account,' he said, 'since you will be alone with the driver at night and that too in isolated areas. Moreover, there's also the fear of elephants.' Although he made it sound scary, we still went ahead and projected this issue another time. This time, the Second-in-Command took us to the den.

'I am not clear about your employability,' the Lion

roared. 'If anything happens to you, who's answerable?' He punched his chest with his index finger. 'Me!'

'Sir,' I said, and gulped nervously. 'Sir, but nothing will happen. We assure you.' I quickly looked at Anju for support.

'Yes, sir,' she said. I was expecting the kind of confidence that had startled the general. So this meek response came as an anticlimax.

For about a minute, his eyebrows danced between the two of us, studying us. Finally he said, 'Hmm, let me think about it.'

He thought about it and our names were entered in the duty officer's roster.

We learnt that night duty involved taking rounds of the total unit area. The rounds would take us a few kilometres away from the functional unit area, dotted with dilapidated buildings which had been used during the Second World War. Only an old office functioned here. Before dusk, the clerks hurriedly slapped their files shut and left. It was rumoured that the office mysteriously functioned at night; that there was chaos and noise behind the locked doors but no one in sight.

On entering deeper into the area, away from the main gate, the sights and sounds changed. Roots of old trees grew into crumbling walls. Banyan trees with auxiliary roots hanging down nearly as thick as the main trunk had a queer stillness about them. The roads had degenerated into gravel tracks. Rather than the sounds, it was the lack of any that added to the creepy quality of the place. Even in broad daylight it looked eerie, and with the darkness of the night, I was sure it would feel like a scene from a horror flick.

Dressed in combat fatigues and seated in the front

seat of a one-tonner, I was on my maiden night duty. On my insistence, the driver parked the vehicle slightly away from the guard post. I wanted to ensure that there actually was an element of surprise, since it was to be a surprise check. As I walked to the guard post in pitch darkness, a sudden, shrill piercing sound from the bushes startled me. Something suddenly leapt out. I leapt out of my skin.

It took me a moment to realize that it was only a human; not a jumbo, or a ghost. For one, he wasn't floating. His feet were firmly planted on the ground. But it wasn't much better, as I found myself staring into the muzzle end of a loaded rifle.

'Tham!' I had been challenged by the guard.

A spate of questions followed as I stood frozen. Having forgotten the password in the confusion, I quickly presented my I-card, nearly forgetting my name. Only when the guard said 'Jai hind, sahab' did my heartbeat slow down to normal.

The duty officer also had to stay back in the unit premises for the night since any problem that occurred during these hours was to be first addressed by him – or her. When staying here, what I feared most was nature's call – since there was absolutely no way I could answer. All I could do was rush all the way back and wake up Anju.

On hearing all about my night duty, Anju said, 'Now I know why everybody including the general had their doubts. It sounds difficult.' Then she thought for a moment and added, 'Should we talk to the 2i/c... to excuse us?'

'Hey Anju, you are an army officer. How can you even think like that? Once you have taken a step forward there's no turning back,' I quoted from an ustad in the academy. 'Look, Anju, if I can do it, you certainly can.'

So Anju finally went for the duty officer's rounds and faced an entirely different kind of situation. Her vehicle broke down somewhere deep in the area and she had to call for another vehicle. Later she told me, 'I was terribly scared. A night in the forest, with ghosts, jumbos and a driver for company. Imagine! Anything could have happened!'

But nothing did.

Once we started with our night duties, Lieutenant Gairola seemed to be relieved. But he was not done yet.

'What kind of faujis are you? You don't drink? Come join us in the bar.'

'We are teetotallers, sir,' Anju said.

He then looked at us from head to toe. 'You people don't follow any dress regulations in the mess. Don't the rules apply to you? Why aren't you wearing shoes?'

'Sir, this is what the first lady wants us to wear,' I said, looking down at our salwar-kameezes. He shook his head and walked away murmuring, 'Huh! Lady officers!'

The change in our attire had come about when in one of the parties our first lady opined that we be attired in 'something feminine' instead of the 'manly' trousers, shirt and belt. We were immediately instructed to wear either salwar-kameezes or saris. And we couldn't possibly team those with boots.

Sometimes I felt like a cutlet, sandwiched between the ideologies of two groups – one that saw us as officers and another that saw us primarily as women. I could see Lieutenant Gairola's point, though Anju never agreed. She always thought he was wrong. Given a choice I would have liked to be dressed like the other officers. Anju, on the other hand, had been waiting for this opportunity to open her remaining suitcases. She wore fitted, tailored salwar-kameezes matched with heeled sandals. I wore loose-fitting cotton or raw silk ones.

While I was happy that I didn't have to interact with Major Bhat in an official capacity, there was no escaping him at dinner time in the mess. He would arrive late, down a couple of drinks and have all of us sit facing him, a reluctant audience at his daily sermon. Apart from Anju and me, the audience included Long Nose and Lieutenant Gairola. Although he demanded an attentive audience, it was only Anju he usually addressed.

'You know, the army runs in my blood,' he said one evening, settling down with his drink. 'I am a third-generation army man. In fact, my golfing and horse-riding skills are all inherited. My dad and grand-dad were big guns... It runs in our blood.'

Anju nodded interestedly as he paused for a sip, before continuing some more about what else ran in his blood. When he got into this when-I-was-like-you-I-was-a-boy-wonder mode, I mentally stuffed his mouth with pakodas, cheese balls, potato tikkis or whatever was brought in as snacks. I was usually saved the task since he did it himself. The stuffed mouth however, didn't reduce the bragging. When the snacks were over, he asked for more 'snakes', condescendingly pronouncing it the way the stewards did. I then rushed the cook to make some quickies.

Often, as the night progressed, it became difficult to sit attentively as he slurred, riding high on his Black Knight. I usually drifted off to sleep, sitting in the same attentive position – I had enough practice with this in the academy. When I returned to the sermon, I usually saw the subalterns desperately battling their yawns. Anju enjoyed his speeches however, and didn't seem to mind that most often we sat into the wee hours of morning.

'You know if a cobra bites you in a dream...,' he slurred one night, looking my way, '...it's a good sign, especially when it's the start of something.'

My sleep vanished. I threw Anju a look. Except her, I hadn't mentioned this to anyone. How could she share it with him, a relative stranger?

Anju nodded and puckered her lips, as he continued, 'I know a fair deal about dream analysis. It's part of psychology. Sigmund Freud... you have heard of him?'

'Yes, sir,' I said and pursed my lips. He went on about how our dreams have a manifestation in our waking lives. Anju listened keenly, while once again, I drifted away. Although the subject was interesting, I was convinced Major Bhat's knowledge was very superficial, since he kept repeating most things over and over.

At dinner time, it was usual that he commented about some dish or the other, knowing very well that I was the sole person affected. The comments got worse after we developed a difference of opinion regarding the use of jawans' rations in the officers' mess.

To my surprise, Anju thought there was nothing wrong with what Major Bhat had suggested. 'After all, what is it about getting a kilo or two of the bulk you receive for the five messes? You can easily do that.'

'It's not about that,' I told her. 'It's pilferage. I can't do that.' I looked at her intently – she had certainly changed. At the academy she would have at the most forced her way into the dormitory bathroom feigning nausea or a terribly upset stomach, but this was a new low.

Anju sighed. 'Your principles always make it tough for you – at the academy and now here. You just want to do the right thing, always.' She jerked her head and looked away. Then she turned to me again. 'Sometimes, you need to be practical and smart. That's how it works.'

Anju was never convinced by my explanations and after a point I didn't try hard.

So it didn't come as a surprise that Major Bhat always found anything served 'not up to the mark'. The dal was a 'misery', the sabzi 'even the buffaloes would refuse' the dosa too 'crumbly' to be jabbed by a fork and the idlis 'so rubbery they slipped under the knife'.

'I will instruct the cook,' I usually told him.

'Pull up their socks!' he would say, his eyes boring into mine. 'Learn to extract work from these Johnnies.'

Sometimes when the fault finding became too much, Anju would try to come to my aid, but I gestured with my eyes to stop her from canvassing for me.

Dinner was not the last thing about every evening. Post dinner there was a moonlight coffee session. Caffeine destroyed the few remaining hours of sleep.

The only advantage of being his audience was that like the weather forecast, he told us about the forthcoming events in the unit. We learned that physical fitness tests and range firing were coming up as part of the administrative inspection. Everybody's focus would certainly be the lady officers.

There was more than just the Lion 'closely monitoring our performance'. This was our big opportunity to shut mouths without actually having to tell them to shut up.

5

Choona-Geru

AS PREPARATIONS FOR THE INSPECTION GAINED momentum, the Lion frequently 'expressed his desire' to hear from each officer about the progress in their respective departments. At a meeting in the den, as each one of us briefed him, he mercilessly shot questions at us like a Medium Machine Gun. When Anju floundered somewhere, the mother hen took over. When I floundered, the Lion looked on, his stare increasing in intensity every passing second. 'Sir, I'll get back to you with the details,' I muttered whenever a question had me stumped. 'Hmmm,' he would nod, visibly displeased.

To my relief, soon, he kept his baton aside and ordered for tea and snacks to mark the end of the meeting.

'So, how often do you call home?' the Lion asked me.

'Sir, twice a week,' I said, holding my cup and saucer steady. The last time I was in a similar situation, I had spilled tea on my trousers since his question had hit me like a bolt.

He then turned to Anju, who said, 'Sir, sometimes we call home more often than that, especially when we go to the Apna movie theatre side. And now since we are mobile we also talk longer since we can avail half rates and sometimes quarter rates...' She elaborated more than was necessary. Sitting beside Major Bhat was giving her some extra confidence. Or maybe she was thrilled to see the Lion in his puppy avatar.

'You must, or your parents may worry about you,' he said and moved on to Long Nose. 'Sandeep, I hope your leave was good. So, are you getting married shortly?'

'No, sir,' Long Nose blushed.

'I hope there are no problems finding girls.'

'No, sir,' everyone chorused.

'That could never be a problem in India, sir,' Lala added.

'You're right, Uttam, but then during my times I faced a little problem,' the Lion said, biting into a samosa. Then he sipped his tea and ran his finger over his moustache as everyone wondered what the problem might be. From the way Major Bhat shook his head and smiled, it was obvious that he knew it. He whispered something in Anju's ears. 'You know,' the Lion continued, 'at that time due to the war no one gave their daughters in marriage to army men. So we used to tell them that we didn't go to the battle front, just provided blankets from the rear.'

Everyone laughed.

'Ordnance,' Major Bhat illuminated, in case anyone had missed the joke. It was obvious that he had buttered his way up to become the Lion's confidant.

'So, that's how I got married,' the Lion continued. 'Well, after that, it is an entirely different story.' He chuckled and all the married officers joined him. 'Puttar, it's only a joke,' he said to Long Nose. 'Marriage is not all that bad.'

*

To monitor the progress of my department, Lala walked into my office very often without warning.

'Where are the books, records?' he walked in one day, and plonked himself into a chair, his roving eyes registering everything on my table and every spot on the wall.

I had all the registers produced.

His eyebrows shot up. 'Where's the lipstick work?'

'Sir, lipstick work...' My mind raced. Maybe the books should look more colourful, attractive. Yes, that was it.

'Sir, it's not done yet. We are yet to decorate it with colour pens,' I said confidently, not perturbed by my lack of knowledge. Anju's words about the shit philosophy rang in my mind: you take shit, you get more.

Lala smiled like a hyena. And this expression suddenly transformed into a growl, 'This is not a painting book to be coloured with colour pens. It must be made presentable, not colourful.' He emphasized the word 'prejentable'. 'Find out how and get it done.'

Whenever Lala nitpicked successfully, he asked me to find out and do the task. Most often, I went to the Company Commander Captain Shinde's office, since he seemed to understand the predicaments of a lost new officer. Although he was a busy man, he took out time for me and helped me clear my very basic doubts. The best part about him was that however funny he found them, he never made fun of me.

He told me later that the books had to be bordered by a red tape. It was the standard procedure followed during all inspections, the lipstick work.

'You need to pick up things fast, like this...' Lala snapped his fingers. 'I am finding you to be a slow learner.' He then summoned my staff and gave them instructions, making me feel like an appendage in my own office. After dismissing them, he walked out. I followed him.

'Why is your Quarter Master area looking so bloody dull? No choona-geru?' He walked ahead, one hand busy at his crotch.

'Sir, by tomorrow it will be done.' I marched alongside, taking long strides to match his. Earlier in a meeting at his office, he had emphasized, 'Choona-geru must be applied on anything that doesn't move. The administrative area must look like a bride, red and white.' The red oxide and lime combination were thus beginning to cover tree trunks, walls, borders and even leaves and flowers.

'This will be your first inspection, isn't it?' Lala stopped and turned to face me. His hand got busier and I didn't know where to look.

'Yes, sir,' I said, looking nowhere in particular. He then had me practise the drill of welcoming the inspecting officer. We did re-runs of the route to be followed when taking him around. Posters of 'Devotion to duty', 'Work is worship', 'Teamwork triumphs' and many more had appeared on the walls.

Apart from cleanliness, discipline and morale it was also important to ensure that the inspecting officer had a comfortable stay. Lala had given me the responsibility to ensure that the suite was perfect for his stay. This time I decided to beat Lala's trained eyes by minimizing his scope. I inspected everything just like him, looking at each object from his angle, literally.

But then Lala was Lala.

'What's this Simco doing here?' He took the tube and tossed it on the bed, unceremoniously eliminating it from among other cosmetics that graced the dressing table.

'It's a hair styling gel, sir,' I said confidently, since I had scrutinized every tiny item there.

'Which idiot told you that?' he barked in his trademark style. 'If you don't know at least learn it now.' He made it sound like even kindergarteners knew everything about it. He bent over, picked up the tube and held it at my eye level. 'This is used only on beards and was specially bought for General Sandhu's visit. Understand? Brigadier Agarwal will take offence at it.' His conceited eyes lingered on me as he shook his head. 'Attention to detail. When will you learn it?'

A hair styling gel it was, whether for hair on the head or in a beard. So why was I standing and listening to him treat me like a nincompoop?

'Sir,' I said, trying to pump up my confidence. 'Actually it is a hair sty–'

'Till you have one star,' he butted in, 'you are a one-star general, and you can afford to make mistakes. But when it gets heavier,' he kept shaking his head sideways as though prophesying my doom, 'I tell you...' he wiggled his fat finger at me and left the sentence incomplete.

My crisis was not over yet. Lala marched on the carpeted floor, determined to find more. I followed closely behind. The inevitable came.

'Where's the welcome folder?'

I wasn't aware of such a thing. But this time, I played my card right. 'Sir, I've already told the mess havaldar to get it. He'll be here any minute.'

He about turned, 'Don't just tell. Ensure!'

'Yes sir, I'll *ensure* it is done.' Despite his harsh tone, I didn't let my confidence dwindle. He stared at me a little longer than usual, trying to outdo me with his eyes.

I stared right back and for the first time ever, he broke contact.

The dates for the firing and Physical Endurance Tests were announced. Anju surprised me with an audacious suggestion – more evidence of how she was changing, like earlier thinking it was okay to steal from jawan's rations.

'See, Dips, no one here knows about our physical standards. So, let's make it easier.' She did physical activities only when there was no choice, like in the academy. And whenever she could, she shammed.

'Anju, don't be silly,' I said. 'These BODs won't get us anywhere. You think they can't find out?'

'Not before it gets over,' she shrugged. 'And then it's only next year.'

'C'mon, it's not a big deal. You can do it.'

Anju sighed. 'You know what? I don't want to do it. It's as simple as that.' She then justified her stand: 'Why should I stretch my body so much, when I have a choice?'

'Look, Anju,' I said firmly, 'as an officer you don't have a choice.'

'I have,' she said, imitating my tone.

On the day of the Physical Endurance Test, Anju managed to produce an SIQ slip, and stayed back, Sick-in-Quarters. Except me, no one knew the truth.

I, on my part, ran with the officers, outrunning some and giving a tough competition to the rest. I also ran the five-kilometre BPET, the Battle Physical Endurance Test, with the men and saw quite a few raised eyebrows. Many remarked that my run was going to prove nothing. I smiled: it was a clear sign that some felt insecure.

'Your behaviour was atrocious,' I told Anju later that evening.

She didn't seem to have any feelings of guilt. 'You be the Keen Kumari,' she said, borrowing Long Nose's term for an over-enthusiastic person, Keen Kumar. 'Go ahead, prove what you want to the world. I'm not interested.'

'Do you realize that whatever one of us does affects the other?'

'It won't,' she said flatly, turning and walking away to the mess.

Maybe I was too harsh, I thought. But her act was not justifiable either. From our discussions, one thing was now becoming obvious: Anju had lost the spark we had come into the Army with. So I took it upon myself to revive it.

The opportunity to do this presented itself at the firing range. It was time for our rendezvous with the guns. This is where many doubts about our capabilities were harboured. On the drive to the firing range, I gave Anju a pep talk. If she wanted to, she could do well, since she was a good shot.

Safety announcements were made as everyone waited in their combat dress. The targets were in place, the guns, ammunition and personnel were all ready. This was the first time in three months that we had come to a firing range. I was excited. The sight of the range took me back to an incident in the academy, which I didn't like to think about much. I had removed the very stubborn safety pin from a live grenade, and happily exclaimed, 'Sir, finally it came out!' The instructor produced every possible pitch and

tone from his throat when he yelled, 'THROW IT!'
The grenade burst before hitting the target. A pall of
gloom immediately descended on the range when the
instructor growled and doled out an assortment of
punishments. It didn't end here. My action had stirred
the higher-ups and I was given a firm warning. I felt
terrible and kept wondering how I could have done
something so silly. Perhaps it was exhaustion and lack
of sleep which made me deaf to the instructions given
prior to handling the grenade.

A male snort brought me back to the present. 'So,
have you held a gun before?' Lieutenant Vishal Gairola
asked, thrusting his chest forward. There were a few
sniggers from all around.

Anju and I looked at each other and said, 'Yes, sir.'
Anju wanted to add more, but I stopped her, quickly
whispering in her ear, 'Show them instead.'

We took our positions.

I held my 9mm Sten Machine Carbine, pressed it
firmly against my right shoulder, closed my left eye,
aimed at the target, and fired. Three rounds.

The results came in. Anju and I had hit all three on
the metal human silhouette target. Among the three,
two were in the centre mass akin to the bull's eye in a
circular target, and one was on the periphery. And that
too with guns known to be low on accuracy.

Anju came close to my ears and mimicked
Lieutenant Gairola. 'Have you held a gun before?'
We had just learnt that he had not had a single hit.
Although I would have loved to see the look on his
face, he didn't give us the opportunity. He had hidden
his face from us.

'What is this, Vishal? Even the girls did better,' we
heard Lala taunt him.

'Even the girls? What does he mean by that?' I whispered to Anju.

'He was sure we couldn't do it,' she said, rolling her eyes.

Then Lieutenant Gairola walked over to us. 'You did well,' he said, taking off his cap and running a hand through his hair. 'I think the gun was not zeroed.' He offered us a lame explanation for his poor performance.

'Another try?' he asked, flinging his cap back on.

I knew he wanted another opportunity to show us down. The poor chap would be the butt end of jokes otherwise. His male superego was badly wounded.

With the range officer's permission, we readied ourselves in the prone position, lying face down on the ground, to fire the 7.62mm Self Loading Rifle. The SLRs had a reputation as an accurate machine and the prone position was relatively easy. I held the rifle butt firmly on my right shoulder, aimed through the foresight blade and pulled the trigger. Despite the firm hold, the recoil action thrust the butt into my shoulder.

We were to fire five rounds in the prone position and five in the standing or offhand position. Once we were through with the prone position, we changed to offhand. Lieutenant Gairola looked at me, as if determined upon proving something. Behind us, the other officers talked. From bits and pieces of the conversation, I knew it was something about us. But I shut them out and tried hard to concentrate on my target. My cheek on the rifle stock, feet apart, I aimed, holding the rifle steady since it moved with every breath. Five rounds were emptied.

'Did you hear what they said?' Anju asked once we were through. We were waiting for the results.

'Wasn't it something about us?'

'Yeah, about lady officers... that we are the lipstick of the army, adding colour.'

'Why is everyone here so obsessed with lipsticks?' I exclaimed.

I could now see how they saw us: as walking, talking, firing lipsticks.

As the results of the firing were brought, Lieutenant Gairola rushed to check. The centre mass hits were seven each for me and him, and six for Anju.

'Hey, looks like they do give you guns in the academy,' he said, finding his old voice again. But his face looked perturbed, perhaps at finding competition where he thought none existed.

The main inspection was now only a day away. A special durbar was called to address the problems of the jawans. In this forum, problems or suggestions could be freely raised by the jawans and the Lion was answerable. Solutions were then formulated based on discussions with the administrative officer and the Company Commander. After the durbar, the I-cards of personnel were checked. We produced our I-cards from the chest pocket of our uniform. Lieutenant Gairola, who was the duty officer for the day, took our I-cards in his hand and examined them. I noticed that Anju's card and mine looked different from the others'. Both of ours were bowed. We exchanged a glance and a smile. Lieutenant Vishal Gairola flipped the cards in his hand and gave us a prolonged grin before returning it to us.

'Such a jerk!' Anju said, as he moved away. 'Gorilla!'

'Gorilla saab' was how Lieutenant Gairola was addressed by most jawans, since that's what they thought his name was. Once in the mess, when the mess havaldar informed him about a phone call, addressing him that way, he howled, thumped his chest and thighs and charged, imitating a gorilla, 'Do I look like a gorilla to you?' he yelled. The mess havaldar on his part, stood calm since he was not new to such dramatics. Looking at both of their expressions, we couldn't help a hearty laugh.

After the durbar when I got back, I couldn't recognize my overhauled office. Everything was either choona-geru-ed, polished, lipstick-ed or painted. The unit pond looked like a picture from a nature conservation magazine. Geese and duck swam and flapped about in it. Where there was usually not a bird in sight, to see so many of them was a shocker. I picked up my phone and asked Anju. She usually knew everything, courtesy Major Bhat.

'Yeah, they have been bought. And 20 of them came waddling on the road, blocking traffic. And you know the best part?' she laughed. 'They were stopped at the gate, since the sentries just wouldn't let them pass.'

The inspections went off well except for some minor glitches. Lala however, made it a point to highlight them. I, on the other hand, took a cue from the Lion and appreciated the hard work of my staff.

Inspections always meant parties. By now we had become adept party planners. Anju had proved time and again that she was the best flower artist around. I experimented with the menu, and tasted and approved whatever went out of the kitchen. Whatever advice and tips the ladies copiously gave me, I passed on to the cook. Both of us were slowly being pushed into what was considered the feminine domain. No one seemed to care that we had beat most males in their own domain, the firing range.

It came as a pleasant surprise when the ladies at the party highlighted our performance. Some of them hugged us and told us they were truly proud of us. Lali aka Lala's wife simply said 'Congratulations!' without understanding much of what was being discussed. Mrs Das, the first lady, shook hands with us and patted our backs saying 'Well done!' I looked around to see if any officer took note. No one seemed to be looking. And the Lion, I hoped he had at least taken note of our performance.

Other than the hugs, the highlight of this party was that our first lady sang with the band. While we were watching her, an officer walked up to us, and stood rocking on his feet, creating small waves in his glass. 'So how are the guinea pigs doing?' he stopped rocking and asked.

'Sir, guinea pigs?' Anju had a questioning look.

'Sir, are you referring to us?' I added.

'Yeah, last time you told me you were in the army on an experimental basis.' His hand moved on the glass.

'Oh, we are doing fine, sir,' Anju said. She said this without an iota of objection. I was irritated. People usually took it as a sign that they could carry on, and call us anything they pleased.

I excused myself and dragged her along. 'Why do you answer such questions? Couldn't you see the smirk on his face?'

'C'mon, he was only joking.'

'No, he wasn't. Keep away from him. That chap is a creep.'

A familiar voice interrupted our conversation. 'Where's the table runner? It's almost dinner time. When will the dining table be arranged?'

'Sir,' I said confidently, 'I have instructed the mess havaldar.'

Lala opened his mouth to say something but before he could, I had said, 'I'll *ensure* it's done, sir.'

Lala pursed his lips and stared at me. I stood unperturbed, since I knew Lala's ways now and how he liked to wreak havoc at the last minute.

Lala looked around desperately to find something and bag his winning position. 'Go entertain the ladies,' he said, looking relieved. 'Can't you see they are getting bored?'

I walked up to a group of ladies who sat staring into the scented party air.

'Ma'am,' I closed in on one, 'I hope the snacks are good.'

'Too oily,' the lady said, rubbing her greasy fingers.

'Ma'am, why don't you try the tandoori paneer?' I called for the steward and had it served. I then thought hard of what else to say. I wasn't as good as Anju when it came to making small talk. It was always Anju who took the lead here. As I sat wondering, another lady joined them. Their conversation revolved around feeding toddlers, tuition classes, problems with their maids, and the like. When I realized that there was absolutely nothing I could contribute, I excused myself and joined Anju in another group, where she was busy discussing ladies' tailors, beauticians and dress materials.

'Don't stick too close, or they will include you in,' I told her, as we moved away.

'Oh Dips,' she waved a hand. 'You think too much. These are things we need to know. Can't depend on that unit tailor anymore. Didn't you see how he stitched our trousers?'

*

About a week after the inspections, we were sitting lazily in the corridor, sipping tea. In our room, our sahayak carried out the spit and polish ritual to brighten our shoes. The strong, acrid smell of the brass polish wafted towards us. I flipped through a current affairs magazine and Anju was engrossed in her romance book. On earlier occasions, I had seen tears roll down her cheeks as she flipped the pages. But today she had started a new one and hadn't reached the emotional bits yet.

'Anju,' I said.

'Hmm,' she nodded feebly, her eyes glued to the page.

'Oh nothing,' I said. 'You carry on with your romances.'

'What is it?' She looked up. 'Something about Lala?'

'No, about us... in general... something doesn't feel right.'

She cocked her head, 'Like what?'

'See, I was just thinking about our role here. You do flower arrangement, I tell the cook to add two spoons garam masala, we select curtains for the mess, I learn about the uses of some bloody hair gel...' I slapped the magazine shut and tossed it on the floor. 'Is this why we joined the army?'

She looked at me for a moment. 'No, that's not all. We had firing, we go for games and we also work in our offices.' She paused before continuing, 'And all that you mentioned is part of our work.'

'But what do we do most? Arrange parties, isn't it? And the worst thing is, our seniors are convinced that these are the jobs that we are good at.' I paused as Anju looked on. 'Where's the challenge, the adventure we came looking for? In fact, I am beginning to feel like an OG doormat.'

She leant forward and placed a hand on my knee. 'I think Lala is not treating you well.

'It's not about Lala. It's about everyone, everything. It's the mindset.' I looked away even as I continued, 'Anju, I want to do something really challenging. I want to prove that I can do a task as good as or better than any male officer. I don't like the way they treat us.' I stopped for a deep breath. 'I just don't like this.'

'Dips,' she said, as she closed her book. 'But you hold the guns and ammunition of the whole unit. Isn't that responsible?

'I hold the registers. Everything else is either Lala or CCME. And most often Lala makes me feel he was better off without me. He's constantly pecking at my head.' I paused and looked at the trees swaying in the wind. 'Do you think we can do something about this?'

'Like what?'

'Like... showing our disinterest in the bum jobs we are handed over, learning our jobs very well, volunteering for new jobs...'

'But won't that be tough? And then we'll be stuck in it like when we volunteered for night duties. What did we get out of it?'

'We need to work consistently. The results will show.'

She looked at me long and hard. 'I can't. I don't want to volunteer anymore. I'll just do what I am told,' she said flatly. 'I've realized that it's very taxing. And anyhow, whatever we do, do you think there will be a change in their mindset?'

Both of us looked at each other and sat quietly. Birds chirped on their way home. 'Dips, it's not easy,' Anju said. 'I don't know how you are going to do this.'

'Not "you", "we",' I said.

She sighed, got up and stretched. Then she picked up the book and gave me her hand, 'Come, let's go in. It's getting dark.'

6

Ms Fauji

THE JUMBOS PERHAPS HEARD MY RANT ABOUT THE lack of adventure and challenges. They decided to pay us a visit.

Several visits, actually. So the 'adventure' season began when they paved frenzied paths into the unit, breaking fences and uprooting trees. Store houses caved in. Sacks were ripped open and flour and sugar strewn around. Shattered doors and windows lay scattered all over. Flower pots had been kicked around like footballs. And since all this destruction happened in the Quarter Master area, I had enough challenge to last me for months.

This is when I realized that Lala had done me a lot of good, albeit unintentionally. His regular fault-finding had ensured that I remembered the Standard Operating Procedures word for word, and knew the manuals and reference books by heart. Although the jumbo adventure had piled me with work, with meticulous planning and execution everything began to limp back to normal soon.

'So, finally Lala must be pleased with all your work,' Anju said one morning as we were getting dressed. 'Did he at least make a mention of it?'

'Huh! Do you think Lala would ever?' I said, tucking my shirt into the trousers and pulling it down through the open fly. 'What are you talking about?'

'Your Lala from La-La land!' Anju chuckled as she pulled on her socks. Suddenly focusing on my open fly, she exclaimed, 'What! You even have an OG panty?' She began to laugh loudly. 'An OG panteeee... imagine!'

'That was the only one available in the canteen,' I explained.

'Dips,' she said, still laughing uncontrollably, 'you are OG to the core!'

'Don't laugh so much, okay,' I said. 'Very soon you'll also be OG to the core when you have to buy one.'

'No. Never! I have enough pastels and florals to last me till I go on leave,' Anju chuckled as we left for work. 'Now you can even tell your Lala, "Sir, I'm the best you can have around here since I'm OG to the core!"'

I dropped the giggling bundle at her office and headed to mine. After tackling some files, I went for rounds, checking the stores, the quality of ration received and issues. I also went into the messes to 'feel the pulse of the unit', like the Lion often said. Unlike earlier, on seeing me now the personnel would come forward enthusiastically to greet me. My efforts were paying off: I addressed them by their names and made it a point to exude warmth and concern when I enquired about their welfare: 'Mohan, how is your wife responding to the treatment?' or 'How was your son's entrance exam, Dwivedi?' Nor did I hesitate to pat a back or shake hands, telling myself that gender should never come in the way. I was slowly learning that people responded better when you showed them genuine concern. I learnt these skills from the Lion, by observing how he went about everything; how he could both be liked as well as feared.

There were also manipulators who came to me for favours, adding slyly, 'I am also from Bangalore, ma'am.' With such people I applied a different tactic. I used a low but firm tone asking them to get to the point. It usually worked, but on rare occasions when it didn't, I used my weapon, the expletives. Since I still didn't feel comfortable using the higher-ranked ones, I stuck to a 'bloody' or at the most 'idiot' or 'stupid'.

But just as I was beginning to revel in the authority and respect I had started to command as an officer, a new problem came up.

The Second-in-Command passed an order that we were to meet the first lady at the forthcoming ladies' club meet, a routine activity of the Army Wives Welfare Association or AWWA. I was happier without the ladies' club, but for Anju it was a dream come true. She had always been curious about what the ladies did there.

As ordered, we joined the ladies in the mess. Standing at ease in our uniforms, we were as conspicuous as dark plums in a basket of oranges among the colourfully clad and bejewelled women.

The first lady informed us, 'So, young girls, you will be participating in a fashion show for the upcoming station party.'

On hearing this unexpected announcement, Anju and I exchanged quick glances. While I had a frantic expression, hers was a jubilant one. She then sat as still as a mannequin, absorbed in the animated discussions as to who would wear what. Her radar was tuned for peak performance.

I lost my cool just looking at her. How could she forget all about the office and sit here looking so engrossed, when all the other officers were at work? I was sure they would be talking behind our backs, and once again getting ready to point fingers at us. I hated to give them that chance, but hardly had a choice.

I sat through the never-ending discussion on blouse materials and hairdos and pallu styles, clutching to the last shreds of my patience. When I decided I had had enough, I shook Anju out of her trance and whispered into her ear, 'I need to get back. All my reports and returns are pending.'

Anju looked puzzled. 'But they haven't told us anything about our dress yet.'

I gave her one of my most violent stares.

'Okay,' she said, dividing her attention between me and the ongoing discussion. 'What should we do?'

The first lady's eyes caught us. 'Yes, girls, what would you like to wear?'

'Anything you say, ma'am,' Anju replied, with a charming smile. Her tone and expression were beginning to remind me of Major Bhat.

'Actually, ma'am,' I added, politely, 'if you could tell us, we could get back and complete some pending work.'

'But I told Oshu to spare you people,' she said. It took me a while to figure out that the silly nickname was for her husband, our Second-in-Command. With the dominating air of a Queen Bee, she then looked around at the ladies and then back at us, and said in not-too-pleased tones, 'Today I'm sparing you, but I won't accept this tomorrow.' She paused and looked at her woman Friday, 'Will they be wearing the same...?' The woman Friday nodded and the Queen Bee turned to us. 'I'll tell you about the colour etcetera tomorrow. But for now it has been decided that you will be wearing chiffon saris.'

On our way out, I made no attempt to hide my irritation with Anju. 'I was just thinking you could go change into a fancy sari and sit there with them. You'll make a good assistant for the first lady.'

'Actually I wouldn't mind that,' she chuckled, adding to my irritation.

'I am certainly not going to do this,' I said, looking disapprovingly at her as we marched to the scooter. 'Why should I? I am not a member of AWWA.'

'Nor am I,' Anju gave me a sideways glance. 'But my dear, we have no choice.'

'I just can't do this.' I repeated, shaking my head. 'I work so hard to earn the respect of those men and now I am supposed to twirl around and show them my body. It's ridiculous!'

'It's not.'

'It is,' I said. 'Officers and jawans from the entire station will be there and we will be walking around like models. And then the word will spread,' I fumed. 'In this profession, where we must try to come across as strong, authoritative... as tough no-nonsense officers, do you think they can respect us when they see us swaying our hips in see-through dresses? They can never respect us if they see us that way. They'll just lech at us. You get me?'

Anju sighed and shook her head a couple of times. I kick-started the scooter, then thought of something and switched off the engine. 'Should we talk to the 2i/c about this?'

'Are you crazy? He won't like it. He passed the order after all. And what do you think we'll say to him?'

'I'll do the talking. You just come along,' I said.

She thought for a while and declared, 'I'm not coming.'

'Anju...' I said, trying to get her to agree, 'if I go alone what will he think? Shouldn't we at least appear united?'

'I don't know what he'll think. But I just don't want to go against anything or anybody.'

'Hey, don't be so stubborn. Come along, please...'

'No,' she said and looked away. Then she turned back to me. 'There are two things. First, I just don't want to go against anything. And second, I don't mind doing a fashion parade. What's wrong after all? Women do it everywhere.'

I realized that there was no way I could change her mind.

Once I dropped Anju at her office, I contemplated the move I was going to make. The repercussions could be many. The 2i/c's ego – or rather, his wife's larger ego – could be hurt. In the army, the wife's rank was always one higher. Worse still, if the Lion thought I was wrong, he could easily make my life a living hell. Anju was right. Just doing whatever we were told was a much easier option and also a much safer one. But then if I didn't stand up for myself now, in the next club I might end up demonstrating the preparation of potato mayonnaise or some such fancy stuff. I would end up doing things I didn't like and I was not required to. So, in a stroke of idiocy, I headed to the 2i/c's office.

'Yes, Deepa,' the 2i/c closed a file he had been peering into and looked at me.

'Sir, I have a small problem.'

'Go on.' He looked very preoccupied.

'Sir,' I said, clearing my throat and not feeling too confident anymore, 'Sir, regarding the ladies' club... I am not clear...' I looked at his shining bald pate, the equally shining glass-topped table and then back into his black eyes. 'As I understand, sir, I am not here as a... an officer's wife, sir...'

I stopped. It was tough, but at least I had made a start and got a part of the point across. The 2i/c looked at me and kept nodding without uttering a word. Then he said, 'Come again, Deepa.'

I wanted to throw the paperweight at him for not listening to my painfully uttered words. But I gathered myself and mumbled the same things.

'What are you coming to?' he said, looking searchingly at my face.

I gave up. 'Sir, actually, um... it's not such a big problem, sir,' I said and grinned like an idiot. In my mind, I had already draped a fancy sari around myself and started walking down the catwalk.

'Deepa,' he pushed a glass of water to me and removed the cover. 'Come, have some water.'

I took four quick gulps of water and looked back at him. His gentler expression made me feel brave again. 'Sir, the thing is... I don't feel comfortable doing a fashion parade before the whole station.'

A few seconds of silence followed. My heart thumped as I waited for the ball to return from his court.

'So, that is your problem,' he said, looking into my dilating pupils. 'I understand your point. In fact, when my wife suggested this, I thought you both might be interested. But if you are not, you need not be a part of this. There's nothing hard and fast.'

It was such a relief to hear this that I could have hugged Oshu (though I also anticipated trouble for him at home). But when I announced the news triumphantly to Anju later, she didn't seem too happy.

Eventually Anju walked the ramp and was a huge success. So much so, that from then onwards, the ladies would inform her about their programmes. They also asked her for her ideas and suggestions. The first lady was excited that she had found a showstopper. As for me, I had entered her bad books. She would turn her nose at me whenever she saw me. The other ladies took a cue from her and ignored me. Not that I was dying for their company, but Anju was now spending more time with them, and acting like them – and less like an officer.

'So, Anju,' said the first lady at a party, standing amidst her entourage in the mess lawns. 'For the next fashion show, we would like to see you in something western, maybe an evening gown.'

'Sure, ma'am,' Anju said and smiled, adjusting the sheer fabric of her light blue chiffon sari. She was the centre of the group's attention while I, in my earthy brown salwar-kameez, was as invisible as the air around.

A deep baritone suddenly closed in. 'Ma'am,' Major Bhat addressed the first lady. 'The fashion show was a big hit! It was the best part of the whole evening.'

'Sure, why not?' the first lady said, smiling and putting an arm around Anju's waist. 'We have her.'

Major Bhat turned to Anju and couldn't take his eyes off her. 'You look stunning!' he said, his eyes lingering on her face.

Anju smiled coyly as she said, 'Thank you, sir.'

Their eyes were locked for a few brief moments. Major Bhat then suddenly broke eye contact and exclaimed, 'You don't have a drink? Come, let's go and fix you a drink.' He then excused himself and led Anju to the bar. The ladies gave me a dismissive look. I moved on in search of Long Nose.

All the adulation and popularity at the fashion show seemed to have gone straight to Anju's head.

'Good I didn't listen to you,' she said one evening, as we walked back to our room after dinner. 'Had it not been for the fashion show, I would never have been so popular. The whole station knows me now.'

'Knows you as what?' I said with a snigger, as I opened the door of our room. 'That is the important part.'

She shot me a look of scorn. 'As a team player, not a spoilsport like you, okay! Everyone is pissed off with you since you don't join in the unit activities.'

'But a fashion parade is not a unit activity.'

'Everything that happens in the unit is,' she said, pausing to look at me as she unstrapped her sandals.

'No, I don't think so,' I said. 'If it were, all the other officers would have participated as well.'

She shook her head disapprovingly and marched into the loo, banging the door behind her. I looked on at the vibrating door, unable to come to terms with Anju's changing ideas.

At the barakhana, an official dinner with the troops on the occasion of Republic Day, Anju was once again dressed like she was about to walk the ramp. Watching her pink floral sari flowing behind her, I couldn't help but ask, 'Anju, don't you realize we are going for barakhana?'

'Yeah, so?'

'An army officer in pink! How will that look?' I said, making a face. 'Please downplay your make-up and clothes. You are not here to be a model. Look, Anju, here we have to prove that we *are* assets to the organization, not *show off* our assets. You are an officer. Dress like one. Exude authority... Think Indira Gandhi, Kiran Bedi... You get me?'

'Oh, c'mon, you don't always have to be so serious to be taken seriously. I'll wait outside,' she said and walked out, running a hand through her loose hair, now cut in steps. Her heels went tick-tock in the corridor.

I sighed and inspected my appearance in the mirror. My blue Kancheevaram silk sari was pleated and pinned neatly and my short crop of hair was combed into place. A few months in the relatively less strenuous atmosphere of the unit had also brought about changes in our physical appearance. Our skin tones had improved and we had also put on weight. I had got some of my curves back and looked well-proportioned, while Anju was gradually moving towards plumpness.

'Grab your pallu,' I said as we mounted our vehicle. I tucked mine at the waist and sat astride, being in the driver's seat. Anju sat sideways and rested her hand on my shoulder, as if she were my wife.

Two sari-clad women navigating a two-wheeler on a jagged road was no pretty picture. The silk beneath me slipped and my tucked pallu slipped out. The pleats blew up like a balloon. When I stopped to set things right, my legs stuck out like a plucked chicken's. Anju didn't have half the trouble as me, perhaps the reason why she was so reluctant to learn to drive, often putting all the blame on the gears. I knew if she decided to do something she could, but she just didn't want to.

At the barakhana, Anju flicked her hair every now and then, aware of the attention she got. I didn't like the way the jawans looked at her. I hated her for not listening to me, for not dressing up a little more soberly. I hated it when the woman in her leapt out at the wrong time.

'Jai hind, sahab,' a jawan greeted me as he passed by. I acknowledged the greeting. In the same breath he then wished Anju, 'Jai hind, madamji.' Our attire and attitude confused a whole lot of subordinates. Each developed their own version of greeting us, 'Namaste memsahib', 'Salaam sahab', 'Namaste madamji,' 'Jai hind memsahib' and so on.

'I think we must stick to sahab,' I said, turning to Anju. 'Most of them anyway call us that.'

'Not sahab,' she said. 'It has to be madam. Madam is the feminine equivalent of sahab.'

'But it doesn't work that way here.' I tried to reason with her. 'This is the fauj, and it's the first time ever that women have entered the scene. The jawan respects only the sahab. When they call us sahab, they forget our gender. And that's important if we have to command their respect.'

She looked at me and simply said, 'Madam.'

'It makes sense,' I tried again to impress upon her. 'Think about it...'

She looked unconvinced. I didn't try harder. She had her own ideas – or rather new ideas, perhaps not her own – and she stuck obstinately to them.

A sudden smile flashed across her face as she saw someone walk up. Major Bhat beamed at her and said, 'So, Anju, tired after the long day at work?'

'No, sir,' Anju said and smiled, 'but it was really a fruitful day.'

They were soon engrossed in talking about their office. I got busy tackling the biryani on my plate.

'Oh, poor thing,' Major Bhat said suddenly, as if remembering something. I looked up from my plate. Anju's eyes were wide with concern. 'I forgot to keep drinking water for Rocky,' he said

'Ahh... poor thing,' Anju said melodramatically. 'But hopefully you will get back soon,' she comforted him. 'This party won't take too long.'

'Yeah,' he said, actually looking comforted by Anju's concern. 'You know, you must meet him sometime. He's a great pet. You will love him.'

'I must,' Anju nodded.

'In fact, why don't you come over after dinner?'

I suddenly turned to Anju, hoping she would refuse the offer to meet Major Bhat's dog and even started to say 'But...' Anju however, seemed oblivious of my presence. 'Sure, sir,' she nodded happily.

They rode away to his residence while I looked on, dazed. Long Nose came up and asked me, 'Where is your friend going?'

'I don't know, sir,' I replied rather curtly, before heading back to my room and waiting anxiously for Anju's return.

She returned after about two hours and cooed into my questioning face, 'Aww! He's so lovely!'

'Who?' I asked, irritated at her irresponsible behaviour.

'Both, actually,' she said and smiled, before going to the other room to change. 'His house is such a mess,' I heard her say, her voice soft and mellow. 'So I was just setting things right for him. He doesn't have the time, always so busy...'

'I don't understand what you are up to, Anju,' I screamed at her. 'He's a drunkard, an oldie, a bachelor. What business do you have to go there and clean up his house at midnight? You know what people will say? You are taking things too far.'

'Don't shout!' she said and looked at me in a manner to suggest 'you won't understand'. She then began arranging her sari on a hanger and turned to her closet, ignoring my protests.

After this, on our way to office, at games, at PT, just about anywhere, Anju just needed an excuse to talk about Major Bhat. 'He's so knowledgeable, proficient, smart... Major Bhat, Major Bhat, Bhat, Bhat...' And my head went phut-phut.

Sometimes I told her to shut up. At other times, I pulled the shutters down over my ears. Sometimes, if I was in the mood, I would tease her. She didn't like it much when I suggested once, 'Let's call him Major Show-Off.'

Entering into its seventh month, Anju's infatuation was lasting longer than I had anticipated. Once, reading her latest M&B romance – she stocked up on them whenever someone went to Calcutta – she started giggling like a teenager and told me, 'You know, in this, there is a 43-year-old hero and a 23-year-old heroine, just like Major Bhat and me.'

'You are still reading these books?' I said. 'Read something serious. We are officers now, not college kids.'

'You read the serious boring stuff,' she said, frowning. 'I would rather enjoy these any day.'

'And moreover, that Major sahab doesn't seem to be having a good influence on you. Despite our initial pact, you have now started having hard drinks!'

'Let me tell you, Dips, it's really not that bad. In fact, you must also try it,' she said, dismissing my concern and turning to her book.

Anju's equation with me was slowly changing. Lately, she didn't pay much heed to what I said, about her conduct or dressing or anything at all. At the CCME Captain Shinde's dining out party, she once again dressed and accessorized like a fashion model, looking stunning in a mauve sari matched with strands of pearls: necklace, earrings and bracelets. Men were sure to swoon.

'Come, let's go to the ante room,' she said, sashaying up to me at the party after dinner. 'All of us are supposed to gather there.' In the recent parties, Anju divided her time and attention between Major Bhat and me.

As was customary, the Commanding Officer spoke about the officer on transfer. Then it was Captain Shinde's turn to speak. After the memento was handed over to Captain Shinde, it was time for the send-off. While the ladies remained seated, all the officers gathered at the main entrance. Major Bhat, Lala, Lieutenant Vishal Gairola and Long Nose then lifted Captain Shinde and tossed him up in the air, singing, 'He's a Jolly Good Fellow... and so say all of us.' Anju and I contributed our bit by holding his legs and tossing them up each time he came down. We laughed as Captain Shinde kicked the air, nearly bringing the chandelier down.

When after about a dozen tosses, Captain Shinde landed, his shoes, shirt and even the buttons of his shirt had come off. He moved to a corner to adjust everything.

I looked at Anju and smiled. 'Is this the way they'll toss us?'

'Maybe!' She laughed and rolled her eyes.

We followed the officers as they walked with Captain Shinde to the main gate to see him off. The ladies followed us at a distance. Major Bhat abruptly broke away from the group ahead, walked towards us and whispered something into Anju's ears. He returned as quickly. Anju grinned. 'Let's stop here. They are going to have a joke session. Dirty jokes!'

We stood between two groups, one of gentlemen and the other one of ladies. I couldn't help observing, 'We are neither here nor there...'

'Yeah, it's true,' she said following my gaze. 'But look at it this way, we can have the best of both worlds – the chivalry shown to ladies and the authority of the officer.' She shrugged. 'It's easy. Sometimes you are an officer and sometimes a lady, based on your requirement.'

'Isn't that manipulation?' I said, unable to agree with her. I remembered how Anju had put that into action at the party. She had broken protocol when, right under Lala's nose and closely behind Major Bhat, she served herself dinner while all the junior officers – including me – waited. Lala's steely stare had no effect on Anju. Lieutenant Gairola looked at me as though I was the one doing it. Her Benefits of Doubt were increasingly becoming glaring. Being close to Major Bhat, who in turn was the Lion's confidant, she was making the most of her immunity.

Now the ladies were slowly moving towards us with their joyful chattering. Anju glanced at them and turned to me as she said, 'So what if it is manipulation? We can use it to our advantage. Can't we?'

'It's wrong,' I said.

'You are the height of OG-ness,' she said. 'I wasn't wrong when I said that you were OG to the core. Loosen up a bit. Relax.'

'Maybe because I am OG,' I said, 'no one thinks that I am taking any undue advantage of the system.'

'Look, Dips, to me it doesn't matter what anyone thinks. I can't be stiff and boring like you.'

I looked at her for a moment. 'Have you forgotten everything that we had decided initially?'

'I can't even imagine you are still stuck on that. Move on, buddy. Life in the unit is different. Here there's no right or wrong. What works for us is what's right. Simple.'

Our debate didn't end with Captain Shinde's dining-out party. We continued later, and the more we argued, the more it became evident that Anju's ideas were drifting away from mine. Now I had been left alone to uphold everything that we both had believed in not so long ago.

Sometimes I wondered if Anju had forgotten all the hurdles we had crossed together and all the times that we had shared in the academy – of how unable to eat our breakfast under the glare of the glassy-eyed seniors, we quietly dropped boiled eggs into the pockets of our combat dress trousers and relished the crumbly remains during crawling exercises; how we clung to each other in a dizzy state, after our OTA whisky, a punishment which involved keeping the index finger steady at one point on the ground and running around it, like a carousel, till asked to stop; of how we went 'on our haunches' when caught squad-less taking a shortcut through the canteen. Through the punishments and high-stress atmosphere of the academy, what we enjoyed the most was our togetherness; the belief that we were there for each other. But now it was all changing.

Of late, she had begun to show other symptoms as well, symptoms that pointed only in one direction.

She smiled at the ceiling, the flower pots or even her suitcases. Sometimes she stretched out in bed and read something from loose white sheets, tossing and turning, putting them aside, shuffling and re-reading them. I learnt from her after much cajoling that those were poems Major Bhat had written for her. She then extended them to me, asking me to read them. With blue ink, in a manly handwriting were these lines:

> *A wandering soul was I,*
> *In a harsh barren desert,*
> *When you came along,*
> *Like a gurgling brook,*
> *Filling my heart,*
> *Filling my senses*
> *Like no one ever did before...*

Anju didn't take her eyes off me while I read. 'He writes so well, doesn't he?' she smiled.

I looked at her, long and hard, nodding absentmindedly.

She then got up and played me a song. 'Listen to this. I'm sure you'll like this. "Heart full of love".'

A deep mellow voice took over as she informed me it was Don Williams. The lyrics of the song sounded like they were written just for her, for an unpredictable child woman.

> *One minute she's up, one minute she's down,*
> *Lovin' her's like bein' on a merry-go-round...*
> *She's a heart full, unpredictable...*
> *'Cause she's got a heart full of love...*

I switched off the tape and said, 'Anju, I am worried for you. That man is too clever. He knows how to go about wooing you. Experience, I guess.' I placed a hand on her shoulder, 'Anju, I feel he is too smart and you are too vulnerable... I hope you realize it.'

'Nice song, na?' she said, switching on the tape and gently swaying her head.

As if in retaliation to what I had said, Anju danced with Major Bhat at the next party. His burly hands were around her waist and her head rested on his chest. It was scandalous.

Officers, their wives and even the stewards looked wide-eyed at her and then with the same expression, at me. I didn't know what I had done to deserve that look. True, she was my friend, but she had her own mind and I was not responsible for everything she did.

'What's she doing?' Long Nose whispered to me.

'Dancing, I guess,' I shrugged.

He walked to the bar, banging the door behind him.

Anju's dance party was one of the quietest parties ever. Mouths had taken a back seat, as eyes worked overtime.

As we got ready for office the next day, I said in as calm a voice as I could muster. 'Anju, I hope you realize what you are doing. It didn't go down very well with everyone... not even me... your dancing yesterday.'

'I see nothing wrong in dancing with him,' she snapped.

I maintained the same calm tone. 'Next time, be a little more careful. Maybe it was the alcohol.'

'I wasn't that drunk, okay? I knew what was happening.'

'And you let that happen? You let his hands run all over you?'

'Dips, can't you see I am in love?'

'Love?' I threw her a disgruntled look. 'It's just infatuation stretched a little longer.'

'It is love.' She raised her voice. 'It's nothing like I have experienced before.'

I was quiet for a moment. 'Anju, he's not the man for you,' I finally said, shaking my head. 'I think it's your romance books that are making the decision for you. He's TDH – that's all you see. Tall, dark, handsome.' I shook her shoulder, as if trying to jerk her back into the reality of the situation. 'Please, Anju, think. Look beyond the exterior. How can you be in love with this man? He is too old for you, such a show-off and then there are also rumours that he's divorced.' I turned back and slumped into the chair. 'I can't believe this trash.'

'It's not you...' she said, cocking her head, 'it's your J speaking.'

'J? Over what?' I leant forward, curious to know what she was talking about.

'Obviously, that men don't pay you any attention.'

I stared at her in disbelief for some time. 'Buddy,' I said, as I walked up to her and rested my hands on her shoulder. 'I agree I am no show-stopper or... jaw-dropper like you. But I am a woman and believe me, every woman knows how to get the attention of men. It's not such a difficult thing.' I spoke into her eyes. I then sighed, dropped my hands and continued, 'Haven't I seen what all you do... dress in clingy clothes, laugh at dumb jokes, make them appear knowledgeable... keep inflating their egos... I know these ways, but I am not going to do all that... get it? My idea is not to attract men here. I am here for a different purpose... And till some time back, I thought you were too.'

7

Marriage and Momos

THE DEN WAS NOT A PLACE I LIKED TO VISIT, BUT THAT'S where I found myself one bright morning beside a sobbing Anju. Lala, Major Bhat and the Second-in-Command were also present, their faces looking morose. The Lion's eyes were on Anju as she spoke between sobs, 'Sir, it was Naik Prasad.'

'Where did this happen?' the Lion asked, running a finger over his moustache, looking fierce.

'Near guard post number 6, sir,' Anju said, making no effort to control her copious tears. I patted her shoulder – I had no official business here, but she had requested that she wanted me beside her at this time.

'Was he drunk?' the Lion continued his interrogation.

'Yes, sir.'

He then turned to Lala. 'Wasn't yesterday the rum-issue day?'

'Yes, sir...' Lala said and added quickly: 'He's from the quarter master wing.'

I don't know why he said the last bit, except trying to divert the Lion's attention from himself to me. But the Lion went on with the same expression, 'Uttam, stay back after this. I need to talk to you.'

'Sir,' Major Bhat said leaning forward, 'if I may add something here. Ever since Captain Shinde has left, there has been a fall in discipline. I am sure you would've noticed it, sir.' He then glared at Lala before turning back. 'These incidents happen due to the lack of discipline. I hope you will agree, sir. There are two charges against Naik Prasad: first, that he was drunk on duty and second, insubordination.'

The Lion's eyes were fixed on Lala. 'Should I have to tell you this?' he nearly shouted, his brows knit. 'Pull up the CCME!'

After Captain Shinde, Lieutenant Gairola had taken over as the Company Commander and was away on temporary duty then. Under him, the discipline in the unit had slackened, as Major Bhat observed. He joked too much with the jawans, and mingled with them more than was required. Having interacted closely with Captain Shinde, I had learnt that a good Company Commander was one who played both God and Devil, depending upon the situation.

The Lion's face softened as he turned to Anju, 'Don't worry. We'll take disciplinary action against the individual. We will ensure that such incidents are not repeated.' He then paused for a few seconds. 'I always had my doubts,' he said, not looking at anyone in particular. Then he turned to us again: 'Do you both still want to do night duties?'

'Yes, sir,' I said quickly. Anju was too busy wiping her tears to reply.

The Lion gave me a dismissive look and frowned. Only on very few occasions had I seen him look so nasty, with that expression of complete unhappiness. He voiced his displeasure regarding lack of discipline and gave all of us a piece of his mind. We received ours and left, while Lala stayed back for the lion's share.

Anju was looking a little more composed now, unlike the night before this. She had gone for routine rounds as the duty officer, so I was surprised by her hysterical shouting and pounding on the door in the wee hours of morning. I was even more shocked when I opened the door. Like on the day she had arrived, she was crying and shaking uncontrollably. Two top buttons of her combat dress had come off and she held the shirt together with her hand.

I finally got the details out of her between sobs. 'I was just talking to him normally, about his family, his kids,' she said. 'He told me that they were away in his village in Bihar. Then he told me about his kids and their pranks and I laughed,' she said and paused, on seeing my expression of disapproval. I had told Anju on many occasions before that it was never a good idea to be too friendly with the jawans, or to enquire about their welfare in the middle of the jungle at night. Whenever I told her to maintain a certain distance, she joked, 'How much exactly?' And despite having spent half the time in the academy 'cutting the smile' she still smiled liberally. This was a place where a serious face got better results than a smiling, honey-sweet face. 'I know you will be angry, but I must tell you all this,' she continued. 'He said something about the barakhana.'

'What exactly?'

'That I was looking beautiful.'

I rolled my eyes. 'Look at his audacity! Bloody chap,' I said.

Anju nodded. 'I smiled casually,' she continued, 'and soon after that, he stopped the vehicle. Initially I thought the vehicle had broken down like before, but then I realized that he had done it on purpose. And before I could react, his hands were on me. I freed myself and got off, but he caught up with me. Then I kicked him with all my strength and ran to the guard post.' She wiped her tears.

'Anju, you should have pushed him out, driven off in the vehicle and reported immediately to the CO. The chap should have been put behind bars immediately.'

'I'm not as bold as you,' she said, and started weeping.

'It's not that I am bold. We have to make ourselves bold,' I said. 'Anyway, have you reported the matter to anyone?'

'Why does this only happen to me?' she said, tears rolling down her cheeks. 'You don't face all these problems.'

'Look, Anju, either of us can face these problems. I was just lucky and maybe a little more careful.' She looked at me through her moist eyes. 'I think you must just relax now. We'll talk about this later.' I then went to the mess to call up Lala, the Second-in-Command and the Lion.

'What do you mean, careful?' she asked me when I got back. She was still sitting in the same scruffy, tear-marked state.

'Ever since I joined the OTA and then the unit,' I said, leaning back on my chair, 'I think I look at myself a little differently.' Anju was all ears. 'I realized that I have to play an entirely new role here... that to be successful here, I need to hone the qualities of aggression, authority and strength, the so-called male traits.' Anju nodded as I continued, 'Usually on my rounds, I don't talk much, just a "yes", "no" or a "hmm".'

'But what if the chap speaks continuously? Like in

my case, that chap just wouldn't stop talking.'

'He talks because you let him. See, what I usually do is that I create an air of authority around me, which discourages them from opening their mouths. I think with this what happens is that his eyes just bounce off me. Just a few days back, this happened with me too.' Anju listened intently as I continued. 'The last duty, the chap tried to chat with me and when I didn't oblige, he kept staring at me intermittently. I caught his stare and stared right back, asking, "Any problem, Tomar?" After that he behaved himself.'

Anju's eyes focused on me through a curtain of tears.

'Anju, haven't we learnt from all our previous experiences that people observe us everywhere, right from what we wear to how we conduct ourselves. And that's the reason why I said that we must dress soberly, especially around jawans.'

'I think you are right, Dips.' She wiped away the tears. She then looked down at the floor. 'I am very confused... a woman stepping into a man's profession... we have to walk like a man, talk like a man, laugh like men... do everything like a man... I mean, I am a woman. So why should I act like a man?' She looked hard at me. 'I never felt like this before, but now I think I am in the wrong place.'

'Look, Anju, we always knew we were women stepping into a man's profession,' I said, getting up, sitting beside her and putting an arm around her. 'Wasn't that what all the excitement was about? The challenge? This is just teething trouble. And we have to face it. Aren't we pioneers after all?' I kneeled before her and lifted her chin. Her face was a mess of liquids and grime, but I could see the pain beneath. 'Look here, Anju.

The very fact that we are here is because we are more motivated, bold and determined than the rest of our lot. That means we have something extra, the strength to overcome odds. So, don't let this incident make you feel weak and most of all, don't talk like a loser.'

She was quiet and stared outside into the darkness. Cicadas broke the stillness of the night with their noisy utterances. She had a faraway look in her eyes as she said, 'I want to go on leave. I want to get back to my parents. I think they were right,' she wept. 'This is not the place for me... And Dips,' she turned to me an said, 'I actually feel like a loser.'

I tapped her shoulder, which was now limp and droopy.

'Where's all your josh gone? Get it back. You are not a loser and can never be. Haven't you heard: the finest steel passes through the hottest fire?'

Earlier, Anju would have yelled back, 'I have heard it a dozen times before', since it was one of my favourite quotes. Whenever I found myself in situations that demanded me to stretch myself beyond the usual, this is what I told myself. But today, she didn't look at me nor did she look like she was going to answer me.

I continued with the fire of a preacher. 'All these experiences make us stronger individuals. It just reaffirms the belief in ourselves that we can overcome all odds; that we can be in the worst of situations but still emerge stronger than before.' I paused and looked at her. 'Are you listening?'

She turned her face to me. 'Good. Face problems like a soldier, Anju,' I said, 'you can't run away or sulk.' I patted her shoulder. 'And you have proved time and again that you can fight. The peanut-wala and now this chap... I am really proud of you that you fought back and kicked him where it hurts the most. Excellent job!'

Anju smiled.

After a few moments of silence, she wiped her tears once and for all and peered deep into my eyes. 'Thanks, buddy,' she said, and placed her hand on mine.

The incident revived our wavering friendship, and for a while, it seemed as if the old Anju of the academy, who never lost her naughty smile despite all the punishments and bulldozing seniors, was back. I also noticed a few other changes in her. Unlike before, she wasn't happy to mingle with the ladies now. But she had no choice but to accompany the first lady for her numerous activities.

'The first lady is such a pain,' Anju said, as we got back from office one day. She made a dirty face. 'Actually they do a lot of good work... running schools, educating children, helping those in need.' She removed her shoes and peeled her socks off. 'But the problem is that she orders me around... and I don't like it. I don't know how to get out of this now.'

'Talk to the 2i/c,' I offered.

'Or should I tell Major Bhat to talk?' she said as she walked to the other room. 'Won't it carry some weight?'

It was after a long time that she had uttered that name. After the last discussion we had about him, which made both of us feel miserable, she had refrained from mentioning his name. I wasn't sure how it was between them; whether she had received more poems or letters or anything.

'Look, Anju,' I said. 'Don't you have any confidence? Why do you want somebody else to talk for you? Do it yourself.'

'But Major Bhat isn't "somebody else".'

'Alright, your wish,' I said. 'Do what you want.'

Anju didn't discuss either the first lady or Major Bhat for a while. Busy times were back again, as the unit got ready for the corps day or the formation day. There was to be a fete, games, competitions and more. All the officers were entrusted with responsibilities: mine was the food stalls, while Anju had the handicrafts stalls. We had to frequently go to town to get things organized, and this is when we developed a new addiction: steaming, mouth-watering momos.

We were in our favourite restaurant one day, enjoying the momos, dunking them in the fiery red sauce and devouring them. It's at this time that a far-from-savoury question cropped up in my head. 'What about your problem with the first lady? Did you do anything about it?'

Anju kept chewing on her momo for what seemed to be an eternity. When she was finally done, she said, 'I had discussed it with Major Bhat. He advised me that I must not talk to the 2i/c,' she said and sipped her tea, as I looked on. 'He told me that it always pays to be close to people in authority.'

'Even at the cost of your self-respect?' I said, with a hint of irritation. She didn't answer me. 'Okay, now that he has advised you, you will follow it to the hilt, isn't it?'

'Look, Dips, why are you always so irritated with him? He's not such a bad man as you make him out to be.'

'Please,' I said, waving a hand. 'I don't want to talk about that man. He's a hypocrite.'

'You think so?' She looked squarely at me. 'Okay, then you must know this...' She looked down at the cup and then back into my eyes. Her eyes suddenly shone with a soft faraway look. 'He proposed to me.'

'What?' I yelled. The momo nearly flew out of my mouth. People around turned to look at us. 'When did this happen?' I asked, composing myself. 'And why didn't you tell me?'

'Two days back,' she said, with an expression I was unable to read: a little confusion, a little glumness and maybe a little happiness. 'I wanted to tell you about this,' she continued, 'but you are never receptive when it is something about him.'

'And what did you tell him?'

'Nothing.'

'And what do you plan?'

'I don't know.' She shrugged. 'You tell me.' Both her hands rested on the table and she leant forward slightly. 'But give me an unbiased view.' She then added in a low mellow voice, 'Dips, don't you think you should marry a person you love?'

I nodded. 'I think so, but you also need to know something about the person.'

'Isn't it enough to know that I love him and he loves me?' she asked, cocking her head.

'C'mon, Anju, don't talk like a starry-eyed teenager,' I said, trying to put some sense into her head. 'Be practical. Life is not a Mills and Boon romance. Do you think this is the man for you? I certainly don't think so.'

Anju looked down at her cup, then at me, but said nothing.

'Do you realize that he is 20 years older than you?

Have you thought about it? When you are 33, he'll be 53, not too old, but old.' I paused to look at her downcast face. 'Okay, forget that. In love such things can happen, I agree, but what I feel is you are just swept away by his style and looks. You don't know him well enough. See, all I am saying is, you need to think very well before deciding anything. And then, with time, things change. In two or three years you may not feel the way you feel today for him. And you may regret this decision.'

In fact, this was the only thing that I was worried about concerning Anju – in a few months she would like to move on, and that's when she would see what she had got herself into. As for now, I knew she was partially blind, unable to see things clearly.

'Whatever happens, even when he's old, I'll still love him,' she said with a faraway look, as though beyond the next chair she could see a video clip of their future. She then dreamily brought her eyes back to face me. 'I am worried about how my parents will react. I don't think they will like it much.'

'I am sure they won't,' I said. 'Which parent would want their young, beautiful daughter to marry such a chap? If all the people who care for you think that you are not making the right move, isn't there something to it? Isn't it something to think about?' I sighed and looked away. 'And can't you see he is too much in love with himself to love anybody else? Have you never felt that?'

'No,' Anju said.

'But you must have certainly thought about this one: the way he drinks and smokes, I don't think he'll be around for long even.'

'About that, he promised me that he'll quit it all

after the marriage.'

'You believe him?' I shrugged. 'Oh! Of course you do.'

Anju looked at my face and sighed. 'Dips, I don't know what to do. I think I must give it more thought. I know you wish me well.'

'Anju,' I said, as we got up to leave, 'I can see everything so clearly. Why can't you?'

When we headed back, I felt heavy not only with the momos and masala chai but also with many weighty thoughts and the bundle of guilt I carried. I wondered if I was advising her to do the right thing. If it was love, as she claimed, then perhaps I was wrong.

But I was surer than her that it wasn't.

As we rode back, I had to quickly glance back or stick my hand out to feel if Anju was still there in the pillion seat. Never before had she been so quiet. Maybe she was weighing my words against her own thoughts.

8

'Happy'-ness

A WHOLE WEEK WENT BY AFTER OUR MOMO TRIP.
Anju hardly spoke, and in monosyllables if at all. I
didn't offer her any more advice: she seemed confused
enough already.

I didn't like the state she was in. I didn't like either
that I was unable to do anything to help her: it finally
had to be her own decision. At the most, what I could
offer her was a surprise.

'Hey Anju, today I am also going to drink,' I declared,
trying to stir up some cheer in her. 'Which one would
you suggest?' We were sitting on high bar stools in the
mess, Anju's hands resting on the semicircular wooden
bar counter. With fingers curled around the glass, head
drooping, a leg on the leg rest, another dangling below,
she looked like a female version of Devdas.

'Great!' Long Nose said, lifting his glass high.
'Welcome aboard. Okay, may I suggest something?'

'No, sir, thank you. Let her.' I turned to her. 'Hey,
Anju, didn't you hear me?'

'Try gin and tonic,' she said, without taking her
eyes off the glass.

I could trust Anju with this, since she knew how
to choose her drink. In Major Bhat's company, she
had learnt a good deal about cocktails. When I tried to

dissuade her from drinking, she would wave a hand in dismissal and say, 'Why bother about what others think? Do what you want to do, and be happy. The drunk happy or the other one, just be happy, happy!'

I liked the spirit of that statement. But I wasn't sure if I could apply it to myself. We had our differences. Anju could easily ignore the curious and interested looks on people's faces, when they stared into her glass filled with a hard drink. She could even ignore the comments and carry on as if she heard nothing. I couldn't. Anju lived her mind and I, others'.

I secretly admired her for her boldness, and at times, even envied her. Sometimes, I wished I could be more like her.

'Look, Anju,' I said, as I picked up my gin and tonic, 'I am going to loosen up, relax a bit... chill... like you told me... so here is to your good health and happiness, buddy,' I raised a toast to her. Long Nose joined me with a buoyant, 'Cheers!' After an unenthusiastic clinking of her glass, Anju got back to her Devdas position.

'Hey, what's wrong with you? You don't look well,' Long Nose said, casting a sideways glance at Anju. 'Anything I can do?'

'Nothing, sir,' she said, her eyes still on her glass.

'I think I can tell you a good joke,' he offered nonetheless, holding on to his favourite drink, rum cola. Despite all his Patiala pegs, I had never seen him too 'happy' for his feet. There were others however, who reached the extremities of 'happiness' very soon. Lala for instance. On many occasions, the frail Lali had to support the staggering Lala in a fireman's lift all the way home.

Anju still sat as though grieving for someone.

Long Nose looked at me and raised an eyebrow. I shrugged.

'I am anyway telling it,' he said.

'It's okay, sir, leave her alone,' I said, since I was sure if he told one she might just about weep.

For Long Nose was what you would call a joke-challenged individual. His jokes mostly fell flat. The narration was embellished with his past experiences and the punch-line most often came after over-preparing his audience. Once he told us a popular joke in the army, the essence of which was: a junior zooming on his bike sees a senior on the road with his car broken down. 'Sir, has your car broken down?' asks the junior and the senior says, 'Nope, yours has,' before zooming away on the junior's bike.

Long Nose's version went something like this, 'There was this young smart, lieutenant riding his new Bajaj Kawasaki, red and black, sleek... despite the potholes, he never felt it one bit... the shockers of that bike... too good, man... Anyway... he hummed a song and rode, when suddenly he saw someone on the road. When he came closer he found it was his Commanding Officer...' Long Nose stretched it some more and then right before delivering the punch-line, said, 'This is the really funny bit... get ready for some good laughs... Are you ready?... Here it comes...'

Anju and I usually laughed out of courtesy. The real laughter would come later in our room, when Anju would mimic him telling the entire joke and delay the punch-line even more with some of her own creations, 'You are going to roar now... hold your chair or you may fall on the floor laughing... be ready for some stomach cramps...'

I smiled at the memory.

But today was a completely different day. I sipped my drink and let the alcohol relax me slowly. None of us spoke. I looked around, studying the various paintings on the walls. When we had just arrived in the unit, the bar felt like a forbidden place. Everyone boozed, smoked and let their tongues loose. The portraits of nudes in various degrees of undress had made me wince. It was all art, beautiful, but made us uncomfortable nevertheless. The largest one was a semi-nude portrait of a Rajasthani woman. Her face was stunning and her ample bosom behind a black veil leapt out of the picture. Initially I wished she weren't there. But now I felt nothing. I guess I had got used to her being around.

'Our old man likes that painting,' Long Nose said, following my gaze.

'Really?' I smiled. 'How do you know, sir?'

'Is it difficult to know? The first thing he does after entering here is stare at her.'

We laughed. Anju was still quiet. Unlike other days she wasn't discussing and dissecting the Lion and other senior members of his kingdom. Of late, I had also noticed that Long Nose was cautious in Anju's presence.

There was a knock at the door and the mess havaldar informed me that the administrative officer was on the phone.

'Now what does Lala want?' I mumbled as I got up. It's when I had to walk across the corridor that I realized that the alcohol was at work.

'Meet me tomorrow, first thing in the morning,' was all Lala said, in a murderous tone. I tried to recall all the possible blunders I could have made recently but couldn't think of any.

'So, what did Lala say?' Long Nose asked, smiling, once I was back.

'Oh Lala, he's always...' But hey, who was I talking to? Wasn't it Long Nose? Who told him about the nickname Lala? I immediately looked at Anju.

'You're the one who said it, okay?' she said curtly, before getting back to staring at a bottle of Old Monk in the glass shelf.

'It's an apt name for him,' Long Nose smiled. 'So, let's hear everyone's name. Let's start with the CO.'

'Sir, only the adam officer has a name,' I said.

'C'mon, tell me,' Long Nose said, 'Let's hear it, c'mon, the CO, the 2i/c, me... Major Bhat...'

Even in her dreamy state Anju's radar didn't fail her. She latched onto the name and turned to us. Long Nose and I looked at her, startled. But her eyes were on something beyond us.

The fragrance of a musk perfume wafted over first and Major Bhat followed. It was time for the sermon. Anju smiled at him and he in turn looked at her tenderly. Feeling uncomfortable, Long Nose and I got up to leave, but Major Bhat's loud rumble caught me mid-step. 'Be seated there.' My questioning look only made his voice grow harsher: 'Sit there, I said.'

Long Nose left. I climbed back on the high stool.

Major Bhat got himself a drink, then whispered to Anju. I kept sitting there as ordered, but being totally ignored. After what must have been about 20 minutes, I spoke up, in a polite calm voice, 'Sir, I'll just be outside. You can call me anytime.'

'Hey you! Sit there,' he jabbed a finger in my direction. I felt like a pup being ordered by its master.

Another 20 minutes passed by, and I finished my drink.

'So, she is your friend?' he finally said, giving me a dirty stare.

'Yes, sir,' I said.

'I don't think so.' There was a long pause. 'I have been noticing you right from the start. You wield too much power over her and just don't let her be. And that's not what a good friend does.'

I looked at Anju, but her eyes were glued to the glass.

'I remember the first day,' he continued, bobbing his head, as I looked on. 'I was surprised that she looked at you to answer my question. That's because you control her.' He took a sip of his drink. 'You agree?'

'Sir, I think you are mistaken,' I said. 'There's nothing like that. We are friends and we listen to each other.'

'But she listens to you more, isn't it?'

Anju held his hand and mumbled something to him. He disregarded her and continued, 'You think you have the power to pull her away from me?' His voice was raised and his face took on a nasty look, 'C'mon, tell me.'

I didn't know how to answer him. I looked at Anju. She tugged at his arm and murmured something into his ears. He shoved her hand aside, and continued with a savage expression, 'C'mon, you want to take me on?' His index finger pointed at his chest, hovering about two centimetres away from it. 'You stupid second lieutenant!' The stare remained on me while his head shook, 'What do you think of yourself, huh? You call me an oldie? A hypocrite? How dare you talk about me like that? I am a major with 18 years of service and you, such a junior, what do you know about the army or even the world? Who the fuck are you to decide if I am the right one for her? Huh? It's her life, let her decide. Why the hell are you interfering?'

'Anju…' I said, looking at her, unable to believe that she had regurgitated our entire momos discussion to him.

'Don't talk to her,' he shouted. 'Talk to me.'

My head felt so light that I thought it was drifting away like a kite. It was clearly the wrong day to be baptized with alcohol. 'Sir, since she is my friend…' I said, trying hard to get myself in control, 'I was only advising her to do what I thought was right.'

'No, you are instigating her against me. That's what you are doing.' He banged his hand on the bar counter. 'You are a manipulator, a sly so-called friend. It suits you for her to be with you. You think only about yourself. You selfish creature!' His index finger was dangerously close to my eyes. I jerked back. 'You don't wish her well or else you would be happy that she's getting married, not trying to split us apart. As far as I am concerned, you are her enemy!'

My eyes instinctively moved to Anju. Sitting there with a coldness I was unaccustomed to, she certainly looked like an enemy. If she had so much as an iota of friendship left in her, she would at least stop him from blowing my gin-head off.

Suddenly Anju spoke. 'Prashant, you promised you wouldn't say anything to her if I told you.' She turned her head away and then faced him again. 'This is not done, okay. I thought you would keep your word.'

'She must be shown her place,' he grumbled. 'She must be told that she is narrow-minded, that she…'

'Prashant!' Anju raised her voice, like a teacher annoyed with her pupil.

'Look, Anju,' I said, 'it's for you to see who has selfish motives. Use your brains, Anju…'

'Hey, you're the brainless idiot!' He banged the wooden counter so hard that all the glasses rattled. 'Weren't you the one who nearly blasted everyone in the academy with your grenade? You are so stupid. How could they make you an officer? And you bloody call me selfish? You have the audacity to talk to me like that? You don't know what you get when you rub me the wrong way. If I want to, I can make your life hell. You get that? I have clout here.' Then dramatically his thundering roar reduced to a firm low tone. 'C'mon, apologize.'

'Sir, I did nothing to offer an apology,' I said, imitating his tone. If nothing else, the gin helped me feel braver.

Major Bhat's eyes bore into mine. 'You think you are too smart, eh?' I stared back, fearlessly. All the practice with Lala had helped. 'You just wait and see what I do. It seems you don't know me,' he said, with a wait-till-I-show-you nod. 'I was the one who trained you. And this is how you pay me back? Don't you have any basic decency? I am ashamed that she calls you her friend. You are muck, worse than that. You come from a lower middle-class background, with inhibited thoughts, bloody middle-class ideas...'

'Excuse me, sir,' I said, getting up and walking away.

'Hey, you! Wait there,' his voice followed me. 'You are insulting me. I am talking to you and you're bloody going?'

Anju followed me as I walked back to the room, slightly unsteady after my first ever dose of alcohol. It was for Anju's happiness that I drank; to lift her sagging mood. But it seemed to have had the reverse effect.

'I'm sorry, Dips, I am really sorry,' Anju said, walking

beside me, putting an arm around my shoulder.

I jerked her hand away. 'You big mouth, you don't talk to me,' I screamed at her. 'How could you go and tell everything to that monster? You heard what he called me?' I thrust the door open and flopped on the chair.

'Dips, I am sorry,' she said, sitting beside me. 'I shouldn't have told him all that. But when I turned down his proposal, he knew it had something to do with your advice. I never thought it would turn out this way.'

'But why did you mention my name, you idiot?' I said, my voice quivering, as tears welled up. 'Couldn't you have said that you thought about it?'

'You think I didn't try? He didn't believe it. He said I couldn't have thought it up. He was sure it was you.'

'Stupid, I thought I was helping you. You are such a dumb-head! Just go wherever you want. It's none of my concern, what you do, to whom you get married or anything.' I said, my voice heavy with emotion and tears rolling down my cheeks. 'I don't understand why I got into this messy affair. I am such a fool.'

'I am sorry. It's all my fault,' Anju said, placing a hand on my knee.

'Just go,' I screamed, as I swept her hand aside. 'I don't want to see your face. Go ahead and do whatever. Marry, divorce, remarry, whatever!'

Anju got up and left. I sat there fuming like a hot kettle, and wiping my tears. How could Anju have done this to me? I always knew she loved to talk, but this was not plain, harmless talking. It was backstabbing. What had come over her? Even when she had told him about my dream, I had warned her not to discuss me with him. It was my life, my cobra dream, and why the hell was she discussing it with some arrogant, elitist narcissist? I was now sure that if at all he read books on psychology, as he claimed, it was to identify his own disorder of extreme self-importance. Who was he to talk about my background and class? Why didn't I give it back to him? I thought about it and realized I possibly couldn't. In a hierarchical set-up, the beam always tilted in favour of the senior.

Anju was back again. 'Dips, I've come to call you for dinner. Come along,' she pulled my hand.

'I've had enough. I don't need more,' I said, glued to my position. 'Anyway, thanks for your concern,' I added sarcastically.

I went to bed hungry and thought of all the ways Major Bhat could make my life hell. I knew he wasn't exaggerating.

The following morning, as I woke up and stretched in bed, winking at the clock, I shrieked. The time was 6 a.m. We were late for PT. I looked at Anju's bed. She lay there and yawned lazily. 'Hey, Dips, I'm sorry,' she said, the first thing in the morning.

'Will you stop it? You have done all the damage you possibly could have done. It's because of yesterday's thing, because of you... that we are late for PT.'

'It's okay. Being late for PT once is pardonable. And in any case, I'll tell Major Bhat not to trouble you.'

I raised an eyebrow in an expression of mock wonder. 'Oh, your word is his command? When did you start commanding a major with 18 years of service? My, my, it pays to have an influential boyfriend with clout here! Your Prashant darling!' I got up, gave her a disapproving look and walked to the loo. 'Thanks, buddy. You have helped me enough. I guess I can do without more.'

'Stop being sarcastic.'

'Shut up!' I said and banged the door in her face.

'Look, Dips,' she shouted at the top of her voice for me to hear, 'I told you it was my fault and I am sorry. What else do you want me to do?'

I was mum. When I was uncontrollably angry or upset, I spoke in spurts and then retracted into a cocoon. Anju knew that it would take me time to get out of this state. But for now, she kept talking, trying to tell me her side of the story. She delivered the conversation she had had with Major Bhat down to the comma. I didn't respond. Anju stopped.

We got dressed for work like two people who are invisible to each other.

The first place I headed to was Lala's office.

'Where do you look when you sign?' he bellowed, without preamble. Usually I scanned everything before putting my 'checked and okayed' stamp of approval. But today it was apparent that there had been a blunder.

'Are you fucking still practising your signature?' His eyes burned and nearly popped out of their sockets. 'You sign everywhere and anywhere without looking!' he said, and slammed the file on my end of the table with both hands, like he were swatting a fly. 'If despite my warnings you continue in your La-La land, I tell you...' he intensified his stare, focusing on my face like with a laser beam, 'you will see my real true colours.'

I saw two colours, yellow and blue. One was a report file and another a leave file. 'For all the blunders you make,' he blared, 'I am answerable to the old man. Do you understand that?'

'Yes, sir.'

'The count of weapons in the army can never go wrong. And here, you have done eggjactly that. Irresponsible!' He opened the yellow file and shoved it towards me. 'See, in this, you are showing more than the held quantity. Don't you know that two had been declared unfit for use by the inspection team? If I had not seen this, do you realize what would have happened?'

'I am sorry, sir,' I offered lamely. 'I overlooked it.'

My apology strengthened his position. 'This sorry business doesn't work here, okay. Once a bullet is shot, it is gone. There's no point saying sorry after it hits someone. You understand?'

After the apt example, he continued some more about how astutely he spotted the error. Then he indulged in some well-deserved self-praise. 'I saved you from the old man,' he said. 'Otherwise he would have made a chutney of you.'

'Thank you, sir,' I said, after everything, after he had sunk my morale. But at least he had saved me from the Lion. I had heard that when the mighty Lion was furious, files and papers flew about like birds in his office.

'And why were you not there at the PT fall-in?' Lala had saved this for the last.

'Sir...' I said, my level of confidence at an all-time low, 'I overslept.'

'Overslept? *Overslept?*' He shook his head. 'Take care,' he said, his voice taking on a warning tone, 'if this is the way you plan to go on, you will land yourself in a thick soup. Mark my word.'

I wanted to tell him I was already in a soup.

Everything seemed to be going wrong. Unlike

earlier, this time, I had made the mistake of depending on my senior JCO, the Junior Commissioned Officer. The moustached, glib talker had convinced me that he had checked each figure thoroughly.

As I walked out, I met Long Nose. 'Looks like you got a lot of prasad after Lala's darshan.'

'I am used to it now, sir. I get a lot of prasad every day.' I smiled through the gloom. 'But I can't share it with anyone.' Before Long Nose could frame his reply to comfort me, I was gone.

Back in my office, I summoned my staff and gave them a thorough dressing-down. I must have looked like a wounded tigress, lashing out at them at the top of my voice. All the words I had learnt, I put to effective use here.

The clerk, a young man of about my age, began to weep. It looked odd, but I didn't stop. If I could get it all from Lala, I also had to pass it down the chain of command. With every shout, every expletive, every bang at the table, I felt something leave me. I felt better. All the things I couldn't tell Major Bhat, I let go now. My pent-up emotions found an outlet here.

But despite that, I was in such an emotionally fragile state, that if anyone so much as looked kindly at me, tears would come rolling down. I dismissed my staff, walked around in my office, and then I went out. I looked at the rose shrubs with tiny buds, trees swaying in the breeze and bees buzzing on the frangipanis. I took a few deep breaths and returned to my table.

A yellow envelope carefully placed under a glass paperweight caught my attention. I opened it and swore some more. It was a missive from the Lion demanding an explanation for my absence at the PT fall-in. I was then ordered to do an extra duty as punishment.

At lunch time, my curiosity got the better of me and I asked Anju, 'Did you also get the letter?'

'What letter?'

When I told her in brief, she said, 'Oh, don't worry about that. I can get the letter cancelled.'

'Thanks so much, Anju, you are such a sweetheart,' I said, putting on a fake grin. 'But I'd rather do an extra duty than take favours from your Prashant darling.'

Anju shot me an angry look. I dismissed it and concentrated on the contents of my plate.

A terse silence gave us company for lunch. It was as though our friendship had evaporated overnight.

In the evening as I returned from office, I saw Anju hurriedly emptying her closet into her suitcases. 'Have you applied for leave?' I asked.

'I don't have to tell you anything,' she snapped. 'Major Bhat was right. I must treat you the same way you treat me... with coldness.'

'Just tell me where you are going?' I said calmly.

'I don't need to tell you, okay?' she said, looking up from her kneeling position as she arranged her clothes in the suitcase. 'It's not like whenever you want to talk, you talk and I answer. I said I was at fault, I said I'm sorry, but still... you are so sarcastic... you treat me like dirt!'

'Look, I am not interested in anything else,' I said, leaning on the door frame. 'I just need to know where you are going. That's it.'

'I am not telling you anything!' she said, stressing each word and looking into my eyes, before stomping out with two of her suitcases and loading them in the back of a waiting one-tonner.

Within seconds, she was gone. There was no goodbye, no wave, not even a look. My eyes followed

the one-tonner as it bumped along the road, with the
two suitcases rattling in the back.

9

Long Nose Leaves

A HUNDRED RANDOM THOUGHTS SWAM AROUND IN my head when Anju left. My first reaction was angry indifference, 'Let her go wherever. I don't care.' But as the evening turned to night, this thought was replaced with concern, 'Where could she have gone?'

Maybe she had taken leave to go home after all. I made a few quick phone calls and learnt that her leave had been approved by the Lion – but she had cancelled it.

Then a nagging thought began to take form. Could she have gone to Major Bhat's house? Would she have been so foolish?

On further enquiry, I gathered, to my dismay that the vehicle had indeed dropped her at Major Bhat's residence. I tried to get in touch with her. I thought of all the things I was going to tell her, 'Anju, I'm sorry... please come back... get married if you want to and move in officially... that would be the socially accepted way.' But I couldn't get through to her. Major Bhat picked up the phone at the other end and blasted me. My head spun as I walked back to my room.

That night, I couldn't sleep. I tossed and turned, feeling torn inside. I wasn't sure of what to do or whom to tell. Perhaps she had acted on impulse and all she needed was a call from me. The next day, I called her at her office, but she banged the receiver down without talking to me. I tried again and after many attempts and many rounds of apologizing, she said, 'Look, if you think I am coming back, let me tell you, I am not. And also, Major Bhat doesn't like me talking to you. So please don't try calling up.'

Things hadn't been going right for me for some time now. But with Anju's leaving, every other problem I had was magnified. Perhaps I just felt so because I didn't have her to share them with. Maybe I had got used to her being around, to hear me out, to vent my rage, to offer suggestions, to laugh and sometimes sulk together. When earlier someone had joked that we were like Siamese twins, always stuck together, I didn't quite like the remark, but now I realized they were right. Irrespective of all our differences, we were usually together.

Days and weeks went by. My room was relatively empty ever since Anju had taken away her remaining suitcases. She walked in one evening, packed her things and left. I tried talking to her, but she just wouldn't hear me out. All she said was, 'Good I didn't listen to you. I am so happy now.' All that remained of her was a stash of colourful Mills and Boons.

Anju might have left without a thought but her actions were beginning to affect me.

'So your friend ditched you?' Lieutenant Vishal Gairola cackled. 'With women in the army I knew these problems would come. Earlier I used to be proud to say that I am an army man, but not anymore. You people have spoiled the image completely.'

Lala summoned me to know the details about this incident. Surprisingly, his tone was nothing close to the regular bark. It had a juicy, gossipy note. 'I heard she is staying with Major Bhat. Is it true?' he asked in a forced whisper. I knew he was among the first ones to know about it, but wanted to hear the sizzling hot news from me.

The Second-in-Command, who usually had a warm demeanour, took on a rather unpleasant tone when he said, 'I am ashamed that unit officers display such un-officer like behaviour. I thought you had the maturity and intelligence to understand these things.'

Then it was the Lion. 'You should have informed me when it happened. After all, you are the one who stays with her. I can't tolerate such casual behaviour from my officers.'

No one thought it necessary to give me an opportunity to justify myself. I knew I was the easy target. The Lion needed Major Bhat's services and as for the others, they could hardly speak out against the Lion's own man.

The scene in my office also changed when the details of the incident trickled down to the jawans. Anywhere I went, I heard stifled whispers behind my back. Some even had sly grins on their faces when they talked. All my efforts at image-building were wasted. The respect I had worked so hard to earn disappeared overnight. A senior JCO walked into my office one day and tried to put it as subtly as he could, 'All these things which are happening are not good, sahab. It affects the morale of the unit. Everyone is talking about it.'

'I know,' I said, 'But I think you must project it to the CO. Maybe he can do something.'

'It's not him,' his voice took on a firmer tone. 'Only you can do something. You are the only one who can set things right.'

'I wish I could do that, sahab,' I said, 'but things

are a little more complicated than that.'

He thought for a brief moment and said, 'Everyone had a very good impression about you... so it's very hard to believe...' With a sombre expression, he then went on to tell me the story that had been doing the rounds. He informed me that the jawans thought that both the lady officers were drunk and fought for a man. On hearing it, I wanted to scream and yell in disgust. Everyone had a taste for sleaze and now they had lady officers to spice things up. The incident was distorted beyond imagination.

'This is hearsay, sahab,' I said, trying not to look affected by the story. 'There's nothing of that sort. Don't believe everything you hear.'

'I know,' the JCO continued. 'I told them that our sahab can never be involved in such things.' He then paused for a moment to read my expression. 'What we are hearing is not the true version of the story...'

I sensed he wanted to hear my version, but I didn't oblige. 'Things will be back to normal soon,' I said curtly before sending him away.

With my staff, I managed to evade questions I didn't want to answer, but when it came to the ladies, there usually was no escape.

'Is it true?' they echoed, disbelief writ large on their faces. Some of the more inquisitive ones steered me into a corner at a party and demanded to know every little detail. Most of them were those who till some time back had their noses high in the air, ignoring me. But now that they had sniffed a bone, they wanted me to add the meat.

'Are they having a live-in relationship?' one of them said in a hushed tone bubbling with excitement.

'Haaaw,' added another. 'No shaadi-vaadi? What

a shame!'

'You could have advised your friend,' said a third one.

'It's nothing like you hear, ma'am,' I said, trying to make it sound as dry and uninteresting as possible. 'They got married in the temple. They moved in only after that.'

'But we never heard it,' they chorused. 'If there was something like that, we would certainly know.'

They marched away, disillusioned at not being able to extract much from me. Their conversations though were loud enough for me to hear.

'These girls, I tell you, they are characterless,' said one. 'They come here so that they can get married and they don't hesitate to do anything to hook officers.'

'Till now I never had any worry,' said another, 'but now with these girls around, I am very worried about my husband. God knows who the other girl will trap now.'

Anywhere I turned, any conversation I overheard, deriding remarks ruled. I knew Anju's move would never be considered fair on moral grounds, but I was not prepared for such an onslaught of reactions.

'These things happen only in America and the west, not our India,' our first lady said, addressing a group of ladies. 'And certainly not in a small conservative place like this. I think these girls are breaking all traditions... joining the army, live-in relations and God knows what else.'

Of late, in the parties, I found myself mostly alone. Anju was always beside Major Bhat and made it a point not to look my way. Most officers and ladies were wary around me. If at all I could walk up to someone and talk, it was Long Nose. He seemed to understand the situation I was in. Whenever he saw a morose expression on my face, he told me, 'See, on your part you did the right thing. But finally, it's her life. Let her decide what she wants out of it. She looks happy, so why are you making that long face?'

'I don't know...' I told him. 'Happy, sad... laugh, cry,' I shrugged, 'What must I be? What must I do?'

'Dips, all I can tell you is that if I were in your place I would have done exactly what you did.'

I looked at him and smiled for two reasons. One, I was happy that at least someone thought I was right. And second, that he had called me Dips, not Deepa.

Major Bhat, as promised, was beginning to make my life hell. I found myself more at the railway station than at the unit, since I was sent on temporary duty on some pretext or the other. Sometimes I was informed at such short notice that I had to travel at odd hours and unreserved. Whenever back in the unit, I found myself to be the duty officer on most days. Ranging from stock taking, to preparing statements of case to being a member of some board for assembling, analyzing and recording information about an incident under investigation, a spate of dreary jobs found their way to me. Most often I had to approach Major Bhat at some stage or the other, since he was a major cog in the wheel. Everything and everyone revolved around him. With whatever I put up to him, he was ruthless, sometimes tearing the papers and tossing back the files even without a fair reading. His insults also became denigrating.

'Even Rocky can do better than this,' he said once.

'Sure, sir, get Rocky here then.'

Well, I never said it of course, but there were

occasions when words nearly rolled off my tongue. But then I realized I couldn't possibly get into a verbal duel with him. He was way too senior. He had enough influence to toss me around like a football and he made sure he did that.

But all was not dark. I still had Long Nose to talk to and be with. In many ways, Long Nose replaced Anju in my life. Or maybe he was taking an entirely different place. I couldn't figure it out nor did I bother to. My life was complicated enough and for now all I wanted was a friend who could hear me out. Long Nose fitted that bill. I didn't feel uncomfortable in his company. He was beginning to be a friend I could just talk to, laugh with and generally be happy around. I often discussed my problems with him. I don't know how I developed the confidence to open up to him. Perhaps it was just a belief that he was a good man and most of all, could be trusted. There were times when I spoke my heart out. He listened and that mattered to me.

We usually came early to the mess so we could talk in the absence of Lieutenant Gairola. And now since Anju was living with Major Bhat, the sermons had died a natural death.

'Mistreating a junior is like slapping someone who can't slap you back,' Long Nose said, when he heard me out one evening in the mess. 'I guess that's what is happening with you.'

'Exactly, sir,' I said, elated that he had put my woes into the right words.

'Why don't you apologize if that's what he wants?' he said, curling his fingers around a glass of rum cola. I sipped some mango juice. After my first drink I never tried another.

'Apologize for what, sir? What have I done

wrong?'

'No, just like that. To satisfy his ego. Try it.' He looked thoughtfully at me. 'It's after all a game of ego. He's keeping his and you are keeping yours. Once you let go of yours, things won't be so bad.'

'I don't think it's that, sir,' I said. 'I am sure whatever I do he'll have the same attitude since he believes I am the villainess in his love story.'

'Hmm,' he said, and sipped his drink. 'Or why don't you try talking to Anju?'

'You know she doesn't talk to me at all. I have tried it so many times. She is following Major Bhat's orders. She doesn't even look at me.' I shook my head and sighed. 'This is not the kind of behaviour I expected from her... ever.'

'She's a heartless kind of a woman,' Long Nose said. 'I am sure Major Bhat will realize it someday. She's the kind who doesn't mind walking over anyone to get what she wants. She's selfish... calculating... in fact, I think she doesn't deserve to be your friend.'

The criticism somehow felt unwarranted.

'Sir, I think she just got carried away,' I said.

Long Nose peered into my eyes, his brow furrowed. Then he shook his head and looked away. We sat in relative silence for a while.

'Okay, coming back to you,' he said, swivelling his bar stool to face me. 'Why don't you have a word with the 2i/c?'

'Sir, I have thought about it... But what will I tell him? I can't possibly go and crib to him about another senior officer. Can I?'

'No, but at least project your problem.'

'What problem will I project, sir? Think about it.

Can I say that I am a member of so-and-so boards, that I am duty officer, or that I am sent on temporary duty at short notice? Do any of those sound like problems at all?' I shook my head. 'No. You think they are not aware that I am being targeted? Everyone just keeps mum since if they interfere, they will have problems. And who wants to be on the wrong side of the CO? Don't they have to get glittering ACRs?'

'Okay, okay, I get it,' he said, and then his face lit up. 'I have a better idea. Why don't you just go on leave? Take some time off and you can come back recharged.' He lifted his glass slightly and brought it down with a bang. 'Now, howzatt?'

I smiled. It certainly seemed like a good idea. 'But sir, do you think I can go?' I said, as doubts regarding its feasibility crossed my mind. 'All my boards are still pending.'

'Put up your leave application. As for the boards, I will also help you with whatever I can.' Long Nose smiled with a warmth I hadn't seen before.

'Thanks, sir,' I said, after toying with the idea for a while. 'It's a great idea. I need a break before I can come back and fight some more.'

We laughed and clinked glasses for having found a fairly simple solution.

Without wasting more time, I filled up my leave application and stood before Lala. 'Sir,' I said, presenting my file gingerly, 'this is my leave application.'

He opened it and glanced at the dates. 'Okay, I am signing it,' he said, as he scrawled his detailed signature. 'But ensure that the boards are completed before you leave.'

'Yes, sir,' I said, unable to believe my ears. Here was

where I expected the most resistance but he seemed to offer none at all. What had come over Lala?

'I know you are sincere, you work hard,' he said, in a kind concerned voice that was markedly un-Lala-like. 'But the thing with you is that you are not tactful.' He kept his pen aside and clasped his hands. 'See, just working hard alone is not enough, you also need to let others know about it.' He paused and looked searchingly at my face. I nodded, still unable to believe his transformation. Perhaps he just wanted to let me know that he was aware that I was being treated unfairly. Maybe that was his way.

Lala continued, 'See, you are too young in service. So you need to learn a lot of things. You can never take panga with someone who's in a better position than you. Isn't it common sense, something basic that everyone knows?'

'Yes, sir,' I said, downcast, while he went on in his kind, caring voice.

'Look at your friend. She's so shrewd. She has made her position so comfortable. Not like you. You yourself asked for the way to hell. Anyway, don't worry. Everything will be alright.'

For the first time, I left Lala's office feeling better than when I had entered it. And now, having cleared one hurdle, my leave file then went on to the next, at the den.

The Lion didn't bother to open my file. 'Finish all the pending work before putting up leave,' he said curtly,

'Sir... but...'

He waved an imposing hand at me. 'Do as I say.'

I knew I was not such an important person in the unit that I couldn't be spared. The repercussions of my actions were beginning to have a cascading effect and

I was beginning to feel the severity. If the Lion had formed a negative impression about me, he was most certainly instigated by his man Friday.

When I told Long Nose about this development, he laughed before saying, 'Good your leave is not sanctioned.' As I looked on quizzically, he informed me that we were detailed for the Young Officers' or YO's course.

'Am I also going, sir?' I asked, unable to contain my joy.

'Yeah, your name is there. I just saw the list. Anju's name is also there.'

'Really? I am so happy!' I said. I was thrilled since this course meant being away from the unit for six months. It was the best thing ever to have happened, considering all the muck I was in. 'But Anju, sir? Do you think she will go?'

'She has to go. You can't refuse a course unless you have a solid reason,' he explained.

I thought about it. Perhaps he was right. Even if he wasn't, I hoped against hope that he was. If a course couldn't be cancelled then that meant no one could stop me as well. After a long time, I went to bed happy. There was the excitement that all three of us would go for our course together. Then maybe Anju and I could get over our differences. Maybe without Major Bhat's influence, she could be the same old Anju, my buddy, my friend. I dreamt of bright and cheerful days ahead.

Reality hit me soon enough. Long Nose informed me a few days later in a sad voice, 'They are trying to cancel your course.'

'But you said they can't do that,' I quoted him.

'See, from what I understand, Major Bhat doesn't

want Anju to go. So I think they are trying to cancel it for both of you.'

'But I want to go.' I said.

He looked at me ruefully. 'I think you have landed yourself in quicksand. Everyone who matters in this unit seems to be trying to sink you. But don't worry.' He patted my drooping shoulder. 'And don't give up. Fight, just like you have been doing so far... and maybe you should still talk to the CO or 2i/c.'

I thought hard about the best course of action. If I went up and talked to my seniors, perhaps they might consider my case. But looking at the present scenario, it didn't look like anyone would give me a fair hearing, let alone a fair judgement. What about Lala? In his latest avatar, he looked quite approachable. Maybe he could help me.

'See, I can't influence this decision,' Lala said in his newly developed sweet tone. 'At the most what you can do is take an interview with the 2i/c or CO.' He then quickly added, 'Don't quote me, but.'

The Second-in-Command had a terse expression when I met him. Before he could hear me out fully, he said, 'Deepa, the unit can't spare three officers together. I hope you can understand that. Lieutenant Sandeep Singh is long overdue, so he has to go.'

'But sir, at least two officers...'

'It's the CO's prerogative to decide,' he interrupted. He then clamped both his hands on the table and leant forward. 'I would also like to warn you to be little more courteous with senior officers. I can't tolerate rudeness and arrogance.'

'I'm sorry, sir, if I sounded rude,' I said, before leaving his office. There was absolutely no difference in the way I had spoken to him. I knew it was something else. It was most certainly the result of bad inputs from Major Bhat. This undercurrent was proving much stronger than I had thought. I brimmed with resentment within. I considered talking to the Lion, but eventually decided against it. There seemed to be no point.

Anju's name and mine were taken off the course list. Only Long Nose was to go. If he was happy about it, he didn't express it. He was aware of how bitter I felt. To add salt to my wounds, I learnt he would not return since he was to proceed on transfer to another unit. I knew I would most certainly miss him. In the recent past, our friendship had deepened.

At his dining-out party, I was as lifeless as a corpse.

'Don't worry,' Lala walked up and put an arm on my shoulder. 'Everything will be fine,' he smiled, coming too close to my face for comfort. His hand then slid slowly down my back and lingered there, before continuing on its downward journey. I jerked away.

'Do you know,' he came closer again, 'I have told the CO that you are doing a good job. You are an asset to the unit...'

I wasn't listening to what he said. Instead I concentrated on the movement of his hands. I excused myself and fled.

I looked around for Long Nose, but he was nowhere in sight. My eyes then fell on Anju, who looked like an apsara in her blue sari. She stood beside a beaming Major Bhat and together they made a handsome couple. All eyes were on them. Anju clung to Major Bhat's arm and even when they moved around, her grip never loosened. Major Bhat's confidence seemed to have doubled with Anju by his side. He rumbled louder, laughed thunderously and intermittently gave admiring looks to his lady love. Anju also contributed to the conversations, laughing freely and talking without restraint.

'So when are you tying the knot?' the Lion asked them.

Anju smiled her happiest smile as she said, 'Very soon, sir,' before looking at Major Bhat for approval.

At the end of the party, Long Nose was given the customary bumps and tossed out of the mess. He then went ahead with the joke session. This time, I stood alone between the group of officers and ladies. Behind me, Anju stood alone too. Perhaps she didn't want to join the ladies to avoid being asked too many questions. Our eyes locked for a second, but she quickly turned away.

Even as I stood there, I wondered if Long Nose knew a dirty joke at all. He didn't look like the type who had a stockpile of them. And considering his tendency for over-narration, I wondered how well it would be received. But uproarious laughter wafted from the group. Simultaneously, Long Nose broke away and walked towards me. He extended his hand for a farewell shake. I shook it.

'Dips, come what may, never let your spirits dampen... keep up the josh,' he said, without letting go of my hand. 'Fight, never lose heart.'

From his breath I knew he was more drunk than most days, somewhere in the 'extremely happy zone', in his own words. He tousled my hair and before I knew it, engulfed me in a bear hug.

'You know what I like the most about you,?' He pulled himself back and peered into my eyes. 'That is apart from your never-say-die spirit...'

I shrugged.

'I don't know if I can tell you this or... ' he hesitated. 'Well, I would love to meet you again... somewhere... to see your lovely infectious smile.'

10

Lala's Antics

FIRST IT WAS ANJU, THEN LONG NOSE. ANYONE WHO meant anything to me had moved away, widening a void within. I had never anticipated that Long Nose's departure could have that kind of effect on me. Perhaps if he had stayed back I would never have felt so lonely. Maybe...

But I shook myself out of the daydream by telling myself that good or bad, everything moves on. So just like the good had left my life, the bad would also pass. Until then, I had to use all my reserves of strength and courage to ensure that the strong undercurrents of office politics didn't wash me away.

The kind of situation I had got myself into, there was hardly a soul in the unit with whom I could have a casual conversation. I began to look outside for companionship. I browsed the directory and called up acquaintances from nearby units. I fixed up meetings with them, but more often than not, I returned disappointed. My stomach turned at their repulsive versions of the unit incident. Like in a game of Chinese whispers, with every ear, it changed form until it became a juicy sleaze story.

Having heard these stories, officers from other units evinced newfound interest in my single status. Parties were inevitable and it's at these soirees that they played their cards.

'You know, my wife is not here,' said a middle-aged officer after the briefest of introductions. 'She's in London, a doctor. Everyone thinks it's a great thing. But you don't know how lonely I am. There's really no company here... the days go by with work but the nights...' He poured out his woes, expecting me to do something in return. Perhaps drive his loneliness away. Then there were others too who, with their extra bright smiles, demonstrated fake concern and affection. They invited me to get-togethers, games and clubs. By now, I had fine-tuned my antenna to detect this species from a mile away.

I avoided all males, except the Commanding Officer. I hardly spoke to anyone other than in the office and began to spend more and more time alone. I knew that no company was better than a demoralizing one. I read any book that was available in the unit library, I flipped through all the magazines and pamphlets I could lay my hands on. I played and replayed all my cassettes so many times that I reached a stage when I could play any song blindfolded. Sometimes the songs with their lyrics and soulful music transported me to another world. Many times I had to pinch myself to see if I really existed. To ward off the depression, I tried writing upbeat letters to friends. I looked forward to their replies and when an envelope came, I was thrilled. I went through them several times, touching them, feeling, smelling and preserving them to re-read later.

Despite all my efforts, over a period of time, loneliness gnawed its way into my mind. The more I tried to mix with others, trying to look for their acceptance and approval, the lonelier I began to feel. When it was unbearable, I rode to town and talked to anyone I came across.

On one such trip, I met two young men at my favourite momo joint.

'You are a regular here, right? Have seen you before,' said one of them. He had slit eyes and a goatee.

'Yeah,' I smiled. 'The momos bring me here.'

They were sitting right next to my table discussing a case study when I joined them. From their looks and discussions I had assumed that they were students.

'You also a student?' asked the more stylish among the two. He wore a hooded jacket and his long hair was combed backwards.

'Naah,' I said, flicking my hair and trying to match his style. 'I am in the army.'

'Oh!' both of them said in unison. The goatee rolled his eyes. His friend lifted an imaginary gun and pointed it towards the entrance, 'Dha-dha-dha...' His gun even recoiled. 'You mean Indian army?' he turned to me after the burst firing.

I nodded.

'You don't look like you are in the army...' the goatee said, and shrugged. 'You know what I mean?'

I looked at him quizzically.

'Can you kill?' asked the one with the hooded jacket. His question startled me.

'Kill?' I repeated.

'Yeah, kill a human being,' he said in a matter-of-fact tone.

Killing someone had never crossed my mind this far and despite being in the army I had never asked myself this question.

I nodded. 'Yeah, if there is a requirement,' I said.

'Uh-oh,' he said as he turned to his friend and

smiled. 'But hard to believe. Actually, you don't look like an army officer.'

'Maybe you should see me in uniform,' I said.

'It's not that,' he said. 'It's something else... the kind of image we have of an army officer...' he shrugged.

'Why? Just because I don't have a handlebar moustache?'

They looked at each other and then at me, not in the least amused. I expected them to at least chuckle at my effort at humour. But they left, casting puzzled glances at me, as though I were some maniac.

On the way back, I replayed the conversation in my mind. What could have gone wrong? Was my desperation to make friends coming through? Was I trying too hard to be funny? Didn't they believe I was in the army? And even if they did, did they find a woman in the army strange? Or were they just plain scared? Or why me, was there something wrong with them?

Back in my room, I peered at my face in the mirror. I thought it was a pleasant one. I smiled at myself, a faint smile growing into a full blown one. I held it there. Didn't Long Nose call it infectious? That meant it was good, wasn't it? Beautiful, perhaps. I changed the angle of the mirror and smiled again. My lips curved, revealing an even set of teeth. But something was amiss. My eyes didn't smile. They looked weary and drawn.

I was beginning to have increasing doubts about my looks, my capability and just about everything. Although I tried hard to escape the loneliness, it continued pulling me down. And to add to this depressing state, I was made the officer-in-charge for a board that was to seal the personal belongings of a dead soldier to be sent safely to his next of kin. The soldier was crushed to

death by a speeding vehicle as he was returning to the
unit on his bicycle. In my presence, the members of the
board emptied his trunk and made a note of all items:
a family photo with his wife and two small children, a
large tin of Pond's talc, jasmine-scented hair oil, large
tubes of toothpaste, new clothes that he had bought
for his children. The trunks were sealed and his body
consigned to flames, but the images had made a deep
impact on my mind. The family photo, the flames that
ate his body and the man's face refused to leave me.

Soon there were rumours that the dead man's ghost
chased commuters in vehicles along the deserted patch
at the spot that he had died. People said that he chased
scooterists and motorcyclists, his boots making loud
thumping sounds on the tar as he ran after them – tok,
tok tok. One of the riders even claimed that the ghost
sat on his pillion and held his shoulder, resulting in
an accident.

Each time I went that route to make an STD call
at night, I raced my scooter. I didn't mind the ghost
chasing, but I certainly didn't fancy the idea of giving
him a ride. For whatever reason, he didn't chase me,
nor did he make his presence felt in any way. I assumed
then, that perhaps he was happy with the job I did of
handing over every tiny item of his to his wife.

As I continued in everyone's bad books, my
temporary duties at short notice to other locations
increased. But these trips gave me more joy than being
in the unit did. I observed all kinds of people, talked
to them and learnt about them. I met a variety of co-
passengers, from the silent, do-not-disturb-me kinds
to those who demanded to know everything with an
authority that reminded me of the Lion. I witnessed
a spate of reactions and questions when I told them

about myself. An elderly lady, a professor, was so thrilled to learn about me that she announced it to the entire compartment. Total strangers from various walks of life flocked to me and hugged me. With awe in their eyes, they looked at me from head to toe as though I were a celebrity. 'Continue the great job you are doing,' they echoed. 'It's an honour bestowed upon you,' the professor said. 'We need many more strong women like you.'

When I rose in people's eyes, it helped me rise in my own. Their genuine praise helped me revive my faith in myself and the system.

Meanwhile in the unit, most people had arrived at some sort of a logical conclusion. Anju was a woman of loose morals. I was her friend. So it followed that I was also like her.

Lala called me to his office one day and held out a bunch of papers to me. 'This report is full of errors. You need to redo the whole thing. And in my experience, this is going to take more time than I thought.' He made a sad face. 'In the office, I don't get enough time since I am caught up with routine work. You also see that.' He stuck his pen on his pockmarked cheek and looked thoughtful. 'Why don't you come to my place and we can complete it in peace?'

'Sir, if you can tell me the errors I can correct it,' I said.

'It's not so easy,' he said. 'You will need some reference books. I have them at home. Carrying everything here would be difficult.'

'Yes, sir,' I said, even as I wondered how I could wriggle out of this situation. 'Sir, once I redo it you can then...'

'What's your problem?' he interrupted. Although

his voice was raised, it was nothing close to his regular bark. 'When such an experienced officer is trying to help you out, can't you utilize his knowledge? It will save you a lot of time and effort.'

'Sir...' I said, my heart beginning to beat faster since I knew Lali and kids were away. 'Sir, actually...'

'Be there by 7.30,' he said, taking a blue file from his in-tray. I stood there wondering what to say, but he pretended to be completely absorbed in the file.

The invitation was for the very same evening, which left me hardly any time. Even as I wondered how to get out of this, I bumped into Lieutenant Gairola.

'How's everything?' he asked casually, as he sat on his bike and put on his helmet.

'Everything is fine, sir,' I said. On any other day, I would have steered clear of him after the initial greetings. But today I needed his help. So I stayed on.

I ran a finger on the front mudguard of his bike and said, 'Black bikes look so sleek and smart. Actually sir, I have always admired your bike.'

Praising the bike was the easiest way to engage a guy in an instant conversation. Sure enough, it got me some passionate mumbo-jumbo on stroke, piston, shaft, power, speed, shock absorbers and the like. Even as he went on, I thought hard of how I could get him to come to Lala's house.

'Oh, sir, I forgot,' I said, interrupting him as he described his bike's pick-up. 'The adam officer told me that last time you made that lengthy report very well.'

'He said that?' Lieutenant Gairola looked at me with suspicion. 'He usually never appreciates anyone.'

'Really, sir,' I said. 'That's why he's invited us to

his place. We have to work at it together.'

Lieutenant Gairola looked unconvinced even as he stared into my eyes. 'Why didn't he tell me then?'

'Sir, he asked me to pass the message to you,' I said, realizing if I lingered on some more, the chances of getting caught were high. 'He has called us at 7.30,' I said, and dashed to my room.

On the way to Lala's place, Lieutenant Gairola updated me about Anju. 'I met your Anju in the canteen,' he shouted as he raced his bike. I clung on to the rear grip. 'That Major Bhat doesn't allow her to talk to anyone. He's like her bodyguard.'

'I know,' I shouted back. Actually, Anju was the last thing on my mind. I was more worried about my plan, hoping that it didn't blow up in my face.

Lala's face had a defeated look when he saw the two of us. 'Smart girl,' he said, as he ushered us in, holding my ear playfully and rubbing the lobe through my hair. I jumped away.

'So Vishal, you decided to escort her?' he then turned to Lieutenant Gairola. 'But I have dinner only for two. And one has to be me.' He laughed at his own joke.

Lieutenant Gairola looked at me and then back at Lala. Before I knew it, my plan turned topsy-turvy. 'Why involve me in your affair?' Lieutenant Gairola hissed into my ear before hurrying back to his bike.

This new development had Lala smiling victoriously. He came and sat next to me, placing a few tomes heavily on the centre table. 'So, shall we start?' His lopsided smile and sugar-coated voice were imminent signs of danger and I felt ill at ease. Humming a song, he then got up to bring the drinks. I looked at the tomes and the 'happy' looking man. What was I doing here? Was

I such a fool? Why didn't I just tell him firmly that I couldn't come to his place to do official work? Was it so important to be in his good books? At what cost?

'Make yourself comfortable,' Lala said, sensing my discomfiture. He came and plopped down next to me, 'Come, have your drink.'

I sipped mine cautiously. 'Sir, I just wanted plain orange juice,' I said, realizing instantly that my drink wasn't soft, as I had requested him.

Lala smiled lecherously. 'Oh, slight contamination is okay. I know you drink.'

Looking at this ugly man with his even uglier mind, everything in my hitherto clouded mind cleared. I knew I had to leave.

'I have to go,' I said, as I walked up and unlatched the door. He followed me, 'What happened? Come, sit down. At least have dinner. It will be an insult to me otherwise.' He put an arm around my shoulder.

'Move away,' I said, throwing his hand away. The tartness of my voice surprised me. For a second, I felt I was the senior among us.

'Mind your tone. Don't forget you are talking to a senior officer,' he said, in a threatening tone. Then dramatically, his voice and expression softened. 'Come on. What's wrong with you? Come sit here.'

I shot him a cold look and stormed out, banging the door behind me. Seething in anger, I walked the two kilometres back to the officers' mess. It was dark and I was so preoccupied that I didn't even realize that I had walked right past the ghost patch.

With this latest incident with Lala, my already weak position in the unit became weaker. Anju was right when she said that I made everything tough for myself. But at least I had not let myself down. Most times I braved everything and looked at them as some difficult challenges. But there were also times when I felt exhausted, depressed and worthless.

As things got worse, I considered all the options available. Maybe the only way to make my situation better was to apologize to Major Bhat. Didn't Long Nose also suggest that after all?

But could I get myself to do it?

11

Turning the Tide

BENGDUBI IN BENGALI MEANS A PLACE WHERE IT RAINS so much that even frogs drown. When the monsoons came in July, it rained cats, dogs and frogs.

I would sit in the corridor outside and watch the dramatic performance by Mother Nature. Water poured down and out of everywhere, sometimes with a force that broke giant branches from trees, and at other times, as a gentle shower that sprayed my face like a tingling aerosol. I watched as puddles formed, flower pots filled and overflowed and the evening sun hid behind the black clouds. I would be lost for ages in the refreshing, earthy aroma and in my own thoughts.

Being alone gave me time for retrospection. Nearly a year had gone by. Much had changed. I had learnt many things and unlearnt some. I had seen people and their various faces. But despite having so many people around me, I couldn't connect with anyone.

Maybe I was to blame for my loneliness.

Acting on impulse, I went for a ride in the rain to no particular destination. Rain drops jabbed at my face like tiny needles. It was a bittersweet feeling, quite like my own life. Being in the driver's seat felt good. My scooter empowered me. I was the one who decided which way to go, whether to sink into a pothole, to slow down, or accelerate, to beep or to race. These little things suddenly seemed to matter a lot. I felt in control of everything – the scooter, its brakes, its handlebar and in some way, my career, my life.

I zoomed past the STD booth, then turned around and stopped.

'I hope everything's fine.' My mother's voice on the line was more anxiety-ridden than usual. 'How come you are calling up today? You just called yesterday.'

'I felt like talking to you, Ma,' I said, as I wiped my face.

'You don't sound too cheerful. What happened? Are you sick?'

'Oh, I'm fine, Ma. Everything is fine.'

'Hope you are taking care of yourself... eating well... sleeping well.' Motherly affection came rushing over the telephone line. Unlike at most other times, today it felt soothing. 'I hope you are fine,' she said again.

This time, I made an effort to smile as I said, 'Yes, Ma.'

'Good,' she said. 'You sound better now. Anyway, take care since it rains a lot there, you may catch a cold.' Then after a pause: 'Tell me, is the job very tough?'

'No, Ma. It's not. Okay, you tell me about the news there.'

'Here everything is fine. Oh, I forgot to tell you yesterday, Veena's marriage is fixed.' Veena was our neighbour's daughter, with whom I'd gone to school. We were in the same class. 'I'm worried about you,' Ma said with a sigh. 'Girls your age are getting married. I had given your particulars in the marriage bureau and some people contacted us. In fact, they liked your photo, our family and everything but when we told them that you were in the army, they backed out. You know why? Because they got scared.'

'Scared? Oh, Ma, please don't listen to these silly things and don't put my photos in those horrible bureaus.'

'No, they were actually scared,' she said. 'I came to know from Lalita aunty. You know, she was saying that they said they didn't want a bahu with a gun! I don't blame them. Usually that's not the image that most people have of a bride, that too an Indian bride.' Our chats usually revolved around my gloomy marriage prospects, of how my wrong choice of profession was affecting all her plans, and how while many of her friends were entering grandmother-hood, she had to wait endlessly. Her regret flowed over the phone line to me. She sighed and went on, 'Anyway, I have decided not to tell them about your job. Maybe then we can take things further.'

'Ma, please stop worrying so much.'

'Why? Have you found someone?' she asked quickly, a glimmer of hope in her voice.

'Ma! No! You think the army has a matrimonial corps?'

'Grow your hair now,' she then instructed me. 'Don't cut it again like a boy. That's why I still have to use your old photos.'

'Yes, Ma,' I said resignedly. Each time we had this conversation, it usually got nowhere. It was better to let her pursue her groom hunt if it gave her any satisfaction.

There was silence at the other end. 'I miss you, molé.'

'I miss you too, Ma.'

This was our problem. We missed each other, but

could hardly communicate. My father was different. Although initially he had his reservations about my choice of career, once he finally gave in, he gave me his whole-hearted support.

'You don't sound very cheerful. Is everything fine?' he asked.

'Yes, Papa,' I said. Each time I talked to Pa, I became his little girl. 'There are some small problems, but I can manage fine.'

'I know you can. I have that confidence in you,' he said. 'I had told you right at the start that you need a lot of inner courage to face the demands of your entirely different workplace.'

'Yes, Papa.'

'You are my brave girl,' he said. I couldn't miss the tinge of pride in his voice. 'When you left our safe nest to start a life of your own, to fight it out in the world all by yourself, although it was difficult for me, I let you go... you know why? Because I believed you were capable.'

'Yes, Papa,' I said, even as a lump formed in my throat. I wanted to tell him that I wasn't so brave after all, that I was letting him down. I was slowly losing my battle. Perhaps I should have listened to them and just stayed back. What was I doing alone on a craggy path away from their cosy nest?

'Didn't you tell me once that everything is in the mind?' Pa said. 'So be mentally strong, and problems will slowly disappear. Think of this as a passing phase.'

I wept silently.

'Are you listening?' he asked after a moment of silence. 'I think a break will do you good. Why don't you come on leave?'

'There's a problem about leave,' I said, steadying

my shaky voice.

'Or should we come there?' It was on rare occasions
that Pa sounded so worried.

'No, Papa,' I wiped my tears and held myself. 'I'll
manage. I'll be alright.'

That very instant, I wanted to fly to them, to be
hugged, to feel the warmth of their selfless love. But
there was no way I could go without being granted
leave. As I rode back to my room, I wailed like a child.
No one could hear or see me. It was all between me
and the rains, our little secret.

In the days that followed, I chalked out a plan to alleviate
my problems. Apologizing to Major Bhat came first in the
list of things. I used the earliest opportunity for this as I
stood before him with a draft of an official letter. After he
had scribbled all over the white space with his remarks,
he tossed it to me. The words I could frame an apology
with resounded in my head and refused to come out.

'Anything else?' he asked me haughtily.

'Sir...' I said as I looked into his tan eyes. He leant
back on his chair with a faint smile and blew smoke
rings out of his cigarette.

'Nothing, sir,' I said, before saluting him and
walking away.

One look at him and I knew he had been waiting
for this day, when I would accept defeat and fall at
his feet. Isn't that why he was putting me through the
grind? I decided I was not giving up yet. As for Lala, I
realized that the only way I could keep away from him
was by pretending to be close to Lieutenant Gairola. It
was like walking in a minefield. I had to be careful of
every move I made.

'Okay, let me give you some good news,' Lieutenant

Gairola said as we returned from office one day and parked our vehicles side by side. We removed our helmets and he pulled his beret out from his back, where he usually stuck it in his belt.

'Major Bhat and Anju are going on a long leave,' he said, shuffling his hair and then setting it back. 'In fact they are being forcibly sent on leave.'

'Why, sir?'

'The CO wants them to get married and come back,' he said. 'Their live-in relationship has come to the notice of the higher-ups at Calcutta. And now there is pressure on the CO.'

'Oh,' I said, trying to look disinterested.

'Aren't you happy they won't be here for two months?' he asked as we walked to our rooms.

'I don't know,' I shrugged.

'Since Major Bhat troubles you so much,' he said, 'I thought you might find this piece of news great.'

Later when we met in the mess for dinner, Lieutenant Gairola said, 'Okay, more happy news. I am going on transfer.'

I looked up from my plate. 'Why do you think that will be happy news for me?'

'No, just like that, since you don't seem to like me,' he said tearing a piece of chapatti from the side plate.

'It's just that I usually can't agree with your views,' I said.

We ate in silence for some time, even as the steward filled our glasses with water.

'I know,' he nodded. 'My views were a bit outdated, but you have changed most of them. Actually you are quite different from what I had thought.'

'Different?' I raised my eyebrows.

'No, what I mean is, you are quite...' he paused

and looked at the lamp shade above, 'a... gutsy woman. I hope I have used the right word.' He smiled even as I looked on. 'The thing is, I have been watching you. They have been putting you through so much trouble, but you never complained, nor did you choose an easy way out.' He wasn't looking at me. He was talking to his plate now. 'I must admire your strength of character. Actually, I hadn't seen someone like you before... so that's how I guess my opinions were so biased.'

'Sir, coming from you, it sounds good.' I shrugged and added, 'I mean if you really mean it.'

'Of course I mean it.' He nodded. 'But I can't say the same thing about your friend. She's entirely another...' He laughed and looked at me. 'Anyway, by now you would have seen that I am quite blunt. I say things on the face, good or bad. Usually people misunderstand me for this reason. I think you too...'

'No, sir,' I said. 'I guess over a period of time, we do leave the first impressions behind.'

He chuckled. Since he was busy talking, he hadn't finished his dinner yet. I had finished and waited for him. 'Hey, isn't that your favourite?' he asked when the steward placed a bowl each of caramel custard before us.

'How do you know, sir?'

'Oh, we are just two members here. So we do get to know about each other,' he said, as the caramel custard in his spoon wobbled like jelly before finding its way into his mouth. 'And I also wanted to tell you one more thing.'

'Yes, sir,' I smiled. 'I think you are in different form today.'

He laughed. 'Maybe had a few drinks less.'

'Yeah, maybe. So what's it that you want to tell

me?'

'Well,' he paused for a moment. 'I wanted to say, I'm sorry.'

'Sorry? For all the things you said before?'

'Hmm... that and one more thing. I shouldn't have left you there at Major Uttam Singh's place the other day. It was a mistake. I hope you will pardon me.'

'Oh, that's okay, sir,' I said, wiping my lips with the napkin. 'Since everyone has grudges against me, it didn't come as a surprise.'

'But I have absolutely no grudges against you now.'

Although it felt nice to hear such words after what seemed to be a very long time, I was now at a stage that when people talked to me nicely, I became cynical. I told myself to watch out, although knowing him so far, the possibility that he was genuine was higher.

As Lieutenant Gairola had said, Major Bhat and Anju proceeded on long leave for two months for their marriage-cum-honeymoon. I knew this was the best time to repair all the damage done to my image. Since the unit was deficient in the number of officers, I volunteered for extra work and participated in all unit activities with renewed vigour. Apart from work, I also took extreme care about my conduct and the way I projected myself. I walked tall, minimized wearing womanly clothes and was extra courteous to officers and their wives.

With the jawans, I once again worked hard to earn their respect. I played team games with them. Initially there were reservations when I declared I was joining a team, since it was usually only Lieutenant Gairola who played with them. When playing volleyball, they usually covered for me and anytime the ball came to me, my team-mates expressed their anxiety, hoping desperately that I didn't drop it. When I lifted an easy ball, they showered praises on me. But when they saw I could hit the ball hard, they soon began to forget my gender. Sometimes, in the excitement of the game, even I forgot. It was only when I knocked against someone that I would suddenly – and painfully – be reminded.

Games were also a battleground of expletives. In the thick of the game, everyone hurled abuses and expletives at each other. Although sometimes it was overused, it didn't bother me, since by now the meanings of the words were lost on me. Moreover, I felt that it added to the energy of the game.

On many occasions, the Lion on his rounds of the unit, stopped to enjoy our game. Usually Lieutenant Gairola was the captain of one team and I of the other. I noticed that more often than not, the Lion supported my team, which came as a surprise. When he supported my team, we played really hard, putting up the fiercest fights. Gradually, at the playground, I won the confidence of the jawans. This was the first step towards winning their respect.

Things were beginning to look brighter. Another new development came as a pleasant surprise. Ma and Pa decided to pay me a visit. I was relieved that they came at a time when things were better. They met the Lion and the Second-in-Command.

'Sir, please take care that my child is not troubled,' Ma requested both of them. 'She is very depressed.' I tugged at the pallu of her sari and whispered, 'Ma, stop it!'

Both the officers smiled, looking mostly at me. Mothers were usually forgiven for whatever they said.

But the daughter was now marked.

I was very cross with her. 'Ma, you were embarrassing me... you don't even know what to say,' I said back in our room.

'She's right,' Pa took my side.

'And who's this "child"?' I said, my irritation increasing. 'I am soon going to be a lieutenant. And you still call me a child, that too in front of my Commanding Officer?'

'Whatever you are, lieutenant, captain or colonel, you are still my child,' Ma said, asserting her rights over me. Pa went into his trademark silent mode. 'And if we don't tell them, who will?' she continued. 'That's why we came all the way here. Now you see how well they will treat you.'

'Okay, okay, Ma, enough. And if you meet them again, don't call them "sir". And also, when someone salutes you, you don't have to salute right back. Just acknowledge with a nod. That was the ultimate.' Pa and I laughed.

She waved a hand in dismissal. 'Okay, tell me who was that boy?' Like any normal Indian mother, it was her pastime to mentally dress up the young men around me as bridegrooms for me. And now, she had taken a shine to Lieutenant Gairola, since he behaved so courteously around her. 'He is so well-mannered and so handsome.' She turned to Pa. 'I pray to God that I find a boy just like him for my Deepa.' On my part, I was relieved that she didn't walk up to Lieutenant Gairola and embarrass me by asking him something related to marriage – especially because his own parents were on the lookout for a girl for him. I knew she was quite capable of that.

Since Ma and Pa insisted upon meeting the other

officers, I introduced them to the rest. On meeting Lala, Ma said, 'I am happy to see so many elders here. I hope you take care of the younger ones.'

'Sure, ma'am,' Lala gave her a crooked smile and looked at me.

I pulled her away before she made more embarrassing requests. Ma certainly didn't know what to say to whom. She took everyone by their face value, without realizing what lay beneath a smile. Obviously she had never couldn't see this world in its crude, raw form, the way I did.

Despite Ma's goof-ups, I was glad to have them around. Their very presence had lifted my spirits. Ma came like a whirlwind, shook things up and left. Pa was the silent breeze, soothing and invigorating.

'It was good they were here,' Lieutenant Gairola said when I met him later in his office. 'They are nice and warm people.'

I smiled. As always, the CCME's office was abuzz with activity. People darted in and out, carrying files. Many waited for his signature.

When there was a brief respite, he opened the file I had placed before him to check. Peering into it, he cracked his knuckles. His mind seemed to be elsewhere.

'Sir, anything wrong?' I asked. 'I mean, you are not your normal self.'

He looked at me. 'Yeah, a slight problem. The adam officer just told me that I can't go on posting.'

'Why's that, sir?'

'Since my reliever will arrive late, my leaving has also been delayed. The adam officer is worried that if I go, there will be no CCME,' he said, keeping his pen aside and leaning back.

'I am here,' I said, then cleared my throat. 'So, I can be CCME, and you can be relieved.'

He leant forward and placed his hands on the glass sheet placed over the green table cloth. 'Please don't feel bad, but I don't think they will consider you.'

I opened my mouth to speak, but he waved a hand. 'I will tell you why. It is a tough job. I am a man and I think so. It's a high-tension job and gives you no time for yourself.' A havaldar walked in with a huge open register and flipped the pages for Lieutenant Gairola's signature. 'People walk up to you with problems of all sorts, either personal, official, disciplinary, accommodation-related and just about anything. And then, as a Company Commander you have to set an example, lead from the front.' The havaldar saluted and left. 'You have to do all the exercises with them, run BPET with them, earn their trust and respect. The main problem is also of acceptance. The troops have never had a female company commander before and they may not be ready for it.'

'I get your point, sir,' I said. 'But how can anyone presume that since I am a woman I can't do it. At least I need to get an opportunity before anyone can decide whether I am capable or not. And as for the troops, I just don't have any worry. I know I can handle them.'

He smiled and thumbed the pages in the file I had taken to him. 'So, what's the query?'

Once he cleared my doubt, I thanked him. 'And, sir,' I added before leaving, 'about being CCME, I am confident I can do it. Plus, you can also proceed on leave.' The opportunity to become Company Commander had presented itself, and now it was up to me to push my way forward.

'See, Deepa, think practically. You may be capable

or not, no one knows, but then everyone has a huge mental block. Think about it this way...' he leant back once again and said, 'do you think the troops can consider you one of them? Can you walk into a barrack of half-naked men on your rounds?' He shrugged. 'No offence, but I just think you will not be able to handle these things. Commanding a strength of 600-odd troops is not an easy job... looking into their welfare, keeping their morale high, earning their respect... it's a very challenging job.'

'I realize it's not an easy job, sir,' I said, 'but it's not impossible either. At least I must be given a chance. And if I am not fit, maybe they can remove me from the position. I'll accept that. But being biased just because of my gender is not really fair... I don't know why people think I am incapable. If I didn't want to take up difficult tasks or challenging jobs, I wouldn't be here in the first place. It's that josh that got me here. And, sir, you would agree that josh doesn't have any gender.'

He looked long and hard at me. 'Sometimes looking at you, I feel you can do it. But there are a whole lot of others who think otherwise. Anyway...' he said, swivelling his chair, 'if you can convince the adam officer and the others, nothing like it. It will be of great benefit to me since I can proceed on my leave-cum-transfer. All my plans will be otherwise upset.'

'Sir, can we meet the adam officer together then?'

Soon enough, we met Lala. Lieutenant Gairola voiced his problems – and proposed the solution. Lala looked at me as though he were seeing me for the first time. Maybe he was seeing me in a new light, imagining me playing a new and important role. Or maybe he just thought I overrated my capabilities. I couldn't tell. Although our personal relationship was strained, on the professional front he couldn't find many flaws with me.

Or so I thought.

'No, no, I don't think you are suitable,' he said.

'But sir... is there any reason?' I mustered the courage to ask.

'It's obvious enough, isn't it?' He smiled his crooked smile and looked at Lieutenant Gairola.

'I am not clear, sir,' I soldiered on. 'I am sure I can handle the company commander's job well if given the opportunity.'

Lala gave me a dismissive look and then turned to Lieutenant Gairola, 'Vishal, you'll have to wait till your reliever comes.'

'But, sir, she's actually quite capable,' said Lieutenant Gairola, coming to my rescue. I wasn't sure if his desperation to go on leave made him say that or whether he actually meant it. Whatever the reason, it certainly added to my voice.

Lala fixed his stare on Lieutenant Gairola. 'Son, you don't have a choice.'

When we left Lala's office, Lieutenant Gairola's face was downcast. 'Sir, we will work out something,' I said. 'So the girl and her parents will come all the way from Bombay to Dehradun?'

'Yeah, it was all tied up a long time back and now everything is going wrong.'

'Maybe you should meet the 2i/c,' I suggested. 'Yours is a genuine problem. You are going to see a girl after all. It's about your marriage. I am sure he will be positive.'

Lieutenant Gairola met the Second-in-Command and the Lion. It was then decided that he would proceed on leave-cum-transfer as per the initial programme.

And until his reliever came, I was to hold the appointment of Company Commander.

'Happy?' Lieutenant Gairola asked me when we met in the evening.

'Aren't both parties happy?' I said.

He laughed. 'Yeah, good they finally accepted it. So, within a week I will give you the handing-over notes. And then the office is all yours. All the best for your new appointment.' We clinked our glasses as we sat in the ante room. 'At least have a hard drink for today. Isn't it a happy day?'

I shook my head. 'Hard drinks don't make me very happy.'

'Oh, that reminds me,' he said. 'I got a letter from Lieutenant Sandeep Singh.'

'Oh! He had called me too, day before,' I said. In his letters and phone calls, Long Nose usually talked only about his course, instructors, his course mates and the place. But in his latest telephone conversation, he had told me about Lieutenant Bipin Ghosh who was to join the unit. 'The chap is bindaas,' he had said. 'I think you will get along with him. But take care since he's an expert at pulling strings.' He didn't explain further. 'Just take care and keep smiling,' he had said, before hanging up.

'What? The chap sent me only a letter and called you up?' Lieutenant Gairola narrowed his eyes at me. 'I think the guy likes you.'

I laughed. 'How can you tell?'

He gave a broad grin. 'I know, because in his happy state he told me. Once we were talking about the two of you, you and your friend. He said that she was like vodka and you like whisky. She strikes you immediately, but you take your time to get noticed. And when you do, you linger on.'

'Like a hangover?' I laughed.

'No, seriously. Maybe if he had stayed back...' He swigged his drink. 'Anyway, in the fauj, usually there are no ifs and buts. Here it's an uncertain life.' His eyes drifted to a landscape painting on the wall. 'More than us, it's the infantry men. I have done my tenure with the infantry. I know.'

All I knew was that his drink was taking over.

'Oh, what am I saying,' he said, as though reading my mind. 'Forget all that. Let's talk about something else.'

'Sir, Lieutenant Bipin Ghosh is your course mate, isn't it?' I said.

'Yeah, you know him?'

'No, but Lieutenant Sandeep Singh had told me that he has been posted here. And also something like he pulls strings or something. I didn't understand.'

'Oh! That's because he's in love with his guitar.'

'Wow! He plays the guitar?' I couldn't hold my excitement.

'Yeah, very well. He plays the guitar and mouth organ together. We used to call him a one-man band. And then, he's also charming. Women usually find him irresistible. You better take care.'

12

Madam Company Commander

I WAS NOW A LIEUTENANT, WHICH MEANT THAT MY DAYS of being the 'one-star general' were over: I now had two. My responsibilities had increased, and now I had been entrusted with an important appointment.

The first time I sat in the Company Commander's chair, I felt too small for it, literally. I grabbed the hand rest before leaning back, feeling that if I didn't, I'd fall backwards. I swivelled it a few times and cast a sweeping look over my table. Everything was big, grand and sparkling here – pen stands, pens, paperweights, tabletop calendars. I placed both my hands on the glass-topped table, took a deep breath and said a silent prayer.

I had got what I wanted. It was a privilege, an opportunity. Now it was for me to do the job well, even if it meant stretching myself to my limit. Lieutenant Gairola on his part had briefed me on every aspect of the functioning of the office before leaving; its structure, the appointment holders, pending issues, problems to be resolved and the problem-makers. He also handed over a few manuals to help me understand my role. I was now accountable for all the men I commanded, their discipline, morale, motivation, welfare and logistical requirements, among other things. The responsibilities would ensure that I was constantly on my toes, especially during the initial weeks.

No sooner had I assumed office than I began attending to people and their various problems. Many waited outside to meet me. Suddenly I was beginning to feel the surge of power. I told myself not to get carried away by all the pomp and show, but maintain a level head and concentrate on the work at hand. Many of the junior lot, whom I knew by name from the games sessions, reacted positively at the new development. They were cordial and respectful. When they entered my office, they gave me such thumping salutes that my office shook. The Junior Commissioned Officers, on the other hand, had their mental blocks. They were disdainful about me being at the helm. Their attitude showed in their lax manner around me. I knew that I had to deal with them tactfully, since they often had long years of service behind them and expected their experience to be respected.

The subedar major, the most senior of the Junior Commissioned Officers and the Other Ranks, walked in to my office languidly. He was an elderly man of medium height with sparse but unkempt hair and a slightly protruding belly – he could have been my father.

'Madam,' he said, 'I heard you will be holding the appointment only till the next sahab comes. So I will not trouble you much. I will need only your signatures. I will tackle all other problems,' he offered magnanimously.

I didn't like his condescension. But then, he was the subedar major, and there was no way I could shoot my mouth off at him. He certainly was an important man in the unit, a father figure to the jawans. He knew every man, his problems, strengths, aspirations, motivation levels, family and just about anything. Without his knowledge I was nothing. The unassuming man standing before me was actually so important that he had a hotline to none other than the Lion himself.

'Sahab,' I said, realizing very well that to be a successful company commander, the first thing I had to do was to handle the subedar major with tact, 'thank you for your consideration, but I think the office must function just the way it had been functioning so far. It's in the best interest of the troops.' I paused and produced the most confident modulation in my voice as I said, 'I hope I am clear, sahab.'

He squirmed in his place. 'I think you took offence to what I said,' he said. 'I was only trying to help you out since you don't have much experience here and moreover, you are only my daughter's age.' Playing the age card cleverly, he had brought to fore the age-old battle between youth and experience.

'Sahab,' I said, with a smile, 'that's why I will need your experience here to run this office. I hope you will cooperate.'

I waited for his acknowledgment before continuing, 'I have a few things in mind, but we would not make any changes right away. It would be gradual. You could also let me know what we need to work on first priority.' The subedar major had by now abandoned his languid posture and stood attentively. 'We have to be the role models for our men to follow. We lead by example.' I used 'we' to include him in, to make him feel important and also because from now on, we were to work as a team.

'Yes, madam,' he shook his head.

'And please call me sahab, not madam.'

Before leaving my office, the subedar major saluted

me. I thought it was the best he could muster. For handling this situation, I gave myself a ten on ten. I hoped that as the days ensued, I handled other situations as well as this.

But in my effort to come across as a tough, no-nonsense Company Commander, I sometimes went too far.

'Sahab, he won't be able to run with the haversacks,' the subedar major said one day, walking up a moustachioed man to me.

'Didn't he overstay his leave by two days?' I asked. Being Absent Without Leave was something I couldn't tolerate and had passed an order that anyone who was AWL was to get a fair deal of punishments. 'Does he have a valid reason for overstaying?'

'No, sahab,' the subedar major said. 'But he can't do the punishment since he has hydrocele.'

'Hydro-cell or whatever,' I said in the sternest of voices, 'if he is Absent Without Leave, he has to do the punishment. It applies to everyone and he's no exception.'

'It's a medical case, sahab,' the subedar major explained.

'What medical case?'

'Actually it is...' he hesitated a while and then said, 'Sahab, it is a male problem.'

I wasn't quite clear of what the male problem was, but guessed it was something below the belt. 'Okay, does he have a medical slip to be excused?'

'No, sahab, but he can't even walk properly, then running...'

'Sahab, he is AWL. He doesn't have a valid reason. And he doesn't have any medical slip to be excused. So, he does the punishment like everybody else. There will be no double standards in this office,' I said, giving my final verdict.

The very next day, I promptly received a call from Lala. 'Don't be over-enthusiastic,' his voice fumed on the phone. 'Understand the individual's problem before taking decisions like that. Do you know that his condition has worsened now? And have you found out what his problem is?'

'No, sir,' I said.

'Find out and let me know,' Lala said. 'And henceforth, don't take any decision without consulting me. Understand?' He had slammed the receiver before I could say, 'Yes, sir.'

I called up a lady doctor I knew at the Military Hospital to learn more about this medical problem. 'It's the accumulation of fluid around the testicles,' she said, in the dispassionate tone characteristic of doctors. 'The testicles become heavy and sometimes the condition can be painful. In some cases, even walking becomes difficult.'

'Oh, shit!' I said.

I then explained the whole condition to Lala. Despite my best efforts, I couldn't keep a dispassionate tone like the doctor. I was embarrassed when a havaldar walked up and stood next to me for my signatures, as I explained.

'I hope you also know that it is a common condition among men?' Lala said. 'When you are in command of 600 men, you better know that.'

I promised myself I would bring in an element of compassion in the decisions I took. If the problems were genuine, the rules could be relaxed slightly.

'Sahab, he wants a house out of turn,' said the subedar major this time, bringing in a short, stout man.

'But you know to be fair we maintain a roster.'

'That's true, sahab, but...' he said and turned to the chap. 'Tell sahab your problem.'

The man spoke. 'Sir, I have been married for ten years.'

'That doesn't qualify you for a house,' I said.

'I don't have a child yet,' he said. 'In every station there was a housing problem. And when I went to the doctor, he advised that my family must stay with me.'

'But you just said you don't have children. Then where did your family come from? So you are lying...'

'Sahab, family means wife,' the subedar major intervened. 'That's how all of them say.'

'Oh,' I said and turned to the subedar major, even as both of them continued to look at me for a decision.

'Alright, sahab,' I said, 'I would like to see the accommodation roster and his personal records.'

The moment they left, I called up Lala to discuss the dilemma.

'Can't you take this petty decision?' he screamed back 'What are you sitting there for?'

'Alright, sahab,' I said, looking at the documents the subedar major brought to me later. 'Let him have the house out of turn. His is a genuine case.'

There were also occasions when I found myself perplexed. Two young jawans were walked up to me one day, since they had been caught having a fist fight in the barracks.

'What's the problem?' I asked.

'Sahab,' the shorter of the two said, pointing to the other, 'he gave me *ma behen ki gaali*. And I felt hurt.' I could see that, since he was on the verge of tears.

I looked at the taller man.

'Sahab, he had opened my trunk to look for some letters I had hidden,' he said. 'He didn't have any business to do that.'

A verbal duel began between the two. I waved a hand. 'You are behaving like little school kids. You should be ashamed of yourselves. The first thing is to learn to behave like soldiers.' I then looked at the taller man, 'You wouldn't like it if someone abused you the same way. Would you?' The man shook his head. 'So, refrain from it. Understand?'

I then sent the tall man away and spoke to the shorter one. 'Grow up. You are in the army now and these *gaalis* are used so frequently here that they've lost their meaning. Don't take them to heart. Either get used to it, or learn to use it. There is no third option.'

In the course of my work, I reassessed my approach and then as time went by, reassessed some more. I learnt that I didn't have to do things by the book. All that the higher-ups wanted was a smoothly running office. If problems went up to them, they fired down at me. I could take some decisions myself and for some I had to get their opinion. I had to learn exactly what to send up or down the military ladders, where each person stood at a certain rung.

Despite trying hard to do my best and to do what I thought was right, inadvertent mistakes did happen. Lala never spared me at such times. His micromanagement skills were the most visible now. Although I sat in the Company Commander's office, there were times when I felt it was run by him. He called up every half an hour to check in on me. His lack of confidence was based on two major aspects. The first was my gender. The second, my inexperience, since I was occupying a chair meant for a captain.

Although Lala expressed a lack of confidence in me, I continued as though I was the best person for the job. And the men were beginning to accept me.

'Sahab, I need leave to get my family,' a havaldar walked up to me one day and said.

'Where is she coming from?'

'Sahab, Lucknow.'

'Okay, go on two-day casual leave to Calcutta and pick her up.'

'No, sahab, I need to go to Lucknow, since she can't travel alone.'

'Arrey, just tell someone to help her at Lucknow, and here you can pick her up.'

'Sahab, my family hasn't stepped out of the house alone before. And then it is an overnight journey. It is very risky for ladies.'

He seemed to forget that he was talking to a 'lady'. I took it as a compliment. All my efforts at making the right impression were paying off. By now I knew that being in command meant that I needed to appear composed, in control and professional, whether or not I felt that way. I worked further upon developing an air of confidence around me, holding my head high, standing erect, and feet slightly apart. I looked people in the eye when I spoke and my voice was firm and clear. I walked briskly, sure of every step and tried to look in control of the world, even at times when I didn't know what I was supposed to do. More often than not, I handed down a decision, irrespective of whether it was right or wrong. Taking a stand was important. Leaving decisions hanging was not a sign of good leadership, I had read in the manual.

When I addressed the parade fall-in, I shouted at the top of my voice, looking people in the eye and reiterating points on conduct and discipline. I ticked off people with improper uniforms or those without proper military bearing.

'What's this worm hanging here?' I barked at a Naik whose pocket button on the Olive Green uniform was stitched with a white thread.

'Sahab, my family did it,' he said. 'She doesn't know.'

'She'll know it when you do a couple of extra duties,' I said.

Gradually, dangling buttons reduced, faded crease lines disappeared and shoes sparkled. 'When you wear the uniform, be proud of it and ensure that it is the best,' I told them. 'I will not tolerate dheela attitude.'

Soon, there were visible changes in the subedar major's appearance. He got a haircut, discarded his fading uniform and straightened his sagging nameplate and ribbons. It was a good sign. But despite being tactful, there were times when the subedar major and I developed differences of opinion. I considered newer, better ways to formulate solutions while he stuck to his age-old long-winded way of doing things. Once he told me, 'Sahab, I have more years of service in the fauj than your age. I have 33 years of experience.'

'That's why I value your opinions, sahab,' I said.

And then, I did what I thought was right. When I made a mistake, I admitted it and praised his foresight and knowledge. This office was not about rank alone, I realized. It was more about managing men and their relationships across the ranks.

For PT, I ran with the men and exercised with them. I had to stretch myself to be among those with above-average physical fitness. It was exhausting and sometimes I thought I was not good enough to command them, since I was not the best. I couldn't be further from the truth. I learnt that as their commander I was not required to run faster, jump higher, do more push-ups or make a show of physical prowess. The important thing was the team spirit I built by undertaking physical activities with them.

Although I was successful in changing some of the men's perceptions about a woman military commander being efficient, there were also those whose doubts stayed on.

At a rope-climbing practice session, I found that many men huffed and panted, getting only midway up. 'C'mon, pull yourself up,' I shouted loud enough for the man on the rope to hear. A Junior Commissioned Officer standing beside me said sardonically, 'It's not so easy, sahab. People who have done it know.'

'Is it so tough?' I asked him.

The Junior Commissioned Officer nodded his head in the affirmative.

'I think I must give you a demo then,' I said, as I moved towards the rope, instructing the man hung midway to descend.

All eyes were on me, unblinking, as I held the rope. 'I am now going to give you a demo of rope climbing.' I said. 'First, ensure a firm grip,' I said, stretching my hands to hold the rope at the highest point I could. 'Next, put all your weight on your hands and pass the rope between your knees, gripping it between the heel of one foot and the ankle of the other.' I then pulled myself up and climbed to the top of the rope like an expert climber. They didn't know that this had been one of my favourite exercises in the academy, and all the practice there helped. Clinging on to a rope hanging from a tree, I was hardly a picture of feminine grace. But I was beyond caring.

'Come down the same way you went up,' I said, as I began my descent.

When I came down, awestruck faces stared at me. 'Rope climbing is not about strength alone,' I said, looking at them. 'It is a technique.'

I turned to the Junior Commissioned Officer who had instigated me. His jaw had dropped.

'So, sahab, is it very tough?' I asked him. 'Would you like to try?'

To save face, he walked up to the rope and grabbed it. After a few unsuccessful attempts, he abandoned the rope and walked up to me. 'I am sorry, sahab.'

The new job gave me these kind of thrills and I looked forward to them. But if there was one aspect of my job I didn't look forward to, and dilly-dallied over, it was carrying out the unannounced inspections. I kept delaying it, but when I knew I couldn't stretch it further, I braved it. Despite giving enough hints beforehand, when I walked into a barrack full of men, I was privy to many sights I was happier not having seen. All around, men dived for cover, their hands instinctively clutching their privates. Hairy thighs, chests and backs sprinted in every direction, like primates in the Amazon rainforest scattering at the sight of a stranger. If the glimpses jolted me, I didn't show it. With a hardened face I walked on as though I saw such sights every day.

I stumbled over socks and shoes strewn all over. The place smelt of stale sweat and damp. Beds were a mess of clothes. The rods for the mosquito nets rattled even without a touch. Underwear hung cheerfully on make-shift clothing lines along the beds. Black trunks lay in a crooked line along the wall.

'Sahab, how did the inspection team walk through here?' I turned to the subedar major, who had accompanied me. He held his notepad and pen in the ready position. Behind him was the company havaldar major, another important appointment holder.

'At inspection time, everything falls in order,' the subedar major said.

'Sahab, inspection is not just an eyewash,' I said. 'I am sure you can ensure that they live in a better condition. The place can certainly look tidier.'

The subedar major called the platoon commander and instructed him, using some of his own jargon. Conscious of all the men who had ducked for cover, I walked out with my entourage following me.

'Sahab, there is a shortage of cupboards, racks and paints,' he said, as we walked ahead.

'Please make a list of all the things you think are required here. Let's see how much of it we can procure. But please ensure that they understand something about personal hygiene.' I walked on. 'Maybe we should have some classes.'

Spotting a locked room that had escaped my attention until now, I pointed to it. 'What's in that room?'

'This used to be our soft-drink plant-cum-canteen. But now it's not functional.'

The room was opened at my behest. In the corner of the dusty, cobwebby room was an abandoned soda-making machine, some cylinders and bottles of old soft-drink concentrates. I looked around, studying the place.

'Sahab, it has been like this for two years now,' the subedar major informed me. 'I think the soda-maker is not functional.'

'Oh, is that all?' I asked, turning to him. My eyes traversed the large room. 'What do you think, how will it be if after games the jawans could relax here with a soft drink and a samosa or pakoda?'

'That'll certainly be good, sahab.'

'So then,' I said, turning back to him and smiling triumphantly, 'this becomes operational.'

'But sahab, the finances...'

'We will work on it,' I said.

I was confident that no welfare measure would be turned down by the higher-ups until it was totally unworkable. Welfare measures were something the Lion was touchy about. This ensured that most of my plans aimed at the jawans' welfare were executed, and well received. I found that I just needed to have the will and resourcefulness to make a change for the better and it could be implemented. Sometimes it took a while to convince Lala about the workability of the new ideas I initiated. At other times, the proposals were turned down as 'too ambitious'.

My 'things to do' list kept lengthening since I found there was plenty to do. Every week I made it a point to check back on what I set out to achieve and how far I had reached. Each time I reached an objective, I set my sights farther. The motivation room, library and the new canteen were given a complete overhaul. Classes for promotion courses, language improvement and motivation were streamlined. I constantly thought of new ideas for the improvement of the place and also welcomed them from my staff. I made the appointment holders responsible and delegated work to them, verifying the progress after the stipulated time. The results were slowly beginning to show. When the Lion walked up and looked at the new developments, he raised an eyebrow or nodded incessantly as he said, 'Good.' When he did that, I felt elated.

I had also changed my working strategy with Lala. I could now segregate problems with the efficiency of a tea-strainer, tackling the smaller ones at my level and projecting only the bigger ones to him. I also offered two or three solutions to every problem, to make it easy for him. Sometimes I did see that Lala was pleased, although he never expressed it verbally.

If there was any unit activity I avoided completely, it was the rum issue. Rum-issue days in the unit were like weekly carnivals, when soldiers drank to their fill. Having been in the company of men who love their drink, I had learnt that alcohol affected individuals in different ways. Some became bold, some wept, some let their tongues loose, some got into unnecessary brawls and then there were also those who went down on their fours. On rum-issue days, I avoided going anywhere near the barracks. A man in an inebriated state was capable of doing anything or saying anything and then getting away with it. Being out of sight was the best way to prevent embarrassing comments or situations. The day after the carnival was usually a long one for me, since disciplinary cases abounded.

One night, I was woken up hastily since a jawan was reported missing. Despite having all-in checks and numerous reports, this jawan had managed to leave the unit premises. It was action time for me. After a thorough search operation, the jawan was brought from the town, moaning in pain. His right arm had been crudely severed and dangled near his knees, held only by nerves and ligament tissues. The painful cries of the man, coupled with the bloody, gory sight, made my knees wobble. But I steadied myself to handle the situation.

As soon as dawn cracked, the Lion roared, 'Is this what you call accountability? I want to know every little detail. Where did he go? Why? Who made the all-in report? Everything!'

Next was Lala. 'I thought you were an effective CCME. Then how did this happen?' he bellowed. It took Lala a crisis situation to accidentally praise me.

Back in my office I yelled for the first time at the subedar major, 'Sahab, I need to know every detail about the incident.'

'I have found out all the details,' the subedar major said. 'He used to go to a brothel.' The word startled me since it had never occurred to me that the men I commanded went out seeking that sort of gratification. Maybe then, many of them at one point or the other, looked at me as a woman, an object, like the way they saw those other women. This thought was disturbing.

'There he picked up a fight,' the subedar major continued, 'they then ganged up and struck his hand with thick iron rods.'

'Iron rods? Oh my God!' I nearly squealed, but stopped myself. That would be too feminine a reaction. 'Hmm,' I then simply nodded, as was apt for my chair.

In every situation, I played the strong woman to the hilt. I was living on the edge of my gender, but in doing so I was also gaining the acceptance of the men. Often I asked myself why I was impersonating a man. Sometimes I longed to just be myself, a woman, a little feminine. Not to be utterly feminine like Anju but to be able to do simple things like wear some jewellery, a hint of lipstick or a soft feminine kurta. But when these thoughts came, I quickly put them aside convincing myself that it didn't suit my job profile.

Despite all my efforts, there were still situations that could leave me helpless. Once, the Lion came for a unit inspection and expressed a desire to visit all the religious places in the unit: the temple, gurudwara, mosque and the church. I accompanied him everywhere, and briefed him as we marched along. At the mosque, I was denied entry while the males walked in. I stood like an outcaste at the gate, waiting for their return.

The wives of the men I commanded perhaps had different expectations from me. They expressed their grouse whenever they got the opportunity.

'Madam, when you became CCME, we thought you would be a little soft,' they echoed when I escorted the first lady for her special meeting with the soldiers' wives.

'She is a good company commander,' said the first lady, and thumped my back. 'She knows the job and does it well.'

Gradually, I was getting back into her good books. She was courteous to me. When there was a requirement for the company commander to be present, I accompanied her, and soon after, left. She knew my stand, perhaps the reason why she didn't insist that I participate in the ladies' club activities and programmes. During visits by generals and brigadiers, the ladies put up special programmes. Sometimes, there were occasions when Lala and I had to attend them in our official capacity. At such programmes, Lala gave the senior ladies his smartest salutes. When I didn't follow his lead and looked questioningly at him, he chided me, 'Don't stand there like an idiot. Just do what I am doing.'

*

I realized that two months had flown by only when I saw Anju and Major Bhat outside the canteen one day. They were back after their long leave.

Anju looked like a cartoon in uniform. Her red bindi shone bright and her sindoor peeked from below her beret. An elaborately crafted gold mangalsutra hung heavily over her Olive Green uniform. Her brightly hennaed hands were embellished further with rings and a couple of tinkering gold bangles. And to add to this, she looked too large for her uniform.

'Hi, congratulations,' I looked at her and smiled.

'Thanks,' she said briefly and clung onto Major Bhat's hand, looking lovingly at him. I thought she brought utter disgrace to the uniform. On any other occasion, I would have told her as much, but now she was with her bodyguard.

'Has the canteen closed early today?' Major Bhat asked. He looked smart, as always.

'No, sir,' I said. 'It closed on time.' This was a better way of telling him that they were late.

'Call that bloody bugger and tell him to open it,' he said, referring to the jawan in charge of the canteen.

'Sir, but he has gone home,' I said. 'The CO has passed orders that unless there is an emergency, the canteen will function as per the stipulated time.'

They looked at each other and then at me.

13

She-Man

ONE EVENING AS I RETURNED FROM OFFICE AFTER A tiring day, I was treated to a musical extravaganza in my usually dull corridor. I saw someone's back, a young officer, who was playing a guitar and singing.

Lieutenant Bipin Ghosh had arrived.

He stopped singing and turned around – he had boyish good looks, and his hair was spiked like the leaves of a casuarina tree. 'You must be Deepa,' he said as he got up, and shook my hand. His hand felt cool and strong against mine. 'I am Lieutenant Bipin Ghosh.'

'I know, sir,' I said. 'Lieutenant Vishal Gairola told me.'

He smiled, an attractive dimpled smile. 'Okay, what did he tell you about me?'

'That you play the guitar, sing very well, play the mouth organ.'

'Hey, this news reaches everywhere before I reach. So once again I become the unit clown. So who am I taking over the cap from?'

I smiled. 'There's no official entertainer here.'

'Anyway tell me about the bunch.'

'The CO you would know, the 2i/c is Lieutenant Colonel Ashutosh Das, the adam officer is Major Uttam Singh...'

'Oh, c'mon don't be a bore, yaar. I know this. Gimme the real thing, who's what. You have experience working with them. So tell me.' With his easy manners, he came across as very friendly, much unlike Long Nose.

'That's for you to see yourself, sir. Form your own opinions,' I said playing the diplomatic card. Although his friendliness flowed out to me, I exercised caution. I scarcely knew him.

Moreover, he was the one who was going to take my office away from me.

At a meeting with all the officers, the Lion said, 'So Lieutenant Ghosh, we waited a long time for you.'

'Sir, actually I was detained since...'

'I know, I know,' the Lion intervened. 'Good to have you here finally.'

'That's right, sir,' Lala added. 'Now he can take over as CCME.'

'Yes, sir,' Major Bhat added. 'The office needs to be revived.'

The Lion turned to Major Bhat, 'Revived? How do you know what needs to be done? You were on leave.'

'Yes, sir, what I meant was...'

'Well, gentlemen,' the Lion cut short Major Bhat's explanation with a wave of his hand. 'And ladies,' he added as an afterthought. 'Lieutenant Bipin Ghosh will be my security officer. Everything else continues as it is.'

I was so thrilled that had I not been in the den, I would have broken into a jig. Lala's eyebrows shot up. As for Major Bhat, if he could spit with his eyes... I didn't look at Anju's face long enough to read her expression, but I thought she looked happy with the decision. As the Lion continued to address the officers, I kept an expressionless face.

After he had covered the points from his scribble pad, he turned to Anju and said, 'Are all these things permitted?' Her bindi, sindoor, henna and bangles had come under his glare.

'Sir, the dress regulations for lady officers are yet to be for-mu-la-ted,' Major Bhat ar-ti-cu-la-ted.

'So until then leave the jing-bang aside,' the Lion said, with a frown. 'Should I have to tell you this? At least give the uniform the respect it is due. You are wearing it like it is some fancy dress.'

The Lion's expressions and terminology brought about some sniggers. Anju looked down and I felt bad for her. If only I could have given her at least a hint.

What emerged clearly from the meeting was that the Lion was not planning to continue with Major Bhat as his man Friday. Perhaps he had got inputs and directives from the higher-ups. This new situation worked in my favour since I was now emerging as the new star. My work was not only being noticed, but also appreciated. While all along, people had ignored me, now since the Lion smiled at me, they acknowledged my work. To me it felt fulfilling. I also knew that Major Bhat would now treat me better. There was no permanence guaranteed, however. Office politics were as unpredictable as sand dunes. Crests and troughs changed with every gust.

In the meantime, Lieutenant Bipin Ghosh was getting familiar with the unit officers. 'God! That lady officer is atrocious. Is she fit to be in the army? She looks so heavy, like a baby elephant.'

I gave him a hard stare. 'She put on weight during her leave. Otherwise she wasn't like that.'

'Um, whatever,' he said and leant against the pillar in our corridor. He had moved into Long Nose's room, which made him my immediate neighbour. 'I can't believe it's for this fat chick the he divorced his wife.'

'Please, sir,' I said. 'He was never married. He was a bachelor.'

'Oh, but in Udhampur I heard another version.'

I shook my head. 'I think men are the biggest gossip-mongers around, especially if it's anything about women.'

'Men will obviously talk about women, who else? It's the loveliest topic ever,' he chuckled.

We usually talked in our corridor and sometimes he brought his guitar out to play. A metal contraption fixed around his head was where he positioned his mouth organ, which he told me was called a mouth organ holder. Then the one-man band began performing. He mostly sang old Hindi songs by Kishore Kumar, some with a fast tempo, others slow and sweet. When he began his sessions, the air around resonated with melody and if I closed my eyes, I couldn't tell it wasn't the original version.

'Wow! You are so good,' I told him, after listening to his perfect rendition of 'Yeh dil na hota bechara'. 'I'm sure you practise a lot. Do you?'

'Yeah, but then I enjoy it.'

'Actually, I had also learnt to play the guitar when I was in college, just a few chords,' I said. 'But then I didn't practise. So I guess I've forgotten.'

'Yeah, practice is important,' he said. 'Anyway, I can teach you and you can practise on my other acoustic guitar.'

'Really? That will be great.'

'Umm... but,' he smiled his charming smile, looking

utterly, irresistibly handsome, 'what will you give me in return?'

'Oh, how much is the fees, sir?'

He cocked his head and smiled. 'Okay, what all chords do you know?'

'All the major chords and then the C-major and D-major family chords.'

'Oh, that's enough to start with. Come and play. Let me see.' He passed his guitar to me.

I played the chords I knew. He then taught me some more in the days that followed. During the lessons, he gave me tips about strumming styles. Once my fingers began to move more or less easily on the fret board, he gave me the lyrics of 'Country Roads', along with the chords: 'For this song you only need G, C, D, e-minor and D7. So let's start. Almost heaven is G, West Virginia is e-minor, then D, C and G... river...'

He then handed it over to me and after a few practice sessions, I was surprised at how good I sounded.

'That was good,' he said. 'You have that inborn thing for music, and then you have a decent voice too.' He paused for a moment and studied my face. 'It feels good to meet people with the same interests,' he said. As I handed over the guitar to him, he asked, 'Okay, now you want to learn to play the mouth organ?'

'No, sir,' I said.

'Look, I have cleaned it for you,' he said rubbing it on his sleeve.

'No, thanks. I like the guitar better.'

Lieutenant Ghosh's playfulness and charisma were hard to resist. He was unselfconscious, easygoing, jovial and had a perpetual naughty twinkle in his eyes. He said things with a level of comfort I wasn't accustomed to. When he wasn't with his instruments, he had a song on his lips. And if there wasn't a song, there certainly was a melodious whistle. He was a walking jukebox, a man who looked happy with his life and in love with the world.

Soon, Lieutenant Ghosh became the official unit entertainer. Any VIP visit, any function anywhere, he would be summoned to sing or play. Sometimes he requested me to play the chords for him, and sometimes to lend my voice for a background or duet. For such programmes, we usually practised after office hours. With the appointment I held, finding time was difficult. So, sometimes, I skipped the practice. There were also other times during practice, when I got so lost in the flight of a song, that I didn't hear the phone ring in my room. Then I wished I hadn't got this perk with the appointment, since it rang incessantly.

With Lieutenant Ghosh, now I was also making my presence felt in the social circuit. Officers who had hitherto known me as an ignorable creature at parties now saw another facet of mine. They showered me with praises after performances and expressed happiness that I had unleashed my latent talent. They said that Lieutenant Ghosh and I looked great together on stage.

As a natural progression, Lieutenant Ghosh and I began to spend more and more time together. Usually, after dinner, we went for a walk. There were times when due to exhaustion from a long day at work I refused. But when he insisted, with a 'Please...' or a smile, I more often than not relented.

'It's just plain curiosity, okay,' he said, as we walked past the pruned hedges one night. 'Why do you put up this act?'

'What act?' I stole a sideways look at him.

'Why do you try to behave like a man?'

'Me?'

'Yeah,' he shrugged. 'You want to be called sahab. Then the way you speak, look at others... your mannerisms, your posture, all that?'

I walked a few steps. 'It's required for the job I do, sir,' I said.

'So it was you Vishal had told me about.' He chuckled, as I looked on curiously. 'You know what he had told me? He had told me that there's this gutsy lady officer. "She's got balls, man," he had said "...and we nicknamed her She-Man."'

I was jolted into silence. She-Man? This was not the kind of thing I wanted to hear about myself, especially from a handsome young man like Lieutenant Bipin Ghosh. The 'balls' bit was embarrassing beyond words. I walked on silently trying to hide my embarrassment.

'Tell me,' he said, 'do you mean to say that if you behave like yourself, I mean a little feminine, they won't take you seriously?'

'Yes, sir, I think so,' I said. 'I think they will not respect me the way they do now.'

'And I think you are wrong,' he said. 'You are a woman, and accept that first. You don't have to become someone you aren't. Just be yourself, and believe me, people will respect you.'

'Sir, try to look at it from my point of view. To earn their respect, I need to show them that I am like them, one of them.'

'I think you have a skewed idea in your head about this,' he said, as we reached the water tank, where we usually turned back. Today we walked on.

'You don't understand, sir,' I said. 'For me, being in

the army is a challenge every day. I love every moment of it and I want to make the most of the opportunity given to me, even if it means living on the edge of my physical, emotional and mental capacity. And yes, I even live on the edge of my gender sometimes.'

I sensed his eyes on me, but looked straight as I continued: 'But that's what I believe makes me a good army officer. People have mental blocks and it will take time before they accept women. And now, when I put up a manly act, I earn respect. And that's why I do it.' I turned to him. 'And also, you know about Anju, don't you? She behaved the way you said, and see? I don't think anyone has a good opinion about her.'

'Okay, let's not talk about Anju. She is the other extreme. See, what I feel is that it is an individual thing, nothing to do really with being a man or a woman. Don't you think?'

'Sir, I think, the concept of individual and all will come in later, maybe once lady officers become a regular, routine thing,' I said. 'As of now, everyone sees me as a woman first, and so they doubt my capability.' We walked on silently. The air was damp and it began to drizzle.

'Actually I don't think you will ever understand what I am trying to say,' I said.

'Okay,' he shrugged. 'Let me put it as plainly as this,' he put an arm around my back and gestured that we turn back. 'Stop being so serious all the time. Relax. At least after office hours, loosen up a bit. I mean, why do you always wear pants in the mess? At the most it is some boring drab sack, like this,' he pointed to my kameez. 'I somehow find it funny. And I can bet you don't have a feminine dress like a sari or something. I don't know, but I think a woman should be like a woman, especially someone like you, who's got everything going for you.'

'Sir, I think it shouldn't concern you so much as to what I wear or how I conduct myself as long as it is in the ethos of the army.' Suddenly I went into my defensive form. He had no business to comment on my dressing sense, or for that matter how I looked, or anything at all.

'Hey, I thought women liked to be called desirable, beautiful...' He smiled and looked at me. 'Now I seriously have my doubts... I hope you had a detailed medical test, just like us.'

'This is sick,' I said, and marched back to my room.

I convinced myself that Lieutenant Bipin Ghosh talked nonsense. But even his casual remarks sometimes sent me into self-psychoanalysis mode back in my room. Was it so difficult to see why I had to put up an act? I thought hard and came to the conclusion that whatever method I had adopted so far was the right one or else the Lion wouldn't let me continue, especially when he had another senior male officer who could replace me. It just meant that I was successful. And to me that meant everything.

Despite the fact that Lieutenant Ghosh teased me and pulled my leg very often, I didn't take it to heart, nor did I stop talking to him, although I kept telling myself I would do that sooner or later if it all got too much.

'Let's go to Darjeeling,' he said one day at the breakfast table.

'Isn't it an overnight trip?'

'Yeah, so what? Anyone will easily accommodate

two men.'

'Very funny!' I said, glaring at him.

Lala was by now more or less comfortable with me as the company commander. Since the Lion expressed confidence in my abilities, Lala had no choice but to accede. He was increasingly convinced that I was in control of my office. The problem however, was that the more I did, the more he expected of me. I had set my standard too high and there was no stepping down. Sometimes, during those difficult days of the month, I ran low on energy and enthusiasm, and couldn't meet my own standards. It hindered my physical activities and overscheduled work in the office. On one occasion, my blood sister decided to arrive a tad early and surprise me. I sprang up to check if I had stained the company commander's light blue chair. Fortunately I hadn't. I then rushed through the urgent signatures, standing up and ordered everyone else to wait, rushing past them back to my room.

'Where were you?' Lala asked me when he came for a surprise check as I rode back in.

'Sir, I had gone to the mess to... to ensure everything was procured for tomorrow's party,' I lied, convincingly I thought, using the word 'ensure' since Lala loved it.

'But you could have done that in the evening,' he said, not looking pleased. 'You can't leave the office during working hours! At least you could have informed me. What was the emergency?'

Lala didn't understand my emergency, nor could I enlighten him. But his double standards irked me. On a couple of occasions before, Lieutenant Gairola had left the same office to catch up with a cricket match. Whenever Lala caught him red-handed, rather than charging at him, he demanded details like 'what's the score', 'who's batting', 'how many runs did X make' and so on. Maybe I should also have told him I went to watch a match. Would he ask me the details then? Perhaps not. I didn't qualify for the man-to-man sports talk.

'I want to carry out a surprise inspection,' Lala announced one day and walked out of the office. I marched behind him.

'Look here,' he pointed to a cluster of parked cycles. 'How many times have I told you about dressing?' He then pointed to the flower pots. 'And here.'

'Dressing' meant orderliness. The cycles and flower pots had to be equidistant and in a straight line, as if they were standing in a military parade. 'Military bearing is not about personnel alone, it's also about all things military,' he said.

'Sir.'

'Do you know how to carry out an inspection?' he asked me as we entered the barracks. For some reason, he didn't snarl as much as before.

'Yes, sir,' I said. 'We need to look for dressing, then missing things, problems and cleanliness.' He pretended to listen, but his eyes were fixed on the busty pinup inside an open closet. I didn't feel embarrassed, since I had developed a talent for selectivity. I could hear selectively, see selectively and ignore things that were not meant for me.

Lala hauled up the young owner of the pinup. 'None of these cheap things must be visible here.' He then turned to me. 'Don't you look at these things?' I expected him to stall there a bit longer, but he marched through the aisle between the rows of beds. 'In fauj, everything is done by a method,' he stopped abruptly and turned around. 'For inspection, follow a pattern; first look up at the fans and cupboards, then to your front, then left, then right and finally, the rear.' He demonstrated what he had said. The inmates looked on. 'Then look down at the floor at the walls and doors. This way you can never miss anything.'

'Yes, sir,' I said, grateful to him for having shared his secret formula. If only he had divulged this earlier, I could have avoided many of his demoralizing comments. As he made his observations, looking around with hawk-eyed precision, I made notes in my scribble pad.

'Follow it up,' he said as we walked back to the office. 'The coming week I will come for my next round. I hope you are also planning ahead for the inspections.' He took a seat and gestured for me to sit on my chair. Picking up a file from the table, he began to thumb through the papers and smiled. 'I didn't know you sing so well,' his eyes shifted from the pages to me, and his lips curved in a smile. I thought it looked quite out of place on his face.

'You are a talented girl,' he said.

I smiled politely, but my antennae directed me to exercise caution.

'I apprised the CO about your good performance. That's how he retained you here. You see, as I told you before, right projection is very important in fauj. Everything depends on the way one is projected.'

I smiled inwardly. I knew better than that.

Lala seemed to be in a pleasant, talkative mood. He went on to enquire about my parents, my schooling, my college days and about my city, Bangalore. I wanted to tell him politely that he was wasting my time and his by sitting late into the evening in my office and talking about nothing remotely official. It was dusk by the time he left.

'So, busy doing nothing, CCME sahab?' Lieutenant Ghosh said, emerging from his room as I reached back. He was wearing red football shorts and a grey T-shirt which screamed '18 till I die'.

I parked the scooter and removed the helmet. 'Oh, the adam officer just wouldn't leave me.' I said and simultaneously jerked the scooter on its stand.

'It's not his fault,' he said. 'Few of them get so lucky.'

'Sir, please, I am in no mood for your jokes,' I said. 'I am tired.'

'Okay,' he said, placing his elbow on the handle of my scooter, blocking my way. 'I was thinking, why not plan a trip to Kalijhora tomorrow. I've heard it's a lovely spot. And it will be a good change.'

'No, sir, tomorrow I have to...'

'Oh, c'mon, it's not like if you are not there on a Sunday, your office will collapse. Don't be so hard on yourself. Take a break, look around, see the beauty, enjoy life.'

'I have been there,' I said. I wasn't sure if I wanted to undertake this trip with him.

'So you be the guide. I hope you will come. Please...' he said, leaning forward and brushing something from my shoulder. 'An insect,' he said, as I looked over. 'And I also have another great idea. What about going for river rafting on the Teesta?'

'Wow!' I said. 'When are you planning that?'

Lieutenant Ghosh had once again managed to convince me: we headed to Kalijhora. We stood at a spot that offered a mesmerizing view of the river Teesta, with its emerald-green waters and frothy white interludes.

'Ah! Really beautiful,' he said looking at the river.

I smiled. 'Don't go just by her beauty. She has the might to wreck.'

'I want to feel her might then,' he said, his eyes following the turbulent flow.

'She's moody and flows with a will of her own,' I said.

'She's beautiful, she's strong, she's moody, curvy... wow!' He turned to me, put an arm around my waist and whispered, 'You know what? She turns me on.'

There was an awkward silence between us as we stood facing each other. Transfixed by his intense gaze, I broke eye contact and looked down at my jeans. 'I... I think we must get back.' I mumbled.

For two days after this, I avoided him completely.

'CCME sahab,' he said, when we met at lunch. 'You are avoiding me, right?'

'No, sir, there's nothing like that.' I looked at him briefly before turning back to my plate. I had made a resolution of keeping away from him. So I made a serious expression as I said, 'And please don't call me CCME sahab.'

'Alright, She-Man,' he said in mock seriousness, before turning back to his plate.

I ignored him and continued with my lunch.

'Okay, I am sorry,' he said.

I still didn't look at him.

'I said I am sorry.' He raised his hand. 'Mea Culpa.' I looked at him wondering what he had just said. 'Not for this. For the other day,' he said, as I looked on. 'See, that day, it was all so intoxicating, the place, the river, the atmosphere... I got a little carried away.' As he apologized, holding on to his spoon and fork and a grain of rice stuck on his lower lip, I thought he looked endearing. 'I promise I will be better behaved.'

I wasn't sure how to behave with him. I could not be angry with him for long, but neither did I like the way he behaved sometimes. All I knew was that a certain restlessness began to grow inside me. Although I wanted to be in control of myself, very often I found I was not. He was awakening something dormant inside me. Whenever he planned short trips, I told myself I would refuse, but in the end I would accompany him.

And for some reason, I didn't seem to mind that everyone around noticed that we were together most of the time.

When we went for the river-rafting expedition, both of us were thrilled. Our expedition was to start at Melli and end at Kalijhora. And we were told November was just the right month. After being given safety instructions by the river guide and having secured our cameras and extra pair of clothes in the waterproof drum, we started our adventure trip. I could hardly recognize him with his helmet and life jacket. Soon, our raft bounced dangerously in the swirling and chilly waters of the Teesta. Keeping the oars in control was tough as water leapt up in hungry tongues, drenching us. Many times I felt I would be thrown off when our raft tumbled over the rocks. It was like sitting in a paper boat. After four hours of this thrilling ride, we reached our destination.

'It was fun,' I said, as we headed back. 'I thoroughly enjoyed it. And you?'

'I think you have more testosterone than me.'

'Oh, c'mon,' I waved a hand.

'No, jokes,' he smiled. 'You are one brave chick...

sorry, I mean chap.'

'Again?'

'Yeah, you are a different sort, you know. River rafting, guitar playing... show me your fingers.' He took my hand in his. 'See, your fingertips are callused, probably why girls usually don't like to play the guitar. Then riding... let me tell you, you give me a complex. I mean, I have a sleek bike, but you are faster than me on your jumbo scooter!' He laughed. 'And then the way you kick-start your scooter when you are seated, I find it very funny. I've never seen a woman do that.'

'That's the way I am,' I said. 'Just because I am a woman you think I am not supposed to do these things? That's funny. I don't follow any stereotypes. I do just the things that come naturally to me. Yeah, I think I do everything my way.'

'Good, just be you... yourself. I love it.'

He then took my hand and looked into my eyes. 'Don't you think we are great together?'

14

Company Commander
on Cloud Nine

THE WAR BETWEEN RIGHT AND WRONG, REASON AND
passion brewed within me as I began to feel attracted
to Lieutenant Bipin Ghosh.

I knew that a link-up would affect me at work. I
fretted about ruining the good impression I had made.
But there were also times when I swept aside such
thoughts. Having been through the depressing vortex
of loneliness, I didn't want to go there again. What
was wrong after all? He was good company. He made
me feel good and I was happy around him. And I had
changed. Of late, I had even begun to read some of the
romance books Anju had left behind.

Sometimes he walked into my room with a brief
knock, either to take a cassette he had lent or to discuss
something urgent. I, on the other hand consciously
avoided going to his room, although he invited me often.
But this Sunday, since he was very late for breakfast, I
went to enquire. 'Sir, it's me,' I said as I knocked.

'Come in.'

I gently pushed open the door left ajar. He wasn't
in the living room. I sat on a chair near the door and
looked around. Two acoustic guitars and an electric

one rested in a corner. A music system sat on a low table with cassettes and CDs strewn around. Two large speakers, nearly my height, occupied the pride of place. These were the culprits that gave my dreams a percussion soundtrack.

'Come in,' he said again from the bedroom. 'Where are you?'

'I am in here,' I said.

'Okay, here I come.' He walked out of the bedroom, clad in jeans and a white T-shirt. 'Am I late for breakfast? I slept very well,' he said.

'And I thought maybe you weren't well or something,' I said. Even as I said this, my eyes caught a collage of colours behind him, on his bedroom wall. Huge pinups of half-naked women were spread across the walls.

'Why do you look so shocked?' he asked, looking at my expression. 'These are normal things every normal guy has in his room.' He then walked in and pointed to two sections. 'See, these are my predecessor's and this collection is mine.'

Long Nose's colourful collection came as a shock since I had always thought he was a nice, decent guy. In comparison to Lieutenant Ghosh's collection however, Long Nose's was way better. He had mostly beautiful faces and shapely figures while Lieutenant Ghosh's collection left nothing to imagination. Along with nude women stood rock stars, holding their guitars at dangerous combat angles.

'See, most guys would hide these things from their girls, but I don't believe in that. That is hypocrisy. I just like being honest, with everything.'

My eyes took in his room. I discovered that the walls were the better part of his room since the rest of it was strewn with clothes, shoes, books, socks, newspapers, slippers, cassettes, and pretty much everything else he possessed.

'I live like a pig,' he said. 'In fact, most young men live like pigs.'

'I agree,' I said.

He laughed throatily.

'Aren't you going to office today?' he asked as we walked to the officers' mess.

'Today is a Sunday,' I said.

'So, what? Go, pull out some files and start signing them.'

I smiled and whacked his arm.

We were late for breakfast in the mess, which meant we would have to go into town. Once through, we drove to Sevoke Bridge. Although this Sunday started late, it had started on a happy note. Even without wings, I felt I was flying. Our hands on the balustrade, we gazed at the Teesta flowing below. A crispy breeze blew into my face. He hummed a song. For no particular reason, I smiled.

'I think I am in love with this place,' I said.

He looked sideways at me. Suddenly, I felt my heart flutter inside, like it had just grown wings and wanted to fly away. Or maybe it was doing a front roll. Or backroll. I couldn't figure.

'Today you look very different,' he said, scrutinizing my face. 'Is it the earrings?' He fixed his gaze on one dangling pearl drop. 'I have never seen you wear anything like this... no... it's not that... you have applied some make-up...' His eyes scanned my face so closely that I thought I would lose control of myself and fall into the river below.

'I don't know what it is,' he said, finally giving up. 'But there is certainly something.' He continued staring into my eyes. I expected something to happen. Everything was so perfect. He moved closer to me and his hand reached up to my cheek. Then, it went higher up and pulled out a dry leaf that had lodged in my hair. I smiled awkwardly, hoping fervently that I didn't look transparent.

Once I landed with a thud from my fantasy world, my eyes turned back to the river.

'So, love marriage or arranged, which one is for you?' he asked.

I turned to him. 'I think love.'

'But I am sure your parents are pressuring you for an arranged one.'

'Yeah, they are, but I think I need to know the person I am going to live with.'

'Same here. I think so too. But my parents never understand. For me, it is important that I love the person's company and that we have something in common... you know, things we enjoy doing together.'

That evening, I laughed merrily and enjoyed every minute of being with him. I played the guitar and sang, oblivious to the world around. It was also surprising how I behaved of late. I felt the awakening of a new me. I smiled more often, felt less self-conscious and behaved demurely around him. I had these urges to wear something feminine and look beautiful. In the office, I played the tough army officer, but by dinnertime I had changed inside out. The contrast even surprised me sometimes. Now, I took special care to dress and accessorize well. I began to wear better-fitting salwar-kameezes, with soft diaphanous dupattas.

Where for most parties, I wore a lounge suit/ combination like all other officers, or at the most an official looking sari, now I dressed purely on instinct, especially when not around jawans. That in this party at the officers' mess translated to a maroon chiffon sari. I let the pallu flow over my shoulder, not harnessing it with pins, and teamed it with a pearl necklace, earrings and elegant make-up.

In some way, I had crossed a limit I had set for myself. And for some reason, I didn't feel guilty.

When I walked into the party, many jaws dropped.

'I didn't recognize you,' the Second-in-Command said. He had risen up from his chair to greet a lady, but found me instead. 'You don't look like Lieutenant Deepa Shekhar,' he joked. There were others too who made the same mistake.

'You look different,' said Lala, unable to believe his eyes.

Where on a normal party day, no one even noticed me, on this occasion everyone seemed to be either looking at me straight or through the corner of their eyes. There were more people around me than ever and men were at their most chivalrous. One of them even pulled a chair for me to sit. It was after a long time that I felt like a beautiful woman and I loved the attention I got.

'What happened to you, Deepa?' asked the first lady, with a worried expression, as though I had a fever. 'Everything normal?'

'Yes, ma'am, all fine,' I said and excused myself before the gang could interrogate me further. I spotted Anju leave a group of ladies and head somewhere alone. Instinctively, I caught up with her and beamed a smile.

'Hi, Anju,' I said. She looked at me in wide-eyed disbelief. 'I couldn't even congratulate you properly the other day,' I said and extended my hand. 'Congrats, my friend,' I shook her hand and gave her a brief hug. 'I am very happy for you.'

'Thanks,' she said, with a genuine smile on her face. We stood there tongue-tied for a few seconds. 'You look gorgeous,' she said.

'Thanks.'

'You have changed. Actually I find it hard to believe...' She pointed at my sari and smiled.

'Yeah, I know,' I said. 'See, Anju, I may not have been entirely right with whatever I said or did. And maybe we all change with time.'

She nodded. 'You know what?' she studied me from head to toe. 'You should have worn higher heels with this.'

'What?' I shook my head and smiled. 'Here I am going all gooey-gooey and philosophical and you are giving me fashion tips.'

She laughed.

'Anju, I just wanted to tell you I am sorry. I think I couldn't understand what you were going through. But now...'

'Dips, are you in love?' she asked, looking searchingly at my face.

'No, I don't think so,' I said quickly.

Anju's pleasant face suddenly took on a worried expression, as she looked at someone. I followed her gaze. It was Major Bhat.

'I think I must apologize to him also,' I turned to her.

'No, no,' she said, with an urgency in her voice. 'He's still pissed off with you. He doesn't even like me talking to you. Dips, go. I think he's coming.'

As I walked away, I bumped into Lieutenant Ghosh. Our eyes locked. He didn't smile nor did he say anything. I felt increasingly conscious of myself and began to melt under his gaze. He was the one drinking, but I was the one feeling all wobbly. I broke the eye contact.

'It's such a transformation,' he said finally. 'I mean I can't believe it's you. You amaze me. You are as perfect with a tie-knot as with a sari. You can be so womanly and yet, so much like a man. You are like the Teesta... beautiful and wild... you remember that trip?'

I made the mistake of looking into his eyes and nearly fell off my feet. Lieutenant Ghosh was beginning to have that kind of effect on me.

A company commander on cloud nine can sometimes make it difficult for the jawans walking the unit. I swivelled my chair from side to side, often losing myself in daydreams. When people came to me with problems, midway through the narration I would drift away. I didn't provide the usual feedback to satisfy them that I had understood their problem. I often lost eye contact and sometimes even when the story finished, I kept nodding as if there was more I wanted to hear. Then I laughed at myself and they laughed with me. Unlike earlier, I was now more relaxed.

'Sahab, please, I need 30 days instead of 20 days leave,' said a young jawan to me one day.

'Why?'

'Sahab, it's my marriage.'

'Isn't that why you are going on leave?'

'Sahab, but I need more leave since after marriage we have to visit our relatives and then we also have to... go for our honeymoon...'

'Alright, granted,' I smiled.

The subedar major walked up to me and gave me one of his widest smiles. 'Sahab, you have changed a lot,' he said. 'Earlier you were too strict, but now you are more approachable. And you don't shout as much also.'

'Actually, sahab, you people don't give me the opportunity to shout,' I said. 'In fact, I like it this way too,' I smiled. 'Okay, sahab, tell me. Any problem?'

'Yes, sahab, gas problem.'

'Oh! So you need to report sick?'

He chuckled. 'No, sahab, what I meant was our soft-drink centre. I am not able to get gas cylinders.'

'Aha,' I laughed. 'We'll tackle it,' I said, reassuring him. From hydrocele to gas problem, I had now come a long way.

Lieutenant Ghosh's fame had now spread out of the unit premises. The whole army cantonment knew him as the melody man. Some nicknamed him Kishore-da for his near-perfect renditions of his idol. After almost every performance, attractive young girls, daughters of senior officers flocked to him and were at their flirtatious best. But more often than not, he skirted them and walked straight up to me with his immediate thoughts: 'I think I screwed up', 'Could you make out I had forgotten the lyrics?', 'I think we should have done the song in C-major'. Although he projected his confident self to the world, with me he discussed the insecurities of the artist in him. He valued my feedback since he thought I understood him and his music more than anybody around. These were times when he made me feel special.

'You get a lot of female attention, sir,' I teased him, after an enthralling performance at a high-profile party.

'Why not?' he said and stuck his thumbs in the front pocket of his trousers, shrugging. 'That's me!'

I waved a hand and ignored his pose.

'Actually these PYTs distract me,' he said, looking towards a few floating around. 'Some of them are really pretty, aren't they?' he asked for my opinion as though I was his male friend. 'Especially that one in red?' he said, his eyes still trailing the beauty he had spotted. 'But I can bet her top floor is empty.'

'Just one look and... I mean just because she is dressed attractively doesn't mean she's all empty.'

'Hey, hey, what's wrong with you? I thought you'll be jealous, but here you are, suddenly defending your clan like Jhansi ki Rani.'

'Look, she's coming here,' I cautioned him.

For a moment, his arms suddenly went limp and the colour left his face. Then he got back in control and struck his usual charming pose.

'Hi,' the girl in red said as she shook hands with us. 'I am Tanya.' She then turned to Lieutenant Ghosh. 'You are a fabulous performer and very gifted.'

She praised him some more before telling us about herself. We learnt that Tanya studied at the London School of Economics and was on a term break to be with her parents.

Later, as we waited for dinner in the mess, I teased him. 'Her top floor certainly has more stuff than both of ours put together.'

'Whatever!' he said, 'But she's um, yummy, isn't she?'

'Yummy? Is she dinner?'

'So, you do get jealous, eh?' He looked at me, a faint smile playing on his lips. I felt he had cast a spell on me. He then held my hand that rested on the table, preventing me from wriggling free. Only when the steward arrived with a large tray mounted with two dongas and a casserole did he let go of my hand.

The ice that had formed temporarily between Anju and me melted gradually, opening rivulets of communication. Whenever we were at a safe distance from Major Bhat, we talked, sometimes in person and sometimes on the phone. One Saturday she called to inform me that Major Bhat was out of town. 'Why don't you come over? We'll have dinner together.' I agreed right away.

'Dips, I am so happy you came,' Anju said when she saw me. 'I was scared you might not turn up.'

'Don't be silly, Anju,' I said, as she ushered me in. 'How could I refuse a dinner that you had invited me to?' I handed her the gift I had got for her, a dinner set I picked up at the canteen. 'I want to see everything that you have prepared for me.'

As we settled, she smiled and looked awkwardly at me for some time, unable to decide how to play hostess with me. 'Orange juice, na?' she then confirmed, before going to get it.

I looked around leisurely at her beautifully decorated house. Terracotta, cane, the green of indoor plants and the soft, warm light of strategically placed lamps created a relaxed ambience. Apart from the Military Engineering Service-issue sofas, a low-rise diwan made for comfortable seating, on which I now stretched my legs and leant back. Photographs of the beaming couple were placed in frames of different types and peeped out of various corners.

'You have put all your talents to best use, Anju.'

She looked dreamily at me, as she offered me the juice. 'It was always my dream to have my own home.

And let me tell you, it feels wonderful to have a little place of your own.'

I nodded. Our conversation then drifted to unit matters, the problems, the possible solutions, the officers and so on.

'That guy, Bipin,' she said, 'there are lots of rumours about him that he hangs around with new girls every month.'

'Oh, I don't believe in rumours,' I said. 'You know when your incident happened, the kind of rumours that went around? If I tell you, you will collapse. And moreover, I've seen Bipin for some time now, and let me tell you, the rumours are all wrong.'

'Anyway, just take care. I thought I ought to tell you.' She leant back on the sofa. 'You know, na, YO's is coming up.'

'Is it? Good, we will go together,' I said. This time there was no reason I would have to miss the Young Officers' course. 'I hope I go this time.'

'Yeah, you will, but I won't be coming,' she said. 'I am medically unfit.'

'Why what happened?'

'Guess?' she said and smiled coyly.

'Don't tell me you are pregnant?'

She nodded. 'I am.'

'Oh my God!' I said, getting up to hug her. 'Congrats! How long has it been?'

'Third month,' she said, beaming.

'Cleverly planned, eh?'

We laughed like old times. Chatting, giggling freely and being together after a long time was so much fun. Strangely, when Major Bhat was not around, she looked much happier. She was free, her old self, who talked, smiled and laughed a lot.

Then somewhere over cheese balls, she suddenly took an unexpected deviation. 'Dips, I am sorry,' she said, as I looked on. 'I am really sorry about how I behaved with you and how badly Major Bhat treated you. You know, I had told him not to be so harsh with you, but the more I said, the more damage he did. He is a very revengeful sort of man. He holds grudges... Many times I didn't even know all that he did and when I asked him, he didn't tell me anything. I mostly found out from others.'

Anju looked at the glass in her hand. 'I don't know if you can understand, but when you get married your husband becomes a very important person in your life. Initially I was blinded by his love and must have appeared mean. But believe me, I really feel bad about my behaviour. And I know Major Bhat troubled you a lot, but he's not such a bad person. He's a bit like you, you know, takes his own time to cool.'

'It's okay, Anju,' I said, 'I understand. You don't have to give me such a long explanation. Anyway forget that. Tell me, how is it being Mrs Bhat?'

'Oh, it's good,' she smiled. He is loving and caring, but sometimes I feel he's overprotective. He treats me like a kid, actually.'

'I guessed so,' I said and added immediately, 'and now don't you tell that to him.'

She laughed. 'No, no. I won't even tell him that you were here.'

I helped her lay the table as she talked on about the merits of married life. Then once again, like old times, she began to chant, Major Bhat, Major Bhat... But the tone was different now. Although she wanted me to believe that she was really happy with him, I somehow felt she was not. To me she appeared like a bird whose wings had been clipped. He had put her in a cage.

Anju knew all about my favourite dishes and took pains to prepare them: matar paneer, mushrooms, baked vegetables. Looking at her in this avatar, it crossed my mind that she was cut out for domestic duties rather than military ones.

'Any news of Long Nose?' she asked, placing a bowl of caramel custard before me. 'This was his favourite pudding also, remember?'

'Yeah,' I said, 'But tell me, Anju, haven't you still gotten over his nose? C'mon, you are pregnant now.'

She whacked my back.

'He's fine,' I said. 'He writes and sometimes talks.'

'Good he's still in touch. He is a good guy,' she said. 'Actually, I thought after I moved out that both of you would get very close and then get married. It would have been so good. Both of us married.'

'And pregnant? The CO would have pulled out his long hair and become like the 2i/c.'

We laughed some more.

'Remember our initial days here?' she said. 'And all our blunders? How we started off and where we reached!' She sighed. 'I think I didn't set a good example, but at least you did. Everyone is all praises for the way you handle the company commander's office. And each time anyone says anything good about you, I really feel proud.'

'Even I feel proud when I hear you are doing a great job in the executive side. The difference is that you'll continue with it while I have to leave my office.'

*

The Lion summoned me soon enough and instructed me to proceed for the Young Officers' course. Lieutenant Ghosh was to take over from me.

'I was better off without this headache,' Lieutenant Ghosh said at the 'anda party', a cocktail party with the troops, nicknamed for the main dish served, boiled eggs. 'I have to now become the agony aunt,' he whined.

15

Bip-O-Phony

'IN... OUT... IN... OUT...' EXPLAINED THE INSTRUCTOR, pointing to the cylinder and piston in the diagram.

The bunch of energetic young officers, seated in a high-roofed, airy classroom built during colonial times, began to look at each other in amusement.

'The four-stroke petrol engine is an important part of your curriculum,' the instructor continued, 'since you are required to learn about all types of vehicles used in the army.' He then turned back to the diagram.

'So, to generate power, the piston moves in and out of the cylinder... in, out... in, out...' Suddenly, smiles swept through the class. Some even began to giggle. Soon, the entire class was in guffaws. The instructor then gave a knowing nod and said, 'Okay, in that case, let's make it up, down...'

That did it. The entire class now roared. Perhaps the presence of lady officers in the class added to the fun. But the lady officers were in splits, too.

'It's good fun here,' I told Lieutenant Ghosh on the phone later. 'Wish you were here too.'

'Enjoy all your activities there,' he said. 'Life in the unit will be different.'

'Yeah, I'm enjoying it all... socializing, games, long-distance cycling, trekking... everything... Oh, that reminds me, there's an all-India motorbike rally coming up and I have volunteered. You must, too. It'll be fun together.'

'Yeah, I'll talk to the old man. I think it should be possible.' After a long pause he then said softly, 'Miss you...'

I smiled and felt the warmth spread inside me.

Much had changed in the six months that I was away from the unit. The Second-in-Command had been transferred out and a new one – with a heavy crop of hair – had taken his chair. A captain had been posted in the unit and held the appointment of Company Commander. The soft drink plant and canteen complex which I had so painstakingly made operational, had now been shut down. Another lieutenant had joined the unit and occupied what was once Lieutenant Gairola's room. Anju had bloated further. But the most significant change was that Major Bhat took the initiative to talk to me.

There were also things that had not changed. The araucaria at the entrance to the mess looked as plastic as I saw it last. The potholes on the roads were exactly at the same places.

And Captain Bipin Ghosh's charms were intact.

'Congratulations, sir,' I said, as we went for a post-dinner stroll, 'you picked up your rank.'

'Thanks,' he smiled. 'I hope now I won't be asked to hop into any office that gets vacant. I hate being the spare wheel.'

'You won't be, sir. Now I think it's my turn to be the spare wheel.'

He laughed.

'So, enjoyed your course?' he asked.

'The course was great!' I turned to look at him. 'Actually you should also have volunteered for the rally. I did inform you well in time.'

'I would have loved it too,' he said. Our steps matched inadvertently. 'But the old man didn't spare me.'

'It would have been so much fun, both of us riding bikes for thousands of kilometres. Wow!'

'Yeah, it would have been, but now there's no point cribbing.' He sighed. 'Anyway, if you want you can take my bike to get familiar with bike riding.'

'That's great!' I said. 'Actually I thought of asking you earlier but was reluctant.'

'Reluctant with me? C'mon,' he said, smiling. 'I thought we were more than friends. How could you think I would refuse you anything?' He shook his head. 'C'mooo-n!'

I smiled.

'Can you ride a bike?' he asked.

'No,' I shook my head.

'That's no problem. I'll teach you.'

As promised, the very next Sunday, he started lessons. 'It's the same principle as your scooter,' he said, as both of us stood beside his bike, 'but here the brakes and gears are controlled with your foot.' He then mounted it and demonstrated what he'd explained.

Once the theory was clear to me, he said, 'Okay, so start.' He then slid from the driver's seat to the pillion, gesturing to me to take control of the handles.

'Why are you sitting there, sir?' I said.

'You are a learner, isn't it?'

'Please! It's not like I haven't ridden a two-wheeler before. Now that I know the theory, I'll do it myself.'

'No, but what if you screw up?'

'Don't worry, I won't. Please, sir, I want to do it myself. Alone.'

He shrugged and got off. 'Stop saying "sir" at least now. Aren't we beyond that?'

I smiled and sat astride, feeling a rush of adrenalin at the prospect of riding a bike.

'Anyway, all the best,' he said, giving me a thumbs-up.

I revved the engine and set off on my maiden ride. Changing gears with the foot took me a little time to get the hang of. I had to concentrate hard on the hand, leg and eye co-ordination and the jagged road as I lumbered on.

After an exhausting kilometre, when I returned, Captain Bipin Ghosh greeted me with a hearty laugh. 'Even bullock carts will overtake you if you ride like this in your rally,' he said. I laughed with him. 'Maybe they should have had a scooter rally instead.'

'I'll certainly get better with this. You watch,' I said.

I went for another round. By the third round, I had shown drastic improvement.

'You are excited like a kid,' he said, leaning on to a pillar on the corridor. 'Your grin can be seen miles away.'

'Yeah, actually I am very happy about riding a bike finally,' I said. 'Initially I did think about buying a bike, but then Anju convinced me that it was not practical. I always wanted to ride a bike in uniform. It looks so smart!'

He nodded, his eyes dreamily lingering on my face. 'We can make a pact. You take my bike and I'll take your scooter.'

'Wow! That'll be so great.'

'Only until your rally, okay?'

'That means two and a half months? Thank you so much.' I parked the bike. 'I don't know why, but I find riding a bike so thrilling. Maybe it is the speed, power, style, sense of freedom...'

'And the feeling that you have conquered another male domain. Right?' he said and smiled. 'I think I know you quite well.'

'No, it's not that,' I said. 'It's just the...' I looked around to get the right word, 'uh, wanting to feel new highs every now and then.'

'Does riding a bike give you a high? At least I don't feel anything until girls look my way.'

I smiled. 'At least initially it does. Anything new. And what I look forward to now, in this rally, is not just the ride, but also the travel bit... travelling the entire length of this great country. And by road! Experiencing the sights and sounds, connecting with the soil, the people...'

He looked at my face for a while. 'But thousands of kilometres on the road won't be easy. Have you thought about it?'

'Yeah, but it will also be fun.'

'You are one hell of a woman,' he said, smiling and shaking his head. 'God save the man who marries you.'

From then on, I rode the bike to office, games, PT, STD booth, just about anywhere. Captain Ghosh sometimes accompanied me on the pillion and often chided me, 'A little slow... roads and rains. Careful.' I zoomed on, nevertheless. This new arrangement attracted not only eyeballs and question marks, but also deriding comments. Somehow, it didn't seem to matter much, since somewhere along the way I had found a balance between what (or what not) I was expected to do and what I wanted to do.

We spent more time together, discussing ourselves, our lives, our families, songs, office and work. Usually when we talked, we sat in the corridor. Sometimes we did go to each other's rooms, but more often than not it was he who sat till late in my room. One night, he stayed back in my room till 2 a.m. I pulled him from his chair, 'It's time. You must go now.'

'Please, can I stay back?' he pleaded.

'No, no,' I said.

'Everyone anyway thinks we are together and...' he narrowed his eyes, 'that is... we are together.'

'No, please,' I said, trying not to look at his face as he looked softly at me. 'You must leave.'

Instead, he got up and before I knew it, had pulled me in an embrace. In his arms, I felt like a blob of jelly. It was like being in a dream, until a cacophony of voices emanated from my head. The voices increased in intensity and when it became unbearable, I jerked myself away from him. 'Please go,' I said, not looking at his face. My heart thumped loudly. 'Please...'

'But I love you.'

'See, uh... the thing is I am not very adventurous when it comes to these things,' I told his toe. 'What I feel is since we are serious, we must talk to our parents.'

'We'll get married. So then what's the problem?' he held my arm. 'Come on.'

I smiled, turned him around and pushed him to the door. 'Now go on,' I said and closed the door behind him.

If life, as they said, was a rollercoaster ride, then after the lowest ebb, I was now at the zenith. Everything I ever dreamed of and wished for was coming true. I had a committed relationship with the most eligible bachelor in this part of the country. He would talk to his parents about me and I had already given a hint to mine. The dream rally I had so wanted to be a part of was also finally here, just two weeks away.

What could possibly go wrong now?

I was quite confident and raring to zoom. On the roads, I practised going fast and manoeuvring sharp turns. When in civil areas, if anyone rode alongside me, especially young men who stared incessantly at me, I had this strong urge to race.

One wet day a young civilian without a helmet challenged me to a race by grinning continuously at me. I accelerated and zoomed past him. With a hurt look in his eyes and his injured pride turning into aggression, he zipped past me, grinning broadly again. The sight of his teeth irked me and I wrung the accelerator harder.

As we entered into a neck-to-neck race, I scarcely noticed a colossal truck speeding in our direction. I braked, ran off the road, spun around and fell, my hand hitting something hard. The bike went a few metres on its own, wheels spinning in the air.

I had zoomed my way right into a Military Hospital bed. My right arm suffered a fracture and was now enveloped in a white casing that looked like a giant cocoon. Along with me, my dream of riding in the rally had also crashed.

The only solace was having Captain Ghosh by my side.

'I'd always told you to be a little careful,' he admonished me. 'It's only fools who race on the roads.'

'I learnt that,' I said and smiled.

'Learning from your own mistakes is usually not the best method of learning. Learn from others' mistakes.'

'Point noted,' I said.

He then ran a hand over my cast. 'Don't worry,' he said. 'There will be more opportunities to get you highs.' He then pulled the chair closer to my bed and sat down. 'Or on second thoughts maybe, I didn't want to let you go. So I think it's a blessing in disguise.'

We were quiet for some time.

'I am sorry about your bike,' I said.

'Bike is okay, doing better than you,' he said, and smiled, sending my heart into a spin. By the time he left, after updating me on the unit news and between jokes, he made me so happy that I felt I was floating on the bed.

I was flipping through a glossy, still floating, when Anju stormed in. 'Dips, are you alright?' she asked. 'How could you be so stupid? What had come over you?'

I didn't answer any of her queries, just smiled. She had grown really huge and if that were not shocking enough, was wearing an equally large Olive Green shirt and trousers, with a black leather belt running across her protruding belly. 'You look like a penguin,' I laughed. 'Why, you even walk like one.'

'Shut up,' she said and went on to extract the exact details of my fall. Then she shook her head. 'Go slow. What's the rush?' Sitting on the chair, she looked like she would burst out of it anytime.

'Why don't you wear a sari, like the lady doctors?' I said.

She sighed, leant back and spread her feet. 'I wish I could, but they won't let me. They say it's not in the dress regulations. You can't imagine how uncomfortable this belt is. I find it so suffocating.' She then unclasped the belt and breathed free. 'You know, ever since the CO turned against Major Bhat, everyone has been very mean with us.' She pulled a stool from the side and perched her feet on it. 'Ever since we got back after our leave, people have been troubling us. Right from the CO downwards. Major Bhat worked like a dog for the CO and did everything he said. But now since Major Bhat is not in the good books of the bosses in Calcutta, the CO is also giving him a cold shoulder. All of them have become so petty.' She suddenly stood up and held her belly, startling me. I leant forward from my relaxed position, 'What happened?'

'Baby's kicking,' she smiled excitedly. 'Feel it, feel it.' She pulled my hand and placed it on her belly. I couldn't feel anything, but lied and said I could.

She settled down once again and continued, 'None of them have any consideration that I am a pregnant woman. All they tell me is that I am a lieutenant and I am supposed to do so and so. And the most wretched demon is Lala. You know he didn't excuse my night duties saying that until I was downgraded into a low medical category, I had to continue with everything I was doing before. When I was four months pregnant I had to go bumping in a Shaktiman at night. And I bled.' Her eyes were moist. 'It was awful. And all of them think I am a liability, a big headache. For every little thing, they say "show the regulations", just to make it difficult for us.' She wiped her moist eyes. 'It's getting so difficult for me.'

'Anju,' I said, wondering how to console her, 'I know it must have been bad. But now you are almost there. Your due date is anytime, right?'

'Yeah, I am waiting for that day,' she smiled. 'I only

wish they hadn't made my pregnancy feel like such a miserable time. It's supposed to be the most beautiful part in a woman's life!'

'I think in your case no one knew how to deal with this new situation,' I said, as she nodded. 'Maybe because it was all so fast? You became pregnant before they could formulate regulations.'

'Yeah, maybe,' she chuckled, holding her belly.

'And someone was just asking me what's the rush, eh?'

She held her belly tighter and shook some more in laughter. 'Oh! I would have nearly forgotten it,' she stopped abruptly. 'I must tell you something very important.' I looked on curiously as she dragged her chair closer to me. 'Tell me, are you very close to that Bipin Ghosh?'

'Close? Yeah, I think so. Why?'

'See, Dips, earlier when I told you, you didn't pay any heed. But now I think I must tell you things as they stand. Better keep away from him. He's not a good guy.'

'I think you are mistaken, Anju. He's been very good to me. We have spent a lot of time together and I never felt he was behaving indecently or something. He's helpful, courteous and jovial,' I said.

'He's a smooth operator,' she said. 'I have heard so many ladies talk about him. And you know what Major Bhat calls him?' She came close to my ears and whispered, 'Bed-hopper.' I looked at her in disbelief as she explained further, 'That's because he sleeps around.'

'C'mon, Anju, I have been seeing him for so long...'

'You mean...' Anju interrupted me and searched

my eyes with a worried expression.

'No, no,' I said.

'Good, because you would just have been another addition to his conquests.'

'But tell me, Anju, are you sure? I somehow can't believe this. These must be just rumours.'

'See, you don't know these inside stories, but all the officers in the unit know about him. And when you were away, he used to roam around with that general's daughter from London.'

'Who, Tanya?'

'I don't know her name. But I am sure from what Major Bhat told me, he had taken her to his room many times.'

'Don't tell me,' I said, with an expression of utter disbelief. 'He can't be that kind of a guy.' I suddenly felt drained and fell silent.

'Look, Dips, I thought I must warn you,' Anju said. 'Sooner or later you would anyway have found out. The sooner the better.'

When Captain Bipin Ghosh came to meet me again at the hospital, my first instinct was to confront him. But he went about everything so casually that looking at him I couldn't believe that what Anju said about him could be true. I knew how incidents could be completely mutated when multiple mouths got involved.

I observed him carefully. Could he be lying to me, putting up an act, cheating on me?

'You are not just a good singer, you also act well,' I said, as he poured tea from the flask into two cups.

'Why?' He suddenly turned to me. 'What made you say that?' I noticed that some tea had spilled on the table.

I smiled. 'You are talented. So I thought. You know

the left brain thing... I was reading in this magazine.'

He extended a cup to me. I held it and thanked him. 'How is Tanya?' I then asked in as casual a tone I could muster.

'Who Tanya?' he said, breaking eye contact with me even as my eyes bored into him. 'Oh, that London one?' he suddenly seemed to remember. 'I guess she's fine. She had gone back long ago.'

'Is she very fond of music?' I asked.

'A little bit. Not too much.'

'Then why had you taken her to your room?'

'Oh, that?' he said, looking at me briefly. 'She insisted she wanted some old Kishore Kumar songs.'

'Which ones?'

'Hey, what's wrong with you? Why are you interrogating me?'

'You know why I am doing it, don't you?' I said, in a tone I had never used with him before. It was usually reserved for erring jawans. 'Are you going to tell me or not?'

He sighed. 'What?'

'Should I have to spell it out to you? You know what I am talking about, don't you?'

He didn't seem to be affected. He sipped his tea casually.

'C'mon, tell me. Why are you quiet? That means that everything I heard was right.'

'Maybe,' he said.

'What maybe? Be clear.'

'Now don't irritate me,' he said. 'Even if it is whatever you think it is, so?'

'So?' I repeated, closing my eyes and feeling a burning pain seething inside me. 'How can you do this? Love one girl and bed another?'

'Hey, wait a sec,' he said. His tone was arrogant and aggressive. I wasn't familiar with this side of his personality. 'Who is this girl I love?' He had a mocking expression on his face.

I looked at him through bleary eyes, but said nothing. I had a strong urge to kick his face. That's what he deserved. The cheat! I wiped my eyes and held back the tears. I couldn't cry in front of this jerk.

'This is the problem with girls,' he continued with the same casualness. 'The moment you talk to them nicely, show some interest, all of them think you are head-over-heels in love with them and then the next question that pops up is marriage.' He placed the cup on the side table and pushed it to the wall. 'Ha! Don't tell me,' he guffawed. 'And marry you of all the chicks around? How could you even think that? You are not wife material. Not the homely, comely, demure sort of a girl I would take home to mom. I don't want a wife who gives me competition. I want someone who can stay at home and cook for me, pamper me...'

'God!' I butted in. 'You are such a hypocrite. So insecure! You don't even honour your own words and you call yourself an army officer? It's such a shame that there are people like you here who treat women like... like toilet paper to use and throw!'

'Yeah, that's how I am,' he shrugged. 'I don't believe in love and such crap. I need to move on from one butterfly to the next. The thrill lies only in the chase. Once I catch one, I get bored and move to the next,' he said, getting up to leave. 'Anyway, with you, I am already so bored. You are playing too hard to get.' He scanned me from head to toe. 'What's the point of having bloody women in the army if we can't have some fun?'

From cloud nine, I had now landed in a hospital bed with more than a broken arm. It hurt badly and my tears flowed ceaselessly.

When Anju was around, I sobbed and talked my heart out. She consoled me, held me and patted me when I cried hysterically. In a surprising gesture, one day she brought Major Bhat with her. 'I came to meet you since she insisted,' he said awkwardly. 'That chap, he's always been like that. Even in Udhampur, he screwed around and got into a lot of trouble. He impresses girls with his manners and charm, hooks them and then dumps them. That's his modus operandi.'

'That chap is not worth wasting your tears for,' Anju added. 'He's an immoral jerk of the first order. Think of this as good riddance.'

All the abuses both of them hurled at Captain Bipin Ghosh did make me feel better. But having the offender around in the unit didn't make matters easy for me when I reported back. He acted aloof around me.

Once in the mess, he ticked me off saying, 'Look, whether you like me or not is immaterial. I am your senior and so I have some privileges, like a junior directing the steward to me first.'

'Sure, sir,' I said, and told the steward: 'Go give the fried potatoes to sahab first.'

At unit functions he continued to give his performances. But I was suddenly averse to his songs, his voice, his performance and everything about him. A heartless man cannot produce soulful music, I told myself. Anju even nicknamed him Bip-o-phony. On one occasion Lala told me to join him on the stage like before, and sing with him.

'Sir, my throat,' I said holding it and trying to clear it. 'It's not quite alright. I have a cold.'

'It doesn't matter,' he said. 'Don't have to act pricey.'

So I croaked on the stage even as my erstwhile friend Captain Ghosh looked on. He must have thought I had joined him deliberately to spoil his show. For once I felt happy that Lala pushed me into something; it made me smile for days.

In the meantime, Ma's worries had increased exponentially.

'What about that boy you were talking about?' she enquired. 'The one who sings. You told me he's a very good boy.'

'Yes, Ma. He's fine,' I said, trying to keep my tone neutral. 'But he's gone on transfer.' I lied to evade the how-why-where analysis.

'So soon?' She wasn't giving up on him yet.

'Yes, Ma. His mother is not keeping well and so he's transferred on compassionate grounds.'

'So, then?'

'So then what, Ma? He has gone. That's all.'

My life had come to a standstill, but others were moving on. Anju and Major Bhat were blessed with a baby girl. They named her Piya. Often I went to her place and helped her with babysitting. Although we spent a lot of time talking, now the topics had changed. She talked about pregnancy, delivery and babies. Most of the times all I did was listen.

My long innings with Lala was also coming to an end. He was to move out on transfer. In one of his last conversations with me Lala said, 'You have a lot of potential. But you need to be more tactful. Remember, in the army, senior is God. Never take pangas with seniors.' His hand slid down to his crotch for a scratch. 'And don't think too much.'

Lali added in chaste Hindi. 'Life is not only about marches and salutes. It is time you think about marriage and children, like your friend. There is a right time for everything. *Gharbaar, bachhey*, these things cannot be delayed. I can tell you from my experience. The more you delay these things, the more difficult it becomes.'

Had my mother been around, she would have given Lali a high five.

16

Ciao

IN THE TWO YEARS THAT HAD GONE BY, THE ONE THING I could be fairly certain of was letters or calls from my old friend, Long Nose. Like with Anju, I had not paid heed to the many hints he had dropped about Captain Ghosh. And I had paid for that.

DD, (Dear Dips)

1. Hope you are fine. I had been waiting for your reply for long. You didn't write, but I am writing anyway. Hope you reply to this one. I like receiving your letters. So just take your pen and write, okay. No excuses!

2. It is great to know that you and Anju have patched up. I always thought sooner or later you both would. Buddies in the academy are friends for life. And it's only natural that you fight. But then you patch up. And so on. I know that very well. What came as a surprise was the patch-up with Major Bhat. I can't believe the ego clashes are finally over! But don't they say time heals everything. Sometimes I think time even fades memories and makes people feel distant than they really are. Looking back, I feel there were some great times I spent in the

unit. I think I don't like it very much here. I
have a feeling that I left something behind.
3. Here it doesn't rain too much. But the place
is beautiful. By the way, I still remember your
rain dance. It was wonderful!
4. I hope you have recovered from your fracture
and every other mess. Hope you are fine now,
and smiling.

So, till we meet, take care.

Love,
SS

Long Nose loved the service way of writing in bullet
points. The first time I received his letter, I couldn't
help laughing. But now I concentrated more on the
content.

'I think he still likes you,' Anju said when I told
her about the letter. 'Why else would anyone keep in
touch for so long?'

'He's a good friend,' I said. 'That's why.'

'No, I think, it's something more than friendship,'
she said, as she changed baby Piya's nappy. Little Piya
gurgled happily.

'I don't know,' I shrugged. 'I don't think.'

'He's the shy type. Maybe that's why he doesn't
know how to tell you. You like him?'

'Like? Yes. I used to like him, but now since I
haven't met him for long,' I paused and shrugged, 'I
don't know.'

'If you both ever get married, the only problem is
you'll have to put up with his PJs.' She laughed. Piya
began to bawl. She then baby-talked to Piya for a bit,
and turned to me. 'Actually, he's a good guy... sensible

and caring, someone you will be happy to spend your life with.'

I was quiet for a while as Anju baby-talked some more, holding Piya in her arms, 'My cootchie coo, my peeloo, my dabboo, looloo...'

I looked at her and smiled. 'You look so happy.'

'I am.' She stopped her looloos to look at me. 'Husband, children... these are the things that make life.

'Maybe that's the reason why everyone behaves like I have a time-bomb ticking on my head,' I said. 'But you can't just get married to anyone, isn't it? You need to find the right guy.'

'But you can't wait endlessly for the right guy. There's a time for everything.' She folded her legs and placed Piya in her lap. 'And let me tell you, a girl never feels complete without a guy and vice versa. It's like two pieces of a jigsaw puzzle. Only when they are together does the picture become complete... and beautiful.'

'You are worse than Lali,' I sighed. 'And my mom.' Baby Piya squealed. I looked at her beautiful form and said, 'But this tiny piece of the puzzle is really cute!'

'Stupid!' And Anju slapped my arm.

It was time for the Lion to vacate his den. At his dining-out party he was tossed higher than everyone else. At first, everything seemed fine, but as the tempo of the song increased, things went wrong. A melee of hands worked in unison to pull out his pagdi. 'Put me down. Bring me down,' he fumed and screamed even as he kicked the air. But his voice was stifled by the loud singing of the officers who continued tossing him, 'He's a jolly good fellow...'

'Who pulled at my pagdi?' he bellowed as soon as

he landed on his two feet. He then looked daggers at Major Bhat, before stomping off, flicking his long hair to a side. Everyone sniggered behind his back.

For me, it was devastating to see the once-powerful Lion disposed of like a joker as soon as he stepped down from his throne. If there was anyone I had immense respect and gratitude for, it was him, since he showed confidence and gave me the opportunity when everyone else had serious doubts about my capabilities.

Anju told me later, her voice brimming with excitement, 'Actually it was Major Bhat's idea. The old man had troubled us enough and he had to get it. Everybody had joined hands – Bip-o-phony, the new CCME and the young lieutenants.' There were times such as these when I couldn't agree with her but unlike before I never voiced my disagreement. I didn't want to run the risk of ruining our bandaged relationship, which over time had developed complications like Major Bhat.

Major Bhat had established his warm associations with the new administrative officer and CCME. This camaraderie didn't pose any threat to me now, since I was on good terms with him. The new administrative officer was completely unlike Lala. He was extra sweet with me and lenient with everyone. Although it was easier for me, I realized that after Lala, he didn't make an effective administrative officer.

Sometimes when the company commander went on temporary duty or leave, I was asked to take over his office. After a hiatus, when I went back in my old office, I found the positive response from the staff overwhelming. They placed their trust in me and expected things to happen. But most often, due to paucity of time, there was nothing much I could implement.

'Sahab, it was better when you were here,' the subedar major said. 'Everyone wants you to be the company commander. No one takes as much interest in welfare activities as you.'

'I am happy to hear that, sahab,' I said. 'But why don't you project your problems to Captain sahab and I am sure he will attend to everything. He's a much experienced person and better suited for the job,' I said, playing my diplomatic card.

I had, to some extent, mastered the art of dealing with the jawans, but when it came to junior officers, it got tricky. I knew that the younger lieutenants referred to me by my nick name, She-Man. There's something about nicknames, I learnt. Once you earn one, people around ensure that you keep it. When dealing with the junior officers, my nickname helped, since it was in consonance with my zero-tolerance policy when it came to their Benefits of Doubt. Anju often reprimanded me for this. 'For a few months of seniority, you don't have to act so bossy,' she said.

'It's not about a few months or days. In the army, a senior is a senior. Do you think if there had been a gentleman officer in my place they would act so smart?'

'Dips, I think you need to learn to ignore a few things.'

'You think I don't? I ignore a lot of the things they say behind my back, or sometimes I overhear. But right in front of me, if someone acts too smart then I better check him. I can't let juniors walk over me, ignore me or act superior. I can't stand it.'

'God knows when your OG-ness will fade a little.'

'That will be the day I quit fauj,' I said.

She looked at me quietly for some time. 'I am planning to quit as soon as I finish my contractual period. I think I am tired of fighting. And anyway, I don't even fit in here.'

'Yeah, you don't. You better exercise and get back into shape,' I said and chuckled. 'Anyway we'll be going on transfer soon. And if you look like this, you'll make a very bad impression.'

'But I am a mother now.'

'So what? You are still a soldier!'

Captain Bipin Ghosh was now married. He brought a fair, soft-spoken young lady as his wife. She looked homely, comely and everything he wanted his wife to be. But despite that, I saw him with Tanya a few times, when she came on term break from London and while his wife was pregnant. Maybe he was getting tired of the demure beauty and desired variety. On a couple of occasions, he also accosted me again, trying to evoke emotions and memories from the past. I ignored him and his advances. But he kept at it brazenly – even after he was blessed with a son.

At my dining-out party, he walked up to me and said, 'Hey, you are going, eh? You are the only girl who left me feeling incomplete.'

'That's good news,' I said, 'at least you will remember it.'

His wife walked up with their newborn. 'He's really cute, just like you, ma'am,' I said, picking up the cherubic bundle.

'I thought he was like me,' Captain Bipin Ghosh said. 'At least that's what everyone says.'

'Presently he's not, and I really hope he doesn't

become like you,' I said. Mrs Ghosh giggled. But her mister got the message, for he glared at me.

As everyone gathered in the ante room after dinner, the Second-in-Command called for everyone's attention. 'Ladies and gentlemen, as you know, today we have gathered here to bid adieu to one of our young officers, Lieutenant Deepa Shekhar.' Everyone looked at me as I stood in a corner behind the blue sofa with all the other young officers. Anju was sitting with the ladies, attending to baby Piya's demands. The Second-in-Command spoke on, giving details of when I reported to the unit, the period I served, the appointments I held and so on. Once he was done with it, he said, 'May I now call upon the Commanding Officer to say a few words.'

The Commanding Officer cleared his throat and began the farewell speech. 'Ladies and gentlemen, as you know, Lieutenant Deepa Shekhar has been with us for two and a half years and during this period, she has done a commendable job. Although she served under me only for a short period, I got very positive feedback about her from my predecessor, who was all praises for her conduct and especially her command and control as the Company Commander.' I saw a few nods and heard someone say 'Bravo'.

The Commanding Officer continued, 'From what I have seen of her, she is a very cheerful, positive and spirited young lady who displays altruism in the right measure.'

Altruism, I repeated to myself, I need to check that up in the dictionary.

'She has the right approach towards work. She is the kind of officer whom you can entrust with work and forget about it, in the assurance that it will be done. And

not just done, done in the best way possible.' Everyone
cheered. 'She's also a very socially active person who
gave us many good performances.' He then turned to
me, 'We'll miss your songs, Deepa.' I smiled. 'So, we
wish you all the best for your tenure in the next unit.
All the best.'

Everyone clapped. Next was my turn to speak. This
was my first farewell speech and I had prepared for it
by rehearsing before the mirror many times.

'Respected CO sir, officers and ladies,' I began.
'Firsts always have a very special place in the heart
and being my first unit, this unit will always be very
special to me.' I looked at the gathered faces confidently.
'When I came here, apart from the six months at the
academy, I knew nothing about the army. But in these
years, I have learnt so much, mostly from my seniors.
In their own different ways, my seniors assisted me in
my work and helped me grow. I was lucky to have a
warm, experienced and co-operative set of senior officers
who were always very supportive...'

Baby Piya suddenly began to howl. Perhaps she
didn't agree. A sudden spurt of activity followed. Ladies
leant over to Anju to ask if she needed help. Anju got
up and took the wailing Piya out of the room. Major
Bhat followed her. As an after-effect, Captain Ghosh's
kid began to cry. In all this commotion, I forgot my
speech and began to mumble. Someone prompted,
'Senior officers were supportive and...'

'Supportive and...' I continued, 'and... and... um...
helpful.' What more? I couldn't remember. Think.
Think. 'At work, I tried to do my best although I may
not have been the best...'

'You were,' I heard someone say from the back.

I smiled and once again lost track. So I jumped

to the concluding line. 'I thank each one of you for being present here to give me a warm send-off. As you know I am going to Ahmedabad. So please don't hesitate to let me know if you have any work in the West. Thank you.'

Everyone clapped. I wondered why. The Commanding Officer then presented me with a memento. After this was bump time. I wondered what kind of farewell I would be given. I was also worried after what they had done to the Lion. The first to do that would be Captain Ghosh followed by the bandwagon of youngsters, whom I had often ticked off. In anticipation, I had dressed up for this special occasion with a salwar knotted tightly and a long kurta. I had even prepared a joke, not a dirty one, but just in case I was cornered.

The men looked at each other, confused. It was then decided that I would sit on a chair and the chair would be lifted up like a palanquin. The bumps began. They tossed up the chair as they sang: 'She's a jolly good fellow... she's a jolly good fellow... and so say all of us...'

I crouched so that my head didn't hit the chandelier, and clung to the hand-rest tightly, for fear of toppling over. Ladies and children looked on at this unusual chair farewell, grinning and clapping.

When I landed, I was mostly in good shape except that some locks of hair came loose from my chignon. My dupatta and sandals had also disappeared. Anju was quick to pass them to me. No one asked me to tell a dirty joke. All the officers shook hands with me in turn and wished me the best. When I shook hands with Captain Bipin Ghosh, I expected to feel bitter. But I didn't. I smiled and said, 'Thank you, sir.' He just looked puzzled.

'After all the highs and lows,' Anju said, 'I am

happy that in the end we are together. I will miss you, Dips.' She looked at me with a faraway look in her eyes, which meant that any moment now tears would fill them.

'Hey! Don't be so senti. I am not on my deathbed or something,' I said. 'And please don't cry. Please!'

We hugged. Like the first day, when she arrived in the unit, I felt a wetness on my shoulder. Only, this time she felt it too.

17

Westward Ho!

AFTER BENGDUBI, AHMEDABAD WAS SURE TO BE exciting with all that a big city has to offer: places to hang out, eat, shop, explore. I looked forward to making the most of it before I got transferred to another isolated unit in a far-flung location. But when I arrived, I learnt that my new unit was mobilized in the deserts of Rajasthan. A JCO of the rear party informed me that it would be four months before they returned from the exercise location.

As my one-tonner entered the cantonment, the difference from the city was conspicuous. Large shady trees covered the boulevard, and bungalows with sprawling gardens lined the roads. There was no clutter, fewer people, and so much greenery. I even spotted a pair of peacocks. But to my surprise, we went through another gate and drove right out of the cantonment. The JCO, Subedar Singha then explained that the unit was not a part of the cantonment, but an independent establishment about five kilometres away. The unit premises had a deserted and abandoned look. Roads were strewn with dry leaves, the corridors of the office buildings hadn't been swept for days and the gardens and lawns were grossly neglected. The one structure that stood out was a bungalow painted red and white. It had a large garden and a bamboo fence around it. Our one-tonner stopped in front of this grand structure.

'Who stays here?' I asked Subedar Singha.

'Sahab, you will stay here.'

'Me?'

'Yes, sahab,' he said, 'these are the CO sahab's orders.' He then directed the working party to begin unloading the three small trunks I had brought.

I looked at the bungalow in disbelief. What a magnanimous Commanding Officer! Junior officers such as me usually got something only marginally better than a shack to stay in, and here I was being given a whole bungalow!

The bungalow was not just impressive from the outside, even the interiors were stunning. My room was huge and well furnished. Expensive looking curtains, upholstery, paintings with golden frames and antique furniture gave it a regal aura. I thought this room befitted a rank no less than a general, and certainly not me.

'Is there no other room in the unit?' I asked him, stepping off the intricately patterned maroon carpet on the floor that looked too beautiful to be stamped upon.

'All other rooms are occupied, sahab,' he said, casting a glance around. 'But isn't it a good place?'

'It's too good for me,' I said. 'And don't you think it's a little too big? What is this place? Who stays here otherwise?' I asked, baffled at this situation.

'This is actually the guest room.'

'Guest room? Oh! Is this place haunted or something?' I joked.

'No, no,' he said hastily. The working party suddenly stopped their work to look at us.

'I anyway don't believe in ghosts and all,' I said,

waving my hand, not entirely telling the truth. 'It's all bakwaas. So you don't have to tell me lies.'

It took me a little more prodding to get them to divulge the details. I learnt that the guest room was in a wing that jutted into a graveyard by the banks of the Sabarmati river. The room had not been used since an officer who had stayed there with his family complained of strange happenings and requested a change of accommodation. Apparently, their beds rattled at night, the fridge, cupboards and drawers opened and closed on their own, chairs and tables changed position and there were loud sounds of people talking and laughing. Even their pet dog behaved strangely as soon as night set in. It would howl all night and scuttle about restlessly. Near the bungalow, there were also instances of jawans falling ill after encounters with supernatural beings. The unit pandit had performed a huge havan to appease the ghosts and to implore them to leave the unit premises, but no one was sure they had left.

Well, I was about to find out.

The JCO left as soon as he could, and I was alone in the haunted bungalow. I kept telling myself that I would be fine, that the ghosts wouldn't come, that there was no such thing in fact, and that I just had to be brave.

Till dinnertime everything seemed fine. I even slept since I found everything to be normal. But sometime in the middle of the night, I woke up in a sweat. The air conditioner was off. I got up to find that there was no electricity. This certainly had nothing to do with the ghosts – the municipal corporation was to blame. I tucked the torch carefully under my pillow and snuggled back under the cover, hiding my face too despite the heat.

But I couldn't sleep. Dogs howled outside. All that

Subedar Singha had told me resounded in my head.

Then a loud ring of the doorbell suddenly shattered the eerie silence, 'Ding-dong!' And again, 'Ding-Dong.'

The electric doorbell was ringing without electricity!

Terrified, I curled tighter under the sheet. The doorknob turned and I heard the door open. Then there were all kinds of noises, people talking, laughing, chairs being dragged. The doorbell rang again and the party went on. I lay there sweating and palpitating. Was I dreaming? I pinched myself to check. But I was not. I nearly wet my bed out of fright.

The ghosts, for reasons beyond my understanding, ignored me, for they didn't rattle my bed nor play with my closets and drawers. But the night seemed never-ending.

It's only the next morning that I could gather the courage to peep into the party room. Everything looked perfect, just the way I had seen it the previous day. Was I dreaming then? Or imagining things? I went to the office looking like a zombie.

Subedar Singha and the jawans studied my face.

'How was it, sahab?' Subedar Singha asked me as I took a seat.

'Oh, it was fine,' I said, aware that all ears were waiting eagerly to hear the story. 'Tell me, sahab,' I said after a moment's pause. 'Have the ghosts harmed anyone?'

'No. They are Gujarati ghosts. So they are non-violent.'

There were a few titters.

'I see,' I said. 'I need to talk to the CO sahab, can you please connect me to him at the exercise location?'

After a wait of about half an hour, I finally got

through to my Commanding Officer, Colonel Abhijeet Mishra.

'Sir, I am Lieutenant Deepa Shekhar. I have reported to the unit, sir,' I said.

'Welcome, Deepa,' a warm and friendly voice greeted me. 'You just missed the exercise by a few days. Good for you.'

'Sir, but actually I wanted to join the unit there.'

'No, Deepa, you take over as the officer-in-charge of the rear party. I will instruct Subedar Singha.'

'Sir, could I please join you there?'

'Deepa, you have no idea how we live here,' Colonel Mishra said. 'These are field conditions and not suitable for you.'

'Sir, I am sure I can cope with field living conditions.'

There was silence at the other end. 'No, Deepa, you stay back and enjoy,' he said. 'I hope your stay is comfortable. Did you make any friends in your room?'

'I didn't make friends, sir, but they did come.'

'Alright. Talk to the AQ and tell him you need a room in the Div. officers' mess.'

The Commanding Officer had turned down my request. Not that I expected him to agree readily, but he had dismissed it without a thought. I would have to wait a while before talking to him again on the subject.

The next best thing I could do was to move out of the haunted bungalow. After a few phone calls I gathered that the earliest I could move was after two days. That meant I had to spend two more nights in the company of ghosts! I made a few frantic calls here and there to check if I could be accommodated somewhere else, but to no avail.

Subedar Singha, who had been listening to all the

conversations, offered a suggestion. 'Sahab, do you need someone to sleep in there, to protect...?'

'What?' I said, feeling offended. What did he think I was? A coward? Agreed, I was a little scared when it came to things supernatural. But now, I had to do something to change his opinion about me, whatever it took – even if that meant sleeping with the ghosts. 'No, sahab,' I said, 'I'll manage.'

I spent two more nights in the bungalow and I did hear noises. The last night, it took me all my courage to open the door and peep into the haunted room. I saw nothing and even the voices disappeared. But there certainly was something spooky about it. I was happy however, that I had opened that door and let go of some of the fear trapped inside me.

Within a week, I called up Colonel Mishra and repeated my request. 'Sir, I am confident I will be able to cope with any hardship.'

There was a pause, and finally he asked, 'What appointments did you hold in the previous unit?'

'Sir, Quartermaster and Company Commander.'

'Company Commander?' He sounded like he didn't believe it. 'You mean CCME?'

'Yes, sir,' I said, my voice unwavering.

'That's good,' he said. 'Just give me some time to think. This is something completely new. We haven't had a lady staying with us in field conditions. Give me a week's time.'

By the end of the week, the Commanding Officer called. 'You can come along with the convoy which is to join us in three days. Just to let you know, we live in tents, far away from civilization. So you can get whatever you want, there's nothing you can buy here.'

'Right, sir. Good day, sir.'

I was thrilled at the prospect of going to the field exercise location. I went to the canteen and picked up everything I might require for my four-month stay in the desert.

I was the convoy commander of the convoy that consisted of a one-tonner and two Shaktimans, all full of stores. I was accompanied by a JCO and five jawans. The journey, I was told, would take a day. I had a walkie-talkie to communicate with the naib subedar in the last Shaktiman.

As we travelled through small towns and villages, the residents looked on at me curiously. Some waved at me. I waved back. The landscape transformed before my eyes. The greenery thinned out and the land became more and more arid. I looked out unblinkingly trying to absorb all that I could. Hot mid-noon winds blew into my face, dislodging my cap occasionally.

As the convoy sped into the desert, my discomfiture, which I had been ignoring for some time now, grew. I had an increasing urge to ease my bladder.

Lunch halt came at the perfect time. The convoy pulled over to a dhaba. The humble-looking roadside joint had an excellent menu that consisted of chapattis soaked in ghee made from camel's milk, lal maas, dal baati, spicy chutneys, pakodi and multi-flavoured lassis, but all they had for a toilet was a makeshift enclosure, with corroded tin sheets for cover. On scrutiny, I found that it had more holes than tin, large ones at that. I abandoned the idea of easing myself and walked out, to find what looked like a tiff between the naib subedar and the dhaba owner.

'No, no, I can't take money from you people,' the

dhaba owner said. 'You are faujis. You do so much for us and these are small things we can do for you in return.'

'No, but it's not right,' the naib subedar said and pushed the money across the table. The dhaba owner promptly thrust it back. The naib subedar requested again and the money came right back. The tussle went on for some time, before I intervened. After a great amount of persuasion and pleading, I finally succeeded in clearing the bills.

The convoy journeyed on. To my dismay, I noticed that the little clusters of greenery which I thought could provide me cover, now began to disappear. Along the road, except for a few dhabas, it was mostly uninhabited. By evening, things were getting so urgent that I could barely control myself. I was worried that I would wet my seat.

'Tea break,' I announced hastily, ordering the driver to stop.

'Sahab, but there is no dhaba here.'

'There is,' I said in a commanding tone, before disappearing into a cluster of houses. I hoped to be able to use someone's toilet. No sooner had I neared them than a bunch of children and women mobbed me.

'Look, there's a woman in fauji dress,' one of the women exclaimed. A barrage of questions followed, as they inspected me from head to toe. 'Are you fauji?', 'Where are you from?', 'Where are you going?' I loved all the attention I got, but the timing couldn't be worse. Before it got too late and I fell in the children's eyes, I projected my problem to one of the ladies. She gladly showed me the way to her toilet. The sight of a commode had never before given me such joy. It was sheer bliss to see a clean one in the middle of the desert.

Just when I thought my problem was over, there was another. Even though my bladder was ready to burst, I couldn't expel, since those muscles had become taut. It took me so long that I was worried the convoy would leave without me.

'*Laydeej ho?*' one of the dhoti-clad men asked me as I emerged. I answered in the affirmative. He promptly went on, '*Fauj me?*'

'*Ji.*'

'*Achha. Par laydeej apni fauj me?*' He looked dazed. A round of discussions followed among the men and some of them, after what looked like a heated argument, finally acknowledged the existence of my species: '*Akhbaar me dekha tha.*'

In the meantime, the gracious ladies had arranged tea for the team. Given a choice I wouldn't have had more liquids, but their friendliness and warmth surpassed my unwillingness.

It was dark by the time the convoy reached our destination, a few kilometres from the international border. Not a speck of light was visible on the horizon in any direction. This could well have been another planet. At the unit location, a campfire seemed to be in progress and human silhouettes danced around flickering flames. Were they dancing? Or running? They moved back and forth frenziedly as a human silhouette came rushing out of a burning tent. Cries of 'AAG, AAG!' rang in the air even as the fire fighters continued to douse the flames with water jets. The soot-covered man who had rushed out of the tent, joined the team in fighting the fire and in a matter of minutes, the flames had been doused.

The soot-covered man then dusted his shirt

thoroughly and gave some instructions to the fire fighters. They saluted him and left. A hand running over his hair, he then walked up to me and enquired, 'So you are the convoy commander? All well?'

'Yes, sir,' I said, barely able to figure out his epaulette with three stars. In the light of the petromax, the only features visible on his face were a part of his forehead, eyes and teeth. Everything else was covered in soot. I suppressed a smile.

'Something funny?' he asked me curtly, before running his hand on his forehead and blackening the only visible part.

I tried hard to keep a serious expression and said, 'No, sir.'

He gave me a stare before passing on orders about what to do with the stores.

Later, I was led to a large tent by an officer who introduced himself as Captain Amit Joseph.

'This is the officers' mess,' he said, lifting the flap of the tent for me to enter. I wasn't much used to chivalrous behaviour, so this came as a surprise. He then rephrased his sentence, 'A *makeshift* officers' mess.'

This tent was far removed from the officers' mess I was used to. Here there was no glitz or pomp, just basic furniture, a water filter and a television.

Inside, I saw a group of about six officers. Everyone was eyeing me with curiosity. A stocky man with a receding hairline was introduced to me as the CO, Colonel Abhijeet Mishra.

'Welcome, Deepa. Welcome to the desert,' he said, as I greeted him. 'I hope the journey was fine.'

'Yes, sir,' I said.

'But usually we don't take so long to get here. Was

there a breakdown, a puncture or something?'

'No, sir. Everything was fine.' He didn't need to know the details.

'So, you are here,' he said, hands in his pockets. 'You wanted to come here, isn't it? Now don't complain I didn't warn you. Life is a little tough here. In fact,' he said, smiling at Captain Amit Joseph, 'the fire you just saw was a demo of field life. Our macho young man here set his tent on fire with his cigarette.'

Everyone laughed looking at the man who had accompanied me in. He smiled, brushing aside the mop of hair on his forehead. I turned to Captain Joseph in amazement. I could scarcely recognize him. In the bright light of the mess, his features were clear: deep sparkling eyes, a sharp, straight nose, a square jaw and a cleft in his chin. He was, I realized, quite handsome once he had gotten rid of all that soot.

The CO asked Captain Joseph, 'Have you shown the lady her room... I mean her tent?' He then turned back to me, 'Make yourself as comfortable as you can. This will be home for quite a long time.'

I smiled. 'Yes, sir.'

Post dinner, Captain Amit Joseph walked me to the entrance of a tent. 'Here, this is yours,' he said.

My tent was adjacent to the officers' mess. Each individual dwelling, I noticed, had a snake trench dug around it. 'Sir, are there snakes here?' I asked.

'Yeah, there are snakes, scorpions, deer... a whole lot of wildlife actually.'

'And who lives here?' I asked pointing to the tent adjacent to mine.

'There's now me and then Captain Reddy.'

'Together?' I asked in my naiveté.

'Of course, everyone has to share a tent, except

the CO and you.'

Having put my foot in my mouth, I quietly retired to my tent, tying the two flaps at the entrance together. I then inspected the interiors. A hurricane lamp lit the inside of my tent. There was a bed, a mosquito net and some water in a jug on a foldable table. The other end of my tent flapped open into another mini tent. Someone had thoughtfully erected a urinal tent for me. A few slabs of stones were roughly placed on the sand in here. There was also an iron bucket half filled with water. After freshening up with the available water, I reduced the flame of my hurricane lamp and stretched out in bed.

It was pitch dark outside and the silence was unearthly. I could even hear the fluttering of a moth near the dim light. I felt uneasy that I couldn't at least lock myself up in a new place in the midst of unfamiliar faces. I tossed and turned in bed till late into the night. Suddenly, I felt something on my toe, something moving. And before I knew it, whatever it was, had bitten me. I shrieked, jumped up and switched on the torch, sure to find a snake. But what I saw instead was a mouse, a sand-brown one, scuttling away. I turned up the lamp to find my first-aid kit. The wound was small but bled profusely. I cleaned it up with an antiseptic solution and bandaged it. A lone lamp in the pitch darkness, meanwhile, attracted many insects. I didn't like all of them sharing my tent – but then it was better than sharing it with an unknown human male.

Which is why, when I opened my eyes sometime early in the morning, I was alarmed to see a man in my tent. He was inspecting my room while pouring tea into a cup.

'Jai hind, sahab,' he said, handing me the tea.

'Thank you,' I said and then added: 'You don't have to come in here. Say "chai" from outside. I'll come and collect it.'

The steward looked puzzled. 'Sahab, I usually keep it on the table,' he said.

'That's okay. Just do as you are told.'

'Ji, sahab,' the steward said and left sullen-faced.

While sipping the tea, I got a glimpse of officers walking deeper into the desert. Soon enough, the tea had its effect and I was following in their footsteps. The track led me to another tent a little distance away. The stink suggested that it was the toilet tent. I cleared my throat a few times loudly, since there was no other way to indicate my arrival. What if someone was inside? The least I wanted was to catch a handsome hunk in the act.

Inside was a deep pit, with two planks across it. One had to perch precariously on these planks to do the job. A heap of sand and a shovel were placed in a corner, which was to serve as the flush. But in this toilet, no one had bothered to flush, since flies buzzed and worms wriggled happily in the pit full of fresh excreta. The sight curdled my stomach and the noxious fumes assaulted my nostrils. I held my breath and ran out.

But now what? Where else could I go? There seemed to be no other place since there were hardly any large enough bushes. After surveying the areas nearby, I made up my mind and returned to the same toilet tent. This was the only place where I could answer nature's calls. I stood outside, pinching my nostrils and imagining the worst. What if someone walked in while I experienced peak pressure? What then, if in my urgency to zip up, I fell down into the pit?

After much contemplation, I finally decided against

the tent. I walked farther away from the unit area to find myself a befitting bush, scrutinizing every patch for thorns, snakes and scorpions. A black buck suddenly whizzed by with its calf. I followed them a little distance. And voila! They showed me the perfect spot. There was a small khejri tree with enough foliage around it, and it was not thorny either. Finally, concealed in the cover, I unbuttoned.

I had nearly pulled my pants down when a voice spoke from dangerously close: 'Good morning, sahab.'

It was a jawan. 'Good morning,' I said, pulling my pants up and zipping up in record time. Perhaps, he too, like me preferred the open air to the toilet tent. I then decided nature's call couldn't be answered as yet, and returned to my tent since I was getting late for office.

The office complex was a cluster of tents with camouflage nets over it. Each department had a tent of its own and individuals reported to their respective tents. I walked up to the Commanding Officer's tent to officially report to him.

'Have you done night duties in your previous unit?' he asked after he had enquired about other things.

'Yes, sir.'

'Do you think you will be able to do it here?' he looked at me with uncertainty. 'You can tell me honestly if you have any problem.'

'I have no problem, sir. I will do the duties.'

'Alright,' he said, nodding. 'I would like you to handle the office correspondence from now. You can take over from Captain Joseph in the next tent.'

'Right, sir,' I said, saluting and heading out.

'I hope everything's all right,' Captain Joseph said. 'I thought I heard you scream last night?'

'A rat bit me,' I said.

He laughed like this was the funniest thing he had heard in years. I wanted to tell him that it wasn't as funny as the image of his soot-smeared face. 'A rat bit you? Unbelievable!'

'I hope I don't get fever or anything,' I said.

'Where did it bite, I mean...'

'On my toe,' I said. 'But I have washed the wound with antiseptic. So I hope I will be fine.'

'Yeah, there shouldn't be a problem,' he said. 'Anyway, we have a military hospital detachment here a little farther away in case of any medical problem.' He then smiled again. 'Welcome to the desert.'

18

My Tent and I

MY DAYS IN THE TENT USUALLY BEGAN WITH A DISTANT ringing of 'Chai... Chai.' Sometimes, in my disoriented state, I thought I was at a railway station until I bumped into the bamboo pole holding up the tent as I got out of bed. Nevertheless, this was far better than having the chap walk into my tent and take a peek at my not-so-presentable sleeping angles; so also my undergarments hanging on a makeshift clothing line.

Living close to nature, my resourcefulness was at its peak. Having abandoned the idea of using the toilet tent or going in the open, like primitive humans, I had now discovered that I could use my mini-bathroom tent instead. All I required was a newspaper, spread out, then a discreet stroll in the desert, with a neatly wrapped paper packet and a good throw to dispose the projectile without a trace. It was a neat idea and I prided myself on it, until one day Captain Joseph saw me with the pack near the mess tent. He narrowed his eyes, looking unwaveringly at the pack.

'Good morning, sir,' I said and continued with my walk.

'We have a garbage dump here,' he called out from behind, pointing in the direction opposite to the one I was walking in. 'Maybe you can use that.'

'Oh, alright sir,' I said and turned around. But as soon as he was out of sight, I changed course and walked right into the deep desert to accomplish my mission. I wondered if he could have guessed what it was that I carried. Not a possibility, I assured myself.

From then on, I tried hard to avoid meeting him on my daily morning strolls. When I saw him at a distance, I hurriedly returned to my tent and deposited the pack in a corner to be disposed of at a more opportune time. Within a few days, I had learnt the art of packaging so well that I could stuff the goods in the thigh pocket of my combat trousers. But the packaging required more paper and hence, despite conserving papers, the stock depleted sooner than I thought. I then turned to magazines for help. The occasional newspaper that came to the officers' mess, I whisked away. It never found its way back.

'Where do all the newspapers disappear?' Major Tomar wondered aloud at breakfast one day, jabbing at the egg yolk with a fork. Major Tomar was the Officer-in-Charge (Stores), a middle-aged, well-built man with a habit of twirling his bushy moustache. He liked his eggs served sunny-side up. 'There's nothing to read,' he complained.

'Sir, I have some magazines and novels,' Captain Joseph offered. 'I can lend them to you.'

'That's okay,' he said, forking identically cut squares of egg and toast into his mouth. 'But even then,' he said, chewing, 'where did the papers go?'

The steward walked in just then, with more toasted bread, butter and jam. '*Kyon bhai*, what do you do with the papers?' Major Tomar turned to him. 'Use them in your *choolha*?'

'No, sahab,' the steward took on a defensive stance and looked crossly at me. I squirmed in my chair and gave him the sternest stare I could muster. 'Sahab, someone or the other takes it to read,' he said, before heading back to the attached kitchen tent.

Psychological warfare was imminent in these surroundings. The chauvinistic attitude of most men was evident in their speech and action.

'What's so good about the mornings now?' Major Tomar thwarted my bright spirits, one morning as I wished him a good morning. 'You have spoiled the mornings, afternoons, evenings, everything.' He gave me a look of repugnance. 'Weren't you better there? You didn't have to come here. Now, with you around, we are conscious all the time. I can't even step out of my tent in a towel.'

So that was his grouse. I wanted to tell him he was free to roam around in a towel. But I said instead, 'Sir, as an officer posted in the unit, I go wherever the unit goes. I am very much a part of this unit like anybody else.'

'You get special privileges, a full tent for yourself, an attached bathroom, excuses...'

'Excuse me, sir,' I said, 'but I have got no excuses. I do all the work I am assigned.'

The other officers, including Captain Joseph, stood silently. As for me, I was taken aback by the reaction to a simple 'Good morning'.

Major Tomar continued, 'Tell me frankly, wasn't it easier for you and for all of us if you had stayed back in the rear? What are you going to do here that we can't?'

'You are right, sir,' Captain Reddy said. He was of medium height, hawk-nosed and with neatly parted hair. 'Some jobs are best left to men. We were doing perfectly fine. But now, everything is changing. Ours is becoming a soft army now.'

'Sir...' I said in a polite but firm tone, looking from one to the other. I knew I had to be tactful. 'Deciding whether I must be here or there is the CO's prerogative.'

'That's the problem,' Major Tomar said. 'Our CO...' He looked at the others and left the sentence incomplete. 'At least you should have thought about the consequences.'

'I am sure the CO thought about it and he knows what's best for *his* unit,' I said.

'Huh!' Major Tomar looked away from me and addressed his audience. 'They cry for equality and opportunity and then can't share a tent, like equals. In the US army, men and women live in the same tents. Now that's equality.'

'Their culture is different, sir,' I said. 'We can't make comparisons like that.'

'Why not? Aren't they also women?'

A few chuckles followed.

'Their society is different,' I said. 'They are more open and tolerant when it comes to men and women mingling.'

'Lieutenant Shekhar is right, sir,' Captain Joseph said. 'The scenario is entirely different in India. Probably we can't make comparisons like that. There they have women in the ranks and a much larger strength of women in the army. But despite all the talk of equality,' he continued, looking mostly at Major Tomar, 'even there they have many problems regarding the role of women in the army, that is, whether they must be deployed in combat roles at all or remain only in support roles.' He then paused for a moment as everyone stood quietly, looking at him. He sounded like someone used to having a captive audience. 'Sir, women in the army is a debatable topic the world over, especially the kind of roles they must play. Women on their part ask for equal opportunities but usually we men interpret it wrongly.'

I thought Captain Joseph had spoken like a mature, well-informed and broad-minded officer, unlike the rest. I liked that and looked at him with a renewed sense of respect.

'Impressing the girl, eh?' Major Tomar said, leaning towards him, in what was to be a whisper. I pretended not to have seen or heard anything.

Mess times saw me unusually quiet since I found that the men had their Martian topics, which mostly precluded me. Major Tomar was in love with tinsel-town and had seen every Bollywood movie ever released. He also had a terrific memory when it came to the vital statistics of the reigning heroines and he uttered them with the importance of a seven-year-old saying his mathematical tables. Colonel Mishra usually took off on another tangent with his lessons on the advantages of yoga. He was a teetotaller and vegetarian, and had bitter-gourd juice first thing in the morning to fend off diabetes, causing everyone at the breakfast table but him to contort their face in distaste. The Second-in-Command was usually quiet, and if at all he spoke, it was only about world news and current affairs. Captain Joseph spoke only when it became extremely necessary, and Captain Reddy was the yes-man. The two Lieutenants – that included me – sat like we had only ears and no mouths.

Sometimes though, there were topics I thought I could contribute to, and I did, but usually no one gave my words the importance I thought it deserved. I was a newbie and until I proved my competence all over again in this new unit, no one would pay much heed.

'I miss doing it here,' the CO said, as we sipped our drinks in the mess tent. 'I can't do it outside. Nor can I do it in the caravan, although I tried.'

He meant yoga. The thought of the CO trying to do yoga postures in his caravan, a specially designed Shaktiman, made it hard for me to keep a straight face as he continued: 'We people in the army think yoga is not for us, but the benefits are plenty.' He uncrossed his legs and put his juice on the table. Everyone nodded. 'The stress of living such a life without any creature comforts,' he continued, 'the feeling of being away from loved ones... yoga can help overcome all that stress.'

'You are very right, sir,' Captain Reddy said.

'Reddy, why don't you join me? We can do some exercises outdoors.'

Captain Reddy looked shocked. Colonel Mishra then turned to me, 'And what about you? You can also try it.'

'Me, sir?' I said, unable to picture myself standing beside the CO in combat dress and boots, doing yoga. Captain Amit Joseph, who sat beside me, looked down at the floor, trying to suppress a smile.

'Anyway, you young people won't understand,' he said. 'For the past three years, I have been practising yoga and with my experience I can tell you it has helped me greatly.' Everyone's faces had a bored look, due to being subjected to these sermons on a routine basis. 'In fact,' Colonel Mishra continued, 'I feel so many things in my life have changed. Now there is no tension about BP, sugar and all the ailments that were beginning to show.'

'Sahab, there's a phone for you,' the steward informed Colonel Mishra. Everyone sighed in relief as he excused himself and moved to the telephone table at the corner.

I glanced at the TV. A film heroine was singing a song and running around in a garden full of tulips. Major Tomar's eyes were glued to the screen. Without taking his eyes off, he leant closer to Captain Reddy and got into a hushed discussion. Captain Joseph shifted sights between the TV, the glass he held and the other officers. I overheard Colonel Mishra on the phone, 'That's the third gear, not first. No wonder the thing doesn't move.' I looked at him as he took a deep breath, shifted the mouthpiece from the left ear to the right and said, 'The middle one is the brake, understand? You can't afford to forget that. The middle one, the middle one,' he said, his voice slightly raised. He seemed to forget his yoga lessons, as his voice became sterner, 'How many times have I taught you A, B, C – accelerator, brake, clutch?' Then, suddenly, he brought in a gentle intonation. 'When I teach you, dear, you don't pay any attention and now see...'

Captain Joseph looked at me from the corner of his eyes and smiled. I smiled restrainedly.

Colonel Mishra continued with his tele-driving class, alternatively changing his tone from harsh to soft, taking deep audible breaths in between. I was hungry and waited for the class to get over, so we could start dinner. Even the steward gave him tired looks, suppressing yawns.

'We're going to have Black Forest,' Major Tomar said, leaning towards Captain Joseph. 'So hold fort.'

My eyebrows shot up. 'Black Forest? Here? I can't believe it,' I said, looking from one to the other. 'It's my favourite.'

'It's your favourite? Unbelievable,' said Major Tomar, rolling his eyes and chuckling. The others joined him. 'Yeah, it's my all-time favourite too,' he said, trying to control his laughter. Captain Joseph shot me a look that demanded that I shut up immediately. For the remaining part of the evening, I didn't care to look at him. After dinner, I retreated hastily to my tent. I was in a grumpy mood when I went to the toilet tent to wind up for the day. I pulled the bucket angrily, by its handle. But instead of sliding closer, it fell and before I knew it, all the water disappeared in the parched earth. I kicked the bucket a dozen times.

Every drop of water was accounted for here. Sometimes the rationed water didn't suffice for my needs, especially when it came to bathing. For most of the officers and jawans, having a bath had been relegated to being an unimportant chore. 'What bath?' they echoed. 'Who bathes in the ex-location?' On a couple of occasions however, I was privy to jawans bathing in a group under the sky, chatting, laughing and soaping themselves vigorously, their hands sliding every now and then into their only piece of clothing.

Irrespective of what the men said, I managed to bathe at least once in two days, although it was mostly a high-speed activity. The mess staff usually obliged me with this special request. I only had to take care that no one was around, especially Major Tomar. Now that everyone had left the mess after dinner, it was the best time. I headed towards the mess in the moonlight, wading through the sand.

'Hey, where are you going?' a familiar voice called out. It was Captain Joseph.

I turned around, wondering what he was doing outside his tent at night. 'Oh, nothing, sir,' I said, as I continued walking.

'Look, look, just wait,' he said, coming closer to me. 'Are you going to the mess?'

'Yes, I am.'

'Is there something you need urgently? Maybe I can help,' he said.

'No, sir, thank you,' I said and began to walk.

I walked up to the mess tent and saw a dim light flickering through the gap of the tent flap. Opening the flap, I called out for the steward. But instead of the steward, another sight greeted me. A group of officers sat glued to the TV, on which bodies jerked and groaned rhythmically. Naked bodies! Although the human anatomy was on display, this certainly was no biology class.

I mumbled something, shut the flap and walked back.

'I told you,' Captain Amit Joseph said, as he saw me walk back in a daze.

'Actually, I just wanted a bucket of water and some kerosene for my lamp,' I said.

'I have half a bucket. You can use it. And you can use my hurricane lamp if you need,' he said, getting up and offering me his camp chair. 'Mind sitting here for some time? I'll get another chair.'

'No, I am not sitting here,' I said. 'I need to go.'

'Okay, I'll just get you the water,' he said and went into his tent. I went into mine to fetch my empty bucket.

'I'm sorry,' he said, pouring water into my bucket. 'I was rude with you in the mess. See, that's because I didn't want you to speak more about it.'

'What was the big fuss about?' I asked. 'They were laughing like it was the joke of the year.'

'It's a little embarrassing to tell you,' he said, keeping the bucket down. 'Okay, let me put it this way. In these areas, a little rum can get you everything.' He shrugged and opened his palms. 'Everything... if you understand!'

I looked at him with a blank expression on my face. Then my mouth fell open. If what I understood was right, it just reaffirmed the fact that I was surrounded by men who sometimes were not gentlemen. Their masks of propriety were tucked away safely to be worn on return. I replayed the conversation in the mess with Major Tomar and cringed in embarrassment. I wanted to thank Captain Joseph for telling me to shut up.

'So, now do you mind being here for some time?'

'No,' I smiled.

He gestured for me to sit. 'It's okay, sir,' I said. 'I'll get my chair.'

I pulled out my camp chair and unfolded it. Captain Joseph waited for me to sit, before he settled into his chair. 'Sir,' I said, 'I am not used to anyone being chivalrous with me.'

He smiled. 'So get used to it.'

'No, sir, it's not right. I wear a uniform. So all that matters is the rank. You are senior. So you are always first. And moreover, I am so used to doing all the chivalrous acts. I get up when the ladies come, I open car doors for them, I escort them... so that's why it feels a little odd.'

'Okay, so what about when you are in your civvies?'

I smiled. 'That would depend.'

'Anyway, give me some time,' he said. 'I need time to get over it.'

I wanted to tell him that I found it charming. It was not that I couldn't open a tent flap or pull a chair for myself, but when he paid me attention, it just made me feel good. And it also made him look refined, unlike the rest.

'It's very pleasant outside,' he said.

'Yes, sir,' I nodded.

'Have you seen a night sky so clear?' he asked, looking up into the heavens.

I looked up. The sky looked incredibly clear like a high-resolution image, perfect to the pixel. Stars shone like diamonds, some bright, some big and some nearly invisible. The moon was perfectly round and luminous. Cold breeze, golden sands and the beautiful night sky together, made for a perfect romantic setup.

'Isn't it beautiful?' Captain Joseph turned to me. I nodded again.

'In the places we live, we can never get this kind of view. Nor can we breathe such fresh, unpolluted air.'

'You're right,' I said.

We sat in the moonlight, looking at the beautiful night sky, the cluster of unit tents, the silhouettes of small desert trees and occasionally at each other.

'Mind if I smoke?' he said.

'No, sir. Go ahead. Only don't burn the tents.'

He chuckled as he lit his cigarette. 'Don't worry. Today I'm not sleepy yet.'

'Don't tell me, sir. You fell asleep with a lit cigarette?'

'Yeah, I was tired and dozed off with a lit cigarette in my hand. Only when my book and my bed began burning did I realize that everything was on fire.'

I laughed. 'And I thought there was a huge campfire that evening.'

'Campfire!' he said and shook in laughter.

'And you looked really funny with a black face!'

The quiet desert night rang with our laughter. Then the ripples subsided and we were silent for a while.

'I'm not much of a smoker actually... just once in a while...' he said, holding the cigarette between his shapely lips and puffing on it. Then he looked up, expelling the smoke slowly. 'Have you ever done any stargazing?'

'Not really,' I said. 'Just a little that we were taught in the academy.'

'I enjoy looking at the stars and the patterns they make in the sky. It's very interesting. I am not much of an expert, but I know some basics.' He then pointed to a cluster of bright stars, 'See, that's the great bear or Saptarishi, the seven stars. And you see there,' he drew a line across the sky with his finger. 'That's the Dog Star, Sirius. These three stars make a straight line and you know exactly which side is north.' He then looked down and at me. 'That's how people used to navigate earlier. Just like we read maps, they read the sky.'

I nodded. His mention of map-reading took me back to the map-reading classes in the academy. As a part of the night exercise, our batch of lady cadets was to read the map and reach a destination from a remote area where we had been dropped. We read our maps and kept walking, through grass, hillocks and squishing-squashing through the wet fields, all in torchlight. When daylight broke, we realized that we didn't have our bearings right. So we had to ask for directions from the locals to get to our destination. The gentlemen cadets who always prided themselves as good map readers were worse: they had to board a bus back.

'Thinking of something?' Captain Joseph asked, seeing me smile.

'Nothing,' I said and came back to the topic. 'So, you use a telescope?'

'No, binoculars.'

'You can see stars with binoculars? I thought we use it only to see tents and vehicles far away.'

'Actually the binoculars are used at the initial stage, and then comes the telescope.'

'Oh,' I said. Then we were quiet. I wanted to ask him why he sat alone here, when all the others enjoyed the movies. I also wanted to ask him why he was mostly quiet around other officers, while inviting me to give him company. What was he up to?

'And what do you like to do?' he asked.

'I... er, nothing much,' I said. But, when he prodded, I mentioned my guitar and songs. He said he would like to hear me when we got back. I learnt that he liked reading, cricket and travelling.

'I like travelling too,' I said.

'So let's plan a trip somewhere from here,' he said. 'What about Jaisalmer?'

'Sure, sir,' I said. We then decided we would talk to the Commanding Officer and take a day off for the visit.

That night, I stretched in bed and thought about him. My curiosity about the man increased. In many ways, he was not like the others. He spoke like a well-read man, aware of the world he lived in. His manners suggested a good upbringing. But then was he trying to show he was different? Was he trying to make an impression? Or was he genuine? After Captain Bipin Ghosh, I had developed a cynical attitude towards all young men. I feared their superficiality.

By the end of the first month, I had become reasonably comfortable with outdoor camp living. The discomfiture of living among an all-male population was slowly reducing, although it never vanished fully. To a large extent, I also overcame my fear of insects, since they shared my tent on a regular basis. Like Anju, now all I did with the beetles, moths and cockroaches was to brush them away graciously. A scorpion once decided to make my shoe its home. I treated even the scorpion graciously, since it didn't sting me when I put my foot inside. Ours was a case of mutual respect. Living close to nature was an adventure in itself and I found all the hardships thrilling. Although sometimes this kind of lifestyle felt medieval, overall it satisfied my sense of adventure.

Besides the hard-living conditions, I thrived amidst the psychological warfare too. I did all the tasks given to me like everyone else. I devised plans to carry out all my daily activities effortlessly. I had also excelled at minimalist living. For unique problems, I found ingenious solutions. To dispose sanitary pads, I buried them in the sand far away from the unit premises. A mutt that had followed me one day looked on from a distance as I dug, salivating at the prospect of finding a bone. To my horror, it walked past a group of men, with a used pad in its mouth. No one noticed. Or maybe they pretended not to.

Rum-issue days in the field location were the only days that I experienced a heightened sense of insecurity.

268 / Sajita Nair

To be surrounded by men in an inebriated state far away from civilization made me nervous. The thought that my dignity was protected only by a flap of canvas gave me many sleepless nights. I also disliked being the duty officer on the rum-issue days. But when, as per the roster I was to do the duty, I did not ask for a change. With heavy boots, I waded through the sand at night holding a torch and measuring each step. Although Captain Joseph had warned me against snakes and scorpions, I knew there was a deadlier species to watch out for: the male homo sapiens sapiens. Moonlit nights did provide some light but there were also those new moon nights when the moment I switched off the torch, I thought I had disappeared in the darkness; that I ceased to exist.

My work profile had also completely changed from that of my previous unit. As the Officer-in-Charge (Headquarters), I now handled correspondence, drafted letters and ensured that the dak reached the right sections. This job was not as exciting or challenging as being the company commander, but living in the field conditions made even this exciting. Before any draft reached the Commanding Officer I took utmost care to ensure everything was perfect. For this, first I had to wean the clerks off from a formula they were used to. They usually pulled out old letters from files and copied them verbatim, often even copying the dates. Initially, although the Commanding Officer read through every draft painstakingly, eventually his confidence in me began to rise. Then he reached a stage when he signed with barely a glance at the letter.

'We will be getting our automation software,' he said one day as I went to him with an important letter. 'Would you like to take on the automation in the computer wing?'

'Sure, sir,' I said. 'I can do that.'

'Alright, so when we get back, you head the automation wing.'

'Right, sir,' I said.

This was good news. The unit had to change over from the manual functioning to an automated one. And if I was to head the department, it was a privilege.

'So, anything else for the day?' he enquired as he began to leave the office.

'Sir, actually, I have a slight problem I wanted to discuss with you,' I said.

'Okay, come to my office,' he said, as he walked back to his office. I followed him.

He sat on his chair and gestured for me to sit. He then placed both his hands on the table and leant forward. 'So, what's it that you want to tell me?'

'Here, sir, everything is fine,' I said. 'My stay is very comfortable, but, sir, there's only a little problem... I find it difficult to use the toilet since anyone can walk in anytime... and I am not comfortable with that.' Despite Colonel Mishra's warm demeanour, it took me nearly two months to project my problem. Of late, Major Tomar, suspecting some foul play, whisked the newspapers away before me. That left me with no other option.

'Oh!' he said clasping his hands and looking at his table. 'How come I didn't think about it?' Then he turned to me. 'Don't worry. We will make some arrangement.'

The very next day, the mess havaldar promptly walked me to a newly erected tent. Outside was a cardboard placard with an arrow mark directing to the tent that read, 'FOR USE/ Lt. Deepa Shekhar only'. It was embarrassing to see how the cardboard screamed for attention. But it would also ensure that no one ever strayed into a tent which was now exclusively mine. Major Tomar and his mates did comment on the new structure and how extra resources and manpower were required to accommodate a lady officer in field condition. I didn't quite agree with him. Being a woman, there were some unique requirements I had and these were not privileges but a basic necessity that I should have projected long back, if only I were not embarrassed to communicate it to the CO. Their comments continued, but I had reached a point when I felt justification wasn't necessary.

19

My Desert Friend

'SNAKE, SNAKE!' I HEARD ONE MORNING AS I WAS dressing.

There was a commotion all around my tent. Jawans lifted up the flaps from all sides, shouting. I buttoned up and bolted out. Then I spotted the creature, a thin snake with stripes along the length of its body, slither into Captain Joseph's tent. Once again there was a flurry of activity as jawans ran helter-skelter with mosquito-net rods and sticks.

'Leave it, leave it,' I heard Captain Joseph say, as he rushed out. 'It's not venomous.'

'How do you know?' I asked him when the jawans left.

'Poisonous ones are usually nocturnal.'

'Are you sure?'

'Actually,' he smiled, 'I am not. But that was the only way to let the snake escape. We have encroached into their land and the least we can do is not harm them. At least, minimize the harm.'

'Oh, nature-lover?' I said. 'Yeah, even I agree with you. But I think I'll tell them to re-dig my snake trench. It's nearly filled with sand.'

Captain Joseph laughed. When he laughed, his eyes nearly closed, softening his otherwise masculine face.

Even if it hadn't been for the snake, the day was to start early, since our unit was to organize a lunch for all the Commanding Officers and Seconds-in-Command of the units in the area. That meant a lot of running around to procure things, especially in the mess.

'Arya, carrot, carrot,' I heard the lieutenant say into the phone, as I entered the mess. 'Carrot, Arya, carrot, gajar.'

I joined the other officers at the table and learnt that the pudding was to be *Gajar-ka-halwa*.

'Carrot,' the lieutenant was now shouting into the mouthpiece, trying to outdo the poor connectivity with the sheer strength of his voice. 'Charlie, Alpha, Romeo... can you hear me, ARYA? CA-RR-OT... CHARLIE, ALPHA, ROMEO, ROMEO, OSCAR... CAN YOU HEAR ME?' He nearly blew the tent off.

At the dining table, everyone was now in splits. I didn't laugh, since my turn was next. I was to procure the crockery and cutlery.

The lieutenant now slapped his forehead. '*Abey, gajar,* carrot, *suna kya?* GAJAR! GOLF, ALPHA...'

'PAPA, LIMA, ALPHA, TANGO...' This was me, procuring the plates a little while later.

Nevertheless, everything was in order before the guests arrived. Most of them were from infantry, artillery and armoured regiments, and found my presence curious. Whenever they caught sight of me, they would suddenly hush up and some of them would come and ask me how I was doing in the exercise location. On seeing me cheerful and normal, some of them were even surprised.

'If given a chance, would you join the infantry?' the CO of an infantry battalion asked me.

'Yes, sir, certainly,' I said.

Others looked surprised at my reply. A discussion then ensued between them as to how women were unfit for the infantry.

'What if a woman is taken POW?' said one.

'The atrocities on them can be far worse,' added another.

'They don't have that much capacity to endure torture,' said a third.

Then finally, one of them asked me, 'So, even after hearing all these things, would you still want to join the infantry?'

'Yes, sir,' I said. 'What I think is, to serve my country, I should not be bound by my gender.' Most knit their eyebrows. 'The doors should be open for anyone with courage and patriotism, irrespective of the gender.'

A few nods ensued.

'It will take time in our army,' said one of them with grey hair. 'It all depends on how you and your colleagues perform.'

In a few days, we were heading to their units, since Colonel Mishra had accepted a few of their invitations. I revelled in all the sights of the desert. Scarce thorny bushes and an occasional acacia or khejri were all that broke the continuity of the sandy landscape. Our jonga sped past them, bellowing sand clouds, on narrow, straight, sand-lined roads that seemed to head over the horizon.

The units we visited welcomed us warmly. Each of the officers then interacted with their respective counterparts, the CO with the CO, Major Tomar with another major, Captain Reddy and Captain Joseph with a major and captain respectively and I with a lieutenant – who happened to be my course mate from the academy. He was thrilled to see me and unlike the others, we weren't bound by formality in our chat.

'Hey, what kind of stores do you give us, yaar?' he said. 'Give us some better quality things.' He then called some of his jawans and had the shoes, shovels, pickaxes and other stores shown to me. 'These shoes don't even last for two months. So what are they supposed to do before they get the next issue they are authorized?'

I assured him I would do whatever I could at my level. I then projected the general dissatisfaction to the CO as we drove on towards the border: 'Sir, they were complaining about the stores.'

Colonel Mishra waved a hand disinterestedly. 'Let's stop at that dune,' he told the driver.

We stopped and walked up to a group of completely barren, sandy mounds. Wavy patterns on the dunes gave an illusion of movement. The sand rolled even as the wind blew. But when we stepped on it, its splendour disappeared, trampled under our feet. I clambered up the mound and looked around. Captain Joseph followed me. Plain arid land lay endlessly before the eyes. Although the Thar Desert continued its sandy tracts into the borders and beyond, our boundary stopped at the village of Munabao.

'This side is our land that we defend,' Captain Joseph said, as we stood on the high watch tower at the border. An expanse of arid land lay below. 'Our land for which we wear the uniforms and pledge an oath, for which so many like us have shed their blood, our land that we call the motherland.'

If only I could weave a few words together that had the power to stir emotions, for the sight below brought a feeling of silent pride. Standing there, I knew what patriotism did to your heart.

*

'Even I felt the same way,' Captain Joseph told me later when I told him how I felt. We were sitting outside our tents after dinner. 'I have thought a lot about it. But you know, the more I think, the more confusing it becomes,' he said, leaning back on his camp chair. 'What I think is, these are the intangible things... feelings. Who cares about how you feel? Just look around. What do people respect most? It's the tangible things, money. And we don't have much of that.'

'But, sir, can anything beat the pride of wearing the uniform?'

'Even I used to think that when I was new to the service,' he said, and leant forward. 'But you know what? Last time I went to Mumbai, I met my cousin who had come from the US. He flaunted his money, pulled me along to swanky clubs, threw money around like it were paper napkins.' His hand swung like he was throwing currency notes at the sand. 'What do you have then? What do you show? That you love your country? Do you show your honesty, integrity and patriotism? That's when I thought, it's those that owe allegiance to another flag with utmost ease that gain. They make huge houses, buy the best cars, go to the best hotels... and let me tell you, whether you accept it or not, the world respects money.' He paused for a moment. 'So sometimes, yes, sometimes it pinches me. Sometimes, I ask myself, what am I doing here after all? Why am I going through all this? I can easily live a better life. In fact, there are many of my relatives abroad who think I am a fool.'

'But, sir,' I said, 'when we serve our country, isn't there a sense of satisfaction?'

'You don't get my point,' he said. 'What is satisfaction? It's not measurable, tangible.'

'Why do we have to measure everything?' I said. 'There are some things that we can only feel. For me, every morning when I wear my uniform, I feel a kind of high. I just transform. And then we have such a fun and fulfilling work environment. We live an exciting and enriching life, full of adventure… we travel so much, get such a lot of respect wherever we go, we work as a huge team that an entire nation places its trust in… I'm sure all those guys with all that money would want to be in your shoes sometimes. Only they don't tell you.'

He smiled. 'I am practical and you are passionate. We have very different outlooks.'

On our way to Jaisalmer in a bus that carried way more weight than its capacity, locals looked on at us curiously, although we were in civil dress. An old man, seeing us engrossed in one of our discussions/arguments, said, 'Couples must show more love towards each other.'

'But we are not a couple,' I said, before he could embarrass us further.

The old man adjusted his large turban and asked to see our palms. He stared at Captain Joseph's palm and then mine, which I held out reluctantly.

'You will be a couple soon,' he then said, his wrinkled face lighting up in a smile.

I pulled my hand away.

'It's written in your hands,' he said, looking at both of us, before alighting from the bus at a sleepy looking village.

For some time after this, both of us didn't talk and we mostly looked out of the window.

We walked around the Jaisalmer fort, the town and bought small curios. Sometimes, our hands or bodies brushed against each other as we walked in the crowd, but each time, he moved away. Sometimes he said, 'Sorry.' He didn't let me pay anywhere, saying I was not in uniform. I let him pay for me at a few places while at the others I insisted that I pay for us. After much persuasion, he agreed on this arrangement.

At the Sam sand dunes, we went for a camel ride. When my camel got up from its sitting to standing position, jerking me forward while straightening its hind legs, I clung on to the saddle for fear of sliding down its head. Captain Joseph laughed heartily. Then, suddenly I was pushed backward as the camel straightened its front legs. When the walk began, I swayed gently back and forth. Sitting on my camel I laughed as Captain Joseph went through the same exercise of mounting the camel. We then waved at each other on the dunes, like desert travellers.

On our journey back in the bus, we talked about the places we had travelled through and the interesting people we met. 'You know,' he said, 'I met this elderly man in the train once. He was a social worker. And when I told him I was in the army, he made a face.'

'Face?' I said.

'Yeah, like this,' he said, scrunching up his nose.

I laughed.

'And when I asked him why, he said, he was not for the army... guns, fighting and wars. He said that it did nothing good for humanity. That wars only destroy.' My desert friend then looked out of the window at the setting sun, before turning to me. 'That set me thinking. I felt maybe he had a point.'

I nodded. 'Yeah, he was right,' I said, 'but partly. It's not like we in uniform don't like peace. Who wants war after all? It destroys. But haven't humans proved through history that there will always be wars to claim territories? We protect our borders from intruders, so no one else lays claim to what's ours. And if the social worker in the train talked his mind to you, it's because he has freedom. And who protects his freedom? We. Us! We wear our uniform so that we can protect our freedom.'

'Were you in the school or college debate team?'

I smiled. 'No.'

By way of entertainment, there was nothing much I could look forward to. The video cassettes catered mostly to Major Tomar's tastes. The radio didn't offer much. So the only form of entertainment in the unit was self-entertainment, which meant unit members exhibiting their talents around a campfire. This was an activity the jawans looked forward to a lot. Some of them sang, some danced, some mimicked and some cracked jokes. Many dance moves were an imitation of hit songs from the latest flicks, mostly with suggestive lyrics. One especially gifted jawan accurately mimicked the heroines down to the heaving bosom, gyrations, feminine gestures, and all, to everyone's loud cheering. This and the many Santa-Banta jokes were not to my taste, but all I did was clap along with the rest, joining in the fun.

'Don't you feel like the odd one out?' Captain Joseph asked me after a campfire, as we walked back to our tent. 'I mean, sometimes... I think how I would feel if I were you.'

'Yeah, sometimes,' I said, giving him a side glance and simultaneously tripping on a jutting stone hidden in a shrub. He flung his arm to prevent me from falling and helped me back.

'Thanks,' I said, as we walked on. 'Coming back to that, sometimes, yes, I feel odd.'

'But you have been the CCME, isn't it? So maybe you are a little immune,' he turned to me. 'Any other girl in your place would have died of embarrassment. My sister would have cried even.'

'No, I don't think so,' I said. 'Men usually underestimate women.'

'No, it's not that. She doesn't have the spunk. She's the studious bookworm.'

I smiled. 'Younger?'

'No, older, bossy and all. She's a doctor.'

'Oh, only one sister?'

'Yeah, and my mother. My father passed away when I was ten. My mother single-handedly brought us up,' he said, putting his hands in his pockets as he walked. 'Oh, she's a resilient woman. It's from her that I learnt that toughness doesn't mean brute strength like the kind men flaunt, but the inner strength to carry on through adversities. I think women have more of that kind of strength.' He paused for a moment. 'That's why sometimes I think had I been in your place, fighting all odds to fit into this system, I would have given up by now.'

'I think you are just being nice,' I said.

'And honest,' he said. 'Tell me, did your folks agree to you joining this unusual profession?'

'No, initially they didn't, especially since I am their only child. But my father gave in, eventually. My mother still holds a grudge, although she doesn't show it too often.'

'It's natural,' he said. 'When it comes to girls, mothers are worried about a lot of things. I have seen it with my sister.'

'I think all mothers are the same,' I said. 'They smother you with their love, irrespective of how old you are.'

He laughed aloud. 'But they are the angels on the earth.'

We turned and walked back to our tent. Major Tomar caught us just as we were parting ways. 'You people are always together,' he said. 'Why don't you move into one tent? So I can have a tent for myself. *Kyon* Amit?' He winked.

'Sir, we were just talking... generally,' Captain Amit Joseph said, looking visibly embarrassed. Although I had learnt to ignore it, even I felt a flush of embarrassment.

But I could not stop thinking about what Major Tomar had said. Though Captain Joseph had never really entered my tent, my mind was increasingly filled with thoughts of him, his cultured persona, his words, his smile and charming manners. Although he was reserved with the others, with me, he would talk non-stop. And from what he spoke, I knew he had knowledge and depth, and most of all a thinking mind. What I liked most about him was that he never encroached on my personal space, always keeping a respectable distance. I thought he treated me with dignity and respect and I liked that. Sometimes inadvertently, comparisons drew up. Suddenly Captain Bipin Ghosh seemed shallower than ever and Long Nose, well, Long Nose seemed distant and unsure.

The impression I formed about Captain Joseph kept changing, however. Sometimes I felt he was far too grounded in reality, materialistic and maybe a tad dissatisfied with whatever he was. At other times, I felt that he fitted in as an exemplary gentleman officer. Or maybe he was just going through a confusing phase in his life that most people go through sometime or the other.

Whatever he was, he was my desert friend. Whenever I needed anything, he was the one I approached. Between us, we lent each other things we required for camp life: needle and thread, antiseptic solution, kerosene, water, magazines, novels, refills, pens. His interaction with the other officers was also the bare minimum, which worked in my favour. Being my senior, he also enlightened me on unit issues.

'Sir, that Captain from 16 Grenadiers was so upset,' I said, one day, as we walked to the officers' mess, for evening tea. 'He was saying we never really understand their problems.'

'My friends in the infantry, armoured and artillery also tell me the same thing,' he said, as we sat in the mess, indicating to the steward to get two cups of tea. 'See, what I feel is that we need to make our system more efficient and user-friendly.' He leant back into the chair. 'They are not happy, so they complain. I always think our men who fight on the borders should get the best. They deserve the best. In fact, they are the fighting arm and we, support. On many occasions I have had a difference of opinion with the others on this account.' He paused to sip his tea. 'You may not understand now. When we get back in the unit, you'll see what I am talking about.' He leant forward and said discreetly, 'I sign at places I don't like to. If I don't, my career goes bang.'

'If you feel it's not right,' I said, 'don't sign.'

He smiled at me as though I were in kindergarten. 'It's not easy. You'll know what I am talking about.'

*

Four months had gone by at the exercise location and the unit had to head back to Ahmedabad. I found two important letters in my personal mail. 'Had been in Pune for some work. Took a deviation and thought would meet you. No luck,' Long Nose had written. '...Major Bhat is now posted to Delhi. I am still at same old Bengdubi. Can't wait to get back to civilization. Hoping to join him in another four to five months...' Anju had written among other things.

'Now it's your baby,' Colonel Mishra said, summoning me to his office and handing over the software manuals, floppies and other related text. 'It's all Greek to me.' For some reason Colonel Mishra was terrified of the computer. He kept miles away from it, as though it were a wild beast always ready to charge.

I began work in an enviable office with all the required equipment, personnel and also an AC. To assist me were three young jawans who didn't seem frightened of the computer like the old man. I studied the software, its many options and instructed my team members, 'Let's first fill in dummy data to see how it functions. If this system can be successfully executed, the issue and receipt procedures will speed up. People who come to the unit would not have to wait endlessly to procure their stores.' My team nodded enthusiastically. 'So, the onus of making a smooth transition from an older tried and tested system to a completely new one depends on us. It may seem difficult at first, but I'm sure we can make a successful transition.'

My energetic team soon got down to working day and night to punch in the data of all the stores held. Colonel Mishra gave me a free hand and put me in touch with the concerned people. In four months, the automated system was limping into place. Initial hiccups caused many to complain, but since Colonel Mishra was adamant, the spoilers eventually backed out.

Captain Joseph and I began spending more time in each other's company. Unlike Bengdubi, social interactions here were not restricted to the cantonment. There was a whole vibrant city waiting to be discovered. We teamed up on most of our trips to enjoy the restaurants, cafés, musical and dance performances and parties. We had also made friends from the other units and sometimes all of us would go out together, rocking the dance floor with our energy. Although Captain Joseph accompanied me for the dance parties, he never danced. 'I just can't. I have two left feet,' he would say.

'C'mon, sir, if you can walk, you can dance,' I tried to convince him. He then braved the dance floor but ended up looking as though he were being punished. More often than not, I had to find my own partner. Sometimes it would be an officer from one of the other units, and sometimes a civilian.

Once, as I danced with a civilian, the young man was all smiles, showing me all his teeth, running his hand through his hair and gyrating to the beats. He came closer and closer to me, and finally started a conversation: 'What's your name', 'Where do you stay?', 'What do you do?' When I replied to his last question, his teeth suddenly disappeared and he recoiled looking at me as though I were an alien, before disappearing into the crowd.

Captain Joseph laughed when he heard this later that night. We were sitting at a bakery cum ice-cream parlour enjoying some ice-cream to cool off before heading back home. 'Why blame him? The poor guy was scared.'

I laughed some more, banging the table.

We had barely stopped laughing, when we overheard a guy at the next table say to his girlfriend, 'Hmmm. It's yummy. I love Black Forest.'

We looked at each other and then roared.

Colonel Mishra made for a likeable Commanding Officer, abstaining from abusing and foul-mouthing, and his wife brought cheer and smiles to the unit with her vibrant personality. I thought I couldn't be in a better unit – until I became a member of a board for local purchase of stores.

'They are the usual dealers and they know what we want,' Major Tomar said, while I sat in his office. 'All you need to do is sign here,' he pushed a set of papers towards me and pointed with his pen at the places where I needed to sign.

I held the papers together and looked at him. 'Sir, when I sign, it implies that I have seen the stores. But I haven't.'

'Oh, you go too much by the book,' he said, pulling his papers back. 'You are increasing my work. Anyway, since you insist, you can go see the stores,' he said, lifting up the receiver and grunting into it.

Shoes, shirts and shovels that were then grudgingly laid out outside the storehouse looked far too sub-standard for the price quoted. And these were meant for an infantry unit. I decided I was not going to sign till better stores were procured.

'You mean to say I can't recognize good items from sub-standard ones?' Major Tomar fumed. 'I spent all the years of my military life only in the executive side. Understand? I ensure the quality, quantity, binning, maintenance, everything... every day. It's a far difficult job than sitting in an AC room fiddling with a computer.'

I didn't sign.

My name was replaced with Captain Joseph's.

'Don't sign it,' I told him. 'See, it's not difficult. Just be honest and say it straight.'

'It's not so easy, okay?' This was the first time ever I saw my friend lose his calm. 'There's a lot of difference between the two of us. You are a short service commissioned officer and I am a permanent commissioned officer. You quit after five years or at the most ten and me... everything I do finally comes to my career. Don't I want promotions, courses? You don't understand.'

'I understand,' I said. 'But just ask yourself if you are happy. Remember, you were the one who said that our infantry men deserve better... in fact, the best.'

'It's very difficult to stick to your morals in such a situation. It's not like the ex-location, where I had nothing to lose when I didn't join the group. Here, my career is at stake. Moreover...'

'Your wish,' I interrupted. 'You know what's best for you.'

Despite the arguments, Captain Joseph didn't sign. But in the end, the same twice-rejected stores reached the warehouses.

'What did I gain out of this exercise?' Captain Joseph said as we sat waiting for dinner at a hotel. 'Nothing. I feel it was a blunder.'

'Then why did you do it?'

He looked into my eyes and said, 'I don't know.'

'C'mon,' I said. 'You didn't do it because you didn't want to. Simple. You have the moral courage to stand up against something you thought was not right. That's what it is.'

'Actually I couldn't muster the courage. You gave it to me,' he said. Then he leant back and sighed. 'But I certainly feel light. And I must thank you for it.'

'Don't have to,' I said.

'And now whatever happens, I will blame you for it,' he said, smiling playfully. Then, seeing the waiter heading to our table with our food, he added, 'See, I don't even have the courage to order anything but this.'

Which was true: he never experimented, usually sticking to his favourite chicken biryani or something else he could very well eat in the mess. I on the other hand, tried different cuisines.

'Even with your food you are adventurous,' he said, looking at my spaghetti Bolognese.

'Yeah, I get bored with the same things. You don't?'

'No, I like the tried and tested. I stick to it.' Then he looked around. 'Like this place. Look at the ambience. It's classy. I know what to expect when I walk in here. I don't like unpleasant surprises.'

'I think I am not like you, then. I like adventure, variety. Or maybe it just depends on my mood.'

'Yeah, you have wild streak about you. You are slightly unpredictable.'

I smiled. Soft music played at the dance bar and a few couples danced. He looked at them, at me and then at his plate. And once again at me. I wanted to tell him, this dance required no brisk movement, just holding each other and gentle swaying to the music. He could easily do it. I didn't know what he was thinking. Perhaps of holding me and swaying...

I ran my fingers through my now shoulder-length hair. Then I looked down at the floral patterns on my long skirt.

'You won't believe it,' he said, 'but sometimes I miss the ex-location.'

I looked up. 'Really?'

'Yeah, remember how we used to sit under the night sky and talk? It was so peaceful, quiet and beautiful.'

'Hmm.'

A year had gone by and I was now a captain myself. As head of the automation wing, no one messed around with me. Moreover, I didn't have to follow a long chain of command, manoeuvring my way through various bosses with their individual quirks. I reported directly to the CO. Whenever an inspection team visited the unit, I was directly answerable to the big brass. And I usually knew what I was saying.

While things were looking up in my professional life, in my personal life, there hadn't been much progress. Captain Joseph and I had grown closer – he even took an interest in music now, while I read my way through his collection of fiction books – but our relationship had not otherwise moved beyond the nods, sighs and dinner-time debates of before. I had also lost touch with Anju and Long Nose.

One evening as we walked back after dinner, he informed me that he was preparing to go on long leave.

'My mother seems to be very excited. She wants me to finalize everything quickly,' he said.

'Finalize...?' I said. 'Finalize what?'

'Hey!' he said, beaming. 'I'm getting married, Deepa.'

'Ma...arried?' I asked disbelievingly. 'Oh... congratulations!' I then added lamely, trying not to look aghast. His eyes were on me as I forced my lips into a smile. I was now convinced that I was a marital lucky charm for everyone but myself.

'I'll be going on leave next week,' he said.

'That's good news,' I said, trying to put on a happy face even as I thought to myself, how could he do this to me? Are all men just the same? Roam around with someone and marry someone of their mother's choice? Maybe I shouldn't have ridden his bike or played the guitar or travelled with him or stuck around him. Maybe... I should have... I should have, what? Shut up, I told myself.

'You think so?' he asked brightly.

'What? Yeah, yeah, of course, it's great news.'

'But I don't even know the girl. We'll be strangers.'

'Everything becomes alright after marriage. At least, that's what I've heard,' I said, pseudo-assuring him.

'Well, I just wanted to know your opinion. Now if you think it's a good idea, I think I must go ahead. I was a little reluctant all this while.'

'What's her name?'

'Rebecca,' he said and gave me another killer smile.

But Captain Joseph couldn't go on leave, because another, much larger emergency came up.

20

Conflicts

'TWO INFANTRY BRIGADES TO BE MOBILIZED AND deployed with immediate effect...' stated the letter from the Corps headquarter. It then went on to give details of the deployment. Our unit was to immediately mobilize on the western border: the Kargil conflict had taken everyone by surprise. A flurry of activities began as stores were loaded in Shaktimans. Many leave requests were cancelled. Captain Joseph's was also among those.

The computer wing suddenly found itself very busy when issues of stores had to be carried out even at nights. 'How are we going to issue stores in the field?' the CO asked me, sparing time for me in the midst of phone calls and those waiting to meet him.

'Sir, we'll take our computers.'

'Will it be safe running them on generators?'

'Yes, sir.'

'Are you sure?' he said, looking jittery. 'You must understand that all units will depend on these computers.'

'Sir, I found out from the signals regiment. The last time they ran their computers on generators at the ex-location.'

'Yeah, but they also had problems due to that. Now I want you to understand that even if one of our computers stops functioning, it can create chaos. I hope you get my point.' He pursed his lips and looked at me. 'Anyway, find out again and let me know the feasibility. I don't want a situation where there's an emergency and we can't issue stores. I will hold you entirely responsible.'

Colonel Mishra's slight disappointment in me was a result of him finding out that I was not as malleable as he had thought. But his technophobia usually prevented him from meddling with my work.

'Right, sir,' I said. 'I will get back to you.'

'And also let me know if the thing can withstand heat? There will be no AC or anything there. And it's May.'

'Sir, I will get back to you with all these details.'

Just as I was about to leave, Major Tomar stormed in. 'Sir, the stores to 8 Kumaon cannot be issued. There is no electricity.'

'Has nothing been issued?' Colonel Mishra asked.

'Only about 50% has been issued, sir,' Major Tomar said.

'Okay,' Colonel Mishra took a moment before giving his decision. 'Get the computers working on the generators.' He turned to me. 'It will also be a trial run. Report back to me after that,'

'Sir,' I said and left.

The trial run was successful despite Major Tomar's forecasts of failure. After finding out from the other units, I also convinced the Commanding Officer that we would be able to run the computers successfully in the field location.

Convoy after convoy left for the field location in a matter of days. Once again tents were pitched and a whole unit began to rise from the bare ground. Team spirit showed in every activity, right from pitching tents and setting up each wing, to digging trenches and pits. Everyone helped each other. Suddenly in the face of a common enemy, the esprit de corps had come to the fore. The tent for the computer wing under my direction was pitched near a lone khejri tree for the iota of shade it could provide. Tents were strategically located and then covered with camouflage nets so that an aerial survey would make it impossible to identify it as a fully functional unit.

Days, especially afternoons were unbearably hot as the sand heated up. Sitting in my tent felt like being in a sauna, with sweat trickling down my temples and cheeks. The office tent was a tad better, but I was constantly worried about the computers packing up. The best place among all was the officers' mess tent, since it had a pedestal fan that ran on the generator.

'There's a serious situation,' Colonel Mishra said, as we gathered in the mess for lunch. 'NH 1 is cut off.'

'Oh! That's very bad news,' Major Tomar said, dal dripping from the piece of chapatti that was now held forgotten in his hand. 'That's our only supply route.'

Colonel Mishra nodded gravely. 'Now capturing those strategic peaks is the only solution.'

The senior lot discussed the gravity of the situation and the possible ways it could be tackled. As for me, not being familiar with the terrain, the names of places and high-altitude war strategies, most of the discussion would have gone right over my head if Captain Joseph hadn't explained it all to me later: 'It's the narrow road that connects Srinagar to Leh. It's a strategic point, the highest motorable road in the Drass sector. It's like they are holding our throat.' Having served in Leh, Captain Joseph had a clear understanding of all the developments and all that Colonel Mishra discussed with the others. 'Very tough conditions to live in even during normal times. High altitude, biting cold, difficult access,' he said, 'and war... it's one the toughest terrains on earth to fight a war.'

'Bofors guns are too huge to find a place there,' Colonel Mishra said at breakfast the next day, 'although they are very effective.'

Major Tomar wiped his moustache clean of bread crumbs. 'Good, sir, finally the army is in action,' he said with a grin and twirled his moustache.

'Is war anything to be happy about, Tomar?' Colonel Mishra said. 'Have you thought about what a war can do to a nation's psyche?' The yogi in him had taken over.

'But isn't that what the army is meant to do, sir? To fight the enemies and defend the nation,' Major Tomar said, simultaneously looking at his aides for approving nods. He did receive some.

'Sir, any casualties reported?' asked Captain Joseph.

'Didn't we start off with casualties?' Colonel Mishra said. 'The recce party disappeared. And there are bound to be many casualties since strategic points have to be reclaimed.'

That put everyone in a pensive mood. The usual jokes, gossip and light-hearted banter had disappeared from the mess anyway.

'We lost one of our officers, a JCO and four jawans,' Colonel Mishra said. 'Their vehicle came under heavy mortar fire.'

'But, sir, how could they use that route?' asked Captain Joseph.

'This happened about a week back, on one of the routine trips. But we received the news late.'

The news of the deaths had brought on a pall of gloom.

'Sir, who was this officer?' asked Captain Amit Joseph, perhaps wondering if the deceased could be one of his course mates.

'I think it was one... Captain Sandeep Singh.'

'Sir, Captain Sandeep Singh?' I asked, suddenly sitting up.

'Yes, you know him?'

'I know one Captain Sandeep Singh who was in Bengdubi. This may not be him,' I said quickly.

Everyone was silent.

'The ill-fated officer was posted in Udhampur,' Colonel Mishra continued, 'and was on Temporary Duty to Leh.'

'Sir, posted in Udhampur?'

'That's what I heard,' Colonel Mishra said. 'And yes, he was in Bengdubi before this. A youngster, not married... parents settled in Indore...'

My heart sank. I suddenly felt unwell, nauseous. The sweet orange juice I had been sipping till now suddenly turned metallic in my mouth. I excused myself and went to my tent.

Long Nose, dead? I couldn't believe it. His face appeared clearly before my eyes. His smile, his eyes, his long nose! The first handshake, the drinking sessions, and most of all, his terrible jokes.

I stretched in bed and relived my past, in my first unit, with the subaltern who was there for me when everyone turned their backs, someone who was a very special friend.

The tent flap was lifted and Captain Joseph came in, gently enquiring if I was alright, but I asked to be left alone. He left quietly.

A strange restlessness and anxiety took over me as I thought about Long Nose. I walked out and looked at the starry night sky. The stars shone bright as they always did. Nothing had changed. Or perhaps something had. I felt a void in my heart. How soon he had reached there... a young, energetic man, who didn't stay long enough to see all that the earth had to offer. Was he, as they said, a star now? Was he looking down? Could he see me?

'Hey Dips, what's this long face for?' I suddenly heard him say. 'Bad I couldn't see you again. I was planning to meet you soon. And I am also cross with you. You never replied to my letter?'

I got up and looked around. The desert winds whistled into my tent and the hurricane lamp flickered dimly in the darkness. There was no one there.

The very next day, I wrote him a letter:

Dear sir,

I am really sorry about the delay. It's not that I didn't want to write, but I am at the ex-location and there were a lot of preparations to be done before moving.

I know that you are not amidst us, that you have gone so far that my letter may not reach you. And you went away so suddenly that I feel cheated. But I know it was not up to you to decide, since if you could, you would never have left.

You were and always will be a very special friend. You were someone who stood by me at a stage in my life when I had no one to turn to, when I felt alone and needed someone to make me feel good about my life and my choices. In fact, sometimes I felt you were more than a friend. Maybe if you had stayed, things would have been different. I knew when you embraced me at your farewell party, it was not merely a friend saying goodbye. Sometimes, although we can read minds, we end up waiting for the words.

I thought we would certainly meet, sometime, somewhere... like you said. I don't know how we would have started off where we left. So much has changed. All I know is that I would be very happy. I would certainly have a drink with you and prod you on for a joke. I smile even at the thought.

I am sorry I never told you the nickname we had kept for you. I thought I would tell you whenever we met. It was Long Nose. I know it's not a great name, a little childish too, but it kind of stuck between Anju and me though I learnt later that there was much more to you than just a long nose.

Wherever you are, I hope you are fine. Thanks for being there always, for being my friend. I send my best smile for that wonderful person.

Be happy happy.

Lots of love,

Dips

I smiled between the tears, stuck the envelope and posted it promptly the next day. And felt much better.

But in the next few days, I sank more and more into my grief. Captain Joseph continued to drop in even though most of the times I was quiet. Sometimes, he did nothing but join in my silence. Other times he would remind me, 'As soldiers, as personnel serving in the army we must reconcile to the fact that death walks always by our side.'

One evening, he sat down for longer than usual outside my tent with me. After several minutes of silence, during which I stared at the sky, he spoke up. 'I have seen death from close. When my father died, I didn't even understand what death meant or why everyone looked morose. It took my mother three months to recover from the shock, but when she did, she carried on like nothing happened. It was surprising. "We have to move on," she said. "Your father wouldn't like it if he were to know that I spent the rest of my life shedding tears for him. He would want all of us to be cheerful, smiling and happy."' There was a pause. Then he put his hand gently on mine and said, 'Don't you agree, Deepa?'

I turned to look at him, and nodded slowly.

'Was he the one who wrote to you often?'

'Yes.'

'Was he a good friend?'

'Yes...'

Then I began to tell him all about Long Nose, and all my memories poured out of me. Captain Joseph listened keenly.

'I think he... liked you,' he finally said. 'From whatever you've told me, I can see everything from a guy's point of view. He was a gentleman, which is why he thought and thought about whether to tell you... but never could. He thought maybe if you didn't like it, he would lose a good friend.'

'How do you know that?'

'Some guys are like that.'

*

For about a week, I hadn't involved myself fully in the office work. And things had begun to go wrong.

One of my staff members used a virus-infected floppy and corrupted the main software. It was also at this precise time that the other standby computer chose to hang. A wave of panic broke out.

'What exactly is happening in the computer wing?' Colonel Mishra said. 'Can you please update me?'

'Sir, one system has a virus and the other is hung.'

He looked sternly at me. 'Does that mean that both are non-ops?'

'Sir.'

'Captain Shekhar, how could you let this happen? Our work is stalled. What answer am I going to give to the GOC?'

'Sir, it's not such a big problem. By tonight, everything will be back to normal.'

'It better be.' He whacked the tip of his pen on the table.

After a slack period, it was action time. The software was reinstalled but a part of the stored data was corrupt in both the computers. To update that, I sat with my staff through one whole night and day.

'Isn't the work over?' Colonel Mishra said, his panic threatening to consume him. 'It was so bad and you said it's not a big problem. Can a problem get bigger than this?'

'Sir, by tomorrow morning everything will be in order.'

'I wasn't expecting these kinds of problems to come with you around,' he said. 'Whatever it is, virus, bacteria, bugs or whatever, tell them to stay away.'

*

By next day morning the computer wing began to function normally again. Colonel Mishra on hearing this news let a loud sigh of relief. In his eyes, I was the ringmaster who had tamed the beasts.

That evening after the office staff left, I was browsing through an important file on the computer and making corrections, when Captain Joseph stormed in and banged hard at my table. Before I knew it, the foldable table wobbled and threatened to offload everything. I clung to the monitor, while simultaneously steadying the table with my leg. The keyboard however, couldn't be saved, and dived down with a clatter.

'Just what's wrong? Sir!' I fumed, turning to him. 'I tidied everything today.'

'I'm sorry,' he said and clung to me, teary-eyed. 'Sorry.'

I patted him gently as his body shook in my arms. A few moments passed. Then he rubbed his eyes and settled in a chair. I sat beside him. 'Are you okay?' I asked softly.

'Remember that chap I used to talk about... my buddy, the boxing champion?'

I nodded.

'He died a martyr. Can you believe it... my dost, my buddy... the bloody chap is gone forever!' He banged at the armrest and covered his face with his hand.

'I'm really sorry to hear that,' I said.

'What bloody sorry?' he yelled, looking at me. 'Was this his age to die? It's unjust! I won't accept it.' From a man usually dignified and reserved, this emotional outburst was an extreme reaction. 'Young people who have not really got a taste of their own lives have disappeared. Why? You know, this chap was his parents' only child? Can you imagine what his parents must be going through? Can you?'

I stroked his hand and listened quietly even as he shouted, sometimes abuses, and cried. Then he became calm.

I took his hand in mine and said, 'We must be brave to face any consequences. Anything. That's what makes us soldiers. Didn't you say that?'

Weeks went by and news of many more deaths began to pour in. Someone or the other from the unit knew some of the deceased. The gloomy atmosphere was depressing and news of death got numbing.

'Do you think the war will escalate to these borders?' Captain Joseph asked, as we walked up the hillock near our unit one evening.

'I don't know. But, if it comes, we will fight... like those brave men.'

'Do you plan to continue in the army?'

'Yes. Why?'

'Oh, nothing,' he said.

We sat on the slope. He aimed pebbles at a prominent jutting stone a little distance away. I watched him for some time. Then I collected some pebbles and began to aim at the same stone. He stopped aiming, looked at me and smiled.

'What does the army give you?' he asked.

'Everything it gives you.'

'But do you want to be here for long?'

'Yes.' I stopped throwing the pebbles and looked at him. 'Why are you asking me these questions? You never talked like this before.'

'Maybe I never felt like this before.'

A gust of wind loosened a few strands of my hair. It covered my eye and tickled my nose. It felt fresh, invigorating. And it suddenly felt good and grateful to be alive. I got up and clambered to the summit. Stretching out my arms, I felt the wind rush against my skin. 'Wow... It feels so good,' I said.

'Sit down,' he said. 'You can't do all this. We are in a war zone.'

Suddenly, there was a loud noise. Captain Joseph pulled me down in a jiffy, and we lay flat on the slope. A commotion ensued from below and I saw that one of the supporting bamboos of the officers' mess tent had collapsed in the wind, hitting the camp chairs. Stewards and cooks scampered out. Everyone gathered and tried to push the bamboo pole back in place. To my surprise, I found that Captain Joseph hadn't been looking at the scene below, but at me. I was suddenly conscious of his intense gaze, that held me captive. I felt my heart race and my breath quicken. We were lost in each other, when suddenly there was another loud noise – perhaps the pole fell again – and we snapped out of the magic moment.

'Sorry, I overreacted,' he said, as we sat up. 'Actually I don't know what's wrong with me. I am behaving a bit strangely.'

'Everyone is.'

'And I want to do things I didn't dare before.'

'Like what?'

He looked away and then turned to me. 'Like... talking to the yogi.'

'About what?'

'About... um, my marriage.' He picked up a pebble and threw it down the hill.

'Oh! But you may not get leave now. I don't think... anyway, what's news from Rebecca?'

'Who Rebecca?' he said, as if caught in the wrong moment. 'Oh my God, you even remember that name.'

'Yeah, you told me,' I said. 'Your mother must be eagerly waiting for you to approve. Or would she go ahead without your approval?'

'Actually, Rebecca...'

'Rebecca is such a nice name,' I said. 'I am sure she must be a demure, homely, comely sort of a girl. After all, your mother has chosen her for you.'

'That sounds so boring.'

'That's surprising,' I said. 'Then what kind of girls do you like?' For some reason I was feeling a little angry. 'Oh, that's none of my business.'

'No, no, wait. I'll tell you.' He stopped throwing the pebbles and looked at me, deep into my eyes, before saying, 'I like someone who is not afraid to be herself, who has a mind of her own. Someone who is a very good friend and who is passionate about everything she does.' He kept looking at me.

'Do you mean the kind... who likes adventure, travel...?'

'Yeah, someone with a footloose spirit.'

'And sometimes... rides bikes, plays the guitar?'

'Yeah,' he said and smiled.

'And wears lounge suit/combination?'

He laughed and nodded.

'Really?'

'Really.'

'But you know what? Such kinds usually don't know much about cooking, cleaning and all that stuff.'

'That's no worry. We'll learn it together.'

'And Rebecca?' I said.

'Rebecca was a lie. I lied to you.'

Our eyes locked. Then we looked away and sat in the quiet. The wind had made a mess of my hair.

'It's surprising how sometimes war brings people closer,' he said. 'And it also teaches lessons.'

'Hmm,' I said, thinking about Long Nose.

We sat quietly for some more time.

'But there's a problem,' I said. 'How do you measure this? It's a feeling, remember? It's not tangible, it can't be measured. '

He smiled and looked at me. 'I was wrong about so many things.'

'What? Joseph? A Christian boy? Have you ever heard anyone in our family getting married to a Christian. These inter-caste marriages don't work out.'

'But, Ma, he's a good man...'

'My first mistake was letting you join the army of all places. Now, don't come up with these impossible things. I can never accept him as my son-in law...'

I closed my eyes and listened. I had gone to the nearest town to call home as usual. I didn't intend to tell them about any of the new developments, although I wanted to share it with them. I knew they would have their reservations.

'I hope you are fine.' Mother sounded anxious as always. 'We are worried about you. Every day we see in the news about war and death. Is it affecting you also?'

'This sector is peaceful, Ma. I am perfectly fine. There's no problem at all.'

'You are sounding happy today. Is there anything?' Mothers have a sixth sense, I'm convinced.

'No, Ma, I am not happy or anything... I mean, yes, I am happy, like always.'

'No, there's more, tell me.'

I couldn't hold it in any longer, so I told her in brief. And she wasn't too happy.

Pa didn't approve either. 'Different religions, cultures... it will all be very complicated.'

When I told Captain Joseph about this development, he said his mother was upset too. 'Her first grudge is that you are a Hindu,' he said. 'I know I can convince her on that account since some of our distant relatives have married out of our community. But her main problem is... well... she says she can't accept a bride in army uniform.' Then he added quickly, 'I am sorry. It's her opinion.'

With opposition from both sides, our future together looked bleak, unless we were ready to disregard our parents and carry on our way. I couldn't think of earning my parent's wrath once again. As for Captain Joseph, I had figured, he loved and respected his mother too much to hurt her.

Meanwhile, predicting an imminent war, Colonel Mishra often gave us his expert views. 'The Indian army has captured a strategic point, Pt 4590,' he said at dinner one day. 'It is a very important development.'

The senior lot discussed how the move was going to affect the course of the conflict. Junior officers listened. Captain Joseph and I sat through these sessions preoccupied in our own thoughts. Although we were part of a larger war, we fought battles within ourselves.

We did walk up to the hillock sometimes, but hardly talked. He looked at the horizon while his hands fiddled with the pebbles. I drew patterns on the sand, then erased them and drew some more. Sometimes I wrote my name, sometimes his, sometimes ours together and then in one sweep, erased everything.

'Is there no solution?' he asked.

'I can't think of any.'

'It's awful that we can't decide our own future.'

I didn't look at him.

'After all what's life all about? The only certainty is death. Haven't we seen it with all those guys? So the few days that we are here, can't we be happy?'

'It depends at what cost we want the happiness. We are bound by so many things, relations, religion, ideas, everything.'

Our rants got us nowhere. He did try convincing his mother, but she refused downright. He talked to his sister, but even she requested him not to do anything that would break their mother's heart. As for me, I never tried convincing anyone. I knew there was no point. For a couple of days, I didn't even call up home. Then one day when I thought I had had a long interval, I called.

'You are our only child and sometimes I feel you take advantage of it,' said my mother. 'We thought a lot about what you said.'

'Ma, I am not going ahead with this. So why do you worry?'

'You are 28 now. Time is running out,' she said sombrely. 'Tell me, do you think he's the right man for you?'

'How does it matter, Ma?'

'Answer me.'

'Yes, I think, I mean I thought so...'

'You think you will be able to live happily with him despite the differences in your religion and culture?'

'Yeah, I did think, but...'

'Then we stand by you.'

'But Ma...'

'For once be obedient and do what we say. Whatever anyone says, we have decided to accept him in our family.'

I heard her whisper, 'Ah, finally!'

21

The Return of Anju

EVER SINCE CAPTAIN JOSEPH REALIZED THAT THINGS were not going his way, he expressed his resentment more often. To add to this, Colonel Mishra had given him a thorough dressing down.

'Yogi says he's not happy with my performance, that my command and control are "piss poor",' he said as we walked back from the office tent.

'He said that?' I gave him a sideways glance. 'But I never found you lacking.'

'Don't we know why?' he said, kicking a stone like he were shooting a goal. The stone took off and landed in a cluster of grass nearby.

'Yeah, maybe that's why he's sending me to Jodhpur to collect the stores,' I said. 'Where a JCO would have sufficed, he's sending me. Now I have to go bumping in a Shaktiman.'

'Despite all these problems you still want to serve?'

'What have these problems to do with my serving? Even you face problems, but quitting is not the first thing that comes to your mind. Is it? We are fighters, not quitters.'

'But isn't it irritating when you have to serve under individuals whom you just cannot respect?'

'Yeah, it is, but then such individuals are everywhere. Moreover, we need to look at the larger cause of the organization, not the individuals.'

"But dealing with such people on a day-to-day basis can get exhausting. Isn't it? Tell me, aren't you tired of fighting and proving yourself? I mean now, you have an easy way out.' We came to a halt outside my tent. He stood with his feet slightly apart and spoke softly, looking into my eyes. 'See, now you have a choice since you have finished your contractual period. You can quit anytime.' He paused to study my face. 'At least then we can be together. I think this is our only solution.'

I looked into his eyes, but said nothing.

'Moreover,' he continued, 'even if we look at our future, I don't think this kind of a career for you will suit our family life. Don't you think it will be difficult? Your transfer, my transfer, temporary duties, night duties, uncertainties?'

'Maybe you are right,' I said, after a moment of thought. 'But I still need some time to think about this.'

'I think I am morally wrong in suggesting this, but I don't see any other solution.' He looked deep into my eyes. 'But you are too precious. I don't want to lose you.'

I was on my way to Jodhpur. I had learnt from past experiences that when travelling in a Shaktiman, it was essential to be attired for the drive. The most important piece of clothing was the bra, since otherwise I knew I would end up aching in a place I couldn't even casually massage.

Sitting beside the driver, I looked out at the arid landscape. Hot air blew into my face nearly scorching my eyes. An occasional riot of colour in the form of village women carrying water on their heads was a welcome relief. With their bright swirling ghaghras and big chunks of jewellery, they walked in a file by the roadside. The driver, on spotting this sight, slowed down to let his eyes linger on their shapely backs. Then he slowed down further to ogle some more. I was sure that if I weren't seated beside him, he would most certainly have stopped to ask them for water and drink directly from their pitchers.

Reluctantly, he drove on and crossed them. Then he craned his neck to catch a glimpse of the veiled beauties in the rear-view mirror. That didn't seem to satisfy him either. So he stuck his head out of the window and looked back – while driving forward.

'Should I drive?' I asked him.

'No, sahab,' he pulled his neck in like a turtle. From then on, he more or less looked straight ahead.

We drove past jeeps, camel carts and an occasional truck or bus. I had fleeting views of little children bursting with energy, and of turbaned weather-worn faces. But the only face that came back again and again, was Captain Joseph's. Anywhere I looked, I saw him, his dark eyes, shapely lips, boyish mop of hair, his smile. For this man, I was ready to do anything – even hang up my uniform.

Or was I?

I wasn't sure. Didn't I even have a row with my own parents to be able to wear it? So, should I? How would it feel? What was it that my uniform gave me? Why did I feel so passionate about it? Wasn't he being practical as always, when he said that my career in the army could come in the way of our family life? Wasn't he right? Was I wrong then?

'Sahab, unit,' said the driver.

By the time we reached our destination, my head was spinning. I couldn't find any answers to all the questions whirling in my head. I didn't know what course to take.

I was to stay for the night at the officers' mess. Stores could be issued only the next day. After the officers mess tent I was used to in the exercise location, this mess with its gardens and illumination looked like a palace.

As I walked in, I saw a smart young lady with short hair in a blue salwar-kameez talking to what looked like another young officer. Her back was towards me. But, from the way she stood, bending her torso forward and moving her hands vigorously in the air, I assumed she was in an aggressive mood.

'How can you bloody address me by my name when I am senior to you? Huh...' she said to the officer. He said something back, but I couldn't hear.

Her voice sounded familiar. Surely...? But Anju couldn't have said anything like that, I reminded myself. Moreover, Anju was far plumper. I waited a few seconds to catch a glimpse of the lady, but she didn't turn. I went into the officers' mess and walked up to the bar counter to get myself some juice. Suddenly, the lady I had seen outside walked in. I left my drink on the table and hurried to her.

'Anju!' I could barely contain my astonishment.

'Dips?' she yelled.

Before we knew it, we were entwined in an embrace. Curious eyes were on us. We then moved to a sofa at the far end.

'You have really changed,' I said. 'I couldn't recognize you.'

'Really?'

'Yeah, so much! My goodness!'

'What a surprise,' she said. 'What are you doing here?'

'Temporary duty from the ex-location. And you?'

'Me too, TD, from Delhi.'

We looked at each other, our expressions changing from astonishment to happiness to disbelief. 'Just a moment,' Anju then left me for a few minutes and went to each one of the officers she knew, wishing them and exchanging pleasantries. Most of them were glued to the TV, catching live coverage of Kargil. I got up, got my drink from where I had left it and updated myself on the war front. Reporters spoke animatedly about the latest developments from ground zero.

Anju joined me after the reportage with a mango juice and we settled back at the same corner. 'Now no one can complain,' she said, giving me a naughty wink. 'Their egos need to be fed.' She then placed her glass on the table and leant back. 'So, it's our time. We have so much to catch up with.'

'Yeah.' I placed my glass on the table beside hers and leant back. 'Are you off drinking these days?'

'Not exactly. I drink when I know the people around me well enough. Otherwise, I don't... like here, no way.' She looked around and then turned her torso towards me. 'You know why? The first thing men think is that you are fast and an easy lay. That has been my experience. And that's the reason I stopped smoking too.'

'Smoking? When was this?' I asked, surprised.

'It's just that phase, Dips, when you are trying to make a statement, trying to show that you are different and all that... but now I think I have stabilized.' She leant forward, sipped her drink and placed the glass back. 'I think I have learnt how to be taken seriously.'

'I guess that's what happened outside?' I said. 'I was impressed.'

She laughed. 'The chap, he's a lieutenant and he behaves like he's a bloody senior. If we can respect our seniors, why can't they? But no, they won't. Why? Because we are lady officers. So, they show their doubts. The first thing they try is to impress you.'

'You have changed a lot,' I said, my eyes fixed on her face, which shone with confidence. Her eyes had a streak of determination I had never seen before. She looked like a fierier version of her old self. When she looked around at men, there was no more the I-need-your-protection look. This new look sent a message right across the room, I-can-take-care-of-myself-thank-you-very-much.

'Don't we all change?' she said. 'Don't all the things we go through change something about our thinking, perception, outlook... everything?'

She sighed and waved to the steward to bring the snacks. 'By the way, you have changed too.'

'Me?' I smiled. 'Like what?'

'I think you have mellowed down. At least you look like that to me. You look comfortable in your skin'

'Wasn't I before?'

'Earlier you were constantly trying to put on an act: I am strong, I am like a man, I am better than a man and all that stuff. But now, you look like a strong and confident woman, comfortable with her femininity. There's a lot of difference.' She pointed to my maroon salwar-kameez and my hair tied in a chignon. 'I guess you have finally accepted yourself as a woman with her own limitations and strengths. You have probably realized that you don't have to always come across as physically strong. All you need to be is strong from the inside.'

These sage words coming from Anju's mouth seemed unbelievable. She looked like she had had a complete personality overhaul.

I nodded. 'Maybe you are right. I guess we learn from people we meet along the way.' Even as I said this, I thought of the numerous people I had met and how each one had influenced my life at some point. Many faces danced before my eyes, but one face immediately shone out, a smiling, self-assured face with those deep dark eyes.

'And I am not the ultra-feminine bimbette I used to be,' she said. As she smiled, her dimples deepened. 'It doesn't work at all. People don't take you seriously then. Actually, we need to walk the tightrope. We need to maintain the right balance, not too feminine, but assertive and firm.'

I didn't speak, just continued looking with wide-eyed wonder at her.

'Surprised, na?' she said.

'So, have you sent in your papers?' I said.

'Yeah, I am continuing. And you?'

'I don't know.'

'What?' she said. '*You* don't know?'

'Yeah, I am confused.'

'What confusion?'

'I'll tell you about it,' I said as the steward walked up and informed us that dinner was served.

Post dinner, we went to her room. A middle-aged woman in a floral printed salwar-kameez, who looked like a domestic help, greeted us.

'Ratna accompanies me everywhere,' Anju said as I walked in. Her room was air-conditioned, well-furnished and had a faint fragrance of perfume. I thought about my tent which usually smelt of stale sweat and urine.

'She's the one who takes care of Piya,' Anju said, as I smiled at the lady.

'Is Piya here?' I said in disbelief. 'Where is she?'

'She must've slept.' Anju opened the bedroom door gently, walked up and kneeled before the bed, stroking little Piya's forehead.

I kneeled beside Anju. 'She's such a pretty child,' I said. 'So good to see her. She must be what, about four now?'

'Yeah,' Anju said and got up to sit on the chair, simultaneously instructing Ratna to sleep in the other room.

'But why did you get her along?' I said, getting up and sitting at the edge of the bed. 'Shouldn't she have stayed back at home?'

'Which home?'

'Your home. Major Bhat's and yours.'

'We don't live together anymore,' she said. She looked at me, through me and then finally at the ceiling.

I didn't know how to react to this piece of news. 'But I thought... I mean...'

'We're heading for divorce,' she said, with an unfeeling voice, as though what she said didn't affect her one bit. She looked at Piya and then at me. 'You know, you were right at that time. I was a fool!' she said shaking her head. 'For him, I disobeyed my parents. Now I don't have their support, nor do I have him.'

I didn't say anything, just looked on at her face and the fleeting expressions. She got up and sat beside Piya on the bed, facing me.

'I was naïve,' she said. 'I was so blinded by love that I couldn't think at all. Although you told me I didn't think much about what I was doing with my life. Slowly things began to fall apart. It was all so gradual that I didn't realize what we were coming to. Remember you had said how could a person who loves himself so much love anyone else?'

I nodded although I didn't quite remember having said anything like that. 'You were right again,' she said. 'He has a huge ego and after marriage I began to feel like a duffer most of the times. He would disregard my opinions and suggestions. In fact, I didn't mind being pushed into the second place, but then I didn't like to be walked over always. I couldn't bear to be treated like that.' She perched both her feet on the bed. 'And I didn't like being forced into domesticity. See, it's different when you do it out of choice, but when someone forces something on you, it doesn't feel nice. You feel that there's absolutely no respect for you as an individual.' Tears had welled up in her eyes and were on the verge of rolling down. Hidden beneath a façade of confidence and self-assurance I had found my old friend.

'Anju...' I said.

'And then there was no transparency in our relationship,' she continued. 'He didn't confide in me.' The tears rolled down her cheeks. I leant forward and put my hand on her shoulder.

'I love Piya so much,' she said. 'And she's the one who gives me the strength to carry on. When she grows up, she must see her mother as a strong and independent woman.' She wiped her tears and paused for a moment. 'Sometimes I regret not listening to you. You knew from the start that he was not the guy for me.'

'No, you should not regret anything,' I said, 'because whenever we do something at any point, it feels like the right thing to do. We can't change the past, so let it be. Use your energy for your future, for Piya.'

She nodded and then after a while, wiped her tears. 'I am so happy I could talk to you,' she said, as she got up and poured herself some water. 'I feel really good, like I just had some health tonic.' Her wet cheeks glistened in the light. 'Look at us,' she said. 'Who would ever believe till some time back that we could sit and talk about such serious things?'

I nodded and we sat in silence for some time. Little Piya turned over in her sleep. Anju propped the pillows once again and gave her a peck on her forehead, before sitting beside her.

'That was my long story,' she said, her fingers running through Piya's long, curly hair. 'Now tell me about you. Why are you confused?'

I didn't say anything.

'Okay, let me guess,' she said, 'there's a guy.'

I smiled.

'That's great. Wow!' she said. 'Okay, then?'

'His name is Captain Amit Joseph.'

Anju repeated the name.

'My parents were initially opposed because of his religion,' I continued. 'But finally when they came around, I get to know that his mother has issues about her son marrying a woman in army uniform.'

'So... he wants you to quit?' she said after a thought.

'Hmm.'

'See, when you are in love, you are blind and your brain doesn't function too well, which means you are bound to make stupid decisions. I know it too well.'

'So help me.'

'Is quitting the only solution?'

'Yeah, we tried to think of every other thing.'

'Do you want to quit? I mean if this pressure wasn't there?'

'Um, no, I don't think so.'

'Then you shouldn't,' she said with conviction. 'Firstly I think it is very selfish on his part to make such a demand. How can he?' She paused for a moment. 'And how is this guy otherwise?'

'He's a good chap, polished, well-read, good company and everything. And most of all, he's a good friend.'

'Then how can he talk like that? Can't he consider what your wish is?'

'Actually I never told him anything yet. When I get back, I am supposed to tell him. What should I tell him?'

Anju looked thoughtful, but her silence made it clear that she didn't know what advice to give me. I closed my eyes and took a deep breath, as some quiet moments passed between us.

'I don't want to lose this guy,' I said. 'He means a lot to me. And I may never find someone like him. He's way too different, a gem.'

'I understand,' she said. 'When you are in love, this is what happens. You find everything perfect about the guy. But from whatever you said, I get a feeling that he'll turn out to be a mama's boy. You know the kinds who go, "Mama, can I do this, do that, please tell me..."'

'I don't think so,' I said, interrupting her mimicking.

'So then, if he likes a girl in uniform and he's ready

to spend his life with her, why is he so worried about what his mother will say? Tell her to go hop.'

'It doesn't work like that, Anju. He respects his mother too much. She single-handedly brought them up. So his mother means a lot to him.'

'Okay, this doesn't seem to be getting anywhere,' she said, readjusting her position to face me. 'Just answer the questions I am going to ask you, as honestly as you can. Everything will be clear. Why don't you want to quit?'

'Because I like my uniform.'

'Why?'

I thought for a while. 'Because... when I wear it and look at myself in the mirror, I like what I see. It makes me feel smart, confident, in control... It gives me my identity.'

'Now would you want to trade all that for anything or anyone?'

'Not anything or anyone, but for Amit, I don't know...'

'The thing is, even if you do that, you would have made a compromise, your very first compromise even before marriage. And with this will begin your string of compromises that will go on throughout your life. He will keep telling you, my mother wants you to do this, do that and the like. Would you then do it, even if you didn't want to? Think about it.'

'I am very confused,' I said and closed my eyes.

'I'm not,' she said. 'Let me tell you, the one thing that I have learnt by being married and living with a man is that whatever everyone says about two becoming one and all that, is just nonsense. With all my romance books that's what I had come to believe and even in the initial years I continued with that belief. It's only later that I realized that it's actually two individuals with their own unique backgrounds, mindsets, interests, dreams and aspirations, constantly trying to adjust with each other. If it's a healthy relationship, they have respect and consideration for each other, but if it's not, as women we keep adjusting. I have done that enough and I know.'

I was quiet.

'But now I am in the driver's seat,' she continued. 'Yeah, sometimes, I feel lonely, but overall, it feels good. You know, Dips, I am a fighter now. I don't give up. I make my way and move on. Remember, how in the academy, they pushed us to our limits of endurance, when we thought we just couldn't do it, but still did it and were surprised at ourselves?' She shook her head. 'That's the way I am now. And now, I like being here.'

'Great! So, now you are OG to the core?' I smiled.

'I don't have an OG panty yet,' she chuckled, 'but yeah, I am OG now. And I love it... when I stand out in a crowd and when people look at me with awe in their eyes.' She paused for a moment. 'You know I have also picked up new things, I play tennis, improved my horse-riding skills and even play golf. I have loads of fun re-discovering myself.'

'Wow! That sounds great, but not better than driving a tank,' I said.

'Hey! That sounds just so much like you. I know you love being here. So, then, the choice ahead is tough.'

'Hmm,' I said, looking at little Piya. In her sleep, she looked like an angel. 'She looks like you,' I said. 'Does she have your dimples also?'

'Yeah.'

I took little Piya's soft pink palm in mine. 'Now, the thing is,' I said looking up at Anju, 'sometimes, I also feel, I want an angel like her.'

Anju smiled and put a hand on mine. 'It's a very tough choice then,' she said. 'Only you can decide. I hope you decide wisely.

I nodded.

'Oh, by the way, wise reminds me,' she said, her sober tone giving way to the old girlish excitement, 'I got my wisdom tooth.'

'It shows,' I said.

She leant over and whacked my back.

On the drive back, the Shaktiman was loaded with stores and my head with a thousand conflicting thoughts. The question was not what I wanted, but what I wanted more. As the vehicle trundled across the sand-lined roads, I pondered over Anju's questions and tried to answer them. What did my uniform mean to me? I thought of all the moments I swelled with pride; when I took the oath in the academy to protect my land, when people anywhere trusted me wholeheartedly just because I owned an Olive Green pair, when a whole compartment of passengers came up and embraced me, when a remote desert village came together to extol our virtues, when I stood at the watch tower in Munabao and looked across.

There were countless moments when I felt a deep sense of satisfaction and pride in my uniform, for it represented courage and valour, blood and toil. It was not just a piece of clothing I wore, but the trust and expectations of an entire nation I embodied. I liked to feel its crispness against my skin. And when I wore it, I felt that I belonged to a much larger family which was not divided on petty grounds. I loved it, because like the people of my great land, I loved freedom.

Then I thought of Captain Joseph, his endearing smile, all the good times we had in the desert, streets, restaurants and tents, talking, baring our hearts and gradually growing on each other. A voice spoke loud and clear from within me, 'Nothing else matters more than this one person. He's the guy who loves you with all your quirks.'

From the tar road, the Shaktiman took a deviation into a dirt track, throwing up thick clouds of dust. Everything looked hazy. The vehicle stopped at the unit location in front of the storage tent.

Through the thin veil of dust, I saw Captain Joseph walking towards me.

She's a Jolly Good Fellow

THE LONG DRIVE BOTH WAYS IN THE SHAKTIMAN, WITH hardly any rest in between, had exhausted me. All I wanted to do was to get into my tent and hit the bed. But no sooner had I alighted than I found myself in the thick of commotion.

'Hope the drive was good,' Captain Joseph said.

'Not bad,' I said.

'Okay, now you need to rush to the yogi. He's been waiting for you.'

'Why? What happened?'

'One of your computers has crashed and he's getting jittery about it.'

'Oh, the old chap,' I said in exasperation. 'Whenever anything goes wrong with the computers, he gets so panicky, like the unit has been bombed or something.' I headed straight to the Commanding Officer's office tent.

'What's with these computers?' Colonel Mishra said, a nasty expression on his face. 'They never seem to give me any peace of mind. Do something and get them in order. And make it fast.'

Sometimes I thought Colonel Mishra spoke about the computers as though they were my babies. He assumed I knew everything about how they behaved.

The worst part was that he thought that my presence was imperative to nurse them back to health. Despite the presence of an engineer or technician, he insisted that I be present all along, like a restless mother waiting impatiently by her child's bedside.

Having called for some tea, I immediately got to work. I opened the CPU and blew out the dust, pushed the various components into their slots and fastened all connections. That was about all I knew about my baby. It still showed no signs of life. I had to call for an expert. It was then decided that the CPU be deposited in the EME workshop. Colonel Mishra ordered that I accompany the CPU all the way, which meant some more bumpy rides in the desert. When I returned empty-handed, he was not too happy.

'You should have put some pressure.'

'I did, sir,' I said. 'But they said they need time to replace the RAM. They have to procure it from Jodhpur.'

'Okay, let me also talk to the Officer-in-charge,' he said, and his tone mellowed down. 'You now have an additional responsibility to train someone to handle the computer wing.'

'Sir?' I said, wondering if that meant he wasn't happy with the job I did. Maybe I should tell him how the generator supply and the desert heat were beginning to take their toll on my babies.

'Don't worry,' he said, reading my worried expression. 'You have been doing a good job. But now you will be going on transfer.'

'Sir, transfer?'

'Yeah, you have been posted to Agra.'

'Sir?'

I was too exhausted for a better reaction. I didn't ask him who the Commanding Officer and the Second-in-Command were. Nor did I ask for any other information.

'So, I need to identify someone who can replace you,' he said, 'someone who is young and in sync with modern technology...'

He piled his worries on me, but I wasn't listening.

At dinner time, Captain Joseph broke another piece of news to me. 'I am going to Calcutta,' he said, 'on transfer.'

'What?'

'Things don't seem to be working in our favour,' he said on our way back to the tent. 'Isn't it a bad sign that we are going different ways?'

'I think...' I said. 'Can we please talk tomorrow? I really need to sleep.'

I crashed into my bed. The next day morning, two Commanding Officers from other units arrived and expressed their desire to see how our software was operated. After they saw a demonstration, one of them thumped my back. 'I must tell you, she's doing a great job,' he turned to Colonel Mishra. 'We hardly faced any teething problems when we switched over from the manual to computer systems. Everywhere else the transition hasn't been so smooth. That's what I hear.'

'Yeah, she's doing a great job,' Colonel Mishra looked at me. 'She knows her job well and handles everything without giving me much trouble.'

They nodded and smiled.

The day had started well, and it went well too.

'Very, very busy, eh?' Captain Joseph said when we met outside my tent, post dinner. 'And too much praise in one day.'

I smiled.

'So?' he asked, unfolding two camp chairs.

We then sat quietly for some time.

'So, where are we headed?' he said, finally. 'Did you think about it at all?'

'Lots,' I said.

'And...?' he scrutinized my face.

'I wish things were that easy to decide.'

'Do you mean... you mean... you don't want to quit?'

We looked at each other. His face had a dejected look.

'Please hear me out first,' I said. 'See, it was a big decision I took when I came here against my parents' wishes. So you can imagine, it means a lot to me. I mean... I like you a lot, it's not that. But I think I should not be forced to quit something I took up voluntarily and passionately... especially when I don't feel ready for it. I think it should be my decision when to quit. I must decide it myself... not because you are telling me to, not because anyone is telling me.' He sat attentively, albeit with an expressionless face. I couldn't figure out what he was thinking. 'I thought a lot about it,' I continued, 'even if I listen to you now and quit, somewhere deep inside I will hold a grudge against you. And I don't want our lives to start with a grudge.'

'I should have known,' he said, after a long pause. 'And please, I am not telling you to quit, it's the situation which has come up.'

'I know, but you must understand I have worked equally hard to be where I am and to let go of everything I earned when I don't feel ready for it, doesn't feel right. You have put me in such a dilemma, I feel drained.'

'I am sorry,' he said. 'I didn't mean to do that.'

'Please try to look at it from my point of view. Maybe you can then understand what I am trying to say. Five years down the line, I might think this was one my biggest blunders, but now it seems right.'

He didn't say anything. We sat silently, our faces downcast. I didn't like to see his face so morose. Maybe I should just tell him nothing was as important as him. Maybe that would make him feel better. It would make me feel better too. But didn't Anju have a point when she said my life would start on a compromise? And she was speaking from experience. I didn't want to make the same mistakes she had.

News from ground zero was coming in thick and fast, but it was all good now. Radio, telephones and personnel in uniform had only one story to tell, that of the victory of our troops at Kargil. Within the unit, there was relief and rejoicing. Everyone praised the brave soldiers who fought a difficult war and won. Chants of *'Bharat mata ki jai'* and *'Jai hind'* rang in the air. This victory gave me a sense of pride, despite my own feeling of unsettlement and bewilderment.

'It was a major offensive and this success gives us every reason to be proud of our brothers-in-arms,' Colonel Mishra said.

'And also of ourselves, sir,' Major Tomar added. 'We are also a part of the team.'

Everywhere, everyone discussed Kargil. Smiles and laughter replaced weary and anxious expressions on the jawans' faces. Discussions ensued regarding how the successful offensive was planned. In the officers' mess, everyone was at their thunderous best. Major Tomar laced his dinnertime talk with tactical jargon and spoke with such authority that had a civilian been privy to the discussions, he would have credited Major Tomar with the successful planning and execution of the entire operation.

A victory party was organized for all the units at the sand dunes. It was a night party which was lit only by campfires. Local folk singers sang soulful desert tunes, accompanied by their traditional instruments. The party saw some more animated discussions about the war and the victory. 'Kargil', 'Tiger Hill', 'Drass', 'Leh', 'martyrs' and 'victory' were words that were frequently heard in most of the conversations. The mood was upbeat as a large gathering of army men greeted each other and raised toasts, clambering over mounds of sand, under the starry sky. Some officers had come in from nearby stations. There was also a team of officers from Jodhpur, including Anju, who had decided to give me a surprise.

'Show me, where's your chap?' she whispered urgently.

'He's not my chap,' I said, adjusting the belt of my combat dress.

'You turned him down?'

'I don't know what I did.'

She studied my face in the flickering light of the campfire. 'You don't look happy.'

'How's Piya?' I said, changing the topic.

'Oh, she's fine. Ratna takes good care of her. And anyway I am getting back tomorrow.'

We walked down the slope of a sand dune. 'Did you tell him you wouldn't quit?'

I nodded.

'Really?' she said, looking squarely at me. 'I thought finally you would decide otherwise.'

'But didn't you tell me?'

'I did, but you know...' she said, her eyes drifting away from me. 'Still.'

'What still?'

'Anyway, who's the guy? I want to meet him,' she said, as we walked towards a large group of officers. A steward served us tandoori paneer.

'At the end of it, if you are not happy, what's the point?' Anju said, taking a small bite of the succulent paneer. 'There's always a chance of reconsidering. It's not like you have signed an official contract or something.'

'Look, Anju, now don't confuse me further. My head is about to split with the all the thinking I have done in the past few days.'

'Hey, look,' Anju discreetly pointed at an officer as we neared the group of revelling men. 'That one looks familiar. Doesn't he?'

I looked carefully at the man, who stood holding a glass in his hand. Only a part of his side profile was visible, but I had recognized him.

'I don't want to go there,' I said and turned.

Within no time, Captain Bipin Ghosh had spotted us and walked towards us. Anju stopped me even as I turned. 'Face him. Don't run,' she whispered.

'Hey, good to see you,' he said, coming closer, flashing his attractive smile. 'So, how have you been? It's been such a long time.'

'All well, sir,' I said, feeling awkward that his eyes lingered on my face for longer than was required.

Suddenly coming out of a trance, he said, 'It feels great to be a part of this grand celebration, isn't it?'

'Yes, sir, certainly,' Anju said.

I was quiet as both of them made small talk. He enquired about Major Bhat and Anju didn't bother to tell him the details. He then enquired about Piya and also informed us that he had just been blessed with a baby girl. From the way he talked about himself, it appeared that his life was perfect, with a lovely wife and two kids. I couldn't help thinking how at one point, I pictured myself beside him. But he had moved on and I was still where he saw me last. It was like he had found the highway while I still trudged along a dirt track.

'So, married?' he turned to me.

'No, sir,' I said, trying to look cheerful.

'Still single?' He sounded worse than Lali.

'Sir, she's getting married shortly,' Anju said, 'to an officer in her unit, Captain Amit Joseph.'

'Anju!' I almost yelled.

'Amit?' Captain Bipin Ghosh looked surprised. 'The bloody chap never told me. Where's he?' He then turned to me. 'Congrats.' Transferring his glass to the other hand, he shook hands with me and said again, 'Congratulations.'

I thanked him and smiled weakly, like a person not sure of anything. Anju had just shot her mouth off and in a matter of minutes everyone would congratulate me. I knew Anju was trying to do me a favour, but now I was apprehensive about the outcome.

'Bloody chap!' Captain Bipin Ghosh mock punched Captain Joseph's stomach after he had summoned the latter by yelling out for him. 'You never told me? Thought I wouldn't know, eh?' He then gave him a hug and a pat on the back, 'Congratulations, buddy.' Leaning closer, he then whispered something in Captain Joseph's ear. Both of them laughed. Captain Joseph looked briefly at me. I turned to Anju.

'Good evening, sir,' Anju said. 'I am Captain Anjali Sharma.'

'Oh, Anju! I've heard a lot about you,' Captain Joseph said.

'Me too...' Anju said.

'And from the same source!' He smiled and looked at me.

Anju and Captain Joseph dominated the conversation. From Anju's facial expression I knew that she liked him. She occasionally gave me smiles of approval. Captain Bipin Ghosh and I were mostly quiet. Whenever he stole glances at me, I asked him about his wife and kids. He didn't seem to like that. Then sensing that there was nothing much to gain standing there, he left. 'Don't forget to invite me for your wedding,' he said, slapping Captain Joseph's back and looking at me before leaving.

'I am sorry,' I turned to Captain Joseph, as soon as Captain Bipin Ghosh left. 'There was a little misunderstanding.'

'That's okay,' Captain Joseph said. 'It was fun playing along. And I kind of felt good imagining that everything is going perfectly right.'

'You know what?' Anju said. 'You can make this happen. Only you'll have to tell a small lie to your mom.'

'What lie? If it doesn't hurt anyone, I'll say it,' Captain Joseph said.

'Just tell your mom that she hasn't yet finished the contract period yet and as soon as it gets over, she'll quit.'

Captain Joseph shook his head. 'I have told her that and she didn't agree. I know her. She's too stubborn. She insists that I see the girl she's chosen for me and then go ahead.'

330 / S<small>AJITA</small> N<small>AIR</small>

Anju looked at me and her expression suddenly changed. 'Okay, then go ahead,' she turned to him, a tinge of sarcasm in her voice. 'Marry the girl. So what's the confusion here about?'

'Anju!' I said. What was she saying? I thought she could make things work, but she was playing spoiler.

'Obviously,' she said. 'He can't decide. You can't decide. Then let other people decide for you. The first thing you have to ask yourself is whether you want to be with each other. I think you guys must...'

An officer from the Jodhpur group called out for Anju, interrupting her midway. She shrugged 'What I was saying was, I think you guys must go ahead. I know you have deep feelings for each other,' she said as she left, adjusting her cap.

That left Captain Joseph and me alone. This was not the first time we were alone, but for some reason, it felt very different. I was suddenly conscious of how the desert breeze caressed the nape of my neck, how a tiny lock of hair came undone and flew gently against my cheek.

'I think I must go,' I said and turned to walk away.

'No, no, just wait,' he said. 'Could we just walk to that side?'

We walked a little away from the noise and din.

'Your friend Anju...' he began.

'I am sorry about all that she said.'

'No, in fact, good she said all that. Sometimes having a third person's view makes things a little clearer. I think she's right.'

I looked at the silhouette of his face against the flickering flames of the campfire.

'What do you think?' he repeated. 'Isn't your friend right? That it's we who must decide?'

'Yeah,' I said, peeling my eyes off him. 'Actually, when I think again, I feel maybe I was wrong.'

He chuckled. 'It's this romantic backdrop, the moon, stars, sand and breeze that make you say this. But I know you too well. It was wrong to even suggest that you quit. I on my part should never dampen the spirit in you. That's what makes you, you!'

I smiled. Despite being in the open, I felt short of breath. Never in all our times of togetherness had he made me feel so warm and loved. Had we not been in our combat dress, I was sure we would at least hold hands.

'Will you come with me to Mumbai?' he said.

'To meet...?'

'Yeah. You know she has this false notion that since you are in the army, you must be that over-smart kind, very fast and devoid of values and all that. She worries maybe you will be too smart for me and make my life difficult, or even hers. I am sure if she meets you once, her impression will change.'

'But if I meet her before we are engaged or married, won't she anyway think I am fast or whatever?'

'No, don't worry about that. You can stay with a friend if you like.'

'But are you sure you can convince her?'

'Yes, suddenly I am very sure. And I am surprised it took me so long,' he smiled.

'I will come,' I said.

Anju waved urgently and called out to me.

'So there isn't much time and we need to plan our leave together,' he said, as we walked towards her. 'We also need to get our transfers to the same place, as per the policy.'

'Yeah, we'll plan everything as soon as we get back,' I said, adding, 'I feel so happy.'

'The GOC wants to meet you,' Anju said, walking me to a large group of middle-aged officers with loads of lipstick on their collar, which meant that they were the super-senior lot.

'What? The GOC? Why? And me of all the people?'

'You'll know soon. I think it's something about the computer wing.'

'Computer wing?' I muttered as we neared the group. I wondered what had happened now. Almost all officers in this group were either the Commanding Officers or Seconds-in-Command of units and now all of them turned towards us. Colonel Mishra introduced me to the General Officer Commanding, a tall man with neatly parted salt-and-pepper hair and a stubbly moustache. Although I had heard enough about him and even caught glimpses of him at a distance, this was the first time I stood so close to him.

'So, you are the one handling the computer wing?' he turned to me, even as everyone one else maintained pin-drop silence.

'Yes, sir,' I said. The eyes of all the heavyweights were on me.

'I had heard it was a lady officer handling the wing, but it's only now that I have had the chance to meet you,' he said in his crisp English, even as my heart raced. 'Anyway, I just wanted to let you know you are doing a great job. Keep it up. Everyone is all praises for your work. The speed and efficiency of the unit has increased manifold, that's what I hear. Well, now,' he turned to Colonel Mishra and smiled, 'I think the only problem is the non-availability of stores.'

Colonel Mishra mumbled something unintelligible. 'Anyway,' the general continued, 'we must encourage this young, hardworking officer. And what better time to acknowledge your work than now? It's victory time for all of us.' He then turned to Colonel Mishra, 'Mishra, send me a recommendation for commendation. She must get the Chief of Army Staff. If not, she'll certainly have the army commander's.'

Some of the Commanding Officers of other units cheered me, 'Well done. Keep it up.' Praises rained from all sides and I felt elated. Anju patted my back. 'Too good, buddy,' she said, as we walked away from the senior gang, accosted by a group of youngsters. 'It's a happy occasion,' one of them said. 'Victory, commendation, marriage. Let's celebrate.'

We drank to the good health of our men on the borders and our victory. It was after a long time that Anju and I were having a drink. The mood around was vibrant and happiness spilled over as every few minutes someone or the other raised a toast. Captain Amit Joseph had a glass of whisky in his hand. We clinked our glasses. Anju joined in, 'What a happy day!'

'Yeah, we are also getting happy,' I said, and suddenly remembered Long Nose.

'Cheers, sir,' Anju said, reading my mind and raising her glass to the starlit sky. 'Today we miss you a lot, sir.'

'Cheers!' Captain Joseph and I joined her.

Nearby, a song session was in progress. The Kishore-da of the previous unit, Captain Bipin Ghosh was crooning some golden oldie. Many joined in, albeit with haywire lyrics. Captain Joseph also joined in with the group.

'Any outcome?' Anju asked me. 'Did you guys talk?'

'Yeah, he wants me to meet his mother.'

'Wow! Wear a sari, and yeah, smile a lot, okay?' Then her expression suddenly changed. 'I hope you are going.'

'Yeah, why the doubt?' I said. 'Of course I am.'

'Great!' she said and put and arm around me. 'Too good.'

We stood sipping our drinks and watching the young officers sing and dance. They forced Captain Joseph to sing. I smiled. Anju nudged me. Captain Joseph didn't sing, but told a joke instead. His joke was followed by more jokes.

'Do you plan to get in touch with Major Bhat?' I asked.

'No, I don't think I will. Ever! Forget it, Dips. It'll never be possible.'

'For Piya's sake?' I said.

'No, I don't think so.' She swigged the remaining gin. 'C'mon, don't spoil my mood. I don't want to think about him now.'

Captain Joseph, in the meantime, was being given a desert farewell by all the young officers, most of whom were quite drunk. 'He's a jolly good fellow...' they sang as they gave him high bumps and finally let him fall free on the sand. His boots and belt had come off. The top part of his shirt had also come undone. Everyone laughed. I gave him a hand to help him to his feet, laughing all the while.

'Now it's your turn,' one of the revellers said. 'Commendation, marriage, transfer, in that order – you need to get many bumps.'

I shrieked and protested but no one paid me any attention. They caught me and flung me up into the desert air that rang with loud voices singing, 'She's a jolly good fellow, she's a jolly good fellow... and so say all of us...'

'...and no one can deny...' Anju sang.

'...and she is one of us...' roared a male voice over the rest.

Everyone joined in the chorus and tossed me up again and again. I felt my bra ride up and my belt and boots come off. But I didn't care. There were few occasions when I felt like this, when I felt such a high – I could almost pluck the stars.

Acknowledgments

A book is finally born after long, hard labour. Had it not been for all the support I got, it would perhaps have died an aborted idea. Many thanks are due to so many people who made it happen.

I am deeply indebted to my parents, Radha and Ramanunni Nair, for loving me enough to let me be, for giving me the freedom to make my own choices and the strength to abide by them. Sajan Abraham, my best friend, my soul buddy for lifting my self-belief whenever it slackened, for offering to read my sloppy first drafts despite missing out cricket highlights on Star Sports; for just being there with a quiet assurance. Tejas and Tisha, my lovely children, for brightening my days with their sprightly hugs and moist kisses, for letting me see the wonders of the world through their eyes.

My parents-in-law for always being supportive and understanding. My brother Sanjiv Nair and sister-in-law Amrita for their infectious enthusiasm all along. Vineeta Dixit and Christine Rajachandra, for being my first readers and honest critics. Asha Kale, Ripunjay Kumar, Ananthanarayanan Krishnan, Anurag Uniyal, Ninad Deshpande and all my other friends, who readily answered my queries, shared their experiences and supported me whole-heartedly.

The entire team at Hachette India, Shivmeet Deol in particular, for believing in my story idea right from the start; for her editorial guidance that helped present this story in its best form possible.

The *fauj*, for inspiring me, for enriching my life with a plethora of experiences and for instilling in me the conviction that turns every 'Can I?' to 'I Can'.